also by angela casella

Finding You

You're so Extra

You're so Bad

Fairy Godmother Agency

A Borrowed Boyfriend

A Stolen Suit

A Brooding Bodyguard

A Reluctant Roommate

Bringing Down the House (Nicole and Damien's story)

Highland Hills

(co-written with Denise Grover Swank)

Matchmaking a Billionaire

Matchmaking a Single Dad

Matchmaking a Grump

Matchmaking a Roommate

Bad Luck Club

(co-written with Denise Grover Swank)

Love at First Hate

Jingle Bell Hell

Fraudulently Ever After

Matchmaking Mischief

Asheville Brewing

(co-written with Denise Grover Swank)

Any Luck at All

Better Luck Next Time

Getting Lucky

Bad Luck Club

Luck of the Draw (novella)

All the Luck You Need (prequel novella) by Angela Casella

you're so extra

FINDING YOU

ANGELA CASELLA

In researching this book, I worked as an extra in a made-for-TV film. So this one goes out to my extra besties, DeeDee and Lisa. Our feet may never be the same after wearing those shoes for hours in the freezing cold, but we did create some pretty epic backstories for our characters. (I'm looking at you, Lisa-slash-Mildred.)

And a shoutout to my daughter, Frances, whose devotion to living a colorful life inspired Delia.

one

DELIA

"THIS SAYS I'm supposed to wear 'normal' clothes, Mira," I say, reading through the email again on my phone. Starting tomorrow, I'm going to be a movie extra. This is the something wonderful the universe sent me after I wished for it so hard I nearly popped a blood vessel in my eye when I blew out the twenty-nine candles on my birthday cake a couple of months ago. I would pretty please with a cherry on top like to not screw it up on the first day. "What does 'normal' mean?"

She snorts and gives me a once-over from behind her bar, taking in my skirt with its design of little cats printed over a background of the universe. "Not what you're wearing."

"I *like* this skirt."

"So do I," my sister tells me, "but it's not what someone else would classify as 'normal.' A T-shirt and jeans. A dress without five thousand colors. That's probably what they're getting at."

I sit at one of the stools in front of her. Her cocktail bar, Glitterati, just closed down, all of the tourists and locals in Asheville gone home for the night, so she has a few minutes to spare for my existential crisis. "I'm nervous about this."

She stops wiping the counter, slapping the lavender-colored

1

towel down. We Evans girls have always liked color. Mira jokes that if you cut us open, you'd find twenty different shades of blood inside. Her bar is an expression of that, of *us*—full of glitter and color and *fun*, from the décor, which I helped with, to the drinks—and no one in our family is the least bit surprised by its success. She was born for this. I, apparently, was born to walk dogs, pretend I'm a mermaid at children's events, and run errands for elderly people. I love what I do, but I'm aware it's not the kind of life an adult is supposed to have or want. People never hesitate to tell me so.

"You've got nothing to worry about, Delia. You don't have any lines to memorize. All you have to do is run around and pretend to have conversations with people." She lifts her eyebrows. "The only problem is you're not good at blending in."

"That's a big problem," I say, tugging on a strand of my long red-orange hair. "You told me the whole point is to blend in."

She laughs, her eyes dancing with it. "And that's why I made you submit those boring-ass pictures for your application."

"Was it dishonest?" I ask. "I'll bet Mom would say it was dishonest." Our mother has a very rigid sense of right and wrong, and unfortunately, I have a tendency to end up in the wrong category more often than not.

Mira rolls her eyes. "Our mother thinks too much for her own good. Besides, you're going to show up wearing boring clothes, so what they don't know won't hurt them. You need to look out for yourself."

"I did this, didn't I?" I ask, pivoting back and forth on the stool because I'm nervous, and heck, it's also pretty fun. "Your cat-eye makeup is on point today."

"Thank you, and quit changing the subject."

"Do you think he'll remember me?"

She reaches across the bar to grab my shoulder, her grip firm and warm. Her eyes are a warm caramel, the color of our dad's. Mine are blue in some lights, green in others, and sometimes, or so I've been told, nearly as golden as a cat's. "You're not easy to forget. I *defy* anyone to forget you. And, yes, I know you were less...yourself for most of high school, but you still weren't forgettable."

I don't like being a naysayer, but I'm not convinced she's right. If she *were* right, then she wouldn't currently be my only friend under the age of sixty.

"He's a movie star now," I say. "And before you remind me, I know he's only in made-for-TV movies, but that's more of a movie star than I'll ever be."

She smirks at me. "Untrue, sister dearest. You're there for a week of filming. Seven days over the next month. Maybe more." She'd know. I've made her read the emails multiple times. The first day of filming is tomorrow, Monday. Then Sunday. The following week, it's Tuesday and Wednesday, then Wednesday and Thursday. "You may not have any lines in the movie, but you're gonna be all over that screen." Her eyebrows wing up. "And, if everything goes according to plan, all over *him*."

I can't deny it felt like a sign when I saw Jeremy was starring in a movie filming so close to town. I haven't seen him since high school, but I had the kind of stupid crush on him only teenagers are capable of. He was a drama kid, and I worked on set pieces for the theater club. Back then he was kind of nerdy in a hot way, and now he looks like he should be inspiring sculptors in Italy. Obviously it's a long shot to think he'd remember me, since our most substantial interactions were as follows—Interaction One: he objected vehemently to the amount of glitter I used on a set piece for one of his plays. Interaction Two: he borrowed a pen from me and returned it broken.

On the other hand, I did ask the universe to throw me a bone, and I saw the ad asking for extras that very same night. An even bigger sign? I got an email offering me the gig just three hours after I submitted my photos. Nobody gets offered a job that fast, even at the places that have had "Help Wanted" signs in the window for so long they're dusty and covered in cobwebs.

Mira's been joking for weeks that the universe decided to throw me Jeremy's bone. I'm not convinced, but I'm not *unconvinced*. All I know is that I'm ready for something big to happen. I feel like I'm standing on the cusp of it. If that something big ends up being Jeremy's bone? Well, I'll have given Mira teasing material for at least a year.

"Don't stress," Mira adds. "Just dress like you did for those photos."

"Yeah, you're right," I say, still playing with the ends of my hair. "I wish they'd told me who I'm playing."

All I know about the movie is its title—*The Opposites Contract*—which doesn't give a whole lot away other than that the leads are, presumably, opposites.

She snorts. "I don't think you're playing anyone, but feel free to make up an elaborate backstory. I know you will. And try to calm down."

I'm a mess of nerves, and not just because I'm going to be sharing a set with Jeremy and his much more famous co-star, Sinclair Jones. It's just...this feels like my chance, even if I'm not quite sure what that means or what form it will take.

I've always been told I'm dramatic. My mother says it's the red hair, as if a little pigmentation can shape a person's whole personality. But I *do* have a flair for drama. Maybe the universe isn't giving me a chance at Jeremy but at a new part-time career. This experience could be a stepping stone to other background roles or even a speaking part. Or maybe it'll help me grow in different ways. One of the other extras could be a supremely interesting human being who changes my life.

My heart lifts, and I find myself smiling, good cheer pouring into me like it's one of my sister's cocktails.

"Are you thinking about all the durrrr-ty things you want Jeremy to do to you?" my sister says in a sing-song voice, making a gesture that undermines my epiphany.

"You're sick."

She pops a hand onto her hip, her dark-brown hair bouncing in its ponytail. "You like it."

"Sometimes I like it," I correct.

She points a finger at me. "Now, go home and get ye to bed. You have an early call time, and I happen to know Doris and Ross wouldn't appreciate being woken up."

She's referring to my elderly roommates. I live in their basement apartment in exchange for helping them with various chores. It's slightly embarrassing to admit they're two of my best friends. It wasn't always like that. I did have a best friend other than my sister and my roommates once, but some blessings aren't given to us for as long as we'd like. Hence the birthday wish.

"I'm in the clear. Ross's hearing aid is broken, and I think he ordered the replacement snail mail so he can pretend he doesn't hear Doris when she asks him to do things. Actually, there's no pretending about it. He hears about one or two things out of five without it. Besides, I don't have to be there until one," I point out. True, it'll take me forty-five minutes to drive to the Rolf Estate, or the Discount Bilt-more as people around town call the much smaller and less grand estate, but I'm reasonably confident I can be awake and dressed by twelve. Hell, I'll have walked five dogs by then and picked up groceries for a couple of my clients.

"We all have different definitions of early," she says with a grin. "Now, go! Fly away, butterfly. Make me proud and send me pictures."

"I don't think I'm supposed to do that," I point out, gesturing to the phone sitting on her bar. "They said no photos."

"Like I said," she says, one side of her mouth hitching up, "break some rules. Break a leg too. I'm told that's lucky."

I knock on the wood beneath the bar top. "Doesn't sound lucky."

"Defy the odds. It's the Evans way."

The next morning, I pull into the parking lot attached to the Rolf Estate, doing breathing exercises. Doris and Ross gave me a sweet send-off before I left to walk the dogs this morning, presenting me with a muffin on which Doris had shakily written *Delia's a Star.* The muffin tasted strange because Doris had put a tablespoon of baking soda into the batter instead of a teaspoon. Her vision isn't the best anymore, but she refuses to wear her glasses because she says they don't suit her. I ate it anyway, and now my insides feel like the tangle of wires that's been in the junk drawer of my childhood home since I was a little girl.

What if I fall flat on my face in the middle of an important scene and they have to reshoot it because of me?

It's true that I play a mermaid a couple of times a week for birthday parties and community events, but it's a stationary gig owing to the tail.

Rather than park, I slowly drive through the lot because I feel the inane urge to find the "right" space. And then I see Jeremy walking at the far end of the parking lot. I recognize him immediately because he has distinctive wavy russet hair. Why is he out here in the open? Where is his gaggle of adoring fans and publicists and...

I clearly have no idea what it's like to be a movie star. He's walking toward the house, which lives behind a row of perfectly trimmed trees that are currently concealing it from view. Would it be a bad idea to shout his name?

Obviously. I can't fully see his face from this angle, but I have a fantastic view of his ass, and as I watch, he pushes a tree branch out of his path a little too violently—is he going to hurt the tree?—and it immediately springs back and hits him in the face. What the heck is he doing? He stomps his foot, like he's pissed at the tree, and then—

"What the fuck?" someone shouts, and there's a rapping on the hood of my car that seems to rumble through the whole vehicle.

Oh no, oh no, oh no. I slam my foot down on the brake, my gaze shooting forward. There are two men right next to the hood of my car, and it's obvious that I almost hit them. I'm going about two miles an hour, but no one wants to be hit be a car, even if it's only going two miles an hour.

I roll down my window. "I'm so sorry! Are you okay? Can I—"

I'm not sure how to end that sentence. What is a person supposed to do after they nearly run over another person? Offer them a granola bar?

The guy who hit my hood still has a hand on top of it, and his fierce gaze beats into me. He's attractive—*very* attractive—with black hair, intensely blue eyes, and a tall, muscular build. In fact, from a purely physical standpoint, he's more appealing than Jeremy. His friend is handsome too, but in a rough-edged way, and he's wearing a beanie hat pulled low over his ears despite the heat. My gaze skates back to Blue Eyes. His coloring is pretty rare—usually people with light eyes don't have hair quite so dark.

"You look like Snow White," I blurt.

"W-what?" Blue Eyes sputters. "But...I'm a man."

"Oh, I can tell. You're very manly. I was referring to your coloring." He's looking at me like I'm a puzzle he doesn't care to figure out. "Sorry. I say whatever I'm thinking when I'm nervous."

"You should watch where you're going," he says firmly.

"You wouldn't be the first person to say so," I tell him, laughing slightly.

His expression says he doesn't appreciate the laughter. Crap. Is he someone important? He has the air of someone important, or at least someone who *thinks* he's important. Then again, I suppose nobody would be pleased if their near-murderer decided to laugh about it.

"Sorry," I say again. "I laugh when I'm nervous too." And tap my fingers in the air. And sweat. At this particular moment, I feel like doing all of those things at once. It's not just that I almost hit these guys—it's Blue Eyes's stare. It's the kind of look that would make someone feel naked in a room full of clothed people. It's shiver inducing, and I can't tell whether or not I like it.

His friend nudges his arm. "Let it go, bud. Red here just made a mistake."

"Are you guys in the movie?" It only occurs to me after I say it that it's probably not appropriate to try to carry on a conversation with them.

"Yup," the friend says. "We're extras. I'm Leonard and this is...Lucas."

My glance shifts from Leonard to Lucas and holds. "I'm usually not the best with names, but I'm going to remember you two. That's the bond created by almost hitting someone."

"Do you do that often?" Lucas asks, this time with a glimmer of amusement. His lips curl at the edges, and it strikes me that they're very nice lips. Some men have an upper lip that's better off hidden by a mustache or beard, but his has...presence. Actually, all of him does.

I clear my throat. "No. Before today, my closest scrapes were with garbage cans. The roads around here are too narrow. I'm Delia, by the way."

Lucas glances at Leonard, who laughs under his breath. Then he shifts his gaze back to me. "Delia Evans?"

"Yeah!" I say, surprised. As far as I know, it's not stitched into my shirt. "How'd you know? Do you have grandparents who use Grand-daughter for Rent?"

"Is that some kind of kinky thing?" Leonard asks, his mouth curling with amusement.

Lucas shakes his head disparagingly, but I can't tell whether his annoyance is with me or his friend.

"No," I say, "but you're not the first person to ask." They both look like they're holding in laughter now, and I feel a prick of annoyance. "Maybe I should change the name. I do chores for elderly people. But if you don't have grandparents who use me—"

Leonard snorts.

"Really?" I roll my eyes and shift my attention to Lucas. "How do you know my last name?"

He rubs his jaw, then glances back in the parking lot. That's when I realize there's a car behind me, probably waiting not so patiently for me to shut up. "Because you and I are playing a couple, *light of my life.*" His mouth ticks up at the corners. "I guess we'll be spending a lot of time together, Delia Evans."

two

"THIS WAS PROBABLY A DUMB IDEA," I say as we make our way to the house.

Delia's still finding a parking space. Leonard suggested waiting for her, but I'm in no mood to be nice to anyone. Most of the people I know would find that surprising. Usually I make a point of being charming to beautiful women, and there's no denying Delia Evans is beautiful. *Arresting*. The kind of gorgeous where you wouldn't mind so much if she *did* hit you so long as she apologized really nicely afterward. But I can't bring myself to care. The day's not even halfway over and it already sucks. The several days preceding it weren't any better.

Then again, I guess that's what happens when you purposefully implode your own life.

Leonard gives me a good-natured clap on the back as we pass the sculpted pine trees bordering the parking lot, the big Rolf Estate coming into view. It has a stone façade, covered in vines that look good but are probably ruining the stone work. To one side is a trellis covered in flowering vines, leading into what looks like a well-orga-nized garden. There's a cobbled road that leads around the other side, but from our angle I can't see what's down that way.

I've never been to the Rolf Estate before, even though it's less than an hour away from where I grew up. Whenever anyone suggested a visit to the Rolf Estate, my mother would cluck her tongue and say, "There's little point in visiting someone else's house when ours is so much nicer." We *did* visit the Biltmore once or twice, because even she had to admit the mansion my great grandfather had built wasn't nearly as fine as the Vanderbilts' home.

I rub my chest, feeling a physical soreness from the thought. Because if I ever speak to my mother again, they won't be kind words.

Leonard drags me from my brooding. "I won't argue with you. We could be working on the flip house right now, man, drinking beers on the deck."

I level him with a *you're a lazy asshole* look, even though I'm grateful as hell that he's here with me. "It's 12:50."

"Lunch beer," he says with a shrug. "It's a thing."

"Well, we're here," I say with a sigh as we continue down the cobbled path to the house. "And we promised Sinclair. It would be shitty of us to drop out at the last minute."

His raised eyebrows remind me that any promises that were made were strictly mine. Sinclair Jones is the sister of my best friend, Drew, who's currently hundreds of miles away in Puerto Rico for who knows how long. That means I probably shouldn't bail on her at the last minute, even if they could probably pull a willing replacement extra off the street. There've been articles about this production in the *Asheville Gazette*, and apparently they had over fifteen thousand applicants who wanted to be extras. We got waved in through the door because of Sinclair, but I'm guessing they chose Delia from the stack. With that hair, she'd stand out. It's long and red-gold, as shiny as a burnished penny.

Dammit. Maybe I *do* care that she's beautiful, but I don't *want* to care. I resent that I do.

11

"It's worth mentioning that neither of us should be showing our faces right now," Leonard comments without any heat.

"Sinclair said she wasn't sharing my last name with anyone," I remind him.

"Why, yes, you're going to be Lucas C., I remember," he says, giving me shit for it. To be fair, it does sound like the kind of pseudonym a fashion model or TV personality with a big ego might insist on. The C is for my middle name, Cornelius—yes, fucking Cornelius —meant to throw off anyone who might put things together if I used my real last initial. Right now, my last name doesn't carry the kind of social currency it once did.

Sighing, I add, "And she said no one will be able to see your face."

"That's a shame," Leonard says with a smirk. "This face was meant to be seen."

I shoot him a look as we get closer to the front of the building. There are people bustling in and out and a few anxious-looking security guards watching them closely. One of them has a hand on his belt as if he thinks he's in an Old West shootout, although there's nothing on the belt but an oversized buckle. An old-timey looking trolley pulls away from the front of the building and rumbles down the cobbled road to the right, away from the trellis.

Yesterday, we were sent a list of rules a page and a half long about what we could and couldn't do in the house. Basically, we're allowed to exist there, so long as we don't touch anything, breathe too hard, or make overly heavy footfalls. The house flipper in me wants to ask what kind of shitty craftsmanship will shatter apart if we step on the ground too heavily, but the rules are the rules.

Leonard is sure to break at least half of them.

"If you wanted the freedom to show your face on camera," I tell him, "you probably shouldn't have cycled through half a dozen identities."

It's an exaggeration. Slightly. Leonard ran from Asheville eight years ago and then went into hiding. He left because he learned a horrible truth about my parents, and he wasn't sure he could trust me to be any better than them. Now that he's back, I've decided I'm going to make it up to him. And when I decide to do something, I damn well do it. The first phase is the house we're renovating together.

"Touché," he mutter, rubbing his his hair through the beanie. Why he thinks hiding his hair is going to help him evade being recognized, I don't know. Really, it's a miracle he spent so many years under the radar if a hat is his disguise of choice. Then again, I'm not even wearing a hat. I figure I've spent my whole life in this town. If I'm recognized on set, so be it. Maybe it's the price I should pay for being a Burke.

Some nervous-looking kid spots us from the doorway and comes running toward us. He has light brown hair that sticks up at awkward angles, as if someone plopped a bale of straw on top of his head, and anxious brown eyes.

"Who are you?" he asks. It probably shouldn't feel like an existential question, but it does.

Leonard's mouth tips into a half-smile. "We're Lucas C. and Leonard Smith," he says, "reporting for extra duty. We're *incredibly* excited."

"Didn't they tell you where to go?" Straw Kid asks. He's practically buzzing, as if he washed down half a dozen caffeine pills with a latte.

"If they did, we'd be there," I say, then wave a hand around. "I'm not seeing any signs."

He squints and rubs his nose, his hand shaking slightly, so maybe it's coke that's got him buzzing. "They wouldn't let us tape anything up or stick spikes in the ground. They really didn't tell you where to go?"

"They gave us this address," I say. "And here we are."

"Christian said he sent a follow-up email," he says accusingly. "Everyone *else* seems to have gotten it."

Christian being the coordinator for the extras.

"Well, we didn't," I repeat, annoyed. I hate inefficiency. It's probably the Burke in me. Being a Burke is no longer a matter of pride, though, so I try to harness what's left of my patience. In other words, not much.

"You need to report to costumes and hair and makeup," the kid says.

"Costumes?" Leonard repeats with a laugh.

Straw Kid gives him an up and down look. "They'll make you lose the hat."

"Told you," I say.

Leonard scowls as if he's a woman with a bad haircut he'd rather not reveal.

"So where is hair and makeup?" I ask, questioning every last decision that led me here. I'd wanted a distraction, and this had seemed like it might be an amusing one...a month and a half ago. If Sinclair had asked me yesterday, I would have said no, or maybe even put it more strongly.

Straw Kid gives us meandering directions to The Barn, which amuses me because it's starting to feel like we're human cattle. According to him, though, it hasn't been a barn since the 1800s, and even then, it was a very *nice* barn.

He's nearly finished with his explanation, which amounts to following the cobbled road, when I hear the sound of running feet behind me. I turn to see Delia Evans coming toward us. She has on a simple black dress paired with wedge sandals, and the darkness of the dress only brings more attention to the flame of her hair and the creamy expanse of her tits straining against the top.

"Looks like we're not the only ones Christian forgot about," Leonard comments, lifting his brows.

"Sorry," she calls out, her voice a bit loud but not unpleasant. "Sorry, I had some trouble in the parking lot."

"Were we the trouble?" I ask incredulously. Who *is* this woman?

Her eyes go wide. "Well, some of it," she admits. "I mean, it was my fault, obviously, but it made me take longer than I should have, and then Doris called me. She's my...I guess you'd call her my landlord. She misplaced her blood pressure pills. I knew where she'd put them, but she doesn't walk too terribly fast, so—" I mustn't be the only one watching her with wonder, because she sputters to a stop. "Sorry, you don't need to know all of that. I just...I wasn't going to ignore Doris."

"Is she one of the grandparents?" I ask, interested despite myself.

"Yes," Delia says brightly, as if pleased I remembered. "She used to be a lounge singer back in the day. She's incredible."

There's something endearing about the way she says it, but Straw Kid glances back at me, his eyes full of a *better you than me* look. Acting as if Delia never interrupted, he continues, "Then you pass the wall, and it'll be right there. Ten minute walk, tops. There's a bus doing runs, but you just missed it." He glances down at his watch and then scowls at us. "You're going to be late."

"I think it's Christian you should have words for," Leonard says, but Delia looks upset by the news.

Straw Kid seems to catch sight of someone behind us and hurries off without another word. Then again, he might just be sick of the conversation. If so, it's a pretty slick departure.

"This isn't good," Delia mutters. "I told myself I wasn't going be late. They were really adamant about that in the email. It was under-lined *and* italicized."

"A bit overkill, don't you think?" Leonard asks as we start walking in accordance to Straw Kid's directions. "Almost like they were challenging us."

I can't help but laugh. That's Leonard for you, never a rule he didn't want to break. Maybe I should feel bad about being late, but I couldn't give a shit. I'd rather not be here in the first place, and the stakes of arriving late for a gig like this feel pretty small, especially with the backdrop of everything else that's going on in my life.

"I don't want to get fired," Delia says.

"I doubt you will," I tell her, surprised by my urge to soothe her. I don't know this woman, and I have plenty of trouble without borrowing any from anyone else. "They're filming today. What are the odds they're going to find someone to replace you? Besides, like I said, you and I are supposed to be a couple."

"How do you know that?" she asks, giving me a sidelong look as we hurry down the road. There are a bunch of sculpted bushes to our right—one shaped to look like a horse and another a man's face. I notice Leonard studying them, and I can practically hear him thinking rich people will find any old shit to waste money on.

There's a fancy wall a distance behind the bushes, presumably the one we were told to look out for. It's covered in more of those climbing vines.

"My friend's one of the stars of the movie," I tell Delia.

A gasp escapes her, and she stops walking for a half a second. "Are you talking about Jeremy?"

"Who's Jeremy?" I ask, although the name's familiar.

"Sorry," she says, continuing down the road. "I shouldn't have presumed he's the one you know. There must be a pretty big cast. But Jeremy and I went to high school together. He's the reason I almost hit you guys with my car."

"Well, fuck him," Leonard teases.

A surprised laugh escapes Delia.

"You're talking about the lead actor?" I ask, placing the name. We looked him up at my place a few weeks ago, and Leonard puffed out air and said, "Pretty boy," dismissively. Danny, my roommate, said, "You talking about Burke?" Which led to them razzing me for a good five minutes.

"Yeah," she says, glancing at me, her expression dreamy in a way

16

that sours my mood. She's taken notice of this guy, but I'm so invisible to her that she almost hit me with her car. My buddies would have something to say about that too, probably something about me being an attention whore. "He's from Asheville originally. We went to high school together."

"You don't say. Where'd you go?"

"Asheville High. Are you from around here?"

I nod tightly. "I went to Carolina Day."

"Oh," she says in a knowing tone. *Rich kid*, she's thinking. I can see it on her face.

It makes me uncomfortable. In some ways, it's always made me uncomfortable, although I've obviously seen the benefits. Still am. I may be estranged from my parents, but they can't estrange me from the trust fund I got when I turned twenty-one.

"Well, Jeremy's probably not going to remember me." She grins at us, and it's a smile so wide and artless it hits me center mass. "But I had a crush on him back then. When I saw him in the parking lot earlier, I'll admit I got a little distracted. Sorry about that. Who's your friend on the cast?"

"Sinclair Jones," I say. "She's the one who told me we'd be paired up."

She whistles, her eyes sparkling. "You know, she was nearly the last thing I ever saw. Last year, I almost got run over by this bus with a huge poster of her on the side while I was chasing after one of my clients."

"An elderly person?" I ask, thrown by the image of this ginger-haired woman running after an elderly person waving their cane in the air.

"No," she says, amused, and for a second I have a thought that's damn near fanciful—that she can see the image floating in my mind. "I walk dogs too."

"I'm starting to wish I had a dog," I say. "Or a couple of living grandparents."

She smiles at me, but there's a quizzical look in her eyes, like she's wondering what the hell I'm up to. It would be a good question. She's not my usual type. I prefer women who are sleek and confident. The kind who want the same thing I do—a good time without any strings. But that was the old me. I'm still figuring out who the new me is. This woman is scattered and disorganized, though. I'll bet she couldn't find her sunglasses if they were sitting on the bridge of her nose—not the kind of thing I would normally find appealing.

It's because she comes off as so genuine and sweet, I decide. Almost innocent. Maybe I want to suck it from her like a vampire.

"Don't mind him," Leonard says. "He can't help himself. It's like he's contractually obligated to flirt with gorgeous women." His mouth lifts up. "Hey, bud, it's like this movie was named after you. *The Opposites Contract.*"

"You're a dick," I tell him without any heat.

"It's okay," Delia says, giving us both a smile. "Feel free to practice flirting on me any time."

Those words shouldn't do anything to me, but damn, they really do.

"Is that a volunteer service you offer in addition to your thirty jobs?" Leonard asks.

"You could say that."

"So you're a real jack-of-all-trades," he says, lifting his hand for a high five as we keep walking. She gives it to him. "I don't like being tied down either."

She says, "I wouldn't mind so much, but I can't seem to do just one thing. My mother says I don't apply myself."

Her mother sounds like a bitch, although I'm probably hypocritical for thinking so. I've always been driven to succeed, to be the best, and the thought of having half a dozen half-baked jobs is abhorrent to me.

"Nothing wrong with keeping your options open," Leonard says, lifting his hands in a sympathetic gesture. "Now, if you like this

Jeremy, I'm guessing you have a thing for pretty boys, huh?" he asks as he trains a smirk at me.

I resist the temptation to shove him, barely. We pass the wall, and The Barn comes into view. As advertised, it looks like a barn on the outside, but there's a nearly full parking lot beside it and a few people gathered in a knot by the propped-open double doors.

"Why didn't that kid tell us to drive?" I complain.

"Maybe you looked like you needed the exercise," Leonard says. Given all I've been doing lately is working out or working on the flip house, it's definitely a joke. I'm in better shape than I've ever been. But on the inside, I feel like shit.

"I'm glad we got to walk," Delia says. "I know the main gardens are on the other side, but this place is so beautiful. I've always loved coming here. It makes me feel like I've stepped into another time and place. There's something special about being able to make a short drive from the city and ending up here."

She's like a fucking fairytale princess. I'm surprised birds don't flutter out of the trees to land on her shoulders. It should be annoying, but she seems perfectly genuine.

"It's no Biltmore," I say, for no other reason than I feel like shit, and half the things that come out of my mouth are negative these days.

She frowns at me, which is possibly the only time she's ever frowned in her life. "Maybe not, but not everything needs to be huge. Smaller things can be their own kind of perfect."

A strangled sound escapes Leonard, and it looks like he's going to bite off his tongue.

"No, but sometimes bigger *is* better," I say. "I haven't had any complaints."

Delia laughs, shaking her head slightly. "I walked right into that one, didn't I?"

Suddenly, I feel like a dick for teasing her.

"I'm so —"

But someone at the door calls out to us. The others have gone inside or wandered off, leaving a guy wearing overalls and glasses with yellow frames that make him look like one of the minions in that kids' movie. His hair is chin length, tucked behind his ears. "You extras?" he snips. "You're late. We told no one to be late. I was very specific about that in the email. Italics *and* underlined."

Delia gives me a wide-eyed look but doesn't say *I told you so.*

I instantly want to get the guy fired for being an asshole. Of course, I'm no longer in a position to have anyone fired, except for maybe Leonard on our two-person flip job.

"You didn't send us the directions," I say as we get closer. "We parked in the wrong spot."

He rolls his eyes. "Excuses are like assholes."

"*Excuse* me?" I ask, pissed by his dismissive attitude.

Do you know who I am? nearly escapes my mouth but doesn't. Thank God, because I'd prefer for him not to know. I also don't want to be the kind of person who asks questions like that.

Apparently it's not going so well.

"He was putting us in our place," Delia tells me. To him, she says, "I'm sorry we were late, it was my fault."

"Who are you?" he asks, slightly less annoyed now that Delia has basically prostrated herself at his feet. I don't like that she did that. I like it even less that he let her. I feel a surge of protectiveness toward her, along with the need to defend her from the minion.

I open my mouth to speak, but she gets there first. "I'm Delia Evans."

"Go on in the back," he says, gesturing inside, toward a paper sign reading "Costumes" with an arrow pointing down a hall.

I start, "But—"

I'm about to tell him off, but Leonard drags me inside and then down the hall after Delia, who's already walking. She's moving fast, like a force of nature made human, and I can't help but check out her ass in that dress. It's round and full, the kind a man could grab on to.

The fact that I'm looking—that I've spent the last few minutes half-assedly flirting with her—tells me that maybe my libido hasn't taken the same beating as my ego, even if I haven't brought a woman home with me for weeks. Leonard catches me looking and gives me a *gotcha* smirk.

"I was thinking about our warm welcome," I lie.

"This is how the other half lives, buddy," he tells me in an undertone. "Time for you to get used to it."

He sounds like he's looking forward to humbling me.

three

DELIA

THE COSTUME DESIGNER tells me my dress will work just fine, which is disappointing, because the outfits hanging on the nearby racks are *fabulous*. There's a gold lamé dress, a green velvet gown that I'd gladly give myself heatstroke to wear, and about five dozen outfits better than this one. He *does* give me a gorgeous golden belt that goes around my middle.

The extras coordinator, Christian, followed us into the waiting room after we went inside. He was adamant that he'd emailed the directions to us, and if we didn't get his note, it was somehow our fault. He was so certain about it, I actually started doubting myself and wondering if it had gotten bumped to my spam mail, along with the less-wholesome responses to my Granddaughter for Rent business.

It's obvious Lucas isn't used to negative feedback. He looked like he was ready to blow up at Christian, but after he gave his name—Lucas C.—the extras coordinator's whole attitude shifted. He called him sir and offered him a better place than "this shithole" to wait for filming. This earned several dissatisfied grumbles from the other people packed into the waiting room, several of us standing because there weren't enough chairs.

To my surprise, Lucas glanced at Leonard, then sighed and said, "No, thanks, man. We'll wait in here like everyone else."

I like that he said it. I was expecting him to accept the special treatment with open arms, especially since it's become clear to me that my first impression was accurate and he is both wealthy and possibly important. It's in his bearing and the confidence that leaks from him. It's in the outfit he's wearing—understated but expensive. I also happen to know the Carolina Day School runs somewhere in the twenty-five to thirty thousand a year range for tuition, even for kindergartners.

Lucas probably came to regret his decision, however, because it took twenty minutes for someone to bring more chairs in, and we had to wait another hour and a half before any of us were called over to costumes to get our looks approved. It went by quickly, though, with Lucas and Leonard telling me about the hundred-year-old flip house they're working on in West Asheville and me telling them about Ross and Doris.

It surprised me how genuinely interested they seemed. Usually, when I tell someone below the age of forty about my living arrangements, they look at me like I'm an exotic bug they'd like to smash or scuttle out of their house. But Lucas watched me with warmth.

I confessed that I'd been fantasizing that we would get put in colorful costumes. Big, full dresses with bright skirts, and suits paired with pink shirts. "Wouldn't that be fun?"

Lucas's lips lifted slightly. "Categorically no. If I'm asked to wear pink, I'm out."

"What's wrong with pink?"

"Nothing, as long as I'm not the one wearing it."

Despite his aversion to color, he's interesting. Sometimes he comes off as casually smooth, like the guys who hang out at Mira's bar—all honeyed words and come-hither eyes, another Doris-ism— but there's a darkness in him, simmering down deep. It's like he's at war within himself, and he's not sure which side will win. Maybe I'm just creating stories again, making mountains out of mole hills to make life more interesting, but I don't think so. It makes me want to know more about him, to ask the kind of questions you're not supposed to ask someone you met a few hours ago. I'd also like to know why someone who clearly has money and prestige is flipping houses. He seems more like the kind of man who'd be ruling boardrooms, making and ruining lives, and—

Yes, there's my overactive imagination at work again.

I didn't mean to, but I kept stealing glances at him while we were stuck in the waiting room, taking in his pitch-black hair, the bright blue of his eyes, the amused tilt of his lips. I've always had a weakness for good-looking men, one that dates back to Jeremy of the russet hair. I told myself that's all it was—an appreciation, like I'd admire a work of art, or a decked-out cake in a bakery window.

When I got called back first, Lucas grinned at me and said, "Tell me you won't talk the costume guy into his-and-her outfits."

"I make no promises," I said, and despite myself, I looked over my shoulder at him as I walked away.

I'm still thinking about him now. Then again, I'd still be thinking about that fancy cake if I'd just laid eyes on it.

As the designer, a gorgeous man with dark skin and an outfit much better than mine, finishes arranging my belt, he says, "Would you believe I've been here since seven a.m., sugar?" He heaves the sigh of someone who hasn't had enough coffee.

"Did Jeremy come through earlier?" I ask before I can think better of it. If he'd already been through costumes, I can't think of a good reason for him to have been in the parking lot, but maybe he went out there to make a phone call.

"Didn't he ever," he says, pretending to fan himself. Then his mouth purses to the side. "He's a bit of a tool, hon."

"Really?" I ask, crestfallen but not as disappointed as Mira will probably be. "I knew him back in high school."

He moves the buckle of the belt a millimeter to the left. "Was he a dick then too?"

I consider our two interactions. "Maybe. He broke my favorite pen and didn't apologize." I knew it was less-than-optimal behavior, obviously, but it happened when I was seventeen. I'd done the teenage thing of keeping the broken pen and idolizing it because he'd broken it.

He huffs out a laugh. "All I can tell you is that he strutted in here all high and mighty, as if *he* were the bigger name celebrity. He asked for a seltzer and then said it was too cold."

"On a day like today?" It's early August and nearly sticky.

"Precisely. We let it sit out for a few minutes and then it was too hot. And he made poor Pammy redo his makeup three times without a please or thank you. He wanted every line covered and shellacked. Now, Sinclair Jones, mind you, was as sweet as you please. And everyone knows she's the real star."

I release a sigh. "That's disappointing."

He waves a hand. "Draw your own conclusions."

"I will," I say, "but consider me thoroughly warned."

"You know, I heard Lucas Burke is here as one of the extras, but we were all told not to talk about it." He makes an aggrieved face. "As if they could stop us from talking. They may have stuffed us in a barn, but we're not animals."

"Lucas's last name is Burke?" I ask, my heart thumping.

Does that mean he's one of *the* Burkes? As in the bigwig family that runs Burke Enterprises? I don't want to think so. I *like* Lucas.

"You've already met him?" he asks, his eyes getting wide. This is clearly the most exciting news he's heard all day.

"Yeah...unless there's more than one Lucas. I think he's my scene partner."

The look on his face suggests I've just made his day.

"They didn't tell you that we're supposed to be a couple?" I ask. "Lucas says Sinclair Jones told him." I should have pumped him for more information about that, but I'd gotten side-tracked. Story of my life.

"They don't tell us a single thing more than they want to," he says with a sniff. "Which is ridiculous, because we'll want your colors to coordinate, obviously."

"I thought about mentioning it earlier, but black matches with everything," I say, not managing to sound very happy about it.

"Pity, sugar. You're someone who could carry color."

It's the kind of compliment that can only make me glow, even though my mind is on Lucas and that dark underbelly I sensed. I've always been drawn to wounded people. Like to like, they say.

The costume designer glances back to the end of the corridor, but we're alone other than one extra fussing with the goodies on the accessories table, making a face at all of the pairs of oversized clip-on earrings. "What do you know about the Burkes?" he asks.

"Just what everyone else knows, I guess. They own a lot of buildings all around town." My heart lurches. My voice sounds tight as I add, "And they owned that one building that collapsed eight years ago."

"Don't you watch the news, hon?"

The honest answer is no. The news depresses me nine times out of ten. Some people can watch those horrible stories about lives ripped apart without carrying the weight of it, but I'm not like that. People have been calling me too sensitive all my life, but I don't know how to be any other way.

"Not much," I say, feeling a little ashamed by it. This is something else an adult should be: informed.

"Well, do I have a story for you—"

"You ready for another one?" Christian asks in that harried tone of his, popping out from behind a clothing rack. A shortcut, I'm guessing. It's a wonder he's in this much of a hurry when we've done nothing but sit around for almost two hours, but I can sort of understand. I always feel late for things, even when I'm not. My mind is constantly moving from one thing to the next—it'll be chugging along on one topic when I remember something I wanted to tell Mira. Probably something I wanted to tell her the day before.

"Just a second," the designer says. "I'm finishing up with Giselle here."

"Giselle?" I ask as Christian waves a hand and walks away.

"You remind me of Amy Adams in that kids' movie," he says, giving the belt another micro-adjustment.

This is obviously a huge compliment, so I thank him.

His gaze follows Christian's back before pinging back to me. "Your belt's fine, sweetheart. I just wanted to give you the scoop. But if I do, I'm relying on you to keep an eye on Lucas for me."

I don't like the thought of spying on Lucas, but the designer continues without waiting for me to say anything. "The House of Burke is tumbling down."

"Why?" I ask, my heart thumping faster again. "What happened?" I'm gripped by the sudden certainty that whatever he's about to say next is the *real* reason I'm meant to be here. Not Jeremy. Not acting. But something to do with Lucas Burke. *That's* why I almost hit him this morning, why he's my scene partner even though no one told me so. I'm supposed to be.

"Burke Enterprises has got themselves a whistleblower." He motions for me to follow him and leads the way over to the accessories table. He selects a pair of bright gold clip-on earrings for me that make my heart happy because at least these and the belt add some flair to my outfit. They make me feel more like myself.

"What did they do?" I press him after I clip on the metal, which is uncomfortable but pretty.

"Plenty, it turns out," he says. "But the main thing is that they were responsible for that building collapse. The evidence is pretty compelling. The Burkes knew they were putting people in danger by building the Newton Building too close to a sinkhole, but they chose to build there anyway. And then they set up that general contractor to take the fall for it. Paid off a few folks too, to keep it all quiet." He tsks. "That's rich people for you. Always someone else's fault."

My blood runs cold.

My best friend was killed in that accident.

I'm pacing in the corridor next to the room where the other extras are waiting, my heart thumping an uncomfortable rhythm in my chest.

I need to talk to Mira. She's well informed, so there's no way didn't know about this. She knew and didn't tell me, which feels crappy. At the same time, I get it. She was trying to protect me, and I'd do the same if our situations were reversed.

I tell myself not to jump to conclusions. After all, the costume designer, whose name I somehow still don't know, was speaking off the cuff. He didn't show me any proof.

If only I had my phone, I could do some poking around of my own, but I left it in the car.

"Are you okay, Delia?" a deep voice asks—the sound of my name sending a shock through me—and I turn to see him behind me. Lucas.

He's wearing a belt with a golden buckle, just like mine. It's ridiculous, but the first thought that occurs to me shoots straight out of my mouth. "I guess our characters got his and her belts after all."

He takes a step toward me. I take a step back.

A furrow appears on his brow. "Did I do something to upset you? You've been out here for half an hour."

"You're Lucas Burke," I say much too loudly. "Your family runs Burke Enterprises." In my peripheral vision, I see someone scurrying around a corner.

He sighs and then swears under his breath. "I was hoping not to advertise that."

"Because people have figured out the truth about what your

family did?" I accuse, my heart racing like a scared rabbit's. But I have to confront him. Have to. I would be doing Natalie a disservice if I spent a whole month with this man without confronting him.

"What did he say to you?" he asks, his tone cold now. "It was the costume guy, right? I noticed the way he was looking at me."

"Going to get him fired?" I blurt. "You're used to getting your way, aren't you?"

His jaw hardens. "I didn't realize I'd created such a bad impression."

Something in my stomach sinks, because the truth is, he didn't create a bad impression. Up until half an hour ago, I liked him. He's a Burke, though, and if what the very forthcoming costume designer said is true, then he's my enemy.

Maybe this is why fate brought us together—so I could confront him. So someone could make the Burkes understand what they took from us that day.

"My best friend died in that building collapse," I blurt.

The look in his eyes shocks me. I'd expected him to be defensive, but he seems devastated, his eyes a liquid blue like the depths of the ocean. He takes a step toward me, his hand lifting, then stops himself. Swallows. "I'm sorry. I'm trying to make it right."

"How?" I blurt, knowing I'm speaking too loudly but unable to be quieter. "You can't bring her back. No one can."

Again, there's pain on his face, raw and bone-deep, and I feel another flicker of doubt. Maybe I got this wrong. Maybe, like usual, I should have done more research before leaping in.

"I know that," he says thickly. "It's what keeps me up at night. I'll bet you wish you hit me with your car for real. Maybe you should have." The expression on his face says he half means it, that feeling physical pain would be a relief because of what's been living inside him.

My mind is a traitorous and terrible thing, because it's urging me to comfort him. To trace the shape of his jaw and wrap my arms around him. To give him the forgiveness he's clearly seeking from someone. But I won't. It's not on me to make him feel better, to lift the guilt from his broad shoulders. If his family had acted differently —if they'd acted humanely—Nat would still be alive. We'd be running Rent a Granddaughter together, as we'd planned.

I wouldn't be alone.

"Were you part of that project?" I ask him point blank.

"No," he says, and I believe him. The truth of it is written into every piece of his being. "I didn't know anything about it, and I don't work there anymore. But if you want me to leave, I will. Or I can ask to switch extra roles with Leonard so we don't have to be paired together."

"No," I say. "It's fine."

Except I'm far from sure that's true.

four

LUCAS

I RETREAT to the holding area, feeling like shit on the bottom of Delia Evans's shoe.

As predicted, Leonard was made to lose the hat, but they gave him a replacement—a fedora that suits him but doesn't conceal his hair or his face. He takes one look at me and whistles. "Nice belt."

I'd forgotten about the damn belt. It's gaudy, and I'm certain my mother would call it gauche. I hate anything that compels me to agree with my mother.

I slump into my chair, and he lifts an eyebrow. "Something happened to you. You look even more pissed off than you have recently."

I feel like the inside of my chest has turned to ash and caved in. I didn't know what my parents were doing back then, and I've done my damnedest to take them down over the past couple of months, so why doesn't it feel like enough?

I could have told Delia that, I suppose, but I didn't want to make excuses for myself. Four people died in the collapse. I've looked up their names and photos, and I think about them at night, when I'm supposed to be sleeping. So unless Delia's best friend was a much older woman or a man, I know her name. Natalie Reiter.

31

I wonder whether my grandparents pulled this kind of shit too. For all I know, the money in my trust fund is blood money, earned by cutting the kind of corners that kill people. Maybe my parents aren't just a diseased limb on the tree; maybe the tree itself is rotten on the inside.

"I'm an asshole," I say.

"Well, I didn't want to be the one to say it," Leonard tells me, but it's obvious from his tone that he's trying to comfort me by being himself. By not treating me like I'm damaged.

"Her best friend died in the Newton Building collapse," I say. "I guess she just found out who I am."

He whistles again. "Damn. That's a kick to the nuts."

"We should probably leave." But I don't get up, because if I fuck off, there's a chance they'll cut Delia's role. I rake my hands through my hair, feeling half crazed by our encounter in the hall, and I tell Leonard as much.

He surprises me by squeezing my shoulder. "You did nothing wrong, Burke. You can trust me when I say that, because I've made plenty of bad decisions."

I glance around to make sure no one noticed him calling me that. The closest woman is crocheting what looks like a sock or a small tube top from sparkly pink yarn that make me think of Delia's affection for pink shirts. It's aggressively ugly, the kind of thing that will live in the back of someone's closet for years because they feel too guilty to toss a homemade gift.

No one's looking, and if they're listening, they're being subtle about it.

Part of me likes being called Burke, the nickname I've had for most of my life. When you're the fourth Lucas Burke in a long line of them, you want something for yourself, a name to make you stand out as *that* Lucas. Answering to my first name still feels strange to me, like I'm playacting, but I asked my friends to make the switch before all hell broke loose with my family. Burke is the man I was before I learned the truth about my family. Before I learned they're a scourge on other people.

Then it hits me. Maybe I'm looking at everything the wrong way. Maybe this is my chance to do some good. To right some wrongs. "I'm going to fix her life," I blurt.

"Excuse me?" Leonard says, lifting his eyebrows.

Yeah, that didn't come out quite right.

"I'm going to fix things for her. Help her, you know?" I make a gesture with my hand, frustrated that I'm still not getting it right.

"And how are you going to do that? Don't get me wrong, that woman definitely shouldn't have a driver's license, but other than that, she's doing just fine. Hell, I might ask Doris and Ross if I can move in with them too. What I wouldn't give to have someone around to make me shitty muffins."

"Danny made you some good muffins last week after you complained about having no working kitchen."

"Huh," he says with a shrug, leaning back in his chair like he might drift off into a nap. "I guess you're right, but I'd enjoy them more if they came from a woman."

From my peripheral vision, I see the tube-top woman tuck her questionable work into her bag and take out her phone. I ignore both her and Leonard, my mind churning.

"What about that guy she likes?" I snap my fingers, my pulse picking up because this has to work. I *need* it to work. I have to change the expression that was on Delia's face just now. I'll never forget it. Unlike this guy's name. "Jerald."

"Jeremy," he corrects.

I point at him. "Yes. I'm going to get him for her."

His eyebrows hike a little higher. "How the fuck you going to do that? What if he doesn't go for her?"

The suggestion annoys me. "Why wouldn't he? She's sweet and gorgeous. Funny. She's definitely good enough for *Jeremy*."

He tilts his head slightly. "Sounds to me like *you* have a thing for her."

"She hates me," I say flatly, the words like dust in my mouth. "And she *should* hate me."

He gives me a fake punch in my arm that's hard enough to hurt a bit, which was probably intentional. "Quit dragging yourself down, dumbass. If you want to take a verbal beating, take up your mother's invitation to tea. You don't need to go ham on yourself."

Although it's not public knowledge who the whistleblower is, *they* know. I was raised to be the next Burke CEO, but I quit my job abruptly. My decision was met with shocked disbelief, accusations of ingratitude, and suspicion. A week later, my parents were arrested. They instantly got out on bail, and the company was placed under the leadership of my father's CFO, a distant cousin who probably whispers the party line to his wife in bed. My parents didn't reach out to me a single time while all of this went down. I sure as hell didn't reach out to them either. We were in a silent stand-off, and I liked it just fine that way. But it ended a few days ago, when my mother invited me to tea, possibly to poison me.

"You should hate me too," I mutter.

Leonard used to work at Burke Enterprises, but he left his job—and Asheville—eight years ago, after confronting my parents about the decisions they'd made with the Newton Building.

They'd threatened him—surprise, surprise—and told him what he already knew: he had a checkered past and no concrete evidence. Then they offered to pay him off. Of course, all of this was communicated in innuendos, nothing outright admitted other than that they thought very little of him and his chances of being taken seriously.

He accepted. But my parents aren't the type to leave loose threads. When he found out they were having him followed, he ran—and kept right on running up until a couple of months ago, when Drew and I finally found him and convinced him to come home. To *stay* home.

I may be the whistleblower, the person who helped the feds build a case against my parents, but I never would have known if not for him.

"Yeah, I probably should hate you," he says, leaning back in his chair. "Because you're annoying when you get down on yourself. Be like me, a happy asshole. Let me level with you, though, your little plan to get Delia some dick is flawed on multiple levels."

I feel a rush of annoyance. "I don't want to get her dick," I snap. "I—"

"What you do on your own time is your business," Christian says, clapping his hands. I'm startled by how close he is—no more than three feet in front of me. He has a manic expression behind those yellow glasses, and it's clear he's forgotten he nearly prostrated himself before me a couple of hours ago. "You need hair and makeup."

I give him a flat look. "My hair is about two inches long. What're they going to do, French braid it?"

"Hair and makeup," he repeats in a tone that suggests he'd underline and italicize it if given the opportunity.

His gaze shifts to Leonard. "Who gave you that hat?" he barks.

Which is when I realize Leonard must have nabbed it without permission. It's enough to make me smile, but only for half a second. Because Delia still isn't in the room, and she must need hair and makeup too.

"Can you go find Delia and tell her she needs hair and makeup?" I ask Leonard, who has begrudgingly removed the hat.

He snorts. "You think I'm going to tell a woman that she needs her hair and makeup done?"

"Yes," Christian says. "Do." He taps that watch on his wrist so adamantly I'm shocked it doesn't pop a spring. "We're running an hour behind schedule."

Leonard heaves a sigh and turns to leave the room. I feel like a tool as I watch him go, because I've sent him to do something I want done, like he's a peon or employee. It's the kind of thing my parents would do. "Wait," I call after him. "I'll tell her."

"I need *you* in hair and makeup," Christian insists, sounding annoyed but not so annoyed that he wants to yell at someone with a connection to the star of the movie. I'm a dick for taking advantage of it, but in for a penny.

"Take him first," I say. "His hair is longer than mine."

He gives Leonard an appraising look, then snaps, "Are those visible tattoos on your arms?"

I take my chance and escape, my heart pounding, because I both want to see her and don't. I check the hallway where she was before, but there's no sign of Delia, only the faint smell of vanilla. There are a few people gathered around the craft services table, one of the guys eating a giant soft pretzel. They're bitching about Christian, and while I'd love to join in under different circumstances, I'm getting worried.

What if she left?

What if I ruined this experience for her before it truly started?

I spend about half an hour looking—there's not much space to cover, truthfully—before I finally admit defeat. She's either in the women's restroom, in which case I can hardly go in there without looking like a pervert or a stalker, or she's gone home. So I head back to hair and makeup. There's a wild feeling inside of me, a desperation I don't fully understand and like even less.

"He graces us with his presence," Christian announces as I walk back in, any signs of subservience gone.

"I couldn't find her," I say, sounding defeated. Feeling it too. There's a burning sensation in my chest when I think of that look on her face.

"She's already been and gone, stud," he says. "And you missed the lowdown on what we're doing today."

"Being human scenery? I think I can manage it."

Christian's expression twists with dislike before he regains control of it. I suppose that's fair. *"Hair and makeup."*

Leonard's watching us with a small smile on his face, sprawled in the same chair he was in before. He's still wearing that damn hat, so presumably he persuaded the hair and makeup people to let him keep it. I'm not surprised. Leonard has a profound ability to persuade people around to his way of thinking. I find myself hoping, not for the first time, that I'm not being an idiot for trusting him.

Even though I get the sense that Leonard is closer to me and our buddies than to anyone else in this world, he still hasn't told us much about what his life was like before we met. I don't know where he grew up or how. All I know is that the last name he had when I first met him—Ashford—isn't the one he was born with.

Maybe he'll never tell me more.

Doesn't matter. I'm going to show him that he can count on me. Maybe that'll be enough to get him to fully open up someday, or maybe he'll never want to face up to what he's left behind. That's okay too.

I clear my throat and ask, "She okay?"

He shrugs. "But they made her hair look damn good."

As if that would take effort.

"So what's the movie about, anyway?"

He gives another shrug, this one lazier than the last. "I have an admirable ability to block people out when I don't care what they're talking about. Do it to you all the time."

"Very funny."

"I thought so," he says, his lips tipping up. "It's something about an old house and contracts. Sounds boring as hell. Do you think Sinclair's going to have to make out with that dude for the camera?"

"Probably." I can't imagine what else they'll be doing for the two-hour runtime.

A woman with short curly hair that reminds me of that photo of Natalie Reiter waves me into her chair.

"Are you okay?" she asks as I sit. "You look like you've seen a ghost."

No, I finally admit to myself. I'm not okay.

five

"THAT'S LOVELY," I say to the older woman sitting beside me. She's crocheting a sparkly pink sweater, her stitches much neater than anything I'm capable of. *She* probably doesn't have half a dozen projects sitting in a basket next to her couch.

When we arrived at the Rolf Estate, we were brought to a small building in the back and told it would be our holding area, as if we're criminals and they're not quite sure what to charge us with yet. There's tea and coffee, and it looks like whoever was here before us was treated to a lovely meal, the remnants of which are scattered around at the empty tables. But I've spent the last ten minutes looking at my hands, trapped in my own mind. Thinking about Nat and Lucas and the grief on his face when I told him about her.

He couldn't have been pretending, could he? Yes, we're here as actors, but we're extras, background, and I don't think anyone could have manufactured that look.

I know what grief looks like. My grief was loud and large, an animal that lived inside of me and let itself be known. I cried while walking through the streets. In the grocery store. In line at the post office. Lucas Burke isn't that kind of man, though. He's the kind who'd stuff it down until it bursts from him. That's what I saw, earlier, I think. The beginning of that explosion.

Honestly, the very idea of a man like him serving as background is ludicrous. Surely he'll take attention away from where it belongs. He's so tall and sturdy, and he has that coloring—the raven dark hair and the intense blue eyes. He has *presence*.

I was grateful that I didn't have to see him again before getting on the bus, but I know it won't be a long escape. We'll have to stand next to each other, at the very least.

While we were finishing up hair and makeup, Christian walked us through the scene we'll be filming today. First, he repeated at least three times that we weren't to share the details with anyone, as if gossip columnists might be hiding behind the bushes, hungry for details about the plot. The movie is about a couple of rival developers who want to purchase the Rolf Estate—Jeremy to develop it, Sinclair to preserve it. The current owners insist they both have to stay in it for a week while devising their plans, then present their competing visions at a party. Leonard snorted "the fuck they did" at that part, but Christian ignored him.

Most of the extras are going to be other guests at the house. I guess Lucas and I are supposed to be friends of the owners, only we're silent friends with no lines.

Today, we're going to be filming the scene where the rivals first meet. It's the kind of thing I'd normally enjoy. Part of the reason I had that crush on Jeremy is because I loved watching him act. It swept me away, just like being in this house does. I know it makes me sound childish, but I've never gotten over the fun of playing pretend, of imagining I live in a world where unicorns are real and magic is possible and people can fall in love with you at the drop of a hat. A world where people accept you as you are without feeling the need to make you different.

But I'm not feeling joyful anymore. The excitement has seeped out of the day. I don't really want confirmation that Jeremy is a jerk or that fate didn't send me here as some kind of celestial gift but rather to rub it in my face that Nat is gone forever. I'd rather slide back into my normal life—my comfortable routine that might look like chaos to someone who doesn't get it.

"I was beginning to wonder if something was wrong with you," the crocheting woman says, tutting her tongue. "If you'd gone five more minutes like that, I would have tapped you on the nose. You have lovely hands, dear, but there can be nothing so fascinating about them. Or this sweater. It's for a dog, and he doesn't give two shits about it."

She startles a laugh out of me. "You're right. I got caught in my own head."

"Happens to the best of us."

"Happens to me a lot," I admit.

"You nervous about the movie?" she asks, making a stitch. "Don't be. They may be actors, but they're as human as the rest of us. They all shit. And strip off the pancake makeup, and they have blemishes and wrinkles too, presuming they haven't paid a dermatologist to laser them off."

I'm instantly drawn in by this woman. She says more than she should, like me, but I can tell it's less that she can't help it and more that she doesn't give a crap what other people think. Her hair is long and white, pulled back into a dignified bun, and she has warm hazel eyes with a merry tilt to them.

"What's your name?" I ask. "I'm Delia."

"Constance," she says, setting down her crochet hook and the pink sweater.

We shake hands, and I awaken to the scene around us. There are about six other extras sitting around the table, all of us dressed in innocuous clothing. A couple of other people are wandering around the floor or standing at the large plate-glass windows that overlook the house and grounds. There's a man across the table from us who

41

appears to have nodded off, and a few of the others are having a conversation none of them seem interested in.

"This isn't really like I thought it'd be," I admit. "It's kind of..."

"Boring?" She laughs softly. "Life's like that a lot, isn't it? We expect roses, but we forget they grow in dirt."

"It's not like that," I protest. "I just..."

I trail off, because she's right, really. I had an expectation that was more colorful and exciting than the reality.

"I saw you talking to those handsome young men earlier," she says, fanning herself with a hand. "If I were forty years younger, what I wouldn't do for the one in the hat."

"You don't think the other one is more handsome?" I blurt. "Lucas has presence."

Her eyes light up, and I instantly know I said too much. "They're both good-looking boys," she acknowledges, her eyes sparkling. Then she purses her lips, as if considering something, and says, "You know, I heard them talking about you."

My heart thumps faster. "Really?"

"No one notices an old woman and her crocheting. Well, I may be old, but there's not a damn thing wrong with my hearing."

"What did they say?" I ask, my voice a little too loud. The snoring man grunts and adjusts himself, his head now leaning on the shoulder of the man beside him, who edges away without missing a beat in his conversation with the others.

"Mr. Presence wants to fix your life. Something about making things right."

I feel something curdle inside of me. How many men have wanted to change me? To take the raw material of Delia Evans and shape it into something impressive?

How dare Lucas think changing me to fit his vision could somehow make things right.

"Fuck him," I say, flinching when the word comes out. I've

always wanted to be the kind of person who can swear without feeling like a child being naughty, but it hasn't happened yet.

Constance grins at me. "There's the spirit. I didn't much like the way he was talking either. Sometimes men like that need to be taught the proper way to behave toward a lady, don't you agree?"

I tilt my head slightly to the side. "Oh?"

"I suggest you let him get along with his little project and use it as a teachable moment. You'll be doing him a favor that lasts his lifetime, and we'll have something to entertain ourselves with while we sit around." She scrunches her nose. "Didn't think there'd be quite this much sitting when I agreed to this. I sit on my keister too much as it is."

"At least you thought ahead," I say, gesturing to her crocheting. "They said we couldn't bring phones or books inside the house, so I didn't bring anything."

"A rule follower, then," she says with a nod. "We'll work on that."

I can't help but smile. "Not so much a rule follower as someone who always seems to do the wrong thing. Or so I'm told."

"Next time someone tells you that, give them a good thump and see if they say it again."

I laugh, warming to her more. Being around her is like drinking a cup of chamomile tea after being caught in Storm Lucas. "How'd you end up doing this?"

"My granddaughter, Shauna, knows the star of the movie. Seemed like a reasonable way to spend a few hours. When you get to be my age, you'll do just about anything for some amusement."

"She knows Jeremy?" I ask, startled.

She snorts. "Don't I wish. He's a handsome devil, isn't he? And God knows that girl deserves to find a good man, or at least one who knows how to look good and shut up. No, I'm talking about Sinclair Jones."

Did Sinclair personally hire half the people on set?

"Lucas...I mean, Mr. Presence knows her too," I blurt.

"He does?" Constance says, seeming fascinated by this.

I look around, reassuring myself that we're still being ignored by everyone around us, then whisper, "He's Lucas *Burke*."

"Perhaps that's supposed to mean something to me, my dear, but the only thing I know is that they're rich. When you've been around for as long as I have, all of those hoity-toity families tend to blend together. Rich people soup, I call it."

Part of me is disappointed, but one thing's obvious—Constance is a woman who likes to talk. Something tells me she'll be talking to Sinclair about Lucas—and telling me whatever she finds out. I shouldn't care. He's a jerk twice over, but I can't deny I'm curious. Part of the reason for my three jobs is that curiosity. I have the desire to do and try and *be* everything, because it feels painful to not experience new things. To let them float by like balloon strings un-grasped.

"What do you do for a living?" Constance asks, picking her project back up and taking a lazy stitch.

"I'm a bit of a..."

Handywoman?

Helper?

I settle on the term that Leonard used earlier. "Jack-of-all-trades. I run a business called Granddaughter for Rent. I help people."

She gives me a shrewd look. "What exactly do you do to help them?" Her tone's more direct than it is rude, and I'm not the least bit offended. Still, I wonder if I really should change the name.

"Pick up dry cleaning, clean, mow lawns, that kind of thing."

She lowers the crocheted sweater into her lap. "How much do you charge? Bertie, my sweet fool, is a handful, and my granddaughter can't spend all her free time taking care of us."

Am I about to get offered another job while on this one?

I tell her my rate, and she plugs my number into her phone. "This, my dear Delia, is what they call the beginning of a beautiful friendship."

I have to smile at that. Nat and I used to love *Casablanca*. We thought it made us very romantic, watching classic movies. I also regularly watch old films with Doris, who calls them her black and whites.

"I'm glad," I say. "I look forward to meeting Bertie."

She waves a hand dismissively. "Oh, get ready for a lot of hot air coming out of both ends. But I love him, God help me."

Without meaning to, I'm laughing again. She's so irreverent but effusive, and the combination is charming.

"You and Shauna will get along too," she says, "once she gets over letting someone else do something for us. That girl's always taking the weight of the world on her shoulders."

It's then that Christian bursts into the room in a state of frantic energy, followed by Lucas and Leonard and a couple of other extras. This last group looks like their makeup was forgotten, and one woman has hair that's only half done. "This is it, gang!" Christian says, pressing a hand to his chest. "It's time for you to make me proud."

"Mommy issues," Constance says under her breath, pulling a half laugh from me. "We'll discuss this later."

six

DELIA

WE GET up and join the group, but I haven't made it two steps before I remember the sleeping man. It's obvious Christian hasn't noticed him or is too amped up to care that he's leaving one of his ducklings behind. So I rush over and jostle his arm.

He wakes with a snort, then blurts, "I wasn't sleeping."

It's what Ross always says, too, when he's asleep in his arm chair, his head hanging back, his snore as loud and even as one of the tracks on those white noise machines.

"Of course not," I assure him, "but I was worried you didn't hear Christian. We need to leave."

He gets up slowly, in the joint-creaking way of people who've seen several birthdays, and I reach out to help him.

I can feel Lucas watching me, but I don't look back. We all exit the building in a pack led by Christian, who then herds us in through the front door of the Rolf Estate. A blond man with an intense expression greets us and aggressively shushes us even though no one has spoken.

"We're doing a sound check," he says in a harsh tone.

Christian's eyes go wide, and he beckons us forward. There's a big group of people gathered inside the large, sweeping foyer. A grand staircase twists upward at one side, there's a hearth the size of my bedroom on the other, and large, expensive-looking paintings and tapestries hang on all of the walls that don't have floor-to-ceiling windows. Suited guards are positioned along the perimeter of the room, watching the film crew—and now us—with open suspicion. It's barely organized chaos, overwhelming to the senses after the staid holding space where they stowed us for an hour. *This* is what I expected from this experience, and the life buzzing around me makes me hum with it.

There's no sign of Jeremy or Sinclair, but there are a couple of people wearing oversized badges with their names on them. "Stand-ins," Constance stage-whispers.

I expect her to get shushed, but suddenly no one seems to care about the sound issue anymore.

"I said it in the note, but I'm saying it again. Don't walk too heavily," Christian tells us, snapping his fingers.

"During filming?" someone asks.

"Always. Quiet, soft footsteps. The Rolf people want us to treat the floor like it's a lover."

Lucas doesn't bother to hold back his laughter. The sound sinks into me, like my body wants to soak it up even though my mind isn't in agreement. Christian sniffs as if offended but doesn't comment.

We're handed off to a bald man with fuzzy eyebrows and a bright orange lanyard printed with the logo of a popular orange juice company. He looks like he's not quite sure what to do with us.

"I was told someone would do my hair," the woman with the half-fixed hair says.

"It looks fantastic," Orange Lanyard says dismissively, not even looking at her.

It definitely doesn't.

"But it's an updo with only half of it up," she says hesitantly. "Surely that'll be noticed."

When he glances up at her, he visibly recoils, then glances

around the room. Failing to find any hair and makeup people, he shrugs. "Keep your head angled away from the camera."

I make a mental note to help her, but Orange Lanyard turns on us. "What are your roles?" he barks, sounding annoyed that he can't tell just by looking. We tell him, and he starts moving people around the room.

Five minutes later, he has Lucas and me positioned by a tapestry on the wall. Scowling, Orange Lanyard says, "This isn't a commercial for sleeping pills, for Christ's sake. You're supposed to look like you're in love. If you feel the need to pretend you're in a commercial, pretend it's for little blue pills. Who brought you in?"

I glance at Lucas, fully expecting him to say the star of the movie recruited him. Almost wanting him to say it because it would confirm... I don't know. That he's a jerk? Entitled?

"I wasn't aware we were supposed to start acting yet," Lucas says, lifting his eyebrows. "This is my natural expression."

Orange Lanyard just scowls at him, then says, "When the AD or director says background, that's your cue."

"What's an AD?" I ask.

His expression condescending, he says, "Assistant director." Then he nods at the severe-looking blond man who silenced us at the door. "When your cue is delivered, start talking. Touching each other." He gives me a lingering look. "Like this," he says, jutting his hand out as if he wants to slap a bug off me. I'm too shocked to move as he rubs the hand up and down my side. It's about as sensual as spreading mustard on a sandwich.

Lucas slaps the guy's hand away before I can even think to act. "You'll want to keep your hands to yourself." He's radiating menace, and I'm suddenly deeply aware of how big he is—tall and broad and with that indefinable presence. I'm not attracted to violence—I abhor it—yet a little thrill runs through me. Maybe it's because it's been a while since someone stood up for me in quite this way.

Actually, I'm not sure anyone's ever stood up for me in quite this way.

Orange Lanyard's eyes bug out, and I'm sure he's about to throw both of us out, except then a woman says, "Is there a problem here?"

This time, Orange Lanyard's eyes look like they might actually pop out of his face. I turn and see Sinclair Jones, only this time her face isn't hurtling toward me at sixty-five miles per hour.

Jeremy is standing next to her. He's right there with his curly russet hair, big brown eyes, and perfectly carved nose, as if Michelangelo himself chipped it out of stone. I expect my body to react to his nearness, but my pulse is completely unaffected.

To be fair, the story about the seltzer was very off-putting, and the chatty costumes guy has proven to be a reliable source of information.

Jeremy gives me a lingering look, his brow slightly furrowed.

"Do I know you?"

"You went to high school together," Lucas says, speaking for me. He seems pissed off, like he's not over Orange Lanyard's attempt to feel me up.

Speaking of Orange Lanyard, he sees we're caught up in conversation and takes the opportunity to scurry away.

I give Lucas a frown of disapproval. "I can speak for myself." Shifting my gaze to Jeremy, I say, "We went to high school together."

Lucas really took the wind out of my sails. I shoot him a glare, but when our eyes meet, I feel a little trip in my pulse.

I'm instantly annoyed with myself. How can I be attracted to this man, knowing what I know? Then again, I suspect most people who are into men would be drawn to Lucas Burke.

Jeremy snaps his fingers, then reaches out and touches my arm. I half-expect Lucas to slap him away too, but he watches with a pained look on his face.

"Delilah," Jeremy says. "You were that girl from drama class, but you had black hair back then." He takes another long look at me. "You've *really* filled out."

"Her name is Delia," Lucas says tightly, his jaw twitching.

"Delia," Jeremy repeats, his eyes on me, hand still on my arm. "Even better. I guess there are some upsides to coming back to this dump. So what do you do now?" His mouth forms a smile that should be devastating. "Still into drama, I see."

"Yeah," I say, suddenly hyper-aware of his hand on my arm. It's slightly clammy. I shift slightly, and he moves it. "This is the only time I've done this before, but I do parties and events in a mermaid costume, so I guess I do some acting."

"Like...adult parties?" he asks in a tone that makes me flush.

"For kids," I say, trying not to sound annoyed. This is another one I've heard a lot. Between my mermaid readings and Grand-daughter for Rent, I'm constantly being asked whether I'm a sex worker.

Sinclair clears her throat. I turn toward her, but her expression is polite and unreadable. She nods to Lucas. "Hey, Lucas. Good to see you." Then she glances back at me. "Was that guy being inappropriate with you earlier?"

I'm surprised she cares enough to ask. Her earnestness makes me want to be honest, but I don't necessarily want to get Orange Lanyard fired for touching my arm. "No, it's fine."

"You tell me if he bothers you again," she insists. "That's not the kind of set I want to have."

I catch Jeremy rolling his eyes. Unless Sinclair Jones is lying and he knows it, here's proof that he's a "full bag of tools," to use Nat's term for guys like him.

Did I have terrible taste in high school?

Probably. Mira would likely remind me that we all had terrible taste in high school, or else everyone would still be wearing handker-chief tops.

"We have to go," Sinclair says, looking at Lucas, "but I'll see you later."

"And I'll see *you* later," Jeremy tells me.

"Accurate," Lucas says dryly. "Your stand-in is less than thirty feet from us. I'm assuming that's where you'll be."

Sinclair's lips twitch slightly, as if she wants to smile but won't let herself, and they move forward to take their marks. It's then I realize that everyone in the room has been waiting for us. While they wouldn't dream of waiting for a couple of extras, the stars have a certain leverage.

"I guess we need to get closer to each other," I say to Lucas. He steps toward me, near enough that I can feel his heat, and I don't like the way the proximity wraps around me like a promise.

I don't like him. I can't. Even if he didn't know about the Newton Building, which is unconfirmed, he's a pompous jerk—the kind of man who thinks he knows better. I'm never going to let anyone else tell me who to be, how to dress.

Well, okay, I guess I let the costume department tell me how to dress, but it's one thing to get instructions from your job and quite another to have a man boss you around.

"You seriously like that guy?" Lucas asks me in a whisper.

"I said I liked him in high school," I say, glancing at Jeremy and Sinclair, who's talking to the assistant director in a low voice. Jeremy's watching her with a scornful, almost mocking look. "That was years ago."

I catch sight of Leonard and Constance on the other side of the room. They look like they're conversing in undertones too, but Constance sees me and waves. I'm reminded of her exact wording—"*Mr. Presence wants to fix your life*"—and annoyance stabs into me again and settles. I'm tempted to confront Lucas, but she made a good point. Better to see what he has in mind and foil it. Better to teach him that people aren't pawns to be moved around a board.

"Anyway," I say, returning my gaze to Lucas. His eyes are rooted to mine, so blue they're painful to look at. "It's none of your business who I like. I haven't asked you who you like."

"I've always liked too many people," he murmurs with a half-smile.

I'll bet. With his looks, he'd have no trouble finding women to keep him company, and he has the slick charm of someone whose bed is never empty for long. I don't want to care about that, but the part of me that finds his dubious charm attractive is irritated.

I glower at him. "So who are you to judge me?"

"If you're going to choose someone special, they should *be* special. Otherwise you might as well just have fun."

"God forbid someone should disagree with you about who's special," I snap, pissed—not because of his attitude toward Jeremy, who has all the marks of being a terrible person now that I'm old enough to judge such things, but toward *me*.

His jaw flexes, and he glances away for a second before looking back at me. "I saw you talking to that woman earlier. The one who's making the hideous pink thing. Did you make friends with her?" he says, edging closer. "I figured you couldn't help yourself since she's in your favorite demographic."

I'm taken aback by his insult to Constance's craftsmanship.

"I'll have you know, Constance is making a dog sweater, and it's adorable."

"Huh," he whispers into my ear. "I was guessing tube top or a sock for someone with gout. Why'd you dye your hair black in high school?"

"How'd you know I haven't dyed it red?"

His mouth lifts into a smirk. "I know."

"Because you've slept with a lot of redheads?" I ask before I can stop myself.

Surprise flickers across his face, followed by amusement. "I'm not saying I haven't, but that's not why I know."

"So? Bowl me over with your wisdom and insight."

"Maybe I'll tell you someday."

He's teasing me. I want to tell him he doesn't get to tease me, but instead I find myself saying, "Then maybe I'll tell *you* someday."

"I'll look forward to it," he says, suddenly serious.

That's when someone shouts "Background!"

"You heard Christian earlier. This is our time to shine," Lucas says to me in that low, sexy whisper, then runs his hands up my arms.

It feels nothing like it did when Orange Lanyard or Jeremy did it, and I hate myself a little for enjoying it—for wanting those hands to brush a little higher and lower and all over me.

seven

LUCAS

I LIKE PLANS. I depend on them, especially as the ground quakes beneath me feet, but I'm starting to realize Leonard's right about the plan I made about Delia.

It's total shit.

I can't let that prick Jeremy have her, can I?

Only...based on what she said just now, she still wants him, still thinks he's special.

I glance over as he waves a stack of papers at Sinclair, then see Orange Juice giving me death eyes. Oh yeah, Christian said we're not supposed to look at the stars during filming. That's some bullshit, if you ask me, because if someone was waving a bunch of papers around and shouting at a lady thirty feet from you, you'd be a real tool to keep carrying on with your girl without even giving them a glance to make sure he's not up to any funny business.

Looking back at Delia, I feel a strange tugging sensation inside of me, like my body is physically compelling me to get closer to her. Since that's precisely what I'm supposed to do, I inch toward her, caressing my hands up and down her arms. They're soft, of course, and I notice a speckling of freckles that fascinates me. Do they continue across her chest? Is Delia Evans's body covered in them?

You're an asshole, my inner voice reminds me. Because I'd promised myself I'd help her, not lust after her and imagine what her tits would look like if she tugged her dress down. Besides, we're on the set of a G-rated movie, the last thing I should be doing is fantasizing my way into a hard-on.

"He called the scene," Delia says, stepping back. My hands fall to my sides, and she brushes off her arms as if I might have infected her with something.

For a moment, I'm baffled, because I didn't hear shit. Didn't notice anything either.

"You're a good actor," she says flatly, eying me in a way I don't like.

"Are you suggesting I lied to you earlier?" I say.

"Did you?"

Something inside of me sinks, and I realize that I care about what this woman thinks of me.

"No, Delia. I didn't. I'm not going to make any excuses for myself, but I didn't know what they were doing, and if I had, I would have stopped it."

She holds my gaze while I'm speaking. I feel as if she's holding me on the scales of justice. One word, and I'm damned. One word, and I'm saved.

"I...I memorized all of their names," I blurt. It's not like me to lose my cool, but there isn't enough of it left to freeze an ice cube. "The people who died that day. The man who was blamed for it."

She stares into my eyes for a long moment, unzipping me. Plunging her hand into my chest to see if I have a heart. Finally, she says, "I believe you," just as someone shouts, "Background!"

She takes a step toward me, and when I don't move to touch her, she places her hands on my arms. It feels like she's steadying me. Like I might fall over if she loosens her grip.

Fuck. If she wants Jeremy, I'm going to have to scare him into being a better man, aren't I? In that moment, I'm pretty damn sure I'd do anything for her, foolish as it sounds.

The director or assistant director yells "cut." I can't tell them apart because they're both tall and Nordic looking, wearing identical black on black outfits. They could be twins.

Wait, *are* they twins?

Orange Juice rolls up. He gives me a look that's half cautious, half self-congratulatory, and says, "You nailed it, my friend. That was totally blue pills material."

"I don't need any blue pills," I say, the words rolling out of their own accord because I'm shaken by being so close to Delia. I don't want to be, but there it is.

"I didn't think I did either, brother," he says, positively chatty now that he knows I'm friendly with Sinclair, "but I tried them all the same, and me and my ex had it going on all night long. She was screaming with the dawn, if you know what I'm saying."

"Are you sure she was enjoying herself?" Delia says in that way of hers where you can tell she's not paying attention to what's coming out of her mouth. "Most women don't want to have sex all night long."

I can't help it—I grin at her. "What's your optimal timeline?"

She lifts her brows and gives me an arch glance. "None of your business."

Orange Juice shoots me a "just us guys" look that I'd rather not be on the receiving end of, then says, "Try moving your lips next time, you two. Pretend you're in the middle of a fascinating conversation. You can whisper the word 'watermelon.' It looks visually interesting."

"Speaking of visually interesting," I say. "Is it just me or do the director and assistant director look like clones?"

A startled half laugh escapes Delia, and Orange Juice makes a displeasing sound and says, "Get this—they're not even related. You want to tell them apart? Sinclair Jones gave the director a necklace she made in some workshop. He's been wearing it steady."

This time I'm the one fighting laughter, because I have to wonder if Sinclair did it because she was having trouble distinguishing between them too.

Orange Juice shuffles away, and I whisper to Delia, "You're glad I asked, admit it."

She gives me an arch look and responds with "watermelon."

So we trade "watermelon"s back and forth for the next three takes, her hands on me, mine on hers.

Once more, and the director tells us it's a wrap for this scene. I know it's him, because he is indeed wearing a necklace with an ugly metal charm on it. I make a mental note to tell Sinclair not to quit her day job just yet.

Delia and I aren't doing our happy couple thing in the next scene, so Christian herds us off to a few benches on the opposite side of the cavernous room while the actors who are filming regroup. We collect Leonard and the old lady with the pink sweater thing on the way, along with the woman with half a hairdo and a group of men who look like they're hoping the shuttle will take them to a bar.

"Good job, everyone," he says brightly. "Now sit over here." He motions to the benches. There's room enough for maybe four people to sit. "They may need you again, so you have to stay close. You'll wait here until you're called."

Leonard raises a hand. "What if we need to use the facilities?"

"I told you all to use the restrooms before we came over here from holding," Christian says in a good imitation of a beleaguered teacher.

"I've got a trick bowel," Leonard says.

I'm pretty sure he just wants an excuse to fuck off for half an hour, but I'm not going to call him on it.

Christian heaves a sigh and then announces that he'll take those of us who need the restroom on a group trip, which is clearly not the answer Leonard wanted, but he shrugs and nods to me. "You coming, man? It beats sitting around and watching other people pretend to flirt."

"And get stuck in a room with you and your trick bowel? No, thanks. I'll take my chances here."

All of the older guys go with Leonard and Christian, leaving me alone with Delia, the lady with half a hairdo, and the older lady. They settle on the benches, the older lady immediately slipping off her shoes with zero self-consciousness.

"Just me and the ladies," I say with a grin.

"No need to sound like cock of the walk, son," says the older lady with no shoes. "You've got me, Marlene over there with half of a hairdo, and Delia." She smiles at Delia. "I'll grant you, she's a prize, but she's not *your* prize."

Goddamn, I've never had someone I don't know cut through me so concisely before.

"I was just—"

"Blowing some hot air," she says. "I know. I'm Constance."

"A pleasure to meet you, Constance." I nod to Marlene, next to her, who's now self-consciously patting her hair. "Marlene."

"I'll fix it for you," Delia says, already lifting her hands to take out the pins.

"God bless you," Marlene says.

I noticed the way Delia paused to wake up Sleeping Beauty back in the holding area earlier. How she's helping Marlene now. She's the type of person who gives to other people without even noticing she's doing it. It makes me more determined to follow through on my mission.

"Why are you here?" Constance asks, skewering me with a look even as she lifts one of her socked feet and starts massaging it.

"Maybe I want to be an actor."

"You're certainly charming enough," she says in a tone that suggests she doesn't mean it as a compliment.

I glance at Delia, who's focused on Marlene's hair. Somehow, I can tell she's listening. There's a subconscious message she's sending off.

"I needed a distraction," I tell Constance. "I figured why not. Isn't that why we're all here?"

She gives me a flat look. "Can't you tell I want to be a star?"

I grin at her. She does not grin back.

"I'd like to be a star," Marlene says. "I heard Sinclair Jones is from Asheville. Jeremy too. I figure if it happened for them, it could happen for me."

Probably not. Somewhere in between takes three and four I noticed her on the opposite side of the floor. She looked like she was smiling so hard she'd get rictus of the mouth. I'm guessing no one told her, because she did the same bit of pacing every time someone called action, but I could tell from the way the cameras were angled that she wasn't in the shot.

"Sinclair started when she was a little kid," I say. What I don't add is that her mother is a piece of work who forced it on her.

"You know her?" Constance asks.

Does she think that means I'm a privileged asshole? I'd like to feel offended, but I am a privileged asshole. I've never had to worry about affording the things I need, or even the things I want. And when I went looking for a distraction, my friend's sister offered me a role in her movie. Admittedly, it has every mark of being a shit movie, and my role is to stand around and pretend to talk, but even so.

"I do," I acknowledge.

"So do I," she says with a slight smile. "She's marrying my granddaughter Shauna's friend."

"Oh," I say, taken off-guard. "Sinclair's brother has been my best friend since we were little kids." I pause, then add, "He's in Puerto Rico with his girl for the next few months."

I'm not sure why I felt the need to offer up that information, other than that I miss the bastard. We've talked plenty, but it's strange, knowing that he's not just across town. We've spent most of our lives living ten to fifteen minutes from each other.

I feel Delia watching me, and I glance at her. She instantly fucks up whatever she's doing to Marlene's hair and has to start again.

"Don't you mean his *woman*?" Constance says, her tone hard. "Or do you think all women are little girls, waiting for a man to tell them what to do?"

I stare at her in disbelief for a solid three seconds before I can come up with a response. "Did I do something to offend you, Constance?" I ask, even though I can't imagine what it could possibly be, given this is the first time we've spoken. Unless...

Delia must have told her about my family.

"Oh no, you couldn't offend me if you tried," Constance says, waving her hand dismissively. "You'll have to forgive an old woman for looking for teachable moments. You get to be my age, and you have wisdom to share. Heaps of it."

I glance at Delia, but she won't look at me, which seems to support my theory that she told Constance I'm a Burke—or a "bloody Burke," as the *Asheville Gazette* called us a few weeks ago. Shame coats me, like that one time I was out hiking with the guys, and Danny fell into a mud pit. I went down to get him out, and both of us were covered, head to toe.

"You look familiar," Marlene says suddenly, glancing up at me. "I've been trying to place you all day."

I wait for it. The expression of excitement or disgust. The assessing look of someone who's trying to gauge whether the person in front of them is a murderer or as good as. This is why I haven't been going out much. The only people I've spent time with are my closest friends—Leonard, Danny, and Shane. Drew, but only on the phone or my devices.

Delia glances at me, an unreadable expression in her eyes, and says, "He's just got one of those faces. Hey, have you guys come up with back stories for your characters? I love coming up with stories for things."

Marlene is happy enough to get caught up in Delia's tide, and there's this feeling inside of me that...

I don't have words for it. She's the last person who should be defending or protecting me, yet here she is, doing it.

Delia Evans is someone special, and I'm going to make damn sure she knows it.

Someone dressed in a guard uniform comes around the corner and audibly gasps. "Are you sitting on those benches? Those are from the nineteenth century."

"To clarify," I say. "Is that a bad thing?"

eight

LUCAS

"WHAT WERE YOU SAYING?" Leonard asks, playing with a yo-yo. I don't want to ask where he got it. Knowing him, he probably nabbed it from the director or someone else who's "important." It's late, and we're in the holding area, having just eaten dinner. It was a buffet, and we had to wait for the other actors and crew to buzz through before we were given our shot. Truthfully, Sinclair invited Leonard, Constance, and me to eat in the first wave with her, but Constance said no, and I didn't want to give Delia another reason to think I'm a dick.

By the time we were allowed to serve ourselves, half the tubs were empty, or near enough, and we were left eating rice and salad like a bunch of overgrown rabbits. As we heaped the unappealing food onto our plates, Leonard gave me a sidelong look and said, "This is what happens when you turn down favors, bud. You're stuck with someone else's leftovers."

Now, we've been fed, somewhat, and are sitting in a corner booth by ourselves.

"How much did you listen to?" I ask.

He executes a trick with the yo-yo, the name for which I probably forgot when I was twelve. "Assume the worst."

"We need to get Jeremy talking, see if he's as much of a dick as he seems to be."

"Oh, he most definitely is," Leonard says distractedly, continuing to play with the yo-yo. "I can tell just by looking at him. You get to be a pretty good judge of character when you move around a lot."

"I thought you said you blew through all of my parents' hush money because you made bad decisions and trusted the wrong people."

He laughs, his eyes crinkling at the corners. "That's true. But you're talking to a man with a clear rap sheet."

That's something the feds had agreed to because we'd both helped them build their case against my parents. He hadn't done anything too serious. Petty theft. Gambling. Fights. But it was what you'd call a pattern, started before his time in Asheville, then resumed afterward, when he was living on the run.

"Sure," I say absently, in response to his expectant look.

"Maybe I knew those people were bad news, and I worked with them anyway, kind of like you're working with me."

"You're not bad news," I say, mostly meaning it. Working on the flip house with Leonard is about all I have going on right now, other than silent investing in few different projects, including a computer game that my buddies Drew and Danny made. I don't want my name attached to those things because I wouldn't make the presumption of attaching my name to anything right now. But working outside, doing the hard physical labor required to make an old house shine again, that's something I *can* do, and it makes me feel alive in a way nothing else does. This is always something I've done on the side—one house at a time, no hurry. It's been my refuge, and even more so now. When I'm ripping off rotted boards, it feels like I'm ripping away the parts of myself that don't serve me anymore—like I'm remaking myself as much as the house. It's a fanciful thought, the kind that would make my father, Lucas Cornelius Burke III, sneer, but I like it nonetheless. Or maybe I like it *because* it would make him sneer.

Leonard gives me a look that's at least half serious. "I'm saying this as a friend. When someone tells you they're bad news, it's wise to listen."

"I've never been good at taking direction," I say. "Or so I'm told."

"I guess that's to my benefit," Leonard says with a smirk. He's always giving me outs like this, telling me I can push him into the dirt. For some reason, it makes me want to pull him in tighter. "So we're going to get this guy talking. Let's presume I'm right and he really is a piece of shit."

I glance across the room, to where Delia's sitting at a table with Constance and Marlene. They're both basking in the light she gives off. I have the errant thought that I'd like to do the same. I suspect most of the assholes she meets feel that way.

Constance seems not only resistant to my charm but to actively dislike me. I asked Leonard if she'd interrogated him about me, and he said she hadn't. They'd had a stop-and-go conversation about cheese.

"Well?" Leonard asks, reminding me of his question.

Right. The jackass.

"We'll warn him off her, obviously, and find some other way to help her."

"You got this real Robin Hood vibe going on lately," Leonard says, sighing as he flips the yo-yo into an around-the-world move. That one, I remember. "I can't decide whether I should make you stop."

Christian, who's been sitting at a solo table, watching us all like a mother hen, gets up and claps his hands. "It's your time to shine, my little stars." His yellow glasses are slightly askew, and he looks like he's been sneaking sips from a hip flask. I'm tempted to ask him for some.

Leonard shoots me a rueful look. "You know, this isn't my idea of a good time. Did you overhear the actors' lines?"

"Not really." My attention was on Delia, and they hadn't been wearing mics. The sound will be amped up later.

"Consider yourself lucky. It's like listening to an old married couple argue. It's anyone's guess why someone would consider that romantic."

I shrug and get up, my gaze finding Delia. "It's called banter."

"You watch these movies? On purpose?"

I have to laugh at that. Returning my attention to him as he stuffs the probably stolen yo-yo into his pocket, I say, "Not on purpose, no. But I've dated some women who like them."

"Like Delia?" he asks pointedly. "She seems like the kind of woman who'd enjoy that shit."

"It's like I said. She doesn't like me. She shouldn't. Besides, I'm not a relationship kind of guy."

"You were when I blew town," he says, giving me a significant look as we join the back of the group.

He's talking about my ex-girlfriend Leanne. We dated for a year before I figured out what should have been obvious from her constant requests for gifts and dinner parties with my parents. She wanted me for my name, my position, my money.

She wasn't the first.

After that, I'd changed tactics. If that was what people wanted from me, why not give it to them and take what I wanted?

I haven't been a dick about it. I always tell them going in that I'm not a relationship kind of guy, and the women I've dated haven't cared. But it's hard to have any enthusiasm for that kind of mutual using anymore. I'm not proud of my family name. My money. I don't want to be around anyone who's impressed by them.

"I can see you moping," Leonard says. "It's frankly exhausting. I feel sorry for myself because you feel so sorry for yourself. If you don't want to stop for your own sake, think about me."

I watch Delia step out of the building, trying not to notice the way her ass sways in that black dress—noticing the hell out of it all the same. She's with Constance, who obviously hates me, and Marlene, who'd probably build a statue in Delia's honor because of the hair thing.

We step out after them, and approximately half a second later, Leonard shoves me hard. I have barely enough time to get pissed off before a brick smashes into the cobblestones at my feet.

"That almost hit you in the head," Leonard says, giving me a slightly queasy look.

"What?" Christian squawks. He hurries over to look at the brick, quickly judging that it is a brick and would, indeed, have killed me if it had beaned me in the head. He starts muttering something that sounds a lot like *shit, shit, shit* under his breath, then grabs a walkie-talkie I wasn't aware he had from his pocket. "We have a… Actually, I don't know what this is," he says. "Come to holding. Repeat, come to holding." He looks upset, but there's a note of excitement in his voice, like he's been waiting his whole life for something interesting to happen, and it just missed the mark by a few inches.

I'm still staring at the crushed brick, shock roiling through me. It almost ended right here. Now. What kind of legacy would I have left? Half a day of filming on a movie whose name I don't remember? A family name that I helped tarnish? A fortune sitting in the bank that's spent half my life smothering me?

A warm hand touches my arm, jolting me out of my partial fugue state. It's her. Delia. I can tell from her scent, which is practically burned into my nostrils after spending the whole morning with my hands on her. Vanilla and salt spray, as if she really were a mermaid.

"Lucas, are you okay?"

I look at her, taking in her big eyes, more blue than green in the waning light. She looks…worried for me. She doesn't like me, but at least she doesn't want me to die. That's something, right?

I let myself acknowledge, if only to myself, that I'm interested in her, even if I don't understand the nature of my interest. Then I manage a half smile. "No, Delia, I'm starting to think I'm fucked."

Half an hour later, they send us all home for the night. I watch her go, feeling a strange twinge in my chest. It's just weird, is all—spending all day with someone you don't know and then watching them leave as if they're a stranger again.

She might hate me, but I don't hate her. Far from it.

When I get home, there's a package waiting for me on the table just inside the door. I open it, and a book is tucked inside: *Why Loyalty Matters*.

A shiver runs down my spine. There's no gift receipt or note, but I know it's from my dear old Dad. His way of telling me to go fuck myself, or to answer my mother's invitation.

It's Wednesday, noon, and Leonard and I are having a lunch beer at the flip house after spending half the morning finishing the drywall upstairs. We're sweaty and hot, and it feels damn good to sit out on the huge deck and take in the view of the blue mountains, to catch the breeze sifting through the evergreens and maples.

"What's the next sob story?" Leonard says.

I'm looking at my phone, and he knows what that usually means. I've developed a habit of...helping people, I guess. I'll find a few people on GoFundMe or other sites like that and, well, fund them. Some of them aren't people who are sick or grieving. I'm backing a few other business projects, including Drew and Danny's game, but most of what I've given has been to the people whose need is the greatest, whose grief is the deepest. Nothing can make what happened right or fair, but I figure I can use the Burke fortune to do what the Burkes have not.

But I'm not looking at GoFundMe right now.

"Jeremy says he'll meet us on Saturday night," I say, half

surprised. Sinclair gave me his number, although she didn't seem very pleased about it. The words "piece of shit" were thrown around. Still, I owe it to Delia to try. If he's as worthless as he seems, I can get a recording of his dickery and show it to her. Seeing is believing, after all, and if he's not worth her time, she's better off knowing it.

Leonard hoots and adjust his ballcap. "What's this 'us' you're using so freely? Take Danny or Shane if you need to take someone. I've had about enough of this extras bullshit. I've spent the past few hours daydreaming about what I can do to get kicked off set."

"You can't leave," I say, "you saved my life. If you leave, I'll get struck by lightning or something." I'm pretty sure I'm joking, but I won't lie—I'm shaken. The people who died in the Newton Building were crushed. I'm not a superstitious man, but even someone who's usually immune to superstition can't miss the pie that just hit him in the face. I might have told Delia I'd deserve it if she'd hit me with her car, but that doesn't mean I want to die, especially not like this, in infamy, without having become my own man and not just Lucas Cornelius Burke IV.

The production closed temporarily so there could be a thorough investigation of the Brick-cident, as Leonard is calling it, so the filming schedule's now off by a day. We were supposed to go back on Sunday, but it's been pushed back until Monday.

The consensus about the brick is that the mortar weakened over time and chose that exact moment to give out.

Lucky me.

Then again, it could have killed me and didn't. I guess that's lucky if you look at it in the right light, like a rock that's dull in the dark and proves to be a ruby when you shine something bright at it.

I told the rest of our buddies what happened last night. Shane, who's a lawyer, immediately shot to thinking I should sue. Drew told me I should have kept the brick.

"That was fucked," Leonard says, picking up a stick from the porch and lobbing it. He gives a visible shudder. "If you'd died in front of me, I would have been seriously pissed at you. I've got enough shit to haunt me at night."

I glance at him. "Oh?" My heart starts beating faster. Is he finally going to tell me something real about what brought him here, to Asheville, the first time?

"Yeah, I mean, I'm not the only one who still has nightmares about the time Drew made us climb all the way up Grandfather Mountain."

His deflection tracks. I'm stuck in the past, and Leonard avoids talking about it at all costs.

"I need you to come with me," I say, serious. "I need someone to keep me in check. To help me make sure this guy is what I think he is."

"An asshole?" he says with a snort.

"An asshole," I agree. "But I owe it to her to make sure. She seemed pretty convinced he was someone special." It aggrieves me to admit it, like every word is rubbing sandpaper along my throat as it comes out.

Leonard snorts. "About as special as getting conked in the noggin with a brick." He gives me a look that's half serious. "Maybe it's a sign we shouldn't go back, Burke."

There it is again, that name. *My* name. I don't correct him, though, because there's a weird part of me that wants to be the person I was and the person I'm becoming.

"It was almost certainly a mistake to do the movie," I admit. "But I'm no quitter."

He pulls a face. "That old broad seems to resent the hell out of you."

"I did insult her pink dog sweater." Not to her face, though. There's still a chance Delia told her everything, but she put Marlene off. Would she have done that if she'd already told Constance who I am?

Shaking the thought off, I say, "Meet Jeremy with me."

He sighs and takes a long sip of his lunch beer. "How'd you get him to agree to it?"

"Sinclair did," I admit. "She wasn't too happy about it, to be honest. She told me he's a narcissist, and listening to narcissists' blather just feeds them."

He squints his eyes at me. "Is that what I'm doing right now?"

"Very funny. Anyway. He knows I have funds, and I may have implied I'm interested in funding his new passion project."

He snorts. "What's it about? Does he have some sort of fetish?"

"It's a romantic comedy about a man who switches places with his dog."

He lifts his eyebrows. "You've got to be shitting me. A woman screws a dog in this movie?"

"I didn't read the script, man, I'm just telling you what I know. It's called *Bow-Chicka-Wow-Wow*. I guess he wrote it. Sinclair's the one who told me about it. She figured I could use it as an in. I guess people pretend to be interested in each other's movies all the time in Hollywood."

"Bow Chicka What Now? That guy's more fucked in the head than I thought." He sighs, looking out at the view for a moment, before shifting his gaze back to me. "I'll come, but I won't be nice to him."

I grin and clap him on the back. "I'm counting on it. If he's as much of a dick as we think, we'll document it and make sure Delia knows. I don't want her to try pursuing some douchebag."

He gives me a very Leonard look and says, "Because you'd rather she got it on with one very specific douchebag."

"She's not for me," I insist, even though there's no denying I've been thinking about her. I spent last night Googling her business and trying to brainstorm ways to help her make it more successful. My Burke mindset insists there should be more "granddaughters," that she could be a boss and manager instead of, or at least in addition to, the person doing the actual work.

"Sure, brother, you keep telling yourself that. So where are we meeting the asshat?"

I smirk. "This bar Glitterati. I went there one time with the guys before you came back—"

"Before you dragged me back," he interjects.

"Before I dragged you back to Asheville," I agree, feeling charitable since he's agreed to come. "It's a little...extra, if you don't mind the play on words."

"I do. I absolutely do," he says and takes a swig of his beer. "But I'll come all the same."

I glance at him, taking in the circles under his eyes. He hasn't been sleeping. Then again, neither have I. "You saved my life, man."

Maybe that'll mean something to him.

He grins at me, but it's as forced as if he'd literally pasted it to his face. Leonard doesn't like being thanked. Never has, probably never will, because accepting someone's thanks is as good as admitting you deserve it. "Is it too late to change my mind?"

nine

LUCAS

"IT FEELS like we stepped into a damn disco ball," Leonard says loudly. Luckily, or unluckily, as the case may be, "Barbie Girl" is blasting over the speakers, so it's unlikely anyone heard him. I figure they're playing it ironically. Then again, the bar top in this place is made of clear resin with rainbows of glitter cascading through it, and the décor is, to put it generously, kitsch, filled with the kind of crafts that would be better off in a dumpster. The clientele looks young and hipster, so there's a good chance I won't be recognized here. I'm guessing there aren't a lot of people in Glitterati who keep up with the local news.

"I figured our guy would like this place."

He snorts. "No, you didn't." His gaze turns incisive. "But I'll bet Delia would."

The thought had occurred to me. She seems addicted to bright, shiny things, from the ornament hanging from the mirror of her car to that gold belt she kept smoothing her fingers over and the sweater Constance is crocheting.

"Will we even be able to hear him?" Leonard continues.

It's a good point. Honestly, if you have to listen to someone talk about a romantic comedy in which a dog and a man change places, you're probably better off doing it in a loud bar, but I do want to get that recording.

"What about that booth by the window?" I ask, nodding my head toward it.

Leonard turns, considering. "Yeah, that should do it. I don't see any speakers near it. Now, please, for the love of God, tell me this isn't the kind of new age place that serves only kombucha."

I laugh. "No, but your cocktail might be pink."

"I don't care if it has glitter in it as long as it's alcoholic. The more, the better. It's beyond me how I let you talk me into this shit."

Probably for the same reason I let him talk me into things too. Because he feels guilty for leaving. Because I feel guilty for being related to the assholes who drove him away.

"I'll go get us a round of drinks," I say.

He heads off to the table, and after texting Jeremy to let him know where we're sitting, I approach the bar and acquire two suspiciously colored drinks for us, plus another called the Shining Star for Jeremy. It feels appropriate. The bartender is pretty, with dark hair and bright lipstick. I don't feel any pull to flirt with her, but she's familiar in a strange way. I tell myself it's because I've been here once before. Something about that doesn't ring true, though. I'm halfway back to the table with the tray of drinks when I figure out what it is—she smells like Delia. Vanilla and sea salt. It's a unique scent, or at least I thought it was. For all I know, they give it out for free at Bath & Body Works.

When I get back to the table, Jeremy's sitting there in a suit, looking about as uncomfortable as a diabetic in a candy shop. Leonard's monologuing about his addiction to estate sales. I'm relatively sure he's never been to one.

"How's it going?" I ask Jeremy, setting the tray down. "I got you a Shining Star, my man." I set it in front of him.

"What's mine?" Leonard asks, his eyes gleaming.

I point to one of the remaining two. "The Tool."

"Perfect," he says, taking it.

I sit down next to Leonard, wanting to look Jeremy in the eye as I interrogate him. Talk to him, I mean.

Seeing him here, I'm more convinced than ever that he's not fit for Delia.

"So," I say, "you know—"

"What's your favorite part of the script?" Jeremy blurts, staring at me intently.

Leonard shoots me a look that accuses me of holding out on him. The truth is that yes, I *did* get the script from Sinclair, but no, I didn't read beyond the first page. I didn't hand it over to Leonard, because for all I know he'd stick it up on Reddit, and I want Jeremy to be cooperative.

"When that guy Hughey and his dog switch places," I say, because that happens on page one. "Inspired."

"Yeah," Leonard says, taking off his hat and scratching his head. "So, are you into bestiality or something?"

"What?" Jeremy gapes. "That's only when a dog and a human get it on. When Hughey gets it on with the sexy poodle, it's okay because he's in a dog's body. It's natural. Instinctual, even."

"Huh, so you think dogs are sexy?" Leonard says, leaning back in the booth with his arm slung over the top. A dog grins at me from above his elbow, one of his many tattoos, and an ugly scar sits over top of it.

Jeremy's jaw flexes. "I didn't say that."

He did.

"It's okay, brother," Leonard says, lifting up his hands. "Different strokes and all that. I think there are some issues with consent, is all." He darts me a sly sidelong look, and goddamn, Leonard is smooth.

I reach into my pocket and turn on my phone recorder. I had it set up, so I don't need to look at the screen to manage it.

Jeremy's brow furrows. "You don't need to pretend to be a feminist. No one's around to hear you."

Leonard barks a laugh that would do Hughey the Dog proud. "You're funny." He points at him. "This guy is funny."

Jeremy looks uneasy now, like he's realizing he might not entirely be in on the joke. He takes a sip of his drink, and Leonard and I follow suit. I'm surprised by how good mine tastes. Admittedly, it's sweet and fruity, and I feel less manly for admitting it's the best thing I've tasted since—

I'll bet Delia tastes better, an inner voice suggests.

Nope, not going there. My imagination has already taken too many liberties, especially since the woman in question would prefer if I'd cease to exist.

A woman walks over with a round tray that looks like an old record covered in epoxy. Scratch that. It is a record covered in epoxy. There's a cocktail glass on it with what appears to be effervescent liquid inside. "Bartender told me to send this over to you," she says to Jeremy, setting it down beside his alcoholic drink.

He doesn't look surprised, so I'm guessing this sort of thing happens every now and then when you're a mildly recognizable TV celebrity.

If I'm recognized, I get spit in my drink, not a pat on the back.

Jeremy doesn't thank her, just nods, then takes a sip and frowns.

"Not a fan of free drinks, bud?" Leonard asks. "Personally, I like free things. More things should be free. There are only so many condoms one man can collect."

"No," Jeremy says. "It's just...it's warm seltzer. Why would someone send me warm seltzer?"

I guess I'm not the only person who dislikes him.

"Maybe they weren't a fan of your last movie, huh?" Leonard says. "Tough break. Did you play an asshole?"

"In my last movie, I was a woman's dead husband, reincarnated as a bird."

Leonard shoots me a *what the fuck have you gotten me into?* look, then says to Jeremy, "Maybe it's someone who doesn't like birds. You know they made a whole movie about that once—birds attacking people, pecking at them. I watched that shit when I was a kid, and now *I* don't like birds. I look at one, and I think, that little pecker is up to something underhanded."

I wonder for what has to be the hundredth time what that was like—Leonard as a kid. But we're getting pretty far off track, and I feel the reflexive need to steer us back to the point.

"So, you know the woman I'm acting with," I say to Jeremy. "Small world. What was Delia like in high school?"

He huffs. "Weird and not half as sexy, but who gives a shit? Look at the tits on her now."

I'm deeply annoyed, but I do what my father always told me to when I was a kid with a temper—take in a long breath, in and out, and stuff it down. *"Don't let anyone catch you acting weak,"* he'd say, his face twisting in disgust and maybe a little dislike. *"You're a Burke, and it's time you started acting like it."*

I was raised to be the next Burke Enterprises CEO since I was in training pants, taught to be precise and careful in my words and to show as little emotion as possible, since emotions were something other people could use against you.

"She's a nice-looking woman," I say politically.

Jeremy looks from me to Leonard and back. "Were you serious about that feminism shit?"

"What about Delia?" I say, then clear my throat. "There's a role for a human woman in your movie. You think she'd be good for it?"

"She's always struck me as a few pancakes short of a stack, if you catch my drift, but if you want me to offer her a role so you can bang her, I'm cool with that."

Rage floods my body, and if he were at all smart, he'd sense it and run—literally run—out of the bar. My voice low with menace, I start, "You piece of—"

But Leonard reaches out and grabs the back of my neck, hard. It hurts, and it's meant to.

"I need a minute to talk to my partner, here," he says to Jeremy, his gaze drilling into me.

"Um, okay," Jeremy says, then his eyes go wide, and he says, "Oh, shit. So you two are..."

"We'll be back." Leonard gets up out of his chair and hauls me with him. I almost punch Jeremy anyway, right there in the corner booth in this loud, bright bar. He wouldn't look half so good to Delia if he had a couple of black eyes, but I owe it to Leonard to hear him out. He's played along with this whole ill-thought-out plan, after all.

He pulls me into the hallway leading to the bathrooms.

"Your trick bowel acting up again?" I ask archly, blood still pounding in my veins, arguing that it should be put to use. My hands are balled into fists.

"Don't be an idiot," he tells me. "You hit that guy, and it's going to be all over the news. Sinclair might get in trouble too, for having set up the meeting. You don't want that. I'm the one who makes mistakes, not you. If we're both fucking up left and right, then we'll be in some real trouble."

I hate that he's right. I really hate it, because Jeremy is a disgusting piece of shit, and it makes my blood burn that Delia thinks he could be her someone special. I can't let her go one more day believing it.

"I have to tell her about him," I say, swallowing.

"Want me to find her cell phone number?"

"It's not listed."

"Not a problem. I'm good at finding information."

I lift my brows, because I'm not sure I like the implication of that, but he laughs. "Constance and I exchanged numbers. She wanted me to text her a photo of that Rock-fort cheese you have in your fridge."

So he wasn't exaggerating about the cheese conversation.

"You mean Roquefort?" I suggest.

"You realize you sound like a dick right now?"

"Sorry, Leonard, I—"

Then *she* steps out of the ladies' room. Delia, with her scent of vanilla and sea salt, only today she's dressed in a green sequined skirt that has a scale-like design, paired with a lemon-yellow cropped blouse and at least five different necklaces.

She should look ridiculous. Instead, she reminds me of a mermaid who was just given two human legs to step onto land and into this bar. I'm turning sentimental about this girl—woman—and I don't know what the hell to do about it.

So I do the natural thing.

I act like an asshole. "What on earth are you wearing?"

ten

DELIA

FOR A SECOND, I'm rendered speechless. I've been thinking about Lucas Burke a lot this week. For one thing, he nearly died right behind me—that's the kind of thing that sticks with a person. For another, I've learned a lot about him since Monday. One might even say I did a deep dive. I started with Mira, who'd heard the latest news about Burke Enterprises and was remorseful for having withheld it from me. To make up for it, she poured me a truly fantastic drink and then told me enough about the whistleblower that I'm now ninety percent sure I know who it is, especially after I did research of my own.

It's Lucas Burke IV, the man who's standing in front of me, staring at me as if I defy his understanding. He's wearing a button-down shirt, loose at the collar, the sleeves rolled up in a nod to the warm temperature, which has a side benefit I'm sure he's perfectly well aware of: it reveals his perfectly muscled, tan forearms.

I don't blame Lucas for hurting Nat—he clearly didn't, and he's giving everything he has and is to try to atone for a crime he didn't commit. I don't blame him for his blood.

I do blame him for judging me.

Thank God for Constance. If not for her, I might not have the fortitude to stand strong against him, especially looking like he does tonight.

"They're clothes, Lucas," I say. "If you must know, this used to be one of my mermaid tails and I turned it into a skirt. It's fantastic to see you too, by the way. I'll admit this doesn't seem like your kind of place."

Leonard snorts.

"It isn't," Lucas admits. His eyes dart to a booth near the front window for a half second. A gasp escapes me as my gaze veers that way. Jeremy is sitting by himself, barely visible, talking to a couple of women who are leaning down toward the table in front of him, their cleavage on display. He's having himself a look, as Doris would say.

"Are you here with *him*?" I ask, turning on Lucas.

He sighs. "Unfortunately, yes."

"Why? You've made it perfectly clear what you think of Jeremy."

"That's my cue, folks," Leonard says. He throws us a two-fingered salute and steps off, possibly to join Jeremy.

To my surprise, Lucas takes my hand and drags me to the back of the bar, where the door leads to the alley. The contact makes me feel warm and slightly stupid. So I don't object to his destination even though it always smells back here, no matter what Mira does to try and beautify it.

He steps out, and I follow him—if for no other reason then I'm starting to think he needs to be told off.

Is he trying to convince Jeremy to date me as part of his little scheme? The nerve!

He takes a look at the back alley in bafflement. "Is that glitter paint?"

"Yes. Why are you here with him?"

His jaw firms. "You said he's a special person. I figured I'd check him out. Make sure—" He cuts himself off, swears, then says, "Okay, I *knew* he wasn't a special person. It was obvious to me that he's completely unworthy of you. I wanted to get proof so you wouldn't waste your time mooning over him." His expression intensifies. "And I did. I—"

I lift a hand, disbelief and anger pounding an unpleasant beat through my veins. "You could have just talked to me," I say, seething. "It would have saved you a lot of time and pointless effort."

"I couldn't let him manipulate you."

"So you decided to do it yourself? If you'd asked me nicely, I would have told you that I could never fall in love with a man who complains about the temperature of his seltzer to people who are nice enough to give him seltzer."

His face creases in confusion. "What's up with the seltzer?"

"Forget the seltzer. I know he's a jerk. Anyone who's been in a room with the adult him for five minutes knows he's a jerk. And, fine, he was probably a jerk in high school too, but try and tell me that you've never wanted to sleep with a woman just because of what she looks like."

He seems relieved and possibly amused. For some reason, that escalates my annoyance. "I know all about your little plan to improve my pathetic life, by the way. Constance overheard you. She told me everything."

He flinches and swears—every inch a man who's been caught being a jerk while trying to expose another jerk. "So that's why she doesn't like me."

"You assume you haven't given her other reasons?" I poke a finger into his chest. I immediately regret it, because it's a nice chest. I've been thinking about that chest ever since I was pressed against it the other day for all of those takes.

"You're right." He looks genuinely remorseful, and for half a second, I feel bad for him, but then I remember his question. *"What on earth are you wearing?"*

"And for your information, I look like this more often than I look like I did on set. I borrowed one of Doris's dresses for the first day of filming."

"You and Doris swap clothing?" he asks, seeming genuinely shocked. "Isn't she old?"

"Eighty-two and fabulous, I'll have you know. And, no, I don't usually borrow her clothes. But I didn't have anything black, and my sister said extras were supposed to fade into the background. Which is why it seems so ridiculous they picked *you*, although I guess they didn't really, because you know Sinclair."

There goes my stupid mouth again, saying more than I'd like it to.

He swallows, takes a slight step toward me, as though he can't help himself. "I don't know why they picked *you*. You look like a sunrise."

It's the most bizarre and beautiful compliment anyone's ever paid me, and of course it came from the man who wants to change me. I try to fan the fire of my outrage and then it hits me. He brought Jeremy *here*.

"Why'd you bring Jeremy to my sister's bar? Did you want me to witness something? Were you going to, what, convince him to have a threesome with those women in that booth? Do you realize just how —fuh—" I chicken out halfway through the eff-word and finish "— messed-up that is?"

"This is your sister's bar?" he asks, his eyes convincingly wide. Then he glances at the glitter spray paint. "I guess it makes sense. But what are the odds?"

My heart quickens, because it doesn't escape me that the universe seems pretty invested in throwing us at each other. I'm not sure why anymore, but Lucas Burke is obviously the reason I'm on that set. "I helped her decorate it."

He grins, looking me up and down with a gaze that sets fires wherever it lands. "So it definitely makes sense."

His grin infuriates me. No, what infuriates me is that it's so attractive even though he's been a jerk. I take a small step back to decrease his draw. "I have news for you, Lucas Burke. I'm more than happy with who I am and with the kind of clothes I wear. I *like* my three jobs, and if none of them is particularly ambitious, I'm okay with that. I'm okay being a colorful little no one. I may not have a lot of people in my life, but everyone who's there likes me just the way I am. And that's how I want it to be."

"You're not a no one," he says, his eyes a stormy sea, his voice gritted with menace. "Tell me who's made you think so."

"What? So you can invite them out for drinks too? They should be quaking in their boots."

"They should be."

He takes a step toward me, and I feel my heart racing. My already sensitive skin buzzing with anticipation.

"Why do you even care? You don't know anything about me. Except apparently where my sister works."

"Let's call it a happy accident," he says, taking another half step that I feel down to every bone.

"Are you going to paint a tree over it?" I ask, before realizing it'll sound meaningless to anyone who hasn't had the pleasure of watching Bob Ross on PBS. Which is probably most people my age—and Lucas's age, because my aforementioned deep dive told me a few things about him, including his age—thirty-three—and his birthday—in three weeks.

"I dressed as Bob Ross for Halloween one year," he says, his eyes twinkling.

"I don't believe you." It's hard to imagine this intense man trying to channel Bob Ross, who was probably the most laid-back man alive. It'd be like a wolf pulling on a sheep suit. Sure, his hair has some curl to it, and his smile makes a person take notice, but those are the only similarities I can see.

"I used to tune into that show when I was supposed to be watching recordings of my father's board meetings. I did it to annoy him, but it was calming."

"How old were you when he made you start watching those?" I

ask before I can help myself, because something about the way he said it makes me think it wasn't a couple of weeks ago.

"Since before I can remember. I had a title at the company before I graduated high school."

I make a face. "Kids should be allowed to be kids."

He takes another half step toward me, and he's close to me now, almost like he was the other day, when his body was nearly pressed to mine for all of those takes. "I agree. Were you allowed to be a kid?"

I give him an arch look. "You seem to think I'm *still* a kid."

"You're no kid," he acknowledges. "I'm sorry I made you feel like one. I...didn't express myself well."

"Or deal with the Jeremy situation well," I say, lifting a finger. "Or do a good job of complimenting my outfit." I lift another finger. "Or impress my friend Constance." Another finger.

"I knew you'd make friends with her the second I saw that pink sweater," he says with a half-smile.

"I'm going to do some work for her," I tell him for no reason at all. In fact, I'm going over there tomorrow morning to meet Bertie so I can see what needs doing around the house. I've been looking forward to it.

"That's great," Lucas says, seeming to mean it. "I hope I can improve her opinion of me. I should have been more careful with my words."

"Or not tried to manipulate me in the first place."

"You're right about that," he says, his jaw flexing. He looks down before meeting my eyes again. "I don't want to be like my parents, Delia, but it's hard to unlearn everything they taught me. It's going to take time."

That's something I understand, and I feel a flash of empathy for him. I don't want to soften toward him—to soften toward a man like this is dangerous—but I feel it happening all the same. It's impossible to remain detached when he's looking at me like that, like he realizes I could teach him something. "But you can do it," I say as I look up into his eyes. "I did. I used to try to be what I thought everyone else wanted me to be. But after Nat died, I decided I was done with that. She loved me for who I was, so I owed it to her to try to love myself that way."

He reaches forward and captures the end of a lock of my hair, lifting it slightly. The nerve endings at my scalp light up, sending sparks of awareness through me. "You used to hide. That's why you dyed your hair black."

I back up again, because I feel seen in a way that's alarming.

"The other kids made fun of me for having orange hair and wearing lots of color. A few of the boys used to throw orange slices at me. So one summer I decided I'd had enough of it and dyed my hair and started wearing monochrome outfits. Then they switched to calling me Morticia."

"They were idiots," he snaps. "They couldn't see what was right in front of their faces. You're gorgeous. The most naturally beautiful person I've ever seen."

"You didn't seem to like my outfit very much fifteen minutes ago."

He groans. "I'm an idiot. I didn't mean it like that."

I stare him down. "Yes, you did. You'd never wear something like this."

"Me, personally?" he says with a slight smile. "No, but it looks good on you. I was just...surprised." He gives me another up and down look that seems to take in every curve and crevice of me, and I feel a liquid heat course through my veins. "You're beautiful. You'd look beautiful in anything."

"But you'd prefer it if I wore something else, something more demure and ladylike. More adult."

He slowly shakes his head. "No. That's just what I'm used to. Anyway, that's not what I meant when I told Leonard—" He swallows again, his throat bobbing. It's impossibly sexy, but I won't let it distract me. "I'm not going to repeat what I said. I only meant... I wanted to do something good for you."

"I told you. You had nothing to do with what happened to Nat or the other people in that building. You owe me nothing."

"At first I wanted to do something for you because of what happened with Nat, but you're a good person, Delia. You deserve something good just for you. I didn't like the way Jeremy treated you —or hearing that other people made you feel small."

So did he, but I decide not to say so. He seems to know and regret it, which is more than I can say for most of the people who've let me down.

"Yes, they were mean. A lot of people were mean to me. But don't go tracking them down to ruin their lives. I can deal with my own problems. Or not deal with them, if that's what I choose." I pause, watching him. He looks slightly bemused but mostly chagrined. It smells like boiled Brussels sprouts back here, but the smell is only hitting me now. My focus has been lasered in on him. That presence I sensed when we first met seems to be washing over the whole alley—over me—changing everything it touches. "I know you're the whistleblower. You're trying to make your parents pay for what they did."

He swallows, my eyes tracking the movement of his strong throat. "I am," he agrees. "But it's too late, and it's not enough. I should have seen what was going on and put a stop to it. It shouldn't have taken me years to clue in." One corner of his mouth lifts, but there's no amusement in the gesture. No real pleasure. "I guess I'm like those people who underestimated you, missing what was right in front of my face. I took what my parents said at face value. Believed in what they were selling just like everyone else."

"There you go again," I say, "thinking you can—or should— control every little thing in the world." His brow furrows, and I can tell my point has hit him hard. I didn't mean for it to land like a blow

—or at least I don't think I did—so I say, "Are you going to become a superhero? Extra Man?"

"Maybe," he says, his voice slightly husky. "It has a certain ring to it. What would I do, pop up in the background of other peoples' photos?"

I can't help but smile. He's funny and charming, even when he's feeling low. "It's not a bad plan," I say. "You'd make them prettier. Isn't it funny to think about all of the photographs you're in? The people whose paths you've crossed without even realizing it?"

"No," he says, rubbing the bridge of his nose, his face pained. "Because it makes me think of *them*. Of how I was part of ruining their lives without even realizing it."

He's talking about Nat, and I have a visceral flash of memory—of her soft curly hair, the way her teeth were slightly crooked, and how it made her smile even sweeter. There's a press of longing and loss, but I know she wouldn't have blamed him. It wasn't in her to hold people accountable for circumstances out of their control—like their last name or the blood that ran through their veins or whether they were allergic to peanut butter, her favorite.

"I can't speak for anyone else," I say, swallowing. "But I'll speak for Nat. She wouldn't hold you responsible, Lucas. Neither do I. Maybe instead of trying to figure out how to fix my life, you should find some peace in yours. Have you talked to anyone about all of this?"

"To some of my friends, sure."

"I meant to a professional."

"A professional talker?" he asks, trying to smile, but it slips. "I'm not crazy, Delia. Just your garden variety of fucked-up."

"I never said you were. It helped me, after Nat died." I pause, then add, "My therapist is the one who helped me make the decision to live the life I wanted. Do you think *I'm* crazy?"

"No, of course not. I think you're a lot of things, and crazy isn't even on the short list."

I'm not exactly sure what that means, so I decide to ignore it. "Men can use help too, Lucas. You need to think about what's going to make you happy."

There's a look of surprise in his bright blue eyes, as if this thought had never occurred to him. Or maybe he's just surprised it came from me.

"I'm doing the flip house with Leonard. I figured maybe we could start a business together. He needs—"

"Make sure it's something *you* need too. You nearly died the other day on set. None of us know how much time we have. Make sure you spend yours the way you want to."

It happens so quickly, I can barely process it. One moment he's standing in front of me, inches away, his heat licking at me, and the next I'm pressed against him, his lips half an inch from mine, his head bent to me.

I don't think. I don't remind myself that this is Lucas Burke, son of a legacy I want no part of, a man who's trying to learn a way of living that's different than the one he was raised with but is struggling. No. I span the distance, lifting on my toes to press my mouth to his. The sound he makes deep in his throat shudders through me, then his hand is on the bare part of my waist, pressing me closer—commanding and hot—while his other hand weaves through my hair and tips my head back so he can get a better angle. My mouth opens to him without pausing to consult the rest of me, and his tongue moves with mine as his hand tightens in my hair, the nerve endings lighting up and making the kiss hotter. Before I know it, he's pushing me up against that spray-painted wall, his body caging mine, but in a way that makes me quite satisfied to be trapped.

"Delia." He whispers my name in my ear. And for the first time in my life, my own name feels like a sexual thing, like a live wire that could burn him if he's not careful. Then his lips are pressing beneath my ear, sending out a burst of pleasure I feel down to my toes, and his mouth travels down my jaw to my neck while his hand weaves deeper into my hair. My body arches up to him, begging to be closer, to press against his hard heat and *know* this perplexing man, and when his mouth reaches the top of my shirt, I hold the back of his head, his hair silky on my fingertips, and then—

"We've gotta go—*oh shit*," a voice says.

I glance over and see Leonard. He peers over his shoulder at the back door of the bar, which is closed, and I hear some kind of ruckus going on inside.

Lucas pulls away from me, a bewildered look in his eyes. It's chased by what is clearly regret. "Delia, I shouldn't have—"

But he doesn't have time to expound on what he shouldn't have done, because Leonard is grabbing his arm and tugging him down the alley. "Sorry, Delia," Leonard calls out, giving me a backward wave. "We'll see you on Monday. If we don't get fired."

My hand rises to my lips, my brain still trying to catch up. Am I... pissed? Pleased? Maybe both. All I know is that Lucas has a strange effect on me, one I don't totally understand yet. I think I'd like to understand it, though.

Seconds later, the door cracks open and Mira appears from behind it.

"Did you see a shifty-looking guy come out this way?"

"Yeah," I say, "but I think he might be my friend."

She gives me a dubious look. "That guy just about caused a riot in here."

"What'd he do?"

"So Jeremy was in there. Obviously, I sent over some slightly warm seltzer the second I saw him."

"Obviously," I say with a snort. She was disappointed to learn the truth about Jeremy, but both of us know that an Evans woman deserves better than a man who's a creep to service professionals.

"I looked for you to tell you, but you were in the bathroom, and then I couldn't find you."

She gives me a slightly searching look, but I choose not to say anything. Yet. I'll tell her about the kiss, since she and Doris are both people who get the unredacted version of my life, but I'm not ready.

"What happened in there?"

"All I know is that your buddy in the hat was talking to Jeremy, and suddenly Jeremy climbs up on the table and starts singing at the top of his lungs."

"Was he any good?" I ask, because it seems like an important detail.

She makes a face. "He'd maybe get through the first round of *Idol*. Definitely not the second. That one jerky judge would have words for him."

"And then?"

"And then Hat Guy gets up on the table next to him and starts singing too. I shit you not, they had a sing-off."

"Was *he* any good?"

"Hat Guy could have won the whole competition," she says. "Women started flocking around his table, asking for his autograph like he was some big deal, and Jeremy got pissy and shouted that he was the famous one. Someone asked what movies he was in, and he started listing them off like he was IMDB. So people started flocking over to his table too. I informed both of the guys that our tables were not stages, and if they didn't get off, they would be thrown off. So they did, but suddenly there was this big lineup for autographs from Jeremy. He was pleased, as you can imagine, but then one guy asked if he could get him Sinclair's autograph instead. Jeremy shoved him, and for a second I thought things were going to get ugly. I was five seconds away from setting off my rape whistle, but Hat Guy restrained Sinclair's fan before he could deck Jeremy. No one needed to restrain Jeremy, because he hightailed it out of there the second your friend got the guy in headlock. Anyway, Hat Guy said something in his ear, and whatever it was calmed him down. Some weird shit, huh? Everyone's still kind of going nuts about the whole thing. I should really get back inside."

"Crap," I say. How'd I miss all of that? The chaos should have been loud enough to bleed into the alley, but I didn't notice it until the end. My focus was so totally on Lucas. I can still feel him on my lips, but I remember the look of bafflement in his eyes as Leonard dragged him away, as if he were waking from sleep. Maybe he'd only kiss me like that when he's away from the wheel, as it were.

"Who is that guy, anyway?" Mira asks. "Are you interested in him? Not my type, but—" She theatrically fans herself.

"That was Leonard from the movie," I say with a sigh. "And the answer is no. But Lucas Burke just kissed me, and he *is* my type. I think I'm in trouble."

eleven

LUCAS

"DID you at least win the sing-off?" I ask.

Leonard's at my apartment with Danny, and the three of us are sitting around the kitchen island with bourbons. Shane's at work late, and Drew's on some all-day hike in the rainforest with his fiancée.

Drew's found himself. It's only after what Delia said earlier that I realized that's what I've been trying to do—to locate the kernel of myself that's me and not what I was modeled to be. If there is one. A dark part of me thinks maybe there's not, that I'm all puppet with just enough will to turn around and bite the hand that's fed me.

"Obviously," Leonard says, taking a long sip of the bourbon. "You don't start a fight you know you can't win."

"You took on my parents," I tell him flatly.

He shakes his head. "No, *you* did. I might have confronted them, but let's call a coward a coward. When they gave me pushback, I took their money and ran. Don't make me into something I'm not, Lucas. I'm no hero. Never have been, never will be."

He says it lightly, the way he says everything, but it's clear he means it. He doesn't like being treated like he's done anything good, even though he helped me build a case against them. It's in the lawyers' hands now. I'm not naïve enough to think my parents will end up in jail, where they belong, but at least it will hurt. It needs to hurt.

"He's not a hero," Danny agrees, but with a half-smile. "But he *does* have a reasonably good voice."

"Reasonably good, my ass." Leonard snorts. "If it were only reasonably good, you wouldn't have hired me to do voices for your game."

Danny and Drew are finishing up the final touches on their survivalist computer game, and they're planning to launch it within the next few months. It's good, really good, and I'm grateful that I have the means to back them. The only reason it's an investment and not a grant is because they're stubborn bastards and won't accept my help any other way, especially Danny, who insists I've done enough to help him.

I own this two-bedroom loft—a birthday present from my parents twelve years ago. That sounds pretty legit unless you consider that they did it without consulting me or asking me to choose anything. I wanted to travel for a few years after college but was instead sent my start date and a set of keys. I asked Danny to move in because I knew he wanted to stay in town too. Local rents had already gotten pretty high by then, and he couldn't afford to live anywhere that wouldn't put him with two or three roommates. Danny's not a two- or three-roommates kind of guy. He's an introvert, and when he's hooked on an idea, he can go a full day without saying five words. That's the kind of thing that could make a stranger, someone who doesn't understand him, salty. But he's one of the best people I know. He put together a website for my side gig flipping houses that's much too good for what it needs to be, plus he insists on doing all of the cooking. That's fortunate, because I grew up with a personal chef at home and can't crack an egg without making a disaster.

"So how did this come about, anyway?" I ask.

"Remember how Jeremy said he played a parrot in his last movie?" Leonard says. "He claimed he sang all of his own songs, and

I figured he was full of shit, so I challenged him to prove it. He's the one who started the thing with the tables, so I'm guessing those drinks were strong or he had a buzz going on when he showed up. I didn't think he was all that good, so I said they must have used auto-tune, and he told me to prove it if I thought I could do any better." He shrugs. "So I did. It kind of devolved from there."

That makes me smile. It's just such a Leonard thing to do. "You get us banned from Glitterati?"

"Maybe. I left before anyone could tell me, though, so I get to go back at least once. What are the fucking chances it would be Delia's sister's bar, huh?"

He's right. I still can't believe it. It almost feels—

I don't want be a dumb fuck and say it feels like fate, but it kind of does.

"I wonder if her sister's the bartender," he continues.

"Did she look like her?" Danny asks.

"A bit. But her hair's all dark. Almost black."

He's right. I sit up a little straighter, thinking about Delia dyeing her hair black to fit in. Was she hoping to look more like her sister? I don't like the thought. I like it even less that I made her feel like I object to her appearance in any way. As if anyone reasonable could.

I didn't mean to kiss her. That was never the plan. The plan was to do something good for her, to pay it forward. The last thing I want is to draw someone like Delia—good and giving and sweetly beautiful—into this blackness I've been feeling, the gaping hole where there used to be a person I thought I understood, even if I didn't like him very much. But she tasted like she smelled, and her body felt so perfect against mine, her hair in my fist, her lips opening to me like a blooming flower, and I can't stop thinking about her. I want more of her. But more than that, I want to prove to her that I accept her for who she is. If she's happy to live with three jobs and a wardrobe that looks like a costume closet, then that's what she should do.

"Look at him," Leonard says, nudging Danny's arm. "This is

what I warned you about earlier. He gets this moony-ass look whenever he talks about Delia. It's getting worse. He's got the Drew Affliction, because that's exactly the same way Drew looked before he ran off to Puerto Rico with Andy."

Andy being Andrea Ruiz, Drew's fiancée. He's right about that look. We'd all noticed it. Shane's the one who came up with the term the Drew Affliction, mostly because the rest of us felt pretty confident in saying we didn't want it to happen to us. Shane has handled plenty of divorces, and being the child of one, he has about as much respect for love and marriage as I do for Jeremy.

"I'm not in love with her," I object. "I've only known her for a week."

"Maybe so," Leonard says, running a finger along the rim of his glass. "But you *did* almost die. That does something to a man. I tell you what, I've almost died a couple of times myself, and one time I proposed to a girl just afterward."

"What happened?" Danny asks.

He tilts his head toward one shoulder. "I got lucky. She was already married."

I'm barely paying attention, though, because now I'm thinking of that crushed brick, of the way it whistled by my head before pounding into the pavement. A few inches, and we wouldn't be sitting here having this conversation. Instead, they'd be talking about the trauma Leonard would almost certainly have experienced from having seen my head get smashed in.

"I can't believe I almost died," I say slowly, the reality of it still mind-bending.

"Speaking of which, do we need to go back to that potentially unsafe work environment?" Leonard asks. "And, if so, should we try to upsell them on our house-flipping services?"

I have to laugh at that. "You want to flip the Rolf Estate?"

"Isn't that what our dumb-ass movie is all about? I never thought I'd side with Jeremy, but it's clear the place needs a little TLC.

Maybe some modern updates. Comfortable chairs would not be amiss."

He seems to have absorbed more of the plot than I have. Then again, he didn't spend the whole time he was on camera within a few inches of Delia.

"You saw the email. They had an emergency structural engineer come in on Tuesday morning to take a look at the set after the accident. Everything else is sound."

Leonard snorts. "Emergency structural engineer. Could you imagine having that on business cards? You'd hand them out at bars and tell women, 'If your house is falling down, I'm the person you call, baby.'" He purses his lips and nods. "It could work. Maybe I should have some made."

"So it was just the one brick that had it out for you?" Danny says, ignoring Leonard and staring at me. There's something concerned in his expression.

"Guess so."

"You don't think your parents—"

"Jesus," I say, "no." The thought sticks to me like a burr, though, and the expression on Leonard's face—a flash of worry—says he doesn't much like it either. "They may have more money than they know what to do with, but how could they arrange for a brick to conk me on the head? We would have seen someone up on the roof."

Leonard's face crinkles with thought. "Not necessarily, man. There was a window right above where it fell. A person could have hidden up there."

"They don't even know I'm doing the movie." I take a long sip from my drink. "Anyway, the night it happened my dad sent me a book. *Why Loyalty Matters.* If he'd planned on me being dead, why would he have bothered?

"Shit, I remember bringing that package up from downstairs," Danny says with a shudder. "Why didn't you say anything? That's creepy."

"Deeply," Leonard agrees. "What'd you do with it?"

"Put it in one of those free libraries." I don't add that I did it the night it arrived, because it unnerved me to have it in the apartment, as if the book might develop teeth and bite me.

"Should we send *him* a book?" Leonard snaps his fingers. "Or what if we send him a titty magazine? Maybe he'll be more agreeable if he busts a nut."

Something about his expression tells me he's putting on a front— that he's disturbed by this too.

"Maybe," I say with a half-smile. "We'll revisit the possibility later."

"Sorry to be a naysayer," Danny adds, "but I don't think the book proves they weren't involved. What if he wanted to send a message to all of us? To Leonard?"

"He doesn't think I know how to read," Leonard quips.

"Besides," Danny says, not reacting, "someone could have told them you were doing the movie. Other people know."

I shake my head. "The structural engineer would have been able to tell if the ledge had been tampered with. It was just an accident, and the book was one more example of my dad being passive aggressive. I'm starting to think you listen to too many of those true crime podcasts." It's his go-to listen when he's coding...meaning he's always listening to a new one.

He shrugs. "Probably. But be careful all the same."

"They might not like me, but they don't want to kill me, Danny."

The sentiment doesn't settle, though. It sticks around the edges of my throat, nearly choking me. My mother texted me again this morning, telling me that I'll be going to tea with her and my father next Sunday—eleven a.m. at their home—for a "family discussion." It wasn't phrased as a request.

What if Danny's right? I can't deny that my parents left me alone until I started filming the movie. What if they see it as a personal slight? Bad enough that I brought them low without becoming a personal embarrassment. If they've decided I'm enough of a stain on their legacy, they might be desperate enough to try to get rid of me. They've always said blood is thicker than water, but the only thing I've known them to actually care about is money and power, and I've proven I'm a threat to theirs.

My gaze shifts to Leonard, who's staring into his drink. A sudden fear stabs into me. The last time he thought they were after him, he blew town and disappeared with the payoff they'd given him. Maybe he's thinking of disappearing again.

"It's not them, Leonard," I repeat. "It was just a stupid accident."

He glances up and smiles, but there's no cheer in it. "Let's hope so, bub. Now, tell us more about how you're not infatuated with that hot redhead you were making out with in that alley that smelled like rotten vegetables."

"I want to do something nice for her," I admit, if only to get his mind off my parents and what they might or might not be up to. "I want to show her that I like her just the way she is."

"Do you?" Leonard asks bluntly, putting the thumb screws to me. "Because back on Monday, you told me you wanted to fix her life."

"She made me realize my life's the one that needs fixing."

"And when she says it, you listen," Leonard says, grinning at Danny, who's grinning back at him. "We've only been trying to tell you the same shit for months."

Is that true? I've had my head so far up my own ass I haven't noticed.

"So what's the plan?" Leonard asks. "Danny and I will think of ways to make it more interesting."

"He means he'll think of ways to fuck it up," Danny says, lifting his drink. "To Lucas, and the only woman to have ever made him worry about impressing her. God bless her, because she's going to need all the help she can get."

"I'll drink to that," Leonard says with a smart-ass grin.

twelve

DELIA

I CAN'T STOP THINKING about Lucas—the way his lips felt against mine, the press of his hand on my bare waist, so confident and direct. The way he overtook all of my senses until it felt like I was breathing him in. He said it was a mistake, and he was right.

It's not because he's not my type.

In the past, I've been drawn to men like him, commanding and self-contained, the keepers of schedules and makers of lists. It's like my chaos wants to be balanced. But men like that have always tried to mold me to their ideals, when all I've ever wanted is to be appreciated as myself. To coexist.

He may say he likes me as I am, but evidence suggests otherwise. He's messing with my head, which I don't appreciate, but it's obvious his head is a mess too. In quitting his job—the purpose he was groomed for since he was a child—he's opened a cavern within himself, and he doesn't know how to fill it. Right now, it's a place where guilt and responsibility and desire are in uneasy coexistence.

I'd be a fool to get involved with him. In addition to every other objection, he's made it clear he's a ladies' man, the kind who probably brings a different woman home each night. I can't delude myself into thinking I'm going to be his someone special or that he suddenly sees me as someone whose flaws can be left alone.

The past is meaningless if we don't learn from it.

He may not be my enemy in the literal sense I thought he was a few days ago, but he can still be an enemy to my peace.

"What are you mooning about?" Ross says, puttering around the kitchen. "You've been standing there for two minutes like you got turned into a pillar of salt." He's looking in drawers and cabinets as if he hopes the groceries will suddenly transform into things he likes. Unfortunately, the things he likes—mooncakes and salty snacks and Little Debbie treats—aren't good for him, and Doris and I have scrubbed them from the house. Or at least we've tried. He has little stashes hidden everywhere, ones whose locations all of us have forgotten, Ross included.

"It's that man," Doris says from the kitchen table. She's eating some plain wheat toast while she watches Ross search for treats. Knowing her, she'll let him eat some long-hidden treat without complaint if he manages to find it, just out of appreciation for the effort he put in.

"Yes," I agree with a sigh. I told them both about Lucas, and only her about last night in the alley. "I'll admit he's hard to forget, but I'm good at doing things when I set my mind to them."

When my mind cooperates. Getting it to cooperate is not always an easy thing.

Sighing again, I get a mug from the cupboard and pour myself a cup of coffee, doctoring it with cream and sugar.

"You know, when I met Ross, he was quite a ladies' man," Doris says contemplatively. "Debonair too."

"I told you nothing ever happened with Debby," he grumbles as he closes a cabinet after frowning aggressively at a container of shredded wheat. "For forty years, I've told you nothing happened with Debby, but still you ask. You don't see me getting on your case about Andy Weary."

"Deb-o-nair," Doris shouts, then rolls her eyes at me. She's annoyed with him for having chosen the snail-mail shipping for his hearing aid.

His lips tip up as he moves on to the next cabinet. "Well, I was at that."

I pat him on the shoulder and then bring my coffee to the table, sitting across from Doris.

"You know," she says, "our great-nephew is working on the movie set. I just heard from him this morning after years without any contact. My sister was never any good at staying in touch, and I'm afraid he's a chip off the old block."

"Old cinderblock," Ross mutters, proving he can hear certain things just fine.

"Really?" I ask, excited. I've never met any of their relatives. They don't have any children, and their only niece, presumably this man's mother, moved out west twenty years ago. "What's he look like?"

"He's a bit rotund, I'll admit." Doris says. "With a bald head and thick eyebrows like caterpillars. Looks like his father's side, I always tell Ross. But there's something memorable about him all the same." She taps beside her big brown eyes. I help her with her makeup every morning, because her vision isn't up to it, but she'd be very distressed not to have her face on—her words. "He has the Leach eyes."

My mind flashes to Orange Lanyard. "What's his name?"

Orange Lanyard, Orange Lanyard, my mind unhelpfully supplies. I hope it's not him. He was unpleasant, and when he touched my arm, it felt like insects were creeping up it. I repress a shudder.

"Thomas. He asked to have dinner with us next week. You should come, dear. If this Lucas is too big for his britches, then maybe there are better choices."

I have a feeling Lucas is plenty big for his britches... And now

I'm thinking about what's inside of his britches. I feel my cheeks heat.

"See, you're coming around to the idea."

"Oh, no," I say, jolted back into the moment. Doris is constantly trying to set me up with other single people, from the mailman to the very nice young man she met in the dairy section at the grocery store. It never goes well, and it will go significantly less well if she tries to set me up with Orange Lanyard. "You enjoy your time with your family. I know you don't get to see him much."

She sniffs. "He may not look like that Lucas fellow, but he would probably exercise given the proper motivation."

"He'd need someone chasing him," Ross says with a huff of laughter. "Lazy. Always has been. Used to sit on a swing until someone would push him, even when he was six or seven." He crouches to open a foot-level cabinet and sneaks his hand around the back of a few pots, brightening as he snakes it back out with a packaged mooncake in hand.

Doris snorts but gives him a nod, indicating she won't stop him from eating his treasure. "Well, there's nothing lazy about you when you're looking to add to your waistline. If Thomas had half as much motivation with running, then Delia might give him a second look."

"I don't care about his weight," I say, frustrated. It's that he's a sexist jerk, but I don't want to hurt her feelings by saying so. "There's nothing wrong with carrying around a few extra pounds. That one actor does, and he's very attractive."

I don't know his name, but she knows exactly who I mean, because we discussed this just last night while watching television. She nods in agreement. "That is true."

"And I like well-defined eyebrows. Maybe not caterpillar eyebrows, but eyebrows can always be plucked. Most men don't bother. Anyway, that's beside the point. It's just—"

My mind summons an image of Lucas, who has very defined eyebrows, those intense blue eyes that could cut through a person, and a body that he must have earned by working on his flip houses, something you usually don't see in someone like him. A man raised from early childhood to be a CEO.

Sighing, I add, "I'll look for Thomas the next time I'm on set. Say hello and introduce myself."

She beams at me. "Thank you, dear. I knew I could count on you to be sweet to him. He's an...okay boy."

I fight a cringe. Doris can be a tough customer, but if she's inclined to like someone, as she would be with her great-nephew, she's overly generous with her character assessments. If she thinks her great-nephew is just okay, he's probably a demon. For her sake, I hope he's misunderstood. Maybe he acts like a pig because he has low self-confidence or some secret trauma in his past, like one of the superheroes in all of those movies that blend together.

Forcing a smile, I finish my coffee. Then I wash out the cup and make sure they have everything they need to get going with their mornings. Doris is having a few friends over to play cards, so I've prepared some snacks for them, and Ross is planning to spend the morning in his workshop. He makes wooden vases and curios but doesn't like dealing with the selling part, so I do it for him on Etsy.

I'm going over to Constance's place for the first time to meet Bertie so I can see what they need to have done and we can decide if I'm a good fit for helping them out too.

I'm glad to keep busy because it prevents my mind from straying back to Lucas. To wondering whether he's okay. And whether he still regrets that kiss. Because even if it shouldn't have happened, I'm having a hard time feeling any real regret.

When I get to Constance's little purple bungalow, there's a sporty, red Mini Cooper parked in the driveway, a car that seems the perfect fit for my new friend. I park in front of the curb, and she opens the door as I approach it.

"Come in, come in," she urges, and I hurry to do just that, smiling at the sight of her, because I'm fond of her, and also because there's a barking Welsh Corgi at her feet who's wearing the sparkly pink sweater. It's warm, so I doubt he'll have it on for long, but it's truly adorable. I make a mental note to take a photo of the dog for Lucas, only I don't have his phone number. It seems ridiculous that I don't, although I couldn't articulate why. I guess what it comes down to is that him entering my life caused a shockwave, and vice versa. That's what happens when fate pummels you with a person.

I hurry to the door. Constance takes both of my hands and studies my outfit—a sun dress with layers of orange and pink and red that match my hair—with a fond look. "I knew you had color in you, girl."

"Thank you," I say. And because she's wearing a colorful muumuu with a flower design, I add, "Same." Then I bend to greet the dog, who sniffs me enthusiastically, his little nub of a tail waving frantically. "Meet Bertie," Constance says with a fond smile.

I'm thrown. I'd felt certain Bertie was a person—her husband, specifically. "Bertie's not your husband?" I ask, looking up in shock. It's probably foolish to say so, but I was so convinced. I'd formed a mental image of a kindly old man in a newsboy cap. It was checkered.

Constance snorts and puts a hand on her hip. "Please. Let's not insult Bertie by the comparison."

I shouldn't ask. I shouldn't ask. I shouldn't ask.

"What happened?" I blurt as I stand back up.

"Frank left last month." She shakes her head. "Fifty-four years of marriage, Delia, and he left me for the woman who teaches the water aerobics class at the YMCA. She's only fifty-five, which won't sound young to someone your age. But there's a world of difference between fifty-five and eighty. Most of it is in chronic pain."

I gasp. "Which class does she teach?"

"Wednesdays and Fridays at two p.m.," she says with a sigh.

"My friend Doris takes the Friday class," I say, horrified. Did Doris witness this illicit romance from the get-go? If so, I'm surprised she didn't say anything to me. The only thing she's mentioned is that the instructor has had some sort of plastic surgery that's made her face look like it's in rigor mortis. She said it nicely, with a "poor soul" tacked on for good measure.

I tell Constance as much, and the expression on her face indicates I've made her day. "Your friend sounds like a very sensible sort of woman."

"I'm not sure she'd like being called sensible," I say with a laugh, "but she does have good judgment."

"Would her good judgment allow her to accidentally kick Frank in the crotch?"

"Yes, if I tell her what he did."

"Do. It's bad enough to be abandoned for another woman after this long, but for a fifty-five-year-old hussy?"

She looks genuinely disgusted about the whole thing, and I think maybe she is, but beneath it there are layers of hurt. Constance is strong and confident. She's human, though, and in the end, we all have soft underbellies.

"Why don't you find yourself a fifty-four-year-old?" I ask. "Then he'll be jealous."

She laughs. "I'd prefer not to care what that old bugger thinks about anything, but I like the thought of showing the world that I may be old but I'm not dead. Now, come in and shut the door before we let every bug in creation inside."

I do, and she leads the way into a pretty yellow-painted kitchen with big windows lined with blue. It feels like the sun is beaming from every wall, and I instantly love it.

"Sit down," Constance says, "and I'll make us a pot of tea."

I almost object—I'm here to help her, not the other way around—but I want her to be comfortable when she tells me what she needs, and I don't want to take her utility away from her. She can still make tea, and I won't act otherwise. Bertie settles at my feet, and I reach down to scratch him between the ears.

Sighing as she bustles around, she fills and turns on an electric kettle and then retrieves a pretty teapot and a bin of looseleaf tea from a cabinet. "I'll have to show you the fish room, but I'd prefer to make you tea first so you'll feel obligated to stay."

"What's the fish room?" I ask, fascinated. I've heard of dogs having rooms, in houses big enough for such a thing, but a fish room?

"It's Frank the Fuck's near-death crisis," she says with a snort. "And *of course* he left it here for me to deal with. I'll be solving that man's problems in the afterlife if he has his way."

"Oh," I say, continuing to pet Bertie as the electric kettle starts hissing. I'm not usually at a loss for words—normally there are too many of them, wanting to come out in a torrent—but I'm thrown by this. Still thrown by last night too.

She pauses with the kettle of hot water poised above the teapot. "You want to leave."

"No," I assure her. "I'm actually very curious about this fish room."

She pours the water, snorting in response to my comment. "You shouldn't be. You'll regret ever having had curiosity about anything when you see it."

"Now I'm really curious," I say.

The corners of her mouth lift slightly. "My granddaughter has said she'll take care of it, but she takes care of everything around here, and I'm sick of being a burden on her. I've never wanted to be a burden on anyone, Delia. It's exhausting."

"I'm sure she doesn't feel burdened," I say.

"Even if she doesn't, I still feel like I'm a weight she doesn't need. She's finally getting her dream job, and I don't want to put too much pressure on her." She flattens her lips. "She's in her thirties and still single. Her personal life is a greater priority than the condition of our house."

"Constance, you surprise me," I say before I can stop myself.

106

"You don't seem like the kind of lady who'd think a woman needs a man around to be happy."

A laugh escapes her. "Maybe not, but I'm not going to be around here forever. I'd like to see my girl settled with a man who won't leave her with a fish room and fifty-four years of mediocre memories. If I'm dead before that happens, then no one will be around to tell her it's a bad idea."

"You haven't liked her boyfriends?"

She sniffs as she retrieves a couple of mugs from the cabinet and arranges them and the tea on a tray, finishing it with a small jar of honey. "We thought her last boyfriend was going to stick, but he left her high and dry for her best friend."

"Really? She's not friends with her anymore, is she?

Constance makes a constipated face. "She's going to be a brides-maid in their wedding."

I make a constipated face back at her. "That's horrible."

"I'm hoping she'll come to her senses and use it as an opportunity to make them both suffer."

She brings over the tray, and I'm filled with delight by the mugs, designed to look like sleeping dragons.

"What time is it?" she asks, angling her head to get a look at my wrist.

"Oh, that's not a watch," I say, running a finger along the back, which is a glass evil eye. "It's a bracelet."

"Glory," she says as she pours the tea. "Well, we don't have too much time, I'm afraid, so drink up."

"Why don't we have much time?" I ask in confusion, because she hadn't mentioned having any other plans. Does she have other granddaughters-for-hire coming over for interviews?

Her lips purse. "We'll see whether it impresses us."

This obviously does not clarify anything, but she drizzles honey into the cups and then waves for me to try the tea. My mother's enforced politeness is too burned into me for me to ignore her.

107

"Oh, that's good," I say, because it is. It's a mixture of berry and elderflower, delicious.

"I like a good cup of tea. The stuff they keep on that movie set might as well be from a fast-food restaurant."

"These mugs are delightful too," I say. "Did you get them from somewhere local? One of my favorite things about living here is all the artists. I love walking through the fairs and taking in all the colors and designs. It makes me feel like we live in a special place."

A proud look crosses her face. "That's my granddaughter's handiwork. Shauna's talented, isn't she?"

I agree. It has the advantage of being true, and I know how important it is to take pride in the people we love. She points out another few pieces Shauna made—a vase on the windowsill designed to look like two people hugging, a clock shaped like a blooming flower. They're delightful, and I say so.

We drink the tea, chatting a bit about the movie—about that brick—but Constance doesn't linger on the subject. A perverse part of me is disappointed. I guess I'd be grateful for any opportunity to talk about Lucas and the kiss that's taken up so much of my headspace. At the same time, it's refreshing to have my head full of something other than him—mainly tanks full of colorful fish in shades of red and blue and electric yellow. And, sure, maybe I'm imagining what Lucas would think of this whole thing. But it's impossible to banish a man like him entirely.

"Okay," she finally says once we've finished. "Are you ready to be horrified?"

"That tea was very calming. If I'm ever going to be ready, it's now. You know, I've been sitting here, wondering what the fish room could possibly look like. My imagination can be a wild place."

"Reduce your expectations," she says, "then reduce them further, and you'll be getting somewhere."

"Is the room itself full of water?"

She shakes her head slightly, amused. "Come with me."

Bertie goes to follow us, but Constance lowers to pat him on the head. "Stay here, Bert." Turning to me, she says, "The fish distress him."

"If this is a gambit to trap a mermaid," I say, following her, "I have to admit that I'm not actually a princess of the sea." I told her about my mermaid readings on Monday, during one of the many lulls.

Constance grins. "You can see right through me, can't you?"

She leads the way down the stairs to the finished basement, then into a room with snapping fluorescents. It's aggressively ugly, the floor covered in vinyl squares, the walls painted a dark purple that makes the room feel dingy due to its lack of windows. Every wall is covered in metal racks, three levels per wall, and on every level there are multiple fish tanks. Small and large and somewhere in the middle, like Frank felt the need to accommodate each of Goldilocks's three bear friends. The fish inside are as I imagined—colorful and plentiful—but several of the tanks are a mess, full of algae and dark murk. It's probably because there are so very many, some of them positioned much too high for easy access. The smell is terrible, like the dumpster outside a fried fish restaurant.

I glance at Constance and am shocked to see tears in her eyes. "Constance, do you even want these fish?"

"*No.* Shauna takes care of them mostly, but she's been so busy lately, and we're both too short to take care of the top tanks without a ladder. Neither of us even like fish. But God help me, I'm not going to commit mass murder just because Frank's an asshole."

"Can you make Frank deal with them?" I ask, surprised this strong woman has allowed him to gift her his mistake.

She snorts at this. "I got the house in the separation agreement, and the old boot is bitter. I know that man, and he's going to leave his problem for me to take care of in retaliation. He says he got these fish because he was unsatisfied and needed a purpose. There was something missing in his life."

"And he thought a thousand fish would fill it?" I ask in disbelief.

She laughs through the tears still shining in her eyes. "I never said he was intelligent. For a few weeks, he was all aflutter about how he was going to start breeding and selling fish, but nothing ever came of it. He moved on from the fish to the water aerobics instructor, so I'm guessing he has a water kink he never told me about."

Part of me wants to laugh, but it's obvious she's just joking to deflect the hurt she feels.

"We're going to figure this out, Constance," I say, watching as a little red fish darts after a pink one. They're probably trying to find an escape, and right now, there isn't one. I feel a pang of sympathy for the fish too. This can't be a good life for them, stuck down here in this room with aggressive fluorescent lighting and nothing fun to look at. Admittedly, I don't know how much fish think, if at all, but surely they have some needs that aren't being met. "We'll figure it out in a way that works for everyone. Even the fish."

Maybe I can find a fish store that will take them, or we can give them away one tank at a time. The enormity of the task is daunting, in a way that makes my mind want to move on to something else, something safer, but I can tell how much this has been weighing on Constance—it's like a visual representation of the ways that Frank has failed her. Abandoned her. I won't leave her to that.

Then the bell rings upstairs, and Constance sighs. "Here's where we find out whether we're impressed or not."

I follow her upstairs, and she opens the door to reveal none other than Lucas Burke, holding a couple of wrapped gift boxes like he's Santa Claus. Bertie, who's been dancing around at our feet, darts forward to smell his legs.

"Huh, I guess you were right about the sweater," Lucas says, smiling at me.

thirteen

LUCAS

THE GIFTS SEEMED like a good idea at the time. Buy them gifts to make up for being a tool and show them that I know what they like, that I *care* what they like. Everyone appreciates presents, after all.

Leonard thought it was a bad idea. Danny insisted he knew nothing about women, as evinced by thirty-three years of ineffectual dating, and therefore could not make a judgment one way or another. But they're my friends, so they helped me anyway. Danny and I picked out what to get, and Leonard sweet-talked Constance into letting me come over.

But now, sitting around the table in Constance's kitchen, with Delia staring at those boxes in consternation, I feel like I mucked everything up. Isn't this what my dad used to do?

Fuck someone over in a business deal? Buy them some steaks. Get caught with prostitutes? Buy your wife a diamond necklace. Miss your son's college graduation? Buy him a penthouse apartment, all the better if it's located where you'd like him to live.

I feel myself blushing as Constance pours me a cup of tea. I never blush. But Delia's gaze has shifted from the packages to me, and I'm aware of her in a way that I've never really experienced before. As if her perusal of me is stamped into my skin. As if that kiss last night branded me. I can still feel her soft lips, her vanilla and sea salt scent engulfing my senses. She looks beautiful, her reddish-gold hair tumbling around her shoulders, wearing a dress that blends several different shades. It would look garish on a plastic model but suits her. There are four thin gold necklaces looped around her neck, the bottom one strung with a hunk of stone that hangs in a place that I'd very much like to touch.

"This is totally unnecessary," Delia says, studying me as if I'm a failed exam. "You didn't have to get me anything, Lucas. I'm not upset with you anymore."

But the way she says it suggests the very fact that I did show up with packages has earned her disapproval or, worse, her disappointment. Hell, maybe she's just pissed that I kissed her, told her I shouldn't have, then ran. That's not the kind of thing you do with a woman you'd like to kiss again.

And I *do* want to kiss Delia again. Truthfully, I'd like to do a whole lot more. I'd like to see her dressed in nothing but that hair, flowing down over her glorious tits. I'd like to hear what her moans sound like when my head's buried between her legs or she's pinned to a wall with my cock. But I understand all of that. I've wanted plenty of women, and plenty of women have wanted me. The part I don't understand is that I care more about earning her good opinion than I do about any of that. I'm almost desperate for it, as if only Delia Evans's regard can expiate me. That's something new.

Constance snorts. "Shouldn't we open the presents before we tell him he shouldn't have?" Then she skewers me with a look. "But I tell you what, boy, if it's a new fish tank, we'll have words."

I don't have a chance to ask her why she thinks a relative stranger would buy her a fish tank, because she's handing Delia her present and starting in on the box marked with her name. There's a look in her eyes that reminds me of a kid at Christmas, and Bertie, the little goblin in the pink sweater, is doing a dance beneath the table as if he knows what's in the box. Or maybe he just has to take a piss.

I smile at Delia, but she has a look of consternation on her face as she claims her box. She waits while Constance opens hers—watching Constance while I watch *her*.

"Well, I'll be," Constance says, claiming my attention. She's opened the box, revealing several skeins of alpaca yarn made by a local company. The woman who works at the shop told me about how many she'd need to make another goiter tube top-slash-dog sweater. She smiles at me. "Bertie thanks you." Then she shocks me by getting up out of her chair and wrapping me in a warm hug. I hug her back, surprised by the swell of emotion trying to drown my chest. She murmurs to me, "I'll give you fifteen minutes to talk. Don't you waste it. I'll be using a timer."

Then she heads to the kitchen counter and grabs a bedazzled leash that makes the Burke inside of me cringe. She removes the pink sweater, probably because it's hot as balls outside, and the little dog does a dance as she snaps the leash to his collar. "I'll be right back. Can't ignore the little man's dances. The last time I did, he shit in Frank's shoes, although I can't deny that gave me great pleasure."

Seconds later, she's gone, the front door snicking shut behind her.

Delia's watching me with a slightly bemused expression, as aware as I am that Constance left so we could be alone together.

"Constance is placing an awful lot of trust in a couple of strangers," I comment. "We could rob her blind or throw a five-minute-long rager."

"We're not strangers," she objects. "We all spent more time together on Monday than most friends spend together in a week. That makes us acquaintances at the very least."

"Do you kiss most of your acquaintances?" I ask before my better sense can take over.

"I'll bet you do," she says archly. Then she licks her lips, and I feel that gesture in every inch of my body, most notably in my cock, which reminds me it's been too long since I've been with a woman. "You want me to open this?" She tucks a lock of hair behind her ear. I remember what it felt like under my fingers, glossy and fine.

Yes. No.

I nod, my gaze on her.

She slides her fingers under the glittery pink wrapping paper, chosen with her in mind, and a strange sense of anticipation grabs ahold of me, as if I'm the one opening the gift.

When she finally cracks open the box, a look of instant pleasure and uncomplicated joy crosses her face as she pulls out the mermaid tail. The scales are colored like a sunrise—purples and pinks bleeding into oranges and yellows, almost like her dress. It took some doing to find it on such a limited time frame. Apparently, mermaid tails are considered specialty items. But this is one of the doors I was happy to let money open for me. She runs her hand over the scales with that same expression of pure delight, and for a moment, I have the pleasure of having done something right, of having pleased this perplexing woman.

But then she tucks it back into the box. "It's gorgeous, Lucas—the most beautiful one I've ever seen—but I can't accept it."

"But you love it," I say, shocked. "Of course you can accept it. You know—"

"I know you have the money, yes," she says. "People who know nothing about you can probably tell you have money. It's there in the way you move, the way you talk. Even your T-shirts look expensive." Her lips purse, and I see the longing look she gives the mermaid tail. "But you don't have to spend money to make friends, Lucas. I'll be your friend if you want me to be, not because you bought me something beautiful. This is...you're trying to control the world again. You can't."

Something wrenches in my chest. "It's not like that." Or at least not totally. The other women who've interested me over the past several years have wanted gifts—expensive necklaces, vacations, dresses—and they've been delighted by them. It's what I've learned, from them and from my father. And yet—

"I wanted to do something for you, Delia," I say, standing up and then realizing it was a mistake, because now I'm looming over her. But I can't sit down with this feeling of energy, of purpose, running through me, so I reach for her hand and pull her up. That was a mistake too, because now she's standing right in front of me, like those grapes dangling over Sisyphus's head. My hands want to touch her.

"And I'm telling you that you have other things to offer than just your money." She gives me a small smile, but there's a sad expression in her eyes. "Or your looks."

"You like the way I look?" I ask, my mouth hitching up slightly.

"You know I do. Everyone does. There's no one on earth who would look at you and find what they saw displeasing."

"Because I look like Snow White?"

Her smile widens, and I feel it in my chest. "Yes, I've always had a thing for Disney movies. But there's more to you than what you look like. Or your money."

"Is there?"

"Yes. And no matter how much I want this insanely beautiful present, I can't let you think otherwise. I *won't*."

Her words stab into me in an unexpected way, because I didn't realize that was what I was trying to do—to make up for being who I am, for what I was born into, by spending my way out of it. At the same time, she's wrong. I do have the money, and this is what I want to do with it—to give joy to the people I care about, to help people in need, to support businesses that I believe in.

I don't mean to, but I touch the end of one of her locks of hair. The glossy feeling of it and the pop of bright color make me feel more than I'm accustomed to feeling.

"Thank you," I say, my voice hoarse. "But I still want you to have it. I want you to know that I like you like this...the way you are. I feel it's necessary, because I royally fucked up yesterday. And Monday. And, hell, probably every day in between. Maybe I'm messing up again, being here. Doing this. But I wanted to, and it's been a long time since I've wanted to do anything."

She shocks me by grabbing both of my arms, and from the way her lips part before she speaks, maybe she's shocked herself too. "You're trying. That's more than most people do. You're going to be all right."

"Please keep it," I say, because I need her to. Something inside of me requires it. "Please. I want you to have it."

She studies my eyes for a long moment, and I feel both lost and found—a thought that rattles me. When did I become such a putz?

Maybe finding out your whole life was founded on a lie will do that to a man. I've always known my parents weren't good parents, or even nice people, but I believed that they had a core integrity. But it wasn't true. They're like a pristinely wrapped box filled with toxic vapor.

"Okay," she says softly, her lips tilting into a smile. "I will, but you're going to come to my next mermaid reading."

"I don't consider that a hardship, Delia," I say, my voice betraying me. "I chose it thinking of what it would look like on you."

And what it would feel like if I got to fuck her with it on, if we could figure out a way, but I know better than to mention it. I have a feeling it wouldn't help my case.

"There will be children present," she says archly, as if she can see my dirty thoughts. "You'll have to behave. Besides—" She takes a slight step back. "Last night, you said kissing me was a mistake, and we both know you were probably right."

"Maybe the real mistake was not picking you up and running with you," I say, but I don't span the space between us. I don't want to be another person who acts like her opinion isn't important, and she's the one who stepped away, even if I see in her eyes the same attraction I feel.

"Maybe," she says, her lips twitching. "But you'd have regretted it after a few steps—and not just because you're what Doris would call the love-them-and-leave-them type. I'm heavier than I look."

"You don't think I could carry you?" I ask, raising an eyebrow. "That sounds like a challenge, and I'll have to warn you that I'm not the type of man to turn a challenge down."

She looks at me speculatively, warmly. "No, I don't imagine you are."

Her other words penetrate—*love-them-and-leave-them type*—and I feel a pang in my chest. Almost a hunger. There's a wanting that's been welling up inside of me. A need that I don't really understand beyond the pull to do something about it.

"I..." I pause, trying to gather my thoughts so I can say what I'm feeling. "I'm not..." I pause once more, then try again. "I don't want..." Another strikeout. "I don't want to be the kind of guy Doris would warn you away from."

That much I can admit, to her and myself.

She watches me seriously, her lips twitching as if she wants to smile. They always seem to do that—to be ever in motion, her face a study of different expressions. "Doris is a stern judge of character."

I let myself smile. "I thought Constance was too, but she really liked that yarn. The lady at the shop said it was their most requested type."

"I don't think it was the yarn that did it," she says, surprising me, because I'd been pretty damn sure it was the yarn.

"No?"

"Absolutely not. You wanted to do something nice for both of us, and you went to some effort to do it, plus you got something for Bertie, whom she loves more than any yarn. That being said, Doris will probably be more of a tough customer. She's trying to set me up with her great-nephew. She says he's bald and has caterpillar eyebrows and is working on the movie. I can only assume she's talking about Orange Lanyard."

"Orange Lanyard?" I ask, then my mind rewinds to the movie set...caterpillar eyebrows...little blue pills. A lanyard with an orange juice brand printed all over it. "You mean Orange Juice?"

Her laugher lights up her face, and I feel the satisfaction of having pleased her. "I like your nickname even better," she says. "But we should probably call him Thomas from now on. We need to be nice to him because he's related to Doris."

"What should I do to impress her?" I say, taking a small step toward her because I can't help myself. I feel drawn in. I want to pull her to me. To kiss her. To claim her, even though I have no business doing any such thing. "Shave my head?"

"Don't you dare. I like your hair."

"Put Rogaine on my eyebrows to make them caterpillars?"

Sweet laughter escapes her.

"Take singing lessons from Leonard? I remember you said she used to be a lounge singer."

"Yes, absolutely." She pauses, smiling, and then says, "You know what? I think we got off on the wrong foot."

"Was it because you almost hit me with your car?"

Her smile widens. "I seem to remember you saying you deserved it, but no, I was speaking in a more general sense." She watches me for a moment, making me wonder what's going on in her head. It's a place I'd like to get lost in. "Maybe we were meant to be friends, not enemies, Lucas Burke."

It's more than I deserve and less than I want. "I'm a mess," I warn her. "You should know that. I don't know what I'm doing anymore. With anything."

"I do," she says, her eyes twinkling slightly. "I happen to like messes."

"I don't want you to think you have to fix me." She gives me a look that reminds me that I'm the one who was talking about fixing her not so long ago. "Yes," I agree. "I'm also a hypocrite. It's another of my bad qualities."

"At least I didn't have to be the one to say so." She tilts her head slightly, the angle changing my view of her irises, making them more green than blue, then almost amber. "But I don't need to fix you. You can fix anything inside of yourself that needs fixing. If I can help you, though, I will."

I reach over to touch her arm, feeling a static shock when I do, almost as if our skin can't touch without forming some kind of electricity. "You'd help anyone, wouldn't you?"

She takes a slight step back, her expression closing down a little, and my hand falls. "No, I wouldn't." She swallows. "I know you're going to think this is stupid, but I could tell fate was bringing me to that movie set. At first, I thought it was because of Jeremy."

I must be scowling, because she reaches out and traces my brow, my consternation falling away. "He's a dick," I start. "He said—"

I can't repeat it to her. I can't even think about it without wanting to get into my car to drive to his hotel and punch him repeatedly for disrespecting her. Even now, part of me thinks that's exactly what I should do.

"I don't care what he said. I realized pretty quickly that he was a dick, and when I found out you were a Burke, I thought maybe I was there because you needed to be reminded of what you'd done."

I feel myself shriveling at the words, but she quickly adds, "Then I found out you were the whistleblower, and I realized that maybe we were supposed to help each other heal, Lucas. So, no, I wouldn't want to help just anyone. I wouldn't do anything for Jeremy other than get him a warm seltzer, now that he's revealed his true personality. And I'm only inclined to be nice to Thomas because I love Doris. Otherwise, I'd think he was a real heel."

She says it so easily—*I love Doris.* I grew up in a home where the word "love" wasn't used, where it was code for weakness. I'm envious of how open she is. How artless.

Despite that weird coincidence last night—winding up at the very bar Delia's sister runs without having planned it—I don't believe in fate. And yet, I don't dislike that Delia does.

But I'm not ready to say any of that to her, so I clear my throat. "Seriously, what's with the seltzer?"

She tells me, and I can't help but smile at the thought of that seltzer being delivered to the table last night. Her sister is protective of her, which I like. "Let's buy him a case of it," I say. "Lukewarm, of course. I'll bring it in tomorrow as a peace offering."

She laughs, still standing close enough that I can practically feel it moving her body. The way she laughs is addictive, and I instantly want more.

"You said we'd be friends. Are we friends who get to kiss?" And fuck, preferably. The desire to sink into her, her red-orange hair wrapped around my fist, is pounding through me. I want to know what the rest of her tastes like. I want to bury myself inside of her and lose myself. At the same time...I'm confused by her. I know that having sex with her wouldn't be anything like bringing a woman home from a bar or some event. It would change me in a way I'm not sure I'm prepared to be changed.

"To be determined," she says, but I don't miss the way her gaze dips to my mouth. She's not immune to me. Thank God for that.

"It was a good kiss. I'll bet we can get even better at it if we practice."

I know instantly that it was wrong of me to push her.

She gives her head a little shake. "We won't be doing that today."

"So what will we be doing?"

"You said you like challenges." A wide, almost mischievous grin spreads across her face, and I feel myself leaning toward her, like I can't help it. "Do I ever have a challenge for you, Lucas Burke."

fourteen

DELIA

IT TOOK LUCAS AN HOUR—ONLY an hour—to find homes for the fish and tanks. Unfortunately, they're not going to the same place, so now we have to separate the fish into groups, empty the tanks, and bring them all to their new homes. Reinforcements were needed, so Lucas called his friends. Danny can't make it on account of he's on a bike ride twenty miles away, and Shane is away on some sort of team-building conference, but Leonard said he's coming. Constance also summoned her granddaughter. The second wave of help hasn't arrived yet, though, and so far it's just the three of us trying to sweetly coax the fish into our nets, like we're not terrifying giants hundreds of times larger than them.

I watch while Lucas dips his net into the tank to retrieve an angel fish—I think—a look of utmost concentration on his face. His light blue polo shirt is slightly wet from fish water, and there's a smudge of something on the bottom. I wish I could take a picture of him like this without looking weird, because it's an image I'll want to remember.

Lucas Burke, down and dirty.

Lucas Burke, savior of women and fish.

I like that he instantly jumped into action when presented with a problem. It didn't seem overwhelming to him the way it did to Constance and me. Then again, this is a man who's used to solving complicated real estate problems. What are a bunch of fish to him?

A little voice in my head, which hasn't quite forgiven and forgotten, asks *What are a bunch of humans to the Burkes?*

I know Lucas isn't like his parents, but I hate the thought of them lurking in his brain as if they have a couple of camp chairs set up in the corner. He himself said they've staked out territory there and it's hard to let them go. I want to help him with that.

Maybe I'm naive for thinking that I can be friends with someone who infuriates me and makes me go liquid with wanting from a single glance. But I can't deny the draw I feel to him. I also can't fully give into it.

Constance is watching Lucas too, and it's wonderful to see the hope in her eyes.

"Got the little bastard," Lucas says in victory, scooping up he little fish he was hunting and moving it to its holding tank. The tank is empty of life now, ready to be drained into the sink Frank had custom-built for this room, and I start arranging the suction tubes to get the water out as Lucas sets down the net.

"Maybe your purpose is to work in a pet store," I say glibly, giving him a glance.

He smiles back at me. "This is where I'd usually say I don't see the purpose in having a pet, but I want Constance to like me, and we both know she has an unnatural attachment to that little dog."

"You just admitted to the very thing you said you shouldn't admit to," I point out, arching my eyebrows. "You can't stop yourself from making a point, even if it's a bad one."

He shrugs, still smiling, then shoots a glance at Constance. "Bertie is obviously the exception to the rule. He looks good in his sweater."

I can't help but snort, and Constance clucks her tongue. "No need to sweet-talk me, pretty boy. I'd let you get away with just about anything right now. But you should know that I have a bullshit meter like no other." Even as she says it, though, she's looking around the fish room sadly. "Except for with that infernal man. I let him get away with murder."

"Fish murder, anyway," Lucas mutters. We found several floaters. I was a little upset about it, so Lucas insisted on reading a poem over them before we brought them to their resting place—the trash can, because I'd read that it was frowned upon to flush them into the water supply.

Constance's phone beeps for what must be the thirtieth time since we came down here.

"You're one popular lady," Lucas teases. "You playing half a dozen few salt-and-pepper bachelors against each other?"

She frowns at him. "No, young man. And you'd do best to keep it in your pants too. We don't need more men running around and giving everyone chlamydia."

I gape in surprise, no longer pretending to do anything. "Frank gave you chlamydia?"

"In 1990," she says with a pinched look. "You're probably wondering why I stayed with him."

Well, yes. She doesn't seem like the sort of woman who'd take a cheater back.

"Pardon my language, but it was his dick," she says flippantly, tucking a lock of white hair back into her ponytail. She got changed into leggings and a T-shirt, but neither her clothes nor her granddaughter's would fit me, so I stayed in my dress. Lucas has been very careful about it. "It's marvelous, and worse, he knows how to use it. A dick like that can make a woman do stupid things. Of course, that was long ago. These days it doesn't get above half-mast. At least not for me."

123

I close my mouth and nod, trying desperately not to think of Frank's dick. I saw a photo of him upstairs, and he looks like Mr. Rogers's less kind brother. It should be illegal to think of Mr. Rogers having a dick.

"Still, I should have left him when he gave me chlamydia. I did kick him the balls so hard they turned black and blue."

My gaze shifts to Lucas, because I want to know how he's taking this all in. He said he doesn't want to be the sort of man who'd give Doris reason to worry, but he's obviously had his way with all kinds of women. He's probably slept with enough water aerobics instructors to staff two classrooms.

"What?" he says, his eyes widening. "*I* didn't give her chlamydia."

"I wasn't blaming you," I say.

"Is this one of those situations when I should apologize for my Y-chromosome?"

"Maybe," I concede.

"We've got your ticket, hot stuff," Constance says, wagging a finger at him. "If you let yourself get chlamydia, half the young women in town would have it."

He blushes, and I feel a tug of fondness for him. I like him like this—out of his element, his black hair mussed, his tanned forearms exposed in all their glory. "I don't... It's been a while since I went out on any dates, Constance, but I'll add you to my dance card if you ask nicely."

There he goes again, rolling out the charm like it doesn't cost him anything, but I can tell he's a little upset, maybe even offended.

"Just because he could successfully seduce anyone doesn't mean he seduces everyone," I tell her. "We should give him the benefit of the doubt. It's not his fault that he's—" I gesture to him, but my hand almost falls, because he's giving me a different look—one that reminds me that he's tried to seduce me, or near enough. Now, I'm thinking of the way his lips felt on my mouth, my neck. God help me, I'd like them all over my body.

Then he clears his throat and averts his gaze to Constance. "Not to change the subject or anything, but why is your phone blowing up if you're not getting bootie calls? Is everything okay?"

Constance's expression sours. "It's Frank the Fuck. It's...it would have been our anniversary today. He posted a photo of himself with his water aerobics floozie on Facebook, and most of the people we know don't even know we're separated. He doesn't answer his phone, so who do you think is getting all the texts and calls?"

"Consider this my official apology for my Y-chromosome," Lucas says. He's exuding charm again, but there's nothing studied about it this time. It's just...*him*...and it's hard not to be drawn in. Then his smile turns crafty. "Why don't we take some pictures of our own, Constance? A rebuttal, if you will. We can really get them talking. I could be..." His gaze averts to me, his smile an invitation.

"A collector of rare, tropical fish," I supply.

"No wonder I wound up with you two," he says with a slight smile. "Let's see. Maybe you put an ad up on Craigslist hoping to find a new home for the fish, and I got in touch with you." He rubs his hands together. "This'll be fun."

Then his mouth twists to the side, and I see his brightness fade. He's remembering. Some of the people who see the photos may recognize him, like Marlene did the other day. If they do, they'll be having different conversations with Constance.

"No," I blurt. "She should take them with Leonard. She has a thing for him."

Constance brightens. "I said I'd be interested if I were forty years younger, but it *is* a delightful idea." She laughs, the sound so delighted it lifts my mood automatically. "Oh, to see the look on Frank's face."

"Leonard will do it," Lucas says, giving me a quick glance. I see relief in it. Mutual understanding. It's like there are invisible spider webs between us, connecting us. I don't know why, but in a weird way it's felt like that since the beginning.

Or was it just since you found out who he is? a voice in my head asks.

I don't know the answer, and don't have much time to wonder, because the doorbell rings upstairs.

fifteen

DELIA

"MAYBE THAT'S LEONARD NOW!" I say, wanting to break the moment without really knowing why.

"You go get him," Constance says. "These old bones could use a rest from the stairs, and I'd like to get to know your friend here a little better."

"She means she'd like to interrogate me," Lucas says dryly but not dismissively.

"Yes," Constance tells him. "I should think that was obvious."

I glance at Lucas to make sure he's okay with this, and he gives me a small, conspiratorial smile. It shivers through me and settles low, and I clear my throat unnecessarily as I leave the room, shaken.

I remind myself that I'm not interested in Lucas Burke. I can't be.

When I get upstairs, Bertie rises from his little bed and joins me at the door, his nub of a tail wagging.

"Thanks for the vote of confidence, Mr. Bertrand." I tell him. It's the kind of thing certain people would get on my case for, talking to a dog, making up a nickname for him. But I don't care for the thought, and I stuff it away.

When I open the door, I'm surprised to see a petite woman with

127

short lilac hair and a bright orange jumpsuit on the stoop. I'm instantly delighted with her style, although she does not seem equally delighted to see me.

"You're not Leonard," I comment unnecessarily.

"And you're not my grandmother," she replies with a small smile. "I'm guessing you're Delia. She told me about you and your *business.*"

She's smiling, but she looks suspicious, like she thinks I'm a grifter who wants to bilk her grandmother out of her life savings. It wouldn't be the first time a relative has assumed the worst of me.

"Yes, I'm your grandmother's friend," I say. "We met on the set of the movie."

She gives me a dubious look. "So now you're palling around with a senior citizen?"

"Aren't you?"

"She's my grandmother."

"Why'd you ring the bell?" I ask, apropos of nothing. It's just... she lives here, right? Shouldn't she have a key? Then it hits me. "Oh, you were hoping I'd answer the door so you could interrogate me."

Like grandmother, like granddaughter, I suppose.

I can tell she's about to say something, but a truck pulls in behind Lucas's car as we're standing there on the stoop. It's an old Chevrolet that looks like it's had better decades, not just years, and I'm not surprised to see Leonard come ambling out, heading toward us. He doesn't have a hat on today, and his brown hair has some photic highlights that suggest he doesn't wear one when he's working outside either.

He sees me and salutes. "The lady of the lake. I've heard we have some wet work to do?"

"Who the hell are you?" Shauna asks, turning to him with a look of suspicion. I guess I can't blame her for that. He's wearing a short-sleeved shirt revealing his tatted arms, one of them with a scar cut across it, and he has the general look of someone who's not up to much good. That's delightful, because it will make for some interesting photos for Constance's social media, but it's obvious Shauna isn't pleased with the whole situation.

"Who are *you*?" he asks, eying her up and down.

"A person who lives in this house, and there are pretty forgiving laws about protecting your property in this state, so I wouldn't come any closer if I were you." She skewers me with a glance. "You know this guy? Does my grandmother know him, or did you..."

"I'm helping Constance with the fish tank situation. My..." I don't begin to know how I was going to complete that sentence—friend? Former nemesis? The man I'm interested in despite myself?—"Lucas found homes for them, and Leonard was kind enough to offer his assistance."

"Fuck," she says, giving her head a shake. "Well, that's something at least. First my grandfather goes insane, and now her. She's been staying up until all hours crocheting dog sweaters, and now she has a bunch of decades-younger friends. Sounds about right." She gives Leonard another suspicious look. "Are you here to sell her drugs?"

"No," he says with an easy grin. "But if you have the 4-1-1 on where to score a little green, I wouldn't say no."

She regards him with all the interest a person might show a pile of roadkill that no longer resembles any specific animal. "Pot's basically legal."

"Then it shouldn't be an issue, huh?"

"I'm Shauna. Be aware that if you *do* try anything, I have a black belt in taekwondo. You may be bigger than me, but you wouldn't stand a chance."

"Are you trying to turn me on?" he asks, his eyes dancing as he takes her in. "Because it's working."

"Gross," she says flatly, then heads past me through the door.

Leonard winks at me, and we both follow her in. Or at least try to. Bertie takes one look at him and starts barking furiously.

"I'm good with dogs," he says, lowering onto his haunches to get to Bertie's level. It's a mistake, because Bertie instantly jolts forward and latches on to his wrist. Leonard gives his hand a shake, but Bertie won't break loose.

"Bertie!" I breathe out, shocked. It seems like a betrayal of his gentlemanly character—or at least the gentlemanly character I've invented for him in my head.

His teeth gritted, Leonard turns to Shauna. "A little help? This gremlin's got some teeth on him."

She quickly detaches the dog, who cuddles into her chest. Her eyes narrow at Leonard. "This dog likes everyone."

"That hasn't been my experience."

"I'm going to go put him in my bedroom," she says. "I'll meet you all downstairs."

I wonder if she's going to go call the police on us. Or, worse, Frank the—

"I think she likes me," Leonard says to me in an undertone, grinning. His eyes are on her back as she heads in the direction of the bedrooms.

I laugh. "Then you're not very good at reading body language or listening to what people have to say." I wait a beat, until Shauna disappears through a door, then say, "Would you be up for taking some flirty photos with Constance so she can post on social media to make her ex jealous?"

He grins broadly. "I'd say it sounds like just the kind of job I'm most qualified for. Bonus points for the added toxicity."

"Well, maybe we'd better hurry so we can get it done before Shauna sees."

"Why?" he asks as we start toward the door to the basement. "I'll take some photos with her too if she asks nicely." He gives me a sidelong glance. "Did you like Lucas's present? Our buddies and I have a bet going."

"Yes and no," I admit. "It's beautiful, but he shouldn't have gotten it."

He gives me a rueful glance as I open the door. "Maybe not, but that's never stopped him. He means well, you know."

Yeah, I do.

We climb down the stairs, and Lucas and Constance meet us as we reach the last step. Lucas smiles at me, but his smile's a little brittle, and I can't help but wonder what she said to him. He's not quite himself, although that's a foolish thing to think since I've only known him a week.

"Ah," Constance says with a smile at Leonard, "my good-for-nothing boyfriend."

He gives her a cocky grin, then walks over and links elbows with her. "I've heard we're about to be the talk of the town. Now, I tried that Roquefort, and I have to say—"

They keep walking while Lucas and I stand there frozen for a moment, looking at each other. His regard makes me hot and cold at the same time, and I think for about the millionth time about that kiss. Why he did it. Why it felt like that. Whether he's right and we can get even better at it by practicing. So I clear my throat and say, "Constance's granddaughter is home. I think she's under the impression that Leonard and I are grifters."

He laughs, his gaze darting toward the fish room. "Maybe she's not far off."

Then he glances back at me, and I feel the full power of his blue eyes. Their intensity and the heat they give off, like the hottest point in a fire. "You saved me back there. I didn't even have to ask. Just like you did the other day with Melinda."

"Marlene."

His mouth tips up. "Marlene. You saved her ass too, if I'm remembering correctly."

My body is twitchy to move, so I give a little shrug. "Her hair, yes, but I guess that's beside the point. You said I help everyone. Maybe you were right."

"You said you didn't."

His gaze asks me for an explanation. I give a pointed glance to the fish room, where Leonard and Constance are waiting for us. He doesn't budge.

Sighing, I say, "Marlene's hair made her feel self-conscious. I told you about the orange slices. I didn't want anyone else to have to feel that way."

"And me? Why would you want to help me? Back then, you didn't like me very much."

I repress a smile. "It was less than a week ago."

"And you thought I was a real son of a bitch." He winces. "Or maybe that's a little too on point."

It takes a second for it to click. He's referring to his mother. I feel a shudder of revulsion. In the internet deep dive I did after meeting Lucas, I saw photos of both of his parents. He looks more like his father than his mother, but he got his piercing blue eyes from her. Hers are flat, though, like a frozen pond, and his father has the kind of smile a person only learns from practice. There's nothing genuine about them, nothing warm or soft. Lucas has plenty of edges, but beneath them there's an earnestness, a warmth.

"When you told me you didn't know about Nat, I believed you," I say. "I saw the pain in your eyes. You were there for an escape. You didn't need to have the past rubbed in your face. Even if you were a son of a bitch."

He swallows. Nods. That heat's flaring in his eyes, and I think maybe he wants to grab me. To kiss me again like he did last night, like air was completely superfluous to his existence. In that moment, I'm desperate for him to. I want him with a tugging urgency I can't remember feeling for any of the other men who wanted to fix me.

"You're too good to be true. Like a Disney princess."

His words are like a bucket of water upending on my head. I put a hand on my hip. "I'll have you know that I'm *very* real, and despite my aforementioned admiration of Disney, I find that offensive.

Maybe, instead of putting me into boxes, you should try getting to know me."

"I am, Delia," he says, his voice serious. "But maybe I'm no good at that either."

"So practice. Next time you want to make a blanket generalization about my life, try asking a few questions first."

"I—"

Leonard leans his head out of the fish room. "If you were real photographers, you'd be fired. I'd know."

"You were a photographer?" I ask, surprised.

He shrugs. "I've been a lot of things. I've only been good at a couple of them—the rest were a waste of other people's time." He winks. "But if you're going to waste time, better for it to be someone else's. Just like you two are wasting ours."

"Yes, and I only have so many years left," Constance says, peering out from behind him. There's a slightly shrewd look on her face, and I'm sure she's wondering what we were talking about. Or, darn it, it occurs to me now that they likely heard everything we said. Or at least Leonard probably did. "What better way to spend them than to scandalize my friends by lying about sleeping with a man younger than my granddaughter."

"Oh, he has to be in his mid-thirties at least," I say without thinking. "Shauna looks younger than that."

A strangled sound escapes Lucas, and when I look at him, I see he's trying not to laugh.

"What'd I ever do to you?" Leonard asks, giving me a pained look and placing a hand over his heart. "I'm not a day over twenty-five."

"That's what I'll be telling everyone I know," Constance says with a wicked expression.

There's a creaking upstairs that tells me Shauna's returned from her bedroom and is preparing to come down. Worry ripples through me. We haven't taken those photos yet, and I know Shauna might not like it.

Well, like it or not, I'm determined. I'm not going to let Constance get the crap end of the stick. Frank doesn't want to answer his messages? That's his right, I suppose, but he's about to get a fresh flood of texts to ignore.

I grab Lucas's hand, ignoring the jolt the contact sends through me, and hustle him toward the fish room.

"You don't think she'll approve?" he asks in a low voice that my ears find very pleasing. Doris would call it a bedroom voice.

"I'm not taking any chances," I reply in a whisper. "It's possible she'd side with her grandfather."

Lucas's expression should be in the dictionary under "dubious." "After he gave Constance syphilis?" he asks, pretending to be scandalized.

I try not to smile and fail. It's his presence, his Lucas-ness. "You know it was chlamydia. Now, behave," I tell him, although I doubt I'd like it half so much if he did.

We step into the room hand in hand before I remember and force myself to release him. There are footfalls on the stairs now. Shauna's getting close.

"Get ready for your close up, Mrs. Smith," Lucas tells Constance with a grin. Presumably it's Leonard's last name, because I know it isn't hers.

Leonard slides an arm around her, and she preens for the camera. "Make sure to get my good side," she says but neglects to tell Lucas which side she means.

Maybe it's a test. If so, it's one I'd fail. I find both sides of her equally pleasing.

Lucas doesn't quail—he pulls out his phone and manages to get a few photos in before Shauna steps into the room.

Her expression slides from confusion to surprise as she takes in all of the work we've done—the tanks that have been emptied and are waiting to be cleaned, the fish gathered together in groups for transportation. "You're actually helping her clean up this mess."

"Either that, or we're stealing all of her expensive aquarium equipment and fish," Leonard says. "There are some nice-looking fish down here." He points to one. "I'll bet that one's worth at least a buck fifty."

A laugh escapes me, and there's an amused twist to Shauna's mouth before she smooths it away. "I guess you're wondering why I let it get this bad," she says, looking at me.

"Excuse me," Constance says. "Are you implying I don't have control over what goes on in my own house?"

Shauna gives her a wry look, as if it to remind her that the room we're in is evidence that neither of them was completely in control of what went down in here.

Constance sniffs, and Shauna says, "He didn't ask us, you know? The delivery guy just showed up and started bringing down tank after tank. I figured my friend was pranking me, but sadly, no. Grandpa Frank actually ordered and paid for all of this. He's obviously got several screws loose. I blame *Finding Nemo*. He watched it half a dozen times before this insanity started."

"Why didn't he order any clownfish, then?" Lucas asks.

Shauna snorts. "He said saltwater tanks were too much work. As if he intended to do any work at all. He was all about the idea, but the reality wasn't any fun. That's what he's like." She pauses, then adds, "Say, you look—"

My defensiveness of him kicks in. "That's Lucas," I say. "He's an actor. We're all in the movie together."

His warm gaze lands on me, and I can practically feel him telling me that I'm doing it again—standing up for people. Helping as if it's my job.

"Him too?" Shauna asks, giving Leonard the stink-eye.

"Yes. He gets to wear a fedora on set," I offer. "It makes him look dashing."

She makes a disbelieving sound in her throat, then swallows audibly and glances back at me. Her eyes are shiny with emotion.

"I...thank you for helping Nana. I'll admit that the problem got away from me. I've been working a lot of hours lately, but I should have taken care of this."

"We're happy to help," I say honestly.

"I guess I don't trust people easily."

Possibly because her grandfather is the kind of person who'd give his wife the clap and then run off with an aquatics instructor and leave her with a room full of fish. Admittedly, thirty-three years passed between those two events, but it seems like ample proof that a fish doesn't change his stripes.

Shauna's gaze darts around the room again, taking in the work we've done, and then pauses on Leonard's hand, still wrapped around her grandmother's shoulders. She points. "What's going on here?"

"Oh, don't mind me," he says with a smirk. "But you might want to get used to referring to me as your step-grandfather. Daddy is also acceptable."

"What's going on, Nana?" she asks, ignoring him as if he's another fish tank.

"Your grandfather, that's what," Constance says, unrepentant. "He put some photos of him and his *special friend* on social media, and my friends here have offered to give him a taste of his own medicine."

"Oh," Shauna says, her tone appreciative. "Fuck, yes. We're doing this thing." She looks Leonard up and down, then darts a glance at Lucas. "Shouldn't you take photos with the hot one?"

sixteen

LUCAS

"SHE WAS JUST SAYING that to get to me," Leonard says for what has to be the five hundredth time. He just drove me back to Constance's to pick up my car after we dropped off the last of the fish and tanks using his truck. Delia and I talked the whole time we were cleaning and packing the tanks while Leonard argued off and on with Shauna. At the end, with all the supplies and fish ready to be brought to their new homes, we took more photos. Constance changed into a variety of different outfits, each more outrageous than the last, and Leonard hammed it up. I also snapped one of Delia, saying I wanted a photo of a mermaid in her natural habitat. She objected and said a mermaid would only be in a place like that in a snuff film. Constance sniffed but agreed. Then Delia surprised me by saying *she* wanted a photo of *me*, the savior of the fish.

It felt like a good sign, but when I told Leonard so, he sighed and told me I was as vain as Shane, who famously has a framed photo of himself hanging up in his apartment. He insists he only put it up because it's the headshot they used when they made the announcement about him making partner, but we all like to talk smack about it.

"I mean, she was definitely just saying that to get to me," Leonard repeats, obviously seeking a response of some kind.

"No," I say, mostly because it amuses me to mess with him. "Constance's granddaughter genuinely seems to dislike you. You sure you didn't sleep with her and forget to call?"

He tilts his head as if considering it, then scrunches his mouth to one side. "Nah, I'd remember a woman like her. And she'd be happier to see the man who gave her half a dozen screaming orgasms."

"Uh-huh." I find myself thinking of what Delia said to Orange Juice—Thomas, I mentally correct—about women not wanting to have sex all night long. I'll bet she'd have something to say to Leonard right now too.

Something surprising, because Delia is nothing if not surprising.

Where is she now? Back at home with Doris and Ross? She told us about the way he's always hunting for hidden junk food, and it painted a picture—a happy picture, like those trees we were talking about the other day. I'd like to meet them, I realize. I'd like to be a part of Delia Evans's world.

And now *I* sound like a fucking Disney movie.

I'm tempted to text her, but she set some boundaries earlier, and I don't want to steamroll them. She already thinks I'm too pushy and manipulative. The last thing I want to do is prove her right. I also don't want to *be* any of those things.

They're Burke things, and I don't want to be a Burke anymore.

"You're doing it again," Leonard says in disgust. "You're thinking about Delia. I can tell by the look on your face. The Drew Affliction is about to become fatal."

"Nah, man. She says she just wants to be friends."

He laughs in my face.

"What's so funny?"

"Nothing. Just...good luck with that. I have a feeling it's going to go great."

"Sarcasm doesn't escape me. You know, Constance told me to leave her alone," I admit, because it's been on my mind. I like Constance. I respect her. I don't want to respect this, though.

"Oh yeah? Do I need to have a little talk with my girlfriend?"

"She said she'd kill me and make it look like an accident if I fuck Delia over."

His face lights up with humor. "I know how to pick 'em, huh?"

I feel the side of my mouth hitching up, wanting to smile. Then it drops. "She thinks I'll hurt her."

He studies me for a moment. "Would you?"

"Not on purpose. I like her."

"Yeah, no shit."

"And she doesn't seem to hate me anymore, so that's something."

"Don't be a dick," he says, as if it's just that easy. "Problem solved."

"Maybe it's in my nature to be a dick." The words come out in a rush, because that's been on my mind lately too—whether I can become my own man or if I'm fooling myself by thinking so.

"It's in every man's nature to be a dick. Doesn't mean you can't fight it." He grins at me. "Hell, it's in my nature to live on the run, yet here I am, helping you rehome a bunch of fish. Before now, the only fish I ever gave a second thought was the kind they tried to force-feed us in the cafeteria."

"Don't run," I say, serious. Because I've worried about it happening. After my parents started tracking his movements, he changed his name and took off—then did it again, rinse and repeat, and again. It can't have been only to get away from them, and he didn't get into enough trouble at his various stops to need to reinvent himself so completely. So I believe him when he says it's in his nature to run.

Still, he was in Asheville with us for over three years before he left. He knows how to stay when he wants to.

"I need you around," I add.

"To give you lessons on how not to be a dick? You're barking up

139

the wrong tree, brosef. Give Drew a call. Or talk to Danny. He's not the slightest bit dickish. Shane." He waves his hand in the air dismissively.

"Sure, but Danny and Drew aren't interested in flipping houses with me. You're good at flooring. I can't do this without my flooring guy."

There's a conflicted look on his face, like maybe he wants to argue with me. "Are you doing this just for me, man? The house? Because I could find another gig."

I've given this some thought since the other night. Delia asked me to think about what I want to do—not what I think is best for everyone else—and I realized something. I like what we're doing with the flip house. I've always loved working on flips. Even when I was at Burke Enterprises, my side hustle was what motivated me the most. It felt like real work, honest, completely disconnected from the paper pushing I did for Burke Enterprises. The investments I've been making are fun too—thrilling—but I need this outlet. The high of working with my hands and with a friend who shares my vision.

"Maybe in the beginning," I admit. "But I've realized I need it too. Would you be interested in making it a more permanent arrangement?"

His mouth twitches into a smile. "You asking me to go steady, Burke?"

"Why do you keep calling me that?" I ask, without really meaning to. Sometimes it feels like a mosquito buzzing in my ear, is all.

"It's your name, isn't it?"

"No one else does, after I asked to be called Lucas instead."

He gives me a weighing look. "You might think you're not letting your name define you by using a different one. That's fine, man, you do you. But make sure it's not about running away. You can never run far enough away to escape yourself. I'd know."

He would, at that.

"You get to decide what makes a Burke," he continues. "It's your legacy too."

I'm startled into silence for a moment, my heart pounding. Then I smile at him, making light of it. "Look at you, getting all profound."

He laughs. "Several lifetimes' worth of mistakes packed into thirty-odd years will do that to a man."

"You heard Delia. You're *at least* in your mid-thirties."

His answer is a snort. "I could point out that you're thirty-three too, but I guess you gotta be rich to afford vampire facials." He's silent for a second, and I think he's going to ignore my offer. Then he says, "You want to do other flips?"

"I was thinking we could make it a business," I say, tapping the dash.

"Of course you were." He rolls his eyes. "What would we call it? Better than the Burkes?"

A laugh escapes me. "I was thinking L&L Restoration."

"Only if Leonard comes first," he says with a small smirk.

"So you'll consider it?" I know him better than to think he'll give me an answer now—or that if he did, he'd mean it.

"I'll consider it. And I'm not about to blow town. I wouldn't make it very far anyway. You heard the old girl's death rattle this afternoon. Pick me up tomorrow?"

We're supposed to be on set in the morning, although they haven't sent a call time yet.

His truck's always got some shit going on. Shane's good at fixing that kind of thing, but not me. My dad hired people to work on his cars, and my mother never drove anywhere. Honestly, I'm not even sure she has a license. If she does, she probably paid someone to take the test for her. Bottom line: I'm not any good with cars. Neither is Leonard.

"Did you ask Shane to look at it?" I ask.

"Sure," he says. "But he doesn't seem to be in any particular hurry, and if I show up late, Christian's going to shit a brick."

"Hopefully not the one that almost hit me in the head," I say before thinking. Because that memory's been sneaking up on me. I'll be working in the flip house, and suddenly I start thinking, *I almost died*. Scrolling through GoFundMe, and I see a flash of something in the corner of my eye and think I'm toast. I shake it off. "Sure, man, I'll pick you up."

I get out, and he gives me the one-finger salute before taking off, his truck making the aforementioned death rattle.

I'm grinning as I get in my car, already thinking about showing up on set tomorrow.

Already thinking about *her*.

At midnight, an email comes through from Christian.

Dearest Extras (Future Stars!),

The set of The Opposites Contract is going to be closed for a day, maybe two, because a colony of Vermillion Flycatcher birds was found on the Rolf Estate. Who can blame them for wanting to nest there! Unfortunately, this means that the scenes you're destined to steal won't be filming until Tuesday or perhaps Wednesday, after these adorable little invaders have been safely relocated. Until then, think starring role thoughts!

Yours,

Christian

His excuse reeks of bullshit. Who found this rare bird colony, and why would they move it if it's so ecologically precious?

Christian's not exactly my buddy, though. I'm guessing he's not going to give me real answers, even if he falls all over himself to provide me with fake ones.

Leonard texts me a couple of minutes later.

> Looks like we're mixed up with a bunch of real ornithologists, huh?

I'm not surprised he's still awake. He was always more of a night owl, although we've gotten in some early starts at the flip house.

> Did you have to look that word up?

> Fuck you. And yes. I tell you what, I hope it's a lie. I wasn't lying to Jeremy the other day. Birds wig me out.

> Flip house in the morning? I still need a ride.

> You got it.

I'm glad we'll get more work in. We're getting close. This is the part of the renovation I love—near the end, when you can almost taste it. When you can finally see the house that was in your mind take shape in the one beneath your feet. I'm still curious about the delay, though, and annoyed that I'll have to wait to see Delia. So before leaving the apartment the next morning, I decide to text Sinclair to see if I can get the real story. She and I aren't exactly on texting terms, but I've known her brother since I was six, so I figure I can take some liberties.

I bring my coffee back to my room and sit in my desk chair to type out the message.

> Rare birds, huh?

It's Jeremy. (Eyeroll emoji) He's a menace. He tried hitting on the Rolf heiress at a dinner last night while her husband was sitting right next to her. Her husband didn't take it well. Obviously. We're lucky if we don't get shut down. Maybe they SHOULD shut us down.

So what's happening during the break?

He made an insincere apology to them last night. They still wanted to boot the movie, but a couple of the exec producers came up with a plan of action. They're going to have us do some charity work for the Rolfs tomorrow, but I don't know much yet. I think they're worried about giving Jeremy too many details.

So what you're saying is they won't need us until Wednesday.

Affirmative. There's also some equipment missing from set. They're opening an investigation into it. So that's something else they'll settle during the break.

My mind immediately jumps to Leonard. He couldn't have done it...right? We've only spent one day on set at this point, and although we didn't drive in together last week, we were around each other all day.

Except for when he left to supposedly take care of his trick bowel.

He would have had time to grab some shit then, I guess, but everyone else took a bathroom break with him.

No, it wouldn't have been possible for him to pull something like this off. Nor would he have been able to transfer it without getting caught, unless it was something as small as that fedora.

Maybe I'm naïve, but I don't believe he'd try something like that anyway. Sure, his moral code veers toward gray, but he's not stupid. Things have been good. He seems like he genuinely wants to make this new life work. Stealing equipment that has an obvious origin—hell, it's probably even stamped—wouldn't be the answer.

But will he get blamed anyway? When you have a thief on set and an extra with a rap sheet...

Sure, the feds cleared it for him, but the producers might be able to find out.

> What kind of equipment? How big?

She's probably puzzled, but I'll give her this, she answers.

> Pretty big. Some of the sound equipment. A few other things. That house is huge, so it probably just got wheeled into the wrong place, but they have to find it before we can resume. Happened yesterday.

Relief radiates through me. Leonard could hardly get blamed for that. He doesn't even have a truck that could run him to set, and they wouldn't have let him in if it wasn't a day we were filming.

> Yesterday was not a good day for this movie. Actually, things have gone wrong from the beginning. Starting with that brick.

> Drew would have been really pissed at me if you'd gotten killed on the set of my movie. So thank you for not dying.

> You're welcome. See you Wednesday. Unless more woodland creatures are found at the house.

Then, because I can't help myself, I add,

> Thanks for helping us all ID the director, by the way. I'm guessing you gave him that necklace because you agree that he and the AD must be identical twins separated at birth.

> YES. It's uncanny.

> Happy to help. ;-)

I take a gulp of the coffee, then get up and pace back and forth a few times, my mind hard at work.

Delia needs to know what's really going on, right? I mean, sure, she must have gotten the bird excuse along with the rest of us, but she deserves the real story. She's a woman who likes stories. I glance at the time on my phone—8:15. She's probably up, going through her morning routine, but I can't call this early. That would be a definite stretching of boundaries.

So instead I text her a few of the photos I took yesterday, following up with:

> I have the real story about the birds. Interested?

I smile as her name pops up on my phone with a call.

"A little early to call, don't you think?" I tease when I answer.

"Yes, it is. Although I suppose it's early to text too. Are you saying there are no real birds? I was going to ask Christian for a photo. Ross is a bird hobbyist."

My smile widens. "I'll bet. But no, no birds. There was some trouble with Jeremy."

There's a pause on the other end of the line, and I realize it might not be smart for me to offer up this information. She might take it as further evidence of me being interfering and manipulative.

Then she surprises a laugh out of me by saying, "Did he have a temper tantrum because they ran out of perfectly refrigerated seltzer?"

seventeen

LUCAS

APPARENTLY, both situations are resolved by Tuesday night, because we get a note telling us to show up "bright and early!" on Wednesday. The level of devotion Christian shows to the bird lie is either admirable or troubling, because there's a photo of a bird's nest full of tiny babies attached to the email. I forward it to Sinclair, who responds with a laughing emoji.

> How'd the charitable event go?

> Really wonderful. I visited the children's hospital— the Rolfs financed a new wing.

> I presume you're not talking about birds.

> Not this time. I loved spending time with the kids, but Jeremy didn't get so lucky. They made him pick up trash on a road they sponsor.

> The paps took pictures. He's not pleased.

I show up to hair and makeup with a case of warm seltzer, because I have no issue kicking this particular man when he's down.

Delia takes one look at it and bursts out laughing. She's in another sheath dress, this one blue, and it's impossible not to grin when I imagine her sifting through a little old lady's closet. Things I never thought would give me a hard-on for $500.

"You're incorrigible," she tells me as I lower into the seat beside her and slide the box under my chair. Constance is already present, and she has the satisfied look of a woman who no longer has thousands of fish slowly dying in her basement.

"You like me that way," I tell Delia, but it's a rote response—a *Burke* response—so I add, "I wanted to see you smile."

Leonard makes a vomit face. He's about to sit next to me, when Constance slaps the empty chair beside her. "Over here, hot stuff. I have something to show you."

"Say no more. Actually, maybe I do want you to say more. Are they nudes of your granddaughter?"

She's a woman who takes no shit from anyone but loves to dish it out, so I'm not surprised when she gives him a wry look and says, "What makes you think they're not nudes of me?"

It turns out that the something she wants to show him is her Facebook page, on which there are well over a hundred comments asking about "the young man" on the post she made with her four favorite pictures from the photoshoot—more impressive when you consider she only has a hundred and fifty-three friends.

Delia's clearly delighted with this turn of events, and Leonard takes it as proof that he's not the gremlin Shauna thinks he is. We spend the rest of the wait time talking, all four of us—Constance being downright kind to me. I'm feeling pretty damn good by the time we graduate from hair and makeup to the unnecessary trolley that will take us the short distance to the house. I wasn't permitted to take the seltzer water, but it got that smile from Delia, so I don't regret bringing it.

"When's your next mermaid reading?" I ask Delia as we get situated on the bus. The seats aren't quite big enough, and her body is pressed to mine, creating a line of heat that feels like it might damn well cut me in two.

"You're really going to come?" she asks, beaming at me.

"Nothing could make me miss it."

I'd be lying if I didn't admit that I've been thinking about it a lot. Last night, when I couldn't sleep, I looked up photos of past events, and the sight of Delia in her mermaid tail, her tits hugged by a sequined bandeau topped with oversized shells, her hair down around her shoulders, studded with crystal jewelry, made me so hard I had to jerk off twice.

"Unless a brick fell on your head," Leonard comments, reminding me—annoyingly enough—that we're not alone. "That would probably do it."

"It's Sunday at eleven o'clock in the morning," she says, ignoring him.

Well, fuck me. What are the chances? It's the exact day and time I was told to report to my parents' house for high tea. I get a weird feeling in my gut, a twisting, because there have been a lot of uncanny coincidences with Delia.

"What's wrong?" she asks, eying me.

"Nothing. It's...someone else asked me to do something on the same day and time, and I didn't want to do it. It's almost like—"

"The universe is giving you an out?" she asks.

I can't help but laugh. She's clearly excited about it, and her excitement's like one of those flashing bulbs on a Christmas tree. They should drive a man insane, but there's something oddly compelling about them. Or at least that's what I thought when I visited Drew's house at Christmas. Our tree was professionally deco-rated, and I wasn't allowed within five feet of it.

"You might not believe in inexplicable things, Lucas," she says, pressing her shoulder into me slightly—the contact drying up my laughter, "but that doesn't mean they don't believe in you."

"I'm going to be sleeping with a nightlight from now on," I say.

"Very funny." She rolls her eyes but doesn't pull away. Her soft skin is still pressed to me, feeling like a benediction.

Maybe that's all this is. Maybe part of me feels like if I earn this woman's regard, I'll be acceptable. I'll be a man who can take pride in himself again.

Except I know it's more than that. If I only cared about her good opinion, then I wouldn't have constant fantasies about her. I want this woman—and for more than just a good time.

"You don't have to come on Sunday," she says. "I do a few events a month."

"Do you wear the tail recreationally?" I ask, grinning at her.

"If I'm asked nicely and the magic words are used."

"Good to know," I say, "but I'm still coming on Sunday."

"What are you going to miss?" she asks, then blushes slightly. "Sorry, I guess that's none of my business. People are always telling me I'm nosy."

"Those unspecified people suck." I swallow, then admit, "I was ordered to report to a tea at my parents' house."

"Oh," she says, her voice small, and I hate the way she edges away from me.

"Delia." I slide my hand onto her leg. I honestly only did it to get her attention, but her skin is smooth and warm, and my fingers curl around her knee. Her eyes dart up to meet mine. "I wasn't... I don't want to go. I haven't spoken to them since the day I quit the company. They know what I did. If I went, it would be a dressing down." More like a flaying.

"You haven't personally confronted them?" she asks, watching me. She makes no move to relocate my hand; neither do I.

"No," I say, the word burning in my throat, because I've imagined that confrontation hundreds of times.

"Do you need to?"

"I don't know," I admit. "Maybe. But I'm not ready. They..." I swallow. "They're horrible people, but they're my parents."

"And you still want to impress them." I'd bristle, but there's nothing judgmental about the way she says it.

"Not really. It's more like I wish I could still *be* impressed by them. I gave up on impressing them a long time ago. Nothing I did was ever good enough, and if it was, then they were the ones who deserved the credit for it."

She reaches down to my hand on her knee. I think she's going to move it—I prepare myself for it, because for some damn reason I can't bear the thought—but instead she flips my hand over and takes it in hers, squeezing. "Okay."

"Okay, I can come to the reading?"

"Yes, but if you decide you want to confront them, I'm going with you."

The thought of exposing her to them fills me with horror. But I don't tell her that. I see the determination in her eyes, and I know she means it. I'm grateful, even though I'd never take her up on it.

"Thank you, Sunshine."

Her lips part, and I'm tempted to kiss her right there on the bus. To lay claim to this woman I want. But Leonard clears his throat, and I look out of the window to see we've arrived at the entrance to the Rolf Estate.

I squeeze Delia's hand. "Showtime."

eighteen

DELIA

WE'RE SITTING around on a half-circle of folding chairs in a side room in the house, having been moved from the main room to preserve the benches we sat on the first day. We're far enough away from where they're shooting that we can talk in undertones. It feels intimate, although maybe that's just because I can still remember the way Lucas's hand felt on me on the bus, the way it enveloped my whole knee and made me want to melt into him.

"You need to say we met because of the fish," Leonard says to Constance. "Really hammer home that we never would have met if it weren't because of your ex. That'll fuck him up good."

She cackles and hands him something silver from her purse. It takes me a second to realize it's a flask. I glance around, worried she'll get in trouble, but no one's watching. Christian has taken to leaving us for long stretches of time and coming back smelling like cigarette smoke and cologne. Constance says it's a rookie mistake for him to think one will cancel out the other. There is, of course, a security guard watching us should anyone try to pocket an old napkin or chew gum.

"Maybe *we* should make up a back story," I say to Lucas, eyeing him.

"Because you don't want to tell people you're involved with a guy whose parents murdered people through negligence and then conspired to cover it up?" he asks, lifting his brows.

"We're not dating."

"We may not be dating, Delia, but we are most certainly involved. I don't dismantle fish rooms for just anyone."

That word—*involved*—seems to twine around me. His bright blue eyes are dancing, and I'm grateful to see him this way again. I don't like the effect his parents have on him, or on me.

I clear my throat. "I was talking about our characters."

"You like making up stories for everything, don't you?" he says, his lips tipping up.

"I do. My character's name is Estelle."

His smile widens. "Why am I not surprised?"

"Because you know that I have excellent taste. What's your character's name?"

"Bappy."

I roll my eyes. "Estelle would never go for Bappy. That's not even a name."

"Is so," he says, his voice teasing, but there's an undercurrent of earnestness to it. "I'll have you know, Bappy was the name of my invisible friend when I was little."

The thought of him having an invisible friend is endearing, and I instantly want to know everything. "Mine was Roberta. Consider Estelle renamed. What was Bappy like?"

"A kid, most importantly," he says wryly. "Didn't see much of those until I started kindergarten. My parents didn't believe in play dates. Or children, really. Means to an end."

I'm saddened by the thought of him wandering around a mansion without anyone to play with other than an invisible friend with a terrible name. He must be able to tell, because he starts shaking his head, his mouth lifting at the corners again. "Don't feel bad for me, Delia. I got a horse for my fifth birthday."

"Not a pony?"

"My father doesn't believe in half measures."

No, I guess he wouldn't. Truthfully, I don't think Lucas does either. I'm surprised to realize how close we are to each other. I wasn't consciously aware of moving, but both of us are leaning toward each other, only inches left between our faces. People are still talking in undertones around us, including Constance and Leonard, but my world has once again reduced to Lucas. I notice the slight reddening of a sunburn on his cheeks. Either it's from working outdoors at his flip house or the makeup artist was a bit too free-handed with the blush earlier. I want to run my fingers across it.

Instead, I pull away, and for a second I think he's going to tug me back. He doesn't, but I notice the way his hands wrap around the bottom part of his chair.

"So why do Roberta and Bappy like each other so much?" I ask, managing not to wrinkle my nose at the name.

"Maybe Roberta helps Bappy realize he's been a dick for half his life and he needs to do better."

A smile betrays me. "Only half his life?"

"Definitely. He was the kind of kid who came up with invisible friends with shitty names. More of a nerd than anything."

"Nothing wrong with that."

"And the kind of pre-teen who had acne and lived for playing Dungeons & Dragons with his friends." He makes a show of looking around. "Don't tell anyone, but he might still play it with them occasionally." His smile widens. "And by occasionally, I mean once a week."

"You don't."

He lifts his hands, palms out. "Hey, we're talking about Bappy here. There will be no aspersions to my character."

"Of course we are. Well, *Roberta* doesn't think he's much of a dick at all, actually. She's just...cautious."

"She's been burned before," he says, with an expression that says he'd like to find out who did it so he can do some burning of his own.

"And she doesn't like it when people try to make decisions for her," I say pointedly. "There's been enough of that in the past. From her mother, from the men in her life."

"I've been trying to show you," he says, offering a hand to me, palm up, "I like you the way you are."

My heart speeds up as I take his hand. I know I'm in trouble because holding his hand makes me feel more than my last three boyfriends did. This connection between us is strong and strange, and I find myself thinking again about my birthday cake and those candles and the feeling of fate.

And maybe that means I'm in even bigger trouble than I've accounted for before, because Lucas makes me want to think this is all going according to some celestial plan.

"And I like you the way you are," I admit.

He gives me a dubious look. "You're the one who's helped me put together a laundry list of all the things that are wrong with me."

I'm shaking my head before he's finished. "I just want you to like yourself that way too. Maybe you'd feel like you have less to prove." His expression changes. I can't read it anymore, but he doesn't pull his hand back, so I'm hopeful he's not upset with me.

"I'll be honest. *I'm* the one who has a thing for Dungeons & Dragons."

"You don't say."

"But we haven't been playing anymore since Drew left. I miss him. That's not something I'd admit to everyone."

My heart seems to expand in my chest, demanding more room in my rib cage. "Will you tell me something else no one else knows?"

His smile is self-deprecating. "You already know about my invisible friend. Do you think I roll that one out at parties?"

Christian barges back into the room, smelling so strongly of cigarette smoke and cologne that Marlene instantly sneezes three times. He glares death at her. "You sick? You were told to stay home if you're sick. We can't afford for it to get passed around."

"It's just..."

"You *stink*, Christian," says Constance. She's never the soul of discretion, but I expected she'd have more than to flat-out tell him. I'm guessing the flask has something to do with that.

"Excuse me?" he says, giving her a withering look.

"It's just...I'm allergic to smoke," Marlene chokes out.

A security guard who's been standing against the wall steps forward, a horror-stricken look on her face. "You've been smoking?" she accuses, having somehow missed the cloud of stench that walked in with him.

Maybe the cologne trick really does work on some people.

"Outside!" he insists. "Only outside."

"*On our grounds?*" she asks. Pursing her lips, she walks up to him —careful not to stomp on the floor even though she's clearly angry. Her face wrinkles when she reaches his stench cloud. "You need to watch the training video again," she says. "*Now*. Start to finish."

"But..." he says, his hands lifting to the collar of his shirt as if it's suddenly choking him. "It's two hours long."

"And it's obvious you didn't pay attention the first time. The Rolfs have made it very clear that if there's even one more instance of disrespect, they're pulling the plug."

There are a couple of gasps, and I glance at Lucas, my lips parting.

He looks like he's holding back laughter, barely.

Christian's eyes are wide behind his yellow-framed glasses. "I can't watch the video now. I need to bring a few of the background actors to set."

"They can escort themselves," she says with a withering look. "What would your boss say if she learns you singlehandedly got this movie kicked off the estate?"

His energy frantic, he turns toward Lucas and me. "You two," he barks, then he gestures to another background couple before sighing and telling Constance and Leonard they're also needed. It's obvious he resents the necessity since Constance's intervention is going to result in him having to watch the two-hour training video again.

I only realize I'm still holding Lucas's hand when Constance and Leonard join us outside the door. "Taking method acting a little too far, don't you think?" she says.

Lucas doesn't drop my hand. "If it worked for Daniel Day Lewis, it works for me," he replies.

She snorts. "Leave it to you to compare yourself to Daniel Day Lewis."

But she sounds more amused than annoyed. He's charmed her despite herself, just as he has with me. I love picturing him as the kid he described—fascinated with Dungeons & Dragons and alive with imagination. I love that this handsome man loves dragons and has fond memories of his invisible friend.

We head toward where they're filming, and Orange Lanyard—Thomas, I mentally correct myself—is waiting to collect us. There's a wild, jumpy energy to him, as if he's been sucking down energy drinks. Or maybe he has a stockpile of hidden snacks like Ross.

Should I say something about Doris to him? I imagine I should, but he's talking a mile a minute about the scene we're about to film, another disagreement between Sinclair and Jeremy's characters. Something about sentimentality and houses.

"Sounds like a real banger," Leonard says under his breath as Thomas leads us over to a large potted plant that looks as much like a real plant as a child's scribbling.

"You two will be over here," Thomas says to Leonard and Constance, "pretending to discuss the plant. You know, gesture at it. That kind of shit."

"What's there to discuss?" Constance asks with a scrutinizing look. "It's a piece of inexpensive plastic."

"Maybe I think it's real, and you're trying to convince me it's not," Leonard says.

She barks a laugh. "If you don't know a piece of plastic from a living plant, I've got nothing for you."

Thomas leads us away from them as they continue to discuss the plant, neither of them seeming to realize they're doing exactly what they're supposed to be doing.

Once we're in our position, under some lighting equipment and next to a bookcase that's probably three times older than I am, Thomas pauses next to us.

To my consternation, his gaze instantly narrows on me before slipping farther south than it needs to. "You're Doris's caretaker," he says. "She's told me all about you."

"Oh no," I say instantly. "I wouldn't call myself that. I'm her friend. But yes, she mentioned that her great-nephew was working on the movie. You must be Thomas."

He surprises me, and not in a good way, when he goes in for a hug. I pat his back briefly, but he's attached himself like a limpet, and Lucas has to pull him away from me.

"Aren't you supposed to tell us what to do?" Lucas asks, menace seeping into the line.

"In a second," Thomas says distractedly, still looking at me. "I'm bringing Doris and Ross to dinner on Friday night, my treat. You'll come?"

I don't want to, for reasons that have nothing to do with his caterpillar eyebrows, but I also don't want to disappoint Doris. I avoid doing that whenever possible. "Okay," I agree, regretting it even as the word comes out.

Thomas grins at me, his canine teeth unexpectedly sharp. Maybe he's a social vampire, and he feeds off of making people feel bored and uncomfortable. It's not a charitable thought. Then again, he's groped me twice. "You know," he says conspiratorially, "I think she has her mind set on doing a little matchmaking."

Someone makes a huffing noise, and I don't need to look to know it's Lucas.

"Background!" someone shouts, which is inconvenient, because Thomas hasn't told us what we're supposed to do.

He makes a face, then waves a hand at us. "Just pretend you're whispering sweet nothings to each other. That kind of shit." He winks at me. "Consider it practice for Friday night."

I open my mouth to say something, but he's already retreating. Lucas wraps his arm around me, pulling me close, as the director shouts, "Action."

I look up into Lucas's eyes, and there's an instant jolt, a weakening of my knees.

"I'm surprised you didn't threaten to ruin him," I whisper as Sinclair's character tells Jeremy's character off for not seeing the full potential of Rolf Estate—or her.

I barely gave any voice to the words, but we're so close together, he can hear me, almost like he's seeing the thoughts in my head. We're surrounded by equipment, and the cameras are arranged across the room from us, on the far side of Sinclair and Jeremy.

Lucas's lip hitches up in the right corner, just a fraction of an inch. "You have no idea how badly I wanted to," he murmurs, his hand caressing my back, sending little waves of wanting through me. "But I remembered what you said about letting you make your own decisions. Maybe old Bappy can learn some new tricks."

"What would you have told Thomas?" I whisper back, taking in his face. I like that I have this forced opportunity to study him, to take in his stately brows, the shifting blues of his eyes, the black stubble peppering his jaw, the curve of the hair falling over his forehead. I like the sensation of having my body pressed up against him, and God help me, I remember what it felt like in that alley when he—

"I would have told him there will be no matchmaking, unless it's with me." His hand is splayed over my lower back now, each finger sending sparkles of warmth through me. "Although I might need to suck up to Constance more before I can count on her help."

"Cut!" the director calls, but Lucas doesn't move, and neither do I.

"I'm surprised you didn't insist on coming to dinner," I comment, looking up at him.

"Did you want me to?" he asks, with this knowing smile that punches holes into my will.

Yes.

"Maybe I'm allowed to be a hypocrite too," I admit, just before the director shouts, "Background!" again.

Lucas hitches me a little closer, and my world is so thoroughly eclipsed by him that I feel a twinge of uneasiness.

"Do you want me to whisper sweet little nothings to you and feed you off my plate so he'll back the fuck off?" he asks, his voice a honeyed murmur in my ear. "Because I'll do it. If you ask nicely, I'll even let you sit on my lap."

"I abhor violence of any kind, but if you try to feed me in front of Doris and Ross, I'll stab you with my fork."

The look on his face says he wants to chuckle but knows it's not part of our act. "And the sweet nothings?" he asks, his hand lifting on my back, drawing me closer. Our heads are inches apart—we're meant to be lovers, and in this moment, we *feel* like lovers.

"Action!" the director calls.

"You can call me Sunshine," I whisper to his lips. His head is bowed down to me, so close to mine, only inches away. It would be so easy to take what I want.

"You liked that, huh?" he asks, his words barely audible but threaded with a pleasure I feel down to my marrow.

Yes, I did. Too much.

"What'll I call you?" I whisper to him.

"Snow White, obviously."

This time I'm the one who barely holds back laughter. His hand moves up and down my back, a gesture that's probably meant to soothe me but fires me up instead. It's not worth denying it anymore —I want him. I think maybe I have since that first day, when he slapped the hood of my car. There's been this connection, this kismet, this feeling of fate pushing me with both hands.

"Okay, Snow White," I whisper, smiling up at Lucas. "I'm feeling generous. You can come to dinner. Maybe I'll even buy you an apple."

He grins back at me, and the urge to span those few inches between us is so persistent that I have to grit my teeth against it. "You're probably going to read too much into this, but I'm allergic to apples."

"No, you're not."

He frees one hand from me and makes the Boy Scout sign. "Scout's honor."

"I'll bet you actually were a scout," I whisper. "I'll bet you out-scouted all of them."

"Bappy was even better at all of that shit," he says, his lip barely moving, his voice pitched just for me, as if we're sharing secrets, not discussing our childhood invisible friends. "He could start a fire with a twig and a prayer."

"That's a turn-on for Roberta," I whisper. "She likes it when a man knows how to take care of himself. Even better when a man's honest. So you'll understand if she doesn't just take his word for it."

"Bappy and I would like to take you camping sometime," he says, his eyes intent on mine. "I'd like to see you standing outside while the sun rises."

"You assume I'm an early riser," I whisper, but there's something clogging my throat. Because I'm imagining it too, us lying out there in the mountains, wrapped up in a blanket as we watch the sun lift through layers of color, our bodies curled around each other.

"Most of your friends are over the age of sixty," he says wryly, his mouth curling up slightly. "So, yes. Plus, you strike me as a woman who'd get up early to see something beautiful. And I'd like to see it with you."

There's something so sweet about the sentiment and the way he says it. I'm not thinking. I'm not paying attention to anything or anyone but him as I tip up on my toes just the slightest bit and kiss him. He makes a sound of surprise, and I swallow it, and then he's pressing me closer and kissing me back, his mouth so hot and sure against mine, so *commanding*, and—

And there's a loud pop close to us, followed by a shower of sparks, right before the power cuts out in the Rolf Estate.

nineteen

LUCAS

DELIA STARTLES and breaks the kiss.

"Are you okay?" I ask, alarmed. I run a hand over her arm. Did she get shocked or burned?

"Yes," she says. "Just surprised."

So am I, and not just by whatever fuckery happened with the power in this old place, although I'm starting to think some in-depth work wouldn't be amiss. Delia felt so damn good against me, like she was supposed to be there. I've become a sentimental idiot, a sap, but there's no denying I feel better than I have in months.

I'm also half hard, which isn't great considering we're in this room full of dozens of other people. The lights went off, true, but it's broad daylight, and the front windows are practically floor to ceiling. The temptation to pick her up and carry her off into another room is strong.

"Have dinner with me tonight," I say, our faces still just inches apart.

There are people squawking all around us about the electricity outage, but my attention is on her because I really need an answer.

"Is that a question or a demand, Lucas?" she asks softly.

"A question. Blame force of habit for the phrasing."

"We're already going to dinner on Friday night, remember?" she asks, her eyes full of mischief. It looks good on her, but I can't wait two days. And as much as I want to meet Doris and Ross, I don't want my first date with Delia to be with her elderly roommates. I want to get her alone. And not just because I want to fuck her, something I imagine isn't on the docket yet. I want to experience her smiles for myself. To listen to her talk. To learn more about her.

"Allow me the delight of spending the evening with you and Roberta."

Her smile is as catching as Frank's chlamydia.

It's a terrible analogy—almost as bad as having chlamydia would probably be—but that's all I can think of because I see Constance and Leonard heading toward us in my peripheral vision. We're running out of time.

"Please," I add, because it never hurts to be polite.

She watches me for a few seconds, trying to gauge just how much of a mistake she's making, then nods. "Okay. But I have to go home and get changed, walk a couple of dogs, and then do a grand-daughter chore."

"I'll help."

She laughs. "Not this time. I'm helping Doris's friend Jane pick a bathing suit, and she won't want a man around."

"That's short-sighted of her," Constance says, joining us. "Is she by any chance joining the water aerobics class?"

Delia nods and smiles at her. She looks almost impish. "They're going to be our inside eyes this Friday. Jane was worried about going, on account of she hasn't worn a bathing suit in years, but we convinced her that we'd find something lovely."

"Splendid," Constance says with a wicked look. I'm guessing it's not going to be so splendid for Frank, but then again that's what you get for screwing around with a woman thirty years younger than you.

She glances around at all the bustle that followed that pop of electricity. "Did you kids make the electricity go out?"

The look in her eyes says she saw Delia kissing me. Is she going to drag me outside by the ear and give me another talking-to? Maybe I deserve one, but my intentions are honorable.

Mostly.

"Maybe," I say. "Or it could have been your scintillating conversation about the fake plant. They sending us packing?"

"That's the word," Leonard says. "I'll be really hard up without getting eight bucks an hour and a lettuce leaf lunch."

"You'll power through. They know what caused the outage?"

"Some circuitry issue, probably." He nods just past us. "Heard a pop over there, but they're not saying what's up."

I grin at Delia. "Maybe it really was us."

She rolls her eyes, but there's a hint of a blush on her cheeks, and I feel like I did the first time I hit a home run in a Little League game. Or finished my first flip house. She agreed to spend the evening with me. Just her and me, finally. My whole life is a mess, my head is worse, but this...this is good. This is the kind of life event that makes you feel the fire of being alive deep in your chest.

"I'll text you later," I tell her.

She lifts her eyebrows. "What if it takes Jane hours to find a swimsuit?"

"I'll buy a store full of them for her."

There's a slightly amused, slightly disapproving look on her face, but the former wins out. "Tonight," she says. "I'm looking forward to it."

"Looks like we have some catching up to do," Constance says. She glances at me, probably finds me wanting, and grabs Delia's arm.

"Don't try to talk her out of it, Constance," I say. "If you do, I swear to God, I'll send over a dozen salt water tanks. Maybe a shark or two to keep things interesting."

She snorts. "As if I'd make the mistake of letting the deliveryman in this time.

We'll see you later, fellows." She nods to Leonard. "Lover."

He has a wry twist to his mouth as he tips his fedora to her. "Lady Constance."

She turns and hastens Delia out, for all the world like we're not going to be exiting in the same direction, right behind them. Or so I think. I take a couple of steps and bump directly into Jeremy, who just stepped in front of me like a guy who wants to get mowed down.

He has a nervous, shifty look, like he's been mainlining coffee or something stronger.

"What's up? I haven't heard any updates from you about my script," he says, rubbing his hands together. "Things got a little...out of hand at the bar the other night. I...I guess you could say I have a competitive streak."

"But you got owned," Leonard says. "You can admit you got owned in that sing-off, right?"

"The crowd seemed evenly split," Jeremy replies tightly. "A lot of people asked for my autograph."

Leonard laughs and pats him on the back. "You're a funny man, huh? This guy is funny." He lets the humor drop and gives Jeremy a serious look. "But how open are you to making changes in your movie, man? I really think it would track better if the guy swapped places with a bird. Dogs are so overdone, don't you think? Besides, you put in a hell of a convincing performance in that bird movie. Why waste that kind of talent?"

"A bird?" he repeats, baffled. "I thought you hated birds."

"I did. The whole situation with the Rolf Estate and those adorable little fuckers who got saved really changed my tune," he says. "Tears in my eyes when I saw that photo this morning. Maybe we could get this whole thing rolling—you could be the bird man. First you saved the Rolf Estate birds, then you became one."

"Just some food for thought," I say, both amused by Leonard and annoyed with him for giving Jeremy hope—and a reason to try talking to us every time we're on set. I've disliked Jeremy from the first moment I met him, when he called Delia by the wrong name, and my impression of him has been on a steady downhill track ever since. "I'm weighing my options. I've got a lot of investments running right now, and we all know that productions can be a shitshow."

He glowers. "This one sure is. First that brick and now this mess. They say they're not going to get the power back on for another day, maybe two. Can you believe it? I guess that's what I get for agreeing to come back to this dump."

I don't bother reminding him that I'm the one who nearly got brained by the brick. Maybe he doesn't know, or maybe he just doesn't feel compelled to give a shit.

"Yeah," I say, "that'll be a real disaster. All the seltzer on set will be room temperature." He looks confused, which is probably the appropriate response. It also gives us an opportunity to leave before he gets his shit together. "Bye, man. See you the next time around."

Leonard and I head for the door, in silent agreement it's time to get out. The costume guy is standing by the door with a giant box. "Taking collections."

"Who's going to sort through that?" I ask, because it looks like a fucking nightmare.

"You're looking at him," he says in a weary tone.

"Sorry, man, that sucks."

His mouth purses to the side. "You know, some people are saying this production is cursed." He lists all the maladies that Jeremy just spouted off, adding, "Then there was the sexual harassment mess with the Rolf heiress and that missing equipment that miraculously reappeared overnight."

The bird story obviously wasn't a widely accepted cover, but that's not what had my attention. "Was it the reappeared equipment that blew the power?"

"I don't know," he says in a tired tone. "They don't tell me much, man. I hear people spilling their life stories to each other, acting like I'm not there, and that's the only reason I know anything." He pauses, then adds, "I do know you're Lucas Burke, but that doesn't even seem like news anymore."

"I'm not... I didn't..."

"Oh, I know the whole story," he says, patting my arm. "Delia told me."

I feel a warmth spread inside of me. She didn't want people to misconstrue me, so she went to the trouble of talking to him. We weren't even here for long today, but still she found a chance. Of course she did, though. There's something inside of her that insists on justice for everyone.

"Hey, what's your name, man?" I ask him.

He gives a weary smile. "You know, you're one of the only people who've asked, this whole time. I'm Clancy."

I shake his hand.

Clancy turns to Leonard with a grin. "You're not walking away with that fedora, my friend."

Leonard's brows wing up, and he takes the hat off, flourishing it with a bow before putting it in the box. He's obviously become fond of it, even though it's beyond me why his character would be wearing a hat indoors while discussing the merits of plastic plants. I'm more grateful to turn in the hideous gold belt.

That done, we head toward the line of trees concealing the parking lot.

"You believe in curses, buddy?" Leonard asks.

A week ago, I'd have told him I *was* a curse. "Don't think so."

"I do," he says, rubbing his jaw as we step beyond the cover of the trees, revealing a sea of cars. "And Clancy's right. This movie is definitely fucking cursed. It's never a good sign when the background actors have more chemistry than the two stars. And I'm not even talking about you and Delia practically porning it up in the backdrop. I'm talking about Constance and me and that damn potted plant. There's enemies to lovers, then there's Sinclair wanting to literally murder that dude."

"Can you blame her?"

"Hell no. But I don't think this movie is going to see the light of day."

"You might be right," I say as we reach the car. I pause next to the back of it, my mind whirring, and say, "Delia agreed to go out with me tonight."

He gives me a *no shit* look. "Yeah, I caught that. What are you gonna do, rent out the Biltmore for her?"

He knows I've done some legendary shit before for women I wanted to impress. Okay, the more appropriate word is fuck. Not renting the Biltmore out level of legendary, maybe more like renting out the Rolf Estate.

"No," I say, my mind whirring. "Don't think she'd be impressed by that. I want to show her that she's becoming important to me. That I'm not just looking to get laid."

His mouth hitches up. "So you're learning, huh? That's good."

"Are you?"

"Never, and no, thank you. But one of us should be able to. I volunteer you as tribute. Do you need help coming up with a plan?"

"From *you*?"

He laughs so hard he nearly staggers. "No. Let's see if Danny can meet us for lunch. Or we can call Drew of the aching heart. Shane's a dick about women, so he's out. Speaking of, I told Constance we'd help her paint the fish room on Friday afternoon after we finish at the flip house. She's a very convincing woman."

"Huh," I say, giving him a look. "Maybe you're not such a hopeless case after all."

"Oh, I am, absolutely," he says, grabbing the back of the car. He gives me a look I can't unpack, then says, "Don't you think it's weird that all this shit is happening on set? Like maybe Danny's right about your parents?"

I huff a laugh. "You think my parents would arrange a power outage? If they wanted to kill me—or you, for that matter—they'd pay someone to do it and leave it at that. They wouldn't want to slowly fuck with me in a roundabout way."

"You sure about that?" he asks. "You heard what Clancy said. Everyone on set knows who you are. How hard would it have been for them to slip someone in there to get that brick to go down? Or to mess with that equipment and put it back where it came from? From my understanding, the electricity at this place has never shorted like that, without any kind of bad weather or downed lines."

"They've also never filmed a movie here before." Or so Christian had told us at least half a dozen times, insisting that we should feel privileged and lucky to be the chosen ones.

"They have," he says with a huff of air. "Christian's full of shit. I got one of the ladies who works here talking—"

"Of course you did."

He grins. "What can I say? My charm works."

"Except on Shauna."

"It hasn't worked on her *yet*. But yeah, apparently they've filmed other shit here, they just haven't called it the Rolf Estate in the movies. It's been a stand-in for other moderate to middling estates."

"Still. The electricity in old places just goes out sometimes," I say. "Hell, it went out at the apartment the other night because it was raining. Anyway, this isn't my parents' style. They're straightforward and brutal. They're not the gaslighting type."

This time the look he gives me is pitying. "What about that book your dad sent, bud?"

"Maybe he thought I'd enjoy it," I hedge. "Has anyone been bothering you?"

He gives me a half-grin. "Only my conscience." After a beat of silence passes, he adds, "Maybe the movie really is cursed. But it couldn't hurt to have someone look into it. Make sure they're not screwing with you. I don't like this. It gives me a bad feeling. If someone did screw with the voltage or outlets or something, it could have killed someone." He gives me a look that says *maybe it was meant to.*

"You sound like Danny."

He lifts a hand. "Not gonna lie. He's turned me onto those podcasts. But your folks had me followed before I blew town, Lucas, and I'm not convinced they would have played nice if I'd stayed. Sure, they need to be more cautious now that it's all out in the open, but maybe they have plans for us."

I think again of that stolen equipment. They might have done something like that to try and frame Leonard, but if so, why had it popped back up again? He's right about one thing, there have been enough strange occurrences that I should poke into what's happening. I don't like the thought of my parents watching me, or him, of them lurking like spiders waiting to wrap their silk around us. Whether they've played any role in this movie's disasters or not, they're definitely fucking with me. There was the invitation to tea and that book. They're destroying the peace I'm fighting for.

Shane works with private investigators at his law firm. He'd be able to refer me to someone reputable, no question.

"You're right," I admit. "It's better to be sure. I'll call someone." I pause, worried. "You're not going to split, are you?"

He pats me on the back. "No, man." He's surprisingly serious, no bluster in his expression. "I've got your back now, like I should have had it in the first place. I'm going to help all of you."

"Shane too?" I ask with a laugh.

Shane's gotten...braggadocious is the word Danny uses for it, now that he's a partner at his law firm. We haven't been seeing him as much lately, especially since Drew left for Puerto Rico. It feels like our group, so tightly knit for years, is slowly unraveling, only

Leonard is back now. And it seems he's taken it upon himself to keep us together.

Something about that feels right.

"Maybe especially Shane." He grins back at me. "Need to keep him around in case I get into legal trouble, am I right?"

twenty

DELIA

"I KNOW your vision is going, Doris, but surely even *you* can see the difference between these two boys," Jane says. "It's like comparing a bucket of instant mashed potatoes to a plate of crispy tater tots."

Jane is famously partial to her tater tots, so that's high praise indeed.

We're in the changing room at the Land & Sea store at the Asheville Outlets, Doris and I sitting in a couple of armchairs with a small table in between them in front of the triple-pane mirrors. Jane has just found *the* swimsuit after trying on a dozen different options I chose for her, so we're all flying high. Which must be why I told them about my date tonight.

At Jane's encouragement, I pulled up a photo of Lucas on my phone from the fish room day, and Doris, who was feeling a little downtrodden about the Thomas situation, found an old photo of her great-nephew on hers. In it, he's glowering at the camera, wearing a bright orange shirt the exact shade of his lanyard, so presumably it's his favorite color. That's the one thing I've found to like about him so far. If possible, I try to find at least one likable thing about everyone.

Doris sighs. "I don't want you to have a point, but I suppose it's staring me in the face. God didn't see fit to bless Thomas with the face of an angel, and I'm sorry to say he has the personality of a turnip. I guess I was hoping Delia could pull something out of him. You do have a talent for pulling personality out of people, Delia. I mean, look at you, Jane."

She gestures to her friend, wearing a delightful two piece that shows just the barest hint of midriff between its parts. It's crimson with a design of little seashells.

"She looks magnificent," I say, "but I can hardly take credit for it."

Jane's already shaking her head, posing for the three mirrors with an exultant smile on her face. "I never would have thought. A two piece. Imagine! I thought my bathing suit days were behind me, never mind a bikini. You're a miracle worker."

"She is," Doris says, beaming at me. Then she nods to the photo of Lucas staring up at me from my phone on the table. "And if that boy doesn't treat you like the gem you are, then I will personally make his life hell."

Her friend laughs. "How? Are you going to bake him muffins, Doris?"

I didn't tell Jane about the baking-soda muffins. But apparently there were some left over, and Doris offered one to her despite having tried them.

"Better that than to have an ungrateful man going after Delia's muffin."

"Doris," I say, "let's establish a ground rule right now for Friday night. No talking about my muffin at dinner."

She sniffs as if to say she's making no guarantees.

Goodness, this dinner isn't for another two nights, but it's already going downhill fast. My phone buzzes, and I grab it. It's Lucas, telling me where to meet him.

"Where's he taking you?" Jane asks, peering down at it.

"Are you going to Rhubarb?" Doris asks as she successfully grabs my phone. I'm not sure what she plans to do with it. Despite being both near-sighted and far-sighted, she didn't even bring her glasses with us. "Oh, or Bouchon? Make sure you order dessert. Don't let him sweet talk you into thinking some nookie can serve as dessert."

"No," I say, my brow furrowed. Because the address he gave is in what I'm pretty sure is a residential or mixed-use neighborhood.

Doris shoves the phone at Jane, who's still standing around in the swimsuit. "Read it."

She does, and Doris's expression slips into a scowl. "He's going after your muffin, all right."

"But this isn't where he lives," I say.

"You've been to his apartment?" she asks, giving me a look that questions whether she even knows me.

"No, of course not. I would have told you if I had. He just mentioned what part of town he lives in."

Jane clucks her tongue, moving a little in the mirror to get a side view of herself in the bathing suit. "You sure you trust this boy? I've seen that show *You*. That man seemed charming and sweet, right up until he up and killed that girl."

"Dammit, Jane," Doris says, slapping her heel against the floor. "You've ruined dozens of shows for me."

"Can it, Doris, it's been out for years. Anyway, it's relevant information. Delia needs to be careful."

"He's not a murderer," I murmur, sending Doris a silencing look. Because she knows all about the Burkes and how he fits in with them. Jane doesn't, and I'd like to keep it that way. Maybe that's why Lucas doesn't want to meet at a restaurant for dinner tonight in addition to Friday. It can't be fun, getting those looks, wondering who's gossiping about him or spitting in his food. Still...where is he sending me?

I pick up my phone and type out a response.

> Jane thinks you're going to murder me, and Doris is worried you're after my muffin. I have no comment, except I'm wondering where it is you're sending me. As a rule, I prefer to know my destination.

The three little dots pop up at once, and I find myself smiling, anticipating his response. He'll like the muffin thing, I bet. In fact, I'm pretty sure he's going to like Doris and Ross. They'll like him too as soon as Doris gets over the fact that I wouldn't date Thomas if he were the last man on earth and the future of the human race depended on it.

"Good," says Jane, who's been looking over my shoulder. "He knows that we know. He wouldn't dare try anything when we've seen the address on your phone."

"Oh, don't tell her that," Doris says, tapping her hand. "Now she'll wonder if the only reason he didn't murder her was because he was worried he'd get caught."

I ignore them, because his next message comes through.

> I'd prefer for it to be a surprise. But I'm not planning on murdering anyone tonight. Or eating muffins...although I could be convinced. Hello, Doris and Jane!

"My word," says Jane, who, of course, read everything over my shoulder. She fans herself with her hand. "That man has a silver tongue. Maybe you *should* let him eat your muffin."

I'm nervous as I drive up to the house. It's in a somewhat secluded neighborhood, and while I don't for a minute think Lucas is a serial killer, I've never really been alone with him before. Other than in the alleyway behind Glitterati, and judging by what happened then, it'll probably be five minutes, max, before one of us tackles the other.

It's a bad idea, getting involved with Lucas. He's got so much healing left to do, and I know better than anyone what a tender time that is. How raw it feels, like your skin has been turned inside out, and even the softest brushing of it can create the sort of pain that sets in and lingers. How much your whole perspective of the world can change from one day to the next. He might want me today, but tomorrow he could decide he'd prefer a woman like my sister—confident and driven, capable of the kind of focus that's always eluded me. He says he likes me the way I am, but it's hard to shake the ghost of those words Constance overheard.

Sighing, I listen to the directions spouted by my phone and pull into the gravel driveway of a green house sitting at the top of a hill overlooking the mountains. The closest neighbors must be half a mile away. Or maybe it's less and it seems like more because there are so many trees between the houses. There's a clear plastic sign out front with a printed paper packet inside with a photo of the house on the front. Lucas's Range Rover is parked beside it. My curiosity kicks in as I pull out the host gift I brought—muffins, of course. I picked them up at the grocery store, which I'd normally avoid, but I figured it was worth it for the joke, like the box of seltzer Lucas brought in this morning.

I climb the steps up to the porch, which looks like new construction, and ring the bell beside the door. What *is* this place? It feels like an odd convergence of old and new.

The door opens seconds later, and Lucas is standing in front of me, dressed casually in work jeans and a white polo shirt. The look on his face flusters me and fills me with heat. Then I glance behind him and take in the pure, echoing emptiness of the space.

My first thought is that Jane would most definitely think it was a murder house.

My second...

"Are we intruding at a house that's for sale?" I ask, remembering one of his stories from when he, Leonard, and their friends were in their early twenties.

"Sort of," he says with a grin. "Come in."

"I'd like a full understanding of which laws I'll be breaking."

He reaches for my free hand, and I give it to him without hesitation. So much for being law-abiding.

As he pulls me in, he says, "This is the flip house Leonard and I have been working on. I wanted to show it to you."

He shuts the door behind me, and I take in the great room. The ceilings are high and there's a fireplace across from the door. Next to it is a sliding glass door, and to the left of that is an open kitchen with an enormous stove and the kind of island you can gather around with stools or glasses of wine while one capable person cooks. It smells like fresh paint. Other than that—

"It's empty."

He grins at me. "That's the idea. We're not done yet. We have maybe a week of work left, mostly down in the basement we're finishing. Then we'll stage it with some furniture before putting it up for sale."

I run my fingers over the wall. "It's beautiful."

He's looking at me with eagerness. "I've been thinking about what you said...about helping Leonard. I've always felt the most useful when I'm working on one of these projects. The most like myself. This is what I want to do."

And he brought me here. The thought puts a ball of emotion in my throat. I continue to run my fingers along the wall, getting to know the house, to feel her personality. "You're both clearly very good at it."

"How can you tell without seeing the starting product?" he asks with a half grin.

"Product? Don't you think houses are more like people? I've

always thought so. They have a personality of their own, or at least these old places do."

"Do you name them, Delia?"

It's a teasing question, delivered in a low, sexy voice that travels through me like a quake, but I decide to answer anyway. "Not always. But this house deserves a name, I think. It has old bones. History." There's the feeling that important events have happened here—births and deaths, celebrations and sorrows. My sister would say it's a house that's seen some shit.

"Do you want to do the honors?"

I glance around, taking in the vaulted ceiling, the cozy fireplace, that plate glass door leading outside to a deck that must have the kind of view a person would remember for always. "Peggy."

I'm not sure why, but it fits.

"Peggy it is," he says with a grin. "I like it." Then he's pulling out his phone, scrolling through. He hands it over with an almost eager look. "See what she was like before her facelift."

I hip-check him. "Don't you dare talk about our old girl like that. She didn't need a facelift, just some different clothing, maybe."

He watches over my shoulder as I scroll through the photos, taking in the changes they've made. My mouth parts, because she was nearly ruined, a wreck of rotted wood and walls dotted with mold, and they've restored her to her present stateliness. What a beautiful thing, to take something broken and make it whole again. It strikes me that maybe that's why Lucas loves this type of work so much; he can make improvements here and see them with his own eyes. The work of a CEO must be so much more abstract, so much colder, in comparison. And despite how he was raised, Lucas is a person of deep feelings. "Will you paint her different colors inside? Is that primer on the walls?"

Currently, the walls are a stark, clean white, but the space seems to beg for a different palette—for sage green and rust, maybe. There's an earthiness to Peggy, a connectivity to the mountains, as if she might have grown up out of them, fully formed.

"Wasn't planning on it," he says, his lips pursing as he studies me, "but I could be persuaded."

I share my thoughts with him, and as I'm speaking, he peers around at the space as if visualizing it. I like that he's taking me seriously even though he's the expert—and also that he's trying to see what I'm sharing with him, to paint the world I'm creating onto the one that exists in front of us.

"You're right," he says, then his mouth lifts. "Want to paint her with me?"

"Yes," I reply without thinking, because his suggestion put another image in my mind: me wearing overalls covered in color, and Lucas in those jeans, his shirt covered in paint. I glance around, then add, "Are we cooking in here?"

"Nah, the kitchen's not hooked up yet." He grins at me, a wicked grin, then his gaze lowers to the container I'm still holding. Suddenly I feel like I'm Little Red Riding Hood, and I've willingly stepped into the wolf's territory. "You don't want to just sit here in this empty house and eat those *muffins*?"

"Well, we could," I say, because I'm mostly certain he's teasing, "but you *did* invite me to dinner. Doris would be cross with me if I accepted anything less."

"We wouldn't want that," he says, that sly almost-smile on his face. He leads me across the space to the sliding glass door, and a gasp escapes me as he opens it. Rolling blue peaks are laid out before us under the waning sun, a feast for the eyes.

Then my gaze drops to what's right before us. There's a red-and-white checked blanket set out on the deck, along with a couple of floor pillows and a picnic basket.

"You made us a picnic?" I ask, thoroughly charmed.

"I'd like to take credit, but Danny helped me. He's my roommate."

"I didn't know you had a roommate," I say, looking up at him. "Most people around here have a roommate because they can't afford rent."

"So you're wondering why I have one," he says, glancing out at the view. He seems almost embarrassed. "My buddy needed a place to live. I had an apartment with plenty of space."

My heart thrums at the admission. "That was kind of you."

He turns me toward him, the movement just this side of rough. "I didn't do it out of any kindness of heart, Delia. I can't have you thinking I'm a kind man. It was a practical decision. He needed a place to stay, and I needed help around the house. He's good at that kind of stuff. He gives me tech support too."

I raise my eyebrows. "Was spending your day helping Constance with her fish practical?"

"Yes," he says, the muscle in his jaw tight. "You've made it clear you value Constance, and I think *I've* made it clear that I want you."

His confession shivers through me, especially given the way his hands are wrapped around my arms...tightly, like he's worried if he releases me I might float away. "That's not why you did it," I press, because I've started to see the man he's fighting to be, the one who's been trapped inside of him. "That's not why you've let Danny live with you. And it's not why you want Leonard to be your business partner, when he's very upfront about having a colorful past. Why can't admit that you care about them? Why don't you want to believe you're a good man?"

His hands flex on my arms. He looks tormented. "Don't you see?" he finally says. "I can't let myself think that. If I do..."

"You won't be letting yourself off easy," I say, peering into his eyes, trying to get through to him. "You've taken responsibility for what your parents did. You've done everything in your power to stop them. Do you really need to keep punishing yourself?"

"*Yes.*" He releases me, then takes two steps toward the balcony of the deck before pacing back. "Yes. I've enjoyed the benefits this life has given me, haven't I? And I've used people just like my parents have. I've bought them off with gifts and promises. You were right about me. I tried to do the same damn thing with you and Constance. Why shouldn't I feel that, Delia? It's the only way I can become a better man."

I grab his arm before he can pace away from me. "I didn't say you shouldn't be aware of your privilege. Be aware of it. Hold on to your good intentions, your self-awareness, but you're not helping anyone by beating yourself up, by treating yourself like you're not someone who's worthy of love."

"What if I'm not?" he says, but his voice has changed. It's low and charged, like the growl of a big cat. A mountain lion, maybe. He stalks toward me. He was already close, and it was only one step, or maybe two, but there's no better word for it. His space invades mine, claims it. "I've imagined burying my head between your legs. Cutting a slit in that mermaid tail so I can fuck you with it on. Carrying you to a hidden room in that Rolf Estate so I can make you come so hard you want to scream but can't because my hand is over your mouth and we're next to a roomful of people. Tell me, would a good man do that, Delia?"

My knees feel like they're going to collapse. I've never felt such a strong physical draw to someone, like the wanting might actually kill me, and if not the wanting, then the acting out of it, again and again and again until there's nothing left of either of us.

"It is if I *want* you to do those things," I say softly, my voice quavering with the power of this thing that's growing between us, out of control, like a snowball that starts rolling down a hill and becomes a behemoth by the time it reaches the bottom. The reasons I was supposed to stay away from Lucas feel distant and small, voices shouting from such a distance the words themselves are intangible murmurs.

He crowds my space a little more, the height and breadth of him staggering. His heat wraps around me, promising me things. I can feel my whole body bending toward him, trying to get closer. "And do you?" he asks, his voice half growl.

"Yes."

I'm not sure who moves first, but suddenly his arms are around me, and we're kissing as if we'd like to consume each other, hard and desperate, bruising. We've known each other for a week and a half, but we've spent so many hours dancing around this wanting—this strange *need*—that it feels more like we've held back for months. Longer. His hand weaves into my hair and fists as he pulls me closer, our mouths moving together. I slide my hand under his shirt, needing to feel the solid heat of his flesh, the thump of his heart beating fast for me. He groans into my mouth and does the same with the hand that was on my back, slipping it beneath my shirt, his fingers rough from the work he does here. Something about that, about this rich man who works with his hands, makes me even hotter.

It strikes me that this deck, facing nothing but the mountains, no houses within eyesight, is perfectly private. Did he know that? Did he plan it?

Does it matter?

His hand glides down from my back to my butt, pressing me against him, and I feel how hard he is for me.

Sense has nothing to do with this. Neither does practicality. Just a deep, throbbing need. I push his shirt up with both hands, needing to get it off, and he breaks our kiss, panting, his hair messy. He lets me take his shirt off, smiling slightly at this sign that I feel it too, that this great, pulsing thing between us is shared.

"You've been wanting to take my shirt off, Roberta?" he says roughly as he pulls it the rest of the way over his head and throws it to the boards of the deck. Air whooshes out of me, because his body is as beautiful as his face, sculpted with muscle and tan, with a sprinkling of dark hair. Does he work out here shirtless?

I swallow. "If you think I'm calling you Bappy right now, you're out of your mind."

He's laughing as his hands find my hips, his thumbs lifting the hem of my shirt. Then he removes it in one fluid, practiced movement, leaving me in my bra—turquoise lace with red piping—and my silver skirt.

His hand lifts to cup one of my breasts and his face lowers to kiss the top, his hair brushing my flesh and sending pleasure coursing through me.

"So fucking beautiful," he breathes out, reaching back to unclasp my bra. He looks up for permission and I nod, because in this moment, there's nothing I want so much as his mouth on my nipple.

The bra falls to the deck boards too, and he caresses his big hands over my breasts and abdomen, brushing aside my hair, which is everywhere.

"I'd wondered if you'd have freckles here too," he murmurs. "They're like constellations." Then he dips his head to kiss a grouping of them above my breast.

I don't have many freckles, hundreds rather than thousands, but I've always thought them blemishes. But to hear him say that, to see him looking at me with awe in his eyes... I've never felt so beautiful. He breathes out another laugh when I get impatient and press his head down.

"I'm not going to say no," he says as he lowers his mouth to me, sucking in one of my nipples while he holds me to him. Hot pleasure arcs down between my legs, and I press into his mouth, wanting more of it. Of *him*. He complies and then moves to the other nipple, his hair sending awareness across my skin as he makes the shift. My knees are weak as I lean into him, reaching for the front of his jeans and running a hand over his hard bulge. I want to free him. To see him totally bare for me. Lucas Burke, vulnerable and *mine*.

That's the thought of a woman who hasn't let herself get swept away before and lived to regret it, the way I have. I should be troubled by it, but I'm not. He moves my hand and looks up at me, something like regret in his eyes, mixed with heat.

"This wasn't part of my plan," he says.

"Maybe it should have been."

He gestures to the picnic basket and blanket. "I brought a picnic. Champagne."

"Did you bring condoms?"

Heat flashes in his eyes, and he kisses the side of my mouth. "No."

"That lack of foresight isn't like the Lucas Burke I've gotten to know. You pride yourself on your plotting and planning." I'm teasing, sort of. I also want to remind myself to take caution. This is a man who's been with a lot of women, by his own admission.

"I thought about it," he confesses, running a hand through his hair. The action makes his muscles ripple in a way that's pleasing to the eye, and I can't help myself, I reach over and trace the definition of his chest, running my fingers over the hard ridges. He sucks in a breath, then grabs my hand, pressing it flat against the expanse of him. "I chose not to bring any. I didn't want to let myself think it was an option, or for you to think...it meant nothing. That I've done this hundreds of times before."

"And have you?"

"No. Not like this." He swallows again, and I feel the impulse to kiss his throat, to bite it. I don't, though. He needs me to listen. "You insisted there was more to me than what I could buy or do for you, so I figured I'd bring you here. So you could know I'm doing something with my life and not just sitting on my trust fund. I thought maybe you'd like that better than if we went out to a nice restaurant or if I hired a private chef."

I swallow back a *you could do that?* Because clearly he could and has.

"I'm glad you brought me here," I say, reaching up to put a hand in his hair. I like that it's mussed, that he's shown this uncontrolled side to me.

I lift up and kiss his jaw, then his mouth, softly, before pulling back. He's watching me with a warmth that wraps me up.

"Why don't you pour us some champagne?" I suggest. "I don't see why we can't enjoy the picnic *and* other things."

twenty-one

LUCAS

MY COCK IS PRESSING SO hard against my pants it'll probably be bruised. I've never wanted a woman as much as I want Delia. It's fucking painful, but I'm determined that this isn't going to be about me or my needy cock. It's going to be about giving her something to remember, the kind of experience that'll make her blush every time she sees a red and white picnic blanket.

"Why don't you go sit on the blanket?" I suggest, my voice coming out husky.

She smiles at me, so unabashedly beautiful with her gorgeous tits on display, framed by her long red-gold hair. She's like a goddess, come down to earth, and here I am again with the fanciful thoughts.

It's Delia that does it to me. She captures my imagination and makes me feel like I don't need or want to be anchored to the earth.

I watch as she lowers herself to the blanket, then I pour her a flute of champagne.

"Don't you need one?" she asks.

"Not yet," I say, grabbing a plate from the basket and putting some strawberries on it.

"I'm surprised they're not covered in chocolate," she says, some amusement in her voice.

"Did you want them to be?" I ask, glancing up.

"No, it's just... Champagne. Strawberries."

Now that she's saying it, I realize it's hackneyed. Overdone. A rich kid's idea of a fucking picnic. Dammit. I wanted to do something special for her, not something that comes off as a joke or a half-assed effort.

"I—"

"I love it," she says, taking the plate from my hand. My cock finds a way to get even harder as I watch her take a bite of a strawberry and make a little hum of pleasure in the back of her throat. "I always dreamed that someone would take me on a picnic like this."

"A naked picnic?"

"Yes," she says with a small smile. "I read a lot of romance novels as a kid." She shrugs. "And now."

"Does that mean you won't mind if I take off your panties?"

She lifts the champagne flute to her lips takes a sip. "No, I don't think I'd mind at all. Aren't you going to eat anything, though?"

I avoid the temptation to deliver a smooth line, the kind of thing I'd say to another woman—the kind who'd come to me for a splashy good time.

"No," I say, running my palms up her smooth legs. I reach for the band of her panties—silky and turquoise blue like the bra. Did she plan on showing them to me? My cock would like to think so. Then I pull them down and over her feet and smooth my hands up her legs again, spreading them when I reach her thighs. "No, Delia. What I'm going to do is go down on you while you eat strawberries and drink champagne and watch the sun set."

Her sharp inhale makes me grin as I push her legs wider apart and lower my head to kiss her lush thighs. I wasn't lying, I've been dreaming about tasting her, about making her writhe with pleasure.

These past several years, I've only looked for meaningless pleasure with women. Expensive fun. But now that I'm floundering, I've realized that I want something more to hang on to. Something meaningful.

Her.

A sigh of contentment escapes me when I reach her center, my head buried between those soft thighs. I press a kiss there.

"Lucas," she says.

"Eat some strawberries. Enjoy yourself," I tell her, feeling the tickle of her skirt against my forehead. "I am."

I suck in her clit, and the sound she makes as she threads a hand through my hair is the best thing I've ever heard. She tastes like vanilla and sea salt and musk, and if I had to die, it might as well be here, between this woman's legs. At least I'd have enjoyed my final moments. I lick and suck like the desperate man I am, because the sounds she's making and the way she's arcing her body toward my mouth and flexing the hand in my hair are driving me to the edge. I want to give her pleasure so badly, to make her come. Have I ever cared about that as much as finding my own release?

Maybe not.

That probably reflects badly on me, but I do feel that way now, so at least I'm not a hopeless case entirely, selfish to the end.

I glance up at her from beneath her skirt, and she has a strawberry pressed to her soft lips, her eyes fluttered closed. Fuck. I've never wanted anything as much as I want to sink my cock into her right here on this blanket. To take her again and again for hours. To prove to her that having sex all night can be a transcendent thing, if it's with the right person.

"Does that taste good, Sunshine?" I ask. "Because you taste like a fucking revelation."

Her eyes pop open, and she looks startled for a moment, but then she surprises me by biting into the strawberry and licking her lips before setting the stem on the plate.

"It's delicious," she says.

I bring my fingers into the game, tracing her, then curling them up inside of her, seeking the spot that will make her see stars. I can tell when I've found it, because I feel her tightening around me and then that plate falls to the picnic blanket, strawberries bouncing off of it. "*Lucas.*"

"I'm going to put my mouth on you again," I tell her. "I want to feel it when you come. I want to taste it."

"It feels so good," she says, her eyes whirlpools of color. "So—"

She cuts off when I lower my mouth to her again, sucking on her clit while I keep pulsing with my fingers. I want her to remember this, dammit. I want it to count.

Finally, I feel her tightening around my fingers, my tongue, and a beautiful sound escapes her as her whole body goes rigid with pleasure. I keep moving, wanting it to last as long as possible for her, but she surprises me by pulling me up.

She tugs me to her and kisses me, and she tastes like strawberries. That's when realize that she's already reached under my skin and claimed part of me.

When she pulls away, she says, "I want to make you feel good, too, Lucas."

"You have," I say. My cock lets me know that we could both be feeling better, but I didn't want to run after my own pleasure to night. That wasn't the point of this.

I can hear Delia in my head, telling me that maybe there doesn't need to be a point.

She reaches for the button of my jeans. "You don't have to prove anything to me," she says, watching me. "You can just accept that I want you to come the same way you wanted me to. Because we like pleasuring each other."

Her words shiver through me and settle in my needy cock. She undoes the button, then the zipper. She looks up at me as she pushes down my pants. My boxer briefs. I can still stop her. I can still insist that tonight is just about her, not me, but I don't. Because I want her any way I can have her—and when she talks to me like this, I can fool myself into thinking, at least temporarily, that it doesn't matter whether I deserve it. Because I'm still selfish enough that when a beautiful woman asks to suck my cock, I'm not going to say no, especially not when it's this beautiful woman.

Her hand wraps around my cock, and I'm so hard I can barely take it. I'm mesmerized by the sight of her hand pumping up and down and then she says, "Lie down, Lucas. I want to explore you."

The way she says it manages to make me even harder, and it does something else too. Something inside of my chest loosens. Warms.

There's a second where I don't want to. It's a vulnerable position, and I'm already feeling more than I'd like to, more than I know what to do with, but she gently pushes my chest, and that's all that's required. I lie there on that blanket, and she gets down beside me, her glorious tits free in the warm evening air, her hair showering down around her. That silver skirt still splayed around her hips. I reach over and wrap her hair up in my fist, because it's getting in her eyes. And, I'll admit it, I also don't want anything obscuring my view.

Staring up at me, smiling, she lowers her head to my cock and sucks in the head, running her tongue over it like it's a damn lollipop. There's a tingling in my lower back as the sensation and the sight wrap around me. I'm not going to last long, but I won't embarrass myself. Gritting my teeth, I flex my hand in her hair as she slowly lowers her mouth, watching me as she takes more of me in. Pleasure and raw need course through me. She repeats it, out and then in, out and then in, her tongue swirling around as she works me. My hips rise to meet her mouth, and I fight the urge to go deeper—to thrust all the way in—because it feels mind-bendingly good. Even better with her eyes on me. And with the warm breeze curling around us, reminding me that we're outside.

"You feel so good, Delia," I breathe out. "You're so damn beautiful with my cock in your mouth." Then I feel the tingling again, stronger, and I know this time there's no holding back. My hand flexes in her hair, and I release it, letting it waterfall back down. "You better stop, Sunshine," I say. "I'm going to come."

But instead, she grabs the base of my cock and goes deeper than she has yet, sucking, and the orgasm rips through me, almost painful it's so strong. And the sight of her still sucking me, swallowing every drop, is the sexiest thing I've ever seen in my life.

I lift her off, smoothing down her hair. "Delia, you didn't have to do that."

"I know," she says with a small smile, leaning in to kiss the side of my mouth. "I wanted to."

I grab one of the strawberries from the fallen plate and hold it to her lips, watching as she eats it.

I swallow. "Let's put some clothes on, because otherwise I'm never going to make it through dinner."

twenty-two

LUCAS

WE EAT the picnic partially clothed, because Delia insisted I shouldn't put my shirt back on, and I insisted that I'd prefer it if she didn't have her bra or underwear on. We're heathens, or so certain relatives of mine would say. After we finish the food, we watch the sun set with our legs dangling down between the slats of the porch, our hands twined together.

For months, my mind has been full of chaos and anguish, but right now, everything feels still. It feels right.

As darkness begins to fall, I turn on the deck light and sit beside her again, our sides touching. She tells me about Doris and Ross, and growing up with Mira, who's only eleven months older than her, and I tell her about my Dungeons & Dragons nights with the guys, the yearly camping trip we've gone on since college, and the game Danny and Drew designed.

As the last of the sunlight slips over the horizon, she turns to me, our feet bumping between the slats, and says, "I'd better go. I don't want Doris to send the police after you." She makes a face. "Actually, she'd probably send them to the wrong address. She did see your text, but her vision isn't what it once was."

"Did her friend find a swimsuit?"

Her face lights up. "She did, and it's fabulous."

"So are you a style consultant now, in addition to being a grand-daughter for rent?"

She bumps her leg against mine, purposefully this time. "This falls squarely under my granddaughter for rent duties. Any self-respecting granddaughter would help her grandmother pick out an outfit."

"How much do you get paid for that, out of curiosity?" I ask. It's the business side of me that wants to know. There are no prices on her website, no indication of what her services might cost. Maybe that's why she keeps getting messaged by perverts thinking she's selling something other than helpfulness and goodwill.

"Why?" she asks with a slight smile. There's something tremu-lous at the edges of it, though, like she doesn't like my line of ques-tioning. "Need some help picking out a suit?"

"No. If anything, I'd like to get rid of most of my suits. I was just wondering."

"I didn't charge her anything," she says. "I live in Doris and Ross's basement apartment. That's how they pay me." She lifts her eyebrows. "Kind of similar to how Danny pays you."

My natural response is to question her, to push, but I know that rent in this city is high and getting higher. It's perfectly feasible that it's a fair exchange. "I look forward to meeting them on Friday," I say instead, promising myself I'll bring up the business plan later.

"I wonder if Thomas is going to wear an orange shirt to dinner," she says offhandedly.

"Because of the lanyard?" This morning, he had on an orange beanie, despite the warm weather.

She smiles and tells me about the photo on Doris's phone. "I hope he does wear orange. I have this theory that there's something likable about everyone, if you look hard enough, and I think Thomas's predilection for orange is his likable thing."

"Not much of a basis for likability unless you like orange," I point out.

"Doesn't matter," she says, shaking her head. "What I like isn't the color itself but the act of choosing an unlikely color, the kind that most people don't take to. There's a bravery in that, a sense of conviction you don't see in everyone."

"Or maybe he just has bad taste," I quip.

"You'll need to be nice to him," she says sternly, and there's something about the way she says it, reminiscent of my hot teacher, Mrs. Lambert, in seventh grade, that makes my cock stir.

"Oh, I'll be an angel." Wrapping a hand around her waist, I ask, "What's my likable thing?"

She studies me for a moment, her eyes contemplative in the dim light from above the sliding glass door, then the sides of her mouth lift. It's so damn cute, I can't help but lean forward and kiss it. Her smile widens. "You have way more than one likable thing, but if you're forcing me to choose one, it would be this. You say I like helping everyone, that I can't help myself. I think you feel that same need, but you refuse to acknowledge it."

I have to look away, because it feels like she's punched me with something that's true and yet not. "I don't do it because I'm a good guy." I reclaim my hand and rub my chest. "I'm trying to even the scales."

"What scales were you evening when you offered Danny a place to live?"

I look out into the night, taking in what I can see of the view in the inky darkness. There are so few lights ahead, mostly just the warm night, the stars, and her. "He was born poor, to parents who didn't give a shit. That's not his fault. He's a good guy. He's always tried harder than me, been smarter. Why should I get everything while he gets nothing?"

"How about funding his game with Drew?"

"It's a good investment. I'll make money from it in the end."

"If someone else told you all of those things," she says, giving me a sidelong glance, "you'd call them excuses. Just like you told me when I explained why I helped Marlene with her hair."

This has the punch of truth to it too. "What's Leonard's likable thing?" I ask, because I want to change the subject. It's not that I don't believe her, or that she's pissed me off by saying these things, more like she's given me something to think about, and I know I *will* be thinking about it.

"Do you have to ask?" she says with a grin. "He knows how to make anything fun."

"Including painting the fish room on Friday?" I ask. "Have you gotten recruited for that task too?"

"No, but I'll come," she says immediately. "I want to help Constance any way I can."

"You're working for her, aren't you?"

She gives me a look that says she understands where I'm going with this and doesn't care for it. "I don't know about that. She's become more of a friend."

"Are all of your clients more like friends, paying you in marshmallows and good wishes?"

She frowns at me, disapproving. "Not all of them, no. I have a grumpy older male client who pays me to clean his fans and throw out the rotten food in his refrigerator. I'm very happy to charge him my hourly rate."

"But I'll bet there's something likable about him too."

"Yes, the twenty dollars an hour he pays me."

She must see me flinch, although I try to hide it. It's barely anything, if you consider that she has to pay taxes, self-employment, and buy her own health insurance.

"And your dog walking and the mermaid readings and parties... What do you charge for those?"

She abruptly pulls her legs out of the slats and turns toward me, cross-legged. I do the same. "Lucas, I haven't asked you how much money is in your bank account. I don't want to know, honestly. So why the sudden interest in mine?"

Because I want to know you're taken care of.

Because I care about you, and this is the only way I know how to show it.

Because I can't help myself.

"I'm good at this sort of thing," I say defensively. "Business. I thought maybe I could help you with a business plan."

"Are you trying to help, or are you hoping you can make my jobs into something that feels more acceptable?"

It hits me with alarm that her eyes are shiny. I've fucked this up and said it all wrong.

"It's not that," I say, reaching for her but not forcing it on her. It's a soul-deep relief when she lets me put my hand on her knee. "I don't want to change you or for you do to anything other than what you do. I do want to punch whoever the hell made you feel unimpressive."

"Even if one of the people who did it was my mother?"

"I wouldn't even hit *my* mother. And I trust her so much that I'm hiring a private investigator to keep an eye on her and my father."

I called Shane right after leaving set earlier, and he referred me to "his best guy." I'm meeting with him tomorrow morning. I felt weird making the appointment, like I was being some kind of alarmist, but the P.I. didn't seem thrown or particularly surprised. Then again, Shane says the guy's in his sixties or maybe seventies and has been doing this since he retired from the police force. He's seen decades' worth of the shit people do to each other. I'm guessing nothing would faze him.

"Really?" Delia seems alarmed, and I don't want that, so I take her hand, trace the lines on her palm.

"Nothing to worry about. It's a precaution. But this guy comes highly recommended. We were talking about your mother, though. I can throw a pretty good word punch. You tell me where and when, and I'll be all over it."

"Okay," she says, softly, but her eyes are still shining with tears.

"I didn't mean it like that, Delia. I swear. But my background is in business. Business plans are what I do. I'm going to make one for my business with Leonard. I helped Drew and Danny make one for launching their game. I—"

She leans in and kisses me, and I feel like a real piece of shit when I notice her lips are wet from fallen tears.

When she pulls back, she says, "I'm sorry."

"You're sorry?" I blurt, shocked. "I'm the one who's sorry. I didn't want to ruin everything. Tonight has been... This is the best night I can remember having in a long, long time."

Maybe ever, but I don't want to scare her. Thinking that, I'm scaring myself. But it's a fear that's edged with hope.

"You didn't ruin anything. You're right. It's just..." She tucks hair behind her ear. "Nat was the one who was good at that sort of thing. We were supposed to do this together, and I wouldn't be such a hot mess if she was part of the business. Mira tries to help, but it's hard to accept help from her because she's the one who's always had it all together. My mother already thinks I'm worthless."

Her words stab into me. Because here again is the butterfly effect of being an asshole, of taking what you want without caring about other people. My parents did that, and other people are still hurting because of it. Delia is hurting because of it.

I didn't realize I was hanging my head until I feel her fingers under my chin, lifting it up. "You didn't take her away from me, Lucas."

"No, but I can't bring her back for you either."

That's the only thing that would make me feel better, I think. If I could rewind time. If I could walk into that closed-door meeting they must have held and told them there was no way in hell I was letting them build that building where they built it, knowing what they knew.

It feels so good to imagine it—to see and feel it down to the smell of ink in the air—but like most wonderful things, it's impossible. Completely out of reach.

Except *she's* not out of reach.

I draw her to me and kiss her, hard, because I have something to prove to myself—*she's here, she's with you, she wants to be with you*—and she kisses me back just as fiercely.

The last thing I want is for her to leave. I'd like to stay out here, on this deck of the house I rescued from the grave, forever. To fool time so this moment can last and last, so this force building between us can never be broken. But the last of the light is gone. I'm supposed to meet Doris the day after tomorrow, and something tells me her seal of disapproval would be as good as a death sentence, so I pull back. Delia pushes forward to get one last kiss, making me smile, and then I get to my feet and help her up to hers.

"I'm going to take you down to your car." I eye the container of muffins she left on the picnic blanket. "Are those muffins for me?"

"All of them," she agrees, giving me a smile that makes my cock come to attention.

"Good. Because I'm not sharing them with anyone." I pause, not wanting to scare her but needing to establish this firmly. "I know it's early, Delia, but I need you to know that I'm serious. Constance has this impression that I'm some kind of ladies' man, but... Look, I'm not going to say that's never been true, but I haven't been like that for months." I take a breath, my heart beating fast and hard in my chest. "I'm not going to be seeing anyone else, and I don't want to share you either."

The truth is, it makes me want to grind my teeth and punch a wall bloody to think of another man touching her, tasting her heat, and drawing those soft sounds of pleasure from her.

But the gentle smile on her face calms me. She leans in and kisses me, then says, "While I'm disappointed that we won't be having a threesome with Thomas, I respect your decision."

Surprised laughter gusts from me. "Were you hoping he'd tie you up with the orange lanyard?"

"And lend you some of those blue pills so you could make me scream all night long."

"I don't need any blue pills for that."

Her eyes widen, then heat flashes through them. "I believe you, but I'm going to have to insist you prove it."

"Didn't I prove it earlier?" I ask, lifting my eyebrows in a challenge.

"I'd like you to prove it more…thoroughly."

Just like that, I'm all the way hard for her. It's extremely tempting to take her soft hand and show her. To ask *is that proof enough?* But I promised myself that I would be careful with her. That I'd take things slow—or at least slower—and she's already made it clear that Doris will worry if she's home late. Holding back a sigh, I say, "I'll enjoy doing it. After we've convinced Doris and her friend I'm not a murderer. I know better than to make a bad impression on her."

I offer her my arm, and she takes it.

"You'll let me know when you're going to Constance's on Friday?" she asks.

I'm tempted to tell her not to worry about it. She doesn't need to do any more work without pay, because even if Constance offers compensation, I have a feeling Delia will find a way to say no. But, ultimately, I can't pass up the chance to see her.

"I will," I promise, "but you'll be hearing from me tomorrow too. I'm sorry to say you'd have a difficult time getting rid of me now."

She leans in and kisses me slowly, a kiss that promises of many more kisses to come, thank God. "Good."

When we head down to the driveway, I see a car idling on the road. A dark KIA with tinted windows. It moves along, but there's a weird feeling in my gut, like it's no accident. Like maybe they were watching.

I spend the night at the house, lying out on the deck on that blanket, because I'm truly bringing sentimentality to the next level. It's mostly because of her, but I also want to clear my mind, and out on the the deck, I feel a kind of clarity that's new to me.

The next morning, Leonard shows up to the house early. He smirks at the folded-up picnic blanket on the counter of the kitchen island. "I take it the date went well?"

"It did," I confirm tightly, because I won't be providing details to anyone. "Your truck made it?"

"Shane helped me put a little masking tape on the old girl, but the tells me she's not long for this world, so I'm doing my best not to push it."

"Wise."

"So, old Burkey finally met his match," he says, then reaches for the container of muffins.

"Oh, hell no," I say, slapping his hand. "Those are all mine."

"Did Delia give them to you?"

He's teasing, but hell, it's true, so I nod. He starts laughing. "Okay, man, I won't eat your girl's muffins, but you've got it bad."

"I do," I say. "And you know what? I'm surprisingly okay with that."

We work on the basement for a few hours before I have to leave to meet with the private investigator, Deacon Montgomery.

"You want to come with me, bud?" I ask Leonard, wiping off my face with a work towel.

"No," he says, his jaw flexing. "I'll hang out here."

"It's going to be okay," I tell him, feeling a little discomfited. There's something unsettled about him this morning, and I know it has to do with this meeting. I don't want him to run. He can't run.

"I know." Then, as if he knows exactly what I'm thinking, he says, "I'll be here. Bring me back some lunch, will you?"

"You got it."

I make my way to the address that Deacon provided to me. His office, unmarked on the outside except for the unit number and tucked into a building that has foundation issues, smells like mildew, stale coffee, and Doritos. I instantly like the guy. He's the gruff, takes-no-shit type, probably closer to seventy than sixty, although he has a craggy, bearded face that makes it impossible to tell.

"Tell me more about what you're doing here, son, and we'll figure out whether we're wasting each other's time," he says.

He already knows about the situation with my parents, which we covered on the phone yesterday, so I start off by filling him in on the strange incidents on the movie set, other than the problems caused by Jeremy being a dick, which I consider both incurable and probably not my parents' doing. Then I tell him about the car I saw idling outside the flip house the other night, in a place that sees little traffic.

He sits with it for a minute, and I'm prepared for him to say I'm making something out of nothing. The he nods and says, "It's worth looking into. You know anyone in their household? Someone who would see your side of things? If we can get in, that would be best. I can poke around a bit on this end, find out if they hired someone to follow you, but an inside person would be able to get us insights we can't get any other way. If they've hired someone on that movie set, there's a chance the person might have come by the house, or there might be some record of it on their devices. If we can clone one of their phones, that would be gold."

"Isn't that illegal?" I ask.

He places a finger next to his nose. "I'm under the impression they're already being prosecuted. If we get anything good from it, we can hope the evidence comes to light a different way. I might have some ways of ensuring it happens."

Which means he isn't strictly by the books. Good to know. I haven't known many private investigators, but all of them seem to share that same philosophy.

"They've hired new people somewhat regularly," I say. "My mother said she didn't want anyone getting too friendly, taking liberties, but I'm guessing it was more than that."

If he has an opinion about that, he doesn't feel inclined to share it. "So you've got no way into the house."

I sigh, thinking of that summoning that's sitting on my phone. My mother sent a follow-up text this morning. *Please send in your RSVP as soon as possible, Burke. The chef needs a head count.*

As if the tea will go on with or without me. It amuses me, slightly, to think of my mother and father sitting down to a formal tea together. What would they talk about? The possibility of doing jail time? The weather? Their wayward son?

"They invited me over this weekend," I tell him. "My mother made it sound like a demand, not an invitation, but she just asked me to RSVP. So I guess she's pissed that I didn't respond."

He lifts his brows. "There you go. Have you spoken to them since you left the company?"

"No," I say through numb lips.

"You think they might let you bring someone? Someone who can wander around and collect information?"

Leonard would be good at that, obviously. But I don't want to expose him to them again after the way they drove him out of town. Delia would offer to go—she's already insisted on it—but there's no way in hell I want her anywhere near them.

Truthfully, *I* don't want to be anywhere near them. The thought makes my heart race. It makes everything inside of me seize.

"Maybe," I hedge. "But I'm not going on Sunday. I have plans. Truthfully, I'd prefer it if you could figure out what they're up to another way."

He considers that for a moment and then shrugs. "Not a bad idea to keep them on their toes. Drop in on your own timing, your own terms. Because if you went on Sunday, they'd be prepared for you."

"I don't like the sound of that," I admit.

"No, son, I don't imagine you'd like anything about it, although they may still think they can talk you around. Get you to lie on the stand for them or at least be seen with them publicly. If you want my honest opinion, they have more to lose by alienating you or trying to do you harm than they would by buttering you up and making offers. But anyone with half a brain and eyes to see knows that people don't always operate according to their self-interest."

"My parents do," I say, feeling my brow knotting, because shit, they really do. That's why the thought of them messing with me like this doesn't square. And yet, he's right, desperate people didn't always do logical things.

"Which is why there's a very good chance this is a whole lot of nothing. Little incidents that seem to tie together but don't." He sits back in his chair. "I'll be frank with you, that's what my gut is telling me. Can't tell you how many times I've seen that happen in my career."

"And the other times?"

His lips press into a flat line. "The other times my clients had good reason to be happy they'd hired me. I should point out that if your parents are behind what's been happening, they might react if you don't show up."

"But you'll be watching them."

He nods. "I'll be watching."

It feels good hearing that, knowing that someone's got my back. It feels even better hearing him say what I wanted to believe—that it's probably nothing, that I'm twitchy from all the shit that has gone down and caught in a string of both very good and very bad luck.

When I get back to the flip house with a bag of takeout, Leonard is sitting on the front porch, reading an old paperback on one of the camp chairs we keep in the basement. There's an empty one next to him for me.

"Is this what you do whenever I'm not around?" I ask.

"Nah," he says, then shrugs self-consciously. "Constance recommended it."

"So it's not *Why Loyalty Matters?*"

He laughs, but it sounds uneasy. He scrubs a hand through his hair. "I couldn't work while you were gone. I was feeling a little jumpy."

I lean against the front door. "No need for that. He thinks it's sensible to take precautions, but he's not convinced they're out to get us."

A corner of his mouth lifts and he lowers the book to the floor. "Well, halle-fucking-lujah."

Maybe it's that clarity of mind I've been courting, but I look at him and flat-out ask, "Why'd you keep running, Leonard? I get why you left Asheville the way you did, but you can't have thought my parents were still looking for you for all of those years. You changed your name more than once. Went to totally new places."

For a second, I don't think he's going to answer. He's staring out at the road like he expects the Kia to show back up. Then he grins at me. "The only place I ever had a reason to stay was here, and your folks pushed me away from it. I guess I kept looking for another place, another life, one that would make me want to hang on to it, but it never happened." He scratches his chin. "Maybe you want me to say I felt guilty for what I did. For letting your folks get away with it for so long. I *did*. But here's the thing... I'm a survivor, Burke. I'll never feel guilty for surviving. They were right. If I'd tried to take a stand against them by myself, with no concrete evidence to back me up, they would have eviscerated me."

I pause for a second, soaking that in, then ask, "Why'd you change your last name before we met you?"

He smirks, some amusement in his eyes. Some pain. "Because my old man's even more of an asshole than yours, and that's saying something."

"But you tried to convince me to start using my nickname again," I sputter.

"Yeah, man. Like I said, I'm a survivor. You're our rock. That's like apples and oranges."

"I've never understood that saying," I tell him. "They're both fruit. How are they that fucking different?"

"One of 'em's sour," he says, laughing, "and the other's sweet."

"I take it you've never had a Granny Smith apple?"

twenty-three

DELIA

I WORK ALL DAY, starting off with a couple of dog walks and then pinging from one granddaughter task to the next. By the time I get home, I'm exhausted, but I put together a quick meal for Doris and Ross. Doris bombards me with dozens of questions about my night with Lucas, and I can tell she's miffed that I'm not being as forthcoming as usual. She's right, but what Lucas and I shared felt so private, so different from my other experiences with men. I spoke with Mira earlier, while I was walking the second round of dogs, and she also accused me of being stingy with details.

"You'll meet him tomorrow," I assure Doris as we clear the table together.

She pouts but seems cheered when I offer to watch *Dr. Quinn, Medicine Woman* with her—what she calls an oldie but a goodie.

Lucas fulfills his promise and calls me about an hour later, and I make my excuses, my heart pounding, and go downstairs to my apartment to take his call.

"It feels good to hear your voice, Sunshine." His voice radiates through me. I can still hear him telling me that I feel good, that I'm beautiful with his cock in my mouth. Usually, it makes me laugh when men talk to me like that, but it felt different when Lucas said those things. It made me *hot*.

He tells me about his visit with the private investigator and then our conversation moves on, traveling hills and valleys as we discuss the movie and our pasts and try to imagine what Christian's life is like when he's not shut up in the Rolf Estate.

Finally, he says, "I don't want to keep you up too late. We both know you're going to get up with the sunrise. Why don't you go get some sleep and dream of strawberries?" He says it wickedly, like he knows exactly what I'll really be dreaming of. I'm tempted to tell him to come over, but a voice in my head warns me that we're moving too quickly, falling too rapidly, and it would be better to slow down.

"Am I meeting you at Constance's tomorrow?"

"I'll pick you up."

My heart races at the thought, because it feels like he's easing into my life a little more. I like that. Also, despite my fears, he's been nothing but good to me.

Still, by the time Friday afternoon rolls around, I'm a touch nervous. He wants to be exclusive—he was pretty clear about that—but I'm still not sure how it'll be between us around the people we know. Will he want to hold back? My latest ex-boyfriend, Timothy, insisted on keeping our relationship quiet for months before we went public.

Lucas announces his presence by ringing the bell, and when I answer the door, he kisses me and insists on coming inside to say hello to Ross. Doris still hasn't come home from her water aerobics class with Jane, where they hopefully made Frank miserable.

"Isn't Leonard with you?" I ask, because he's making faces at us through the passenger window.

"He is," he acknowledges. "He's having some trouble with his truck, so I've been giving him rides, but he says he wants to stay out of it."

I suspect this is his way of giving us space. Leonard's more thoughtful than he'd like anyone to realize. They're both wearing T-shirts, and Lucas has on the work jeans he probably wears at the house.

He notices me noticing and smiles. "I brought nicer clothes to change into for dinner. I thought about buying an orange shirt to make Thomas feel like he's in his element, but I couldn't bring myself to go through with it."

Smiling, I swing the door wide. "I brought a different outfit too. Come in."

There's a warm tingling in my chest when Lucas smooths his hair before entering the house. It's such a sweet thing to do, like he's a teenager who wants to impress his girl's parents, and it's so wholly unnecessary because Ross isn't at all perceptive about the state of other people's hair. Doris once dyed hers blue temporarily, and it took him two days to notice something had changed.

When we step into the living room, Ross gets up from his favorite armchair, groaning about his muscles not cooperating.

"Do you use Tiger Balm?" Lucas asks. "Works wonders after a day of flooring."

"Tigers, huh?" Ross says.

They exchange a firm handshake and a jovial greeting, and Ross asks "Luca" what he does for a living.

"I've been flipping houses lately, among other things."

Ross shoots me an incredulous look. "Why didn't you say so, Delia? Tigers...backflips. Sounds like one hell of a show. We'll have to bring Doris to see it. She's always liked the circus."

Lucas seems thrown by this. He opens his mouth, pauses, then says, "I flip houses, sir. There's no circus."

"You do the flips in someone's house? Isn't that a liability issue?"

I should probably take the trouble to explain, but Leonard's been waiting out in the truck for several minutes by now, and it's Ross's own fault for not getting faster shipping on his hearing aid. "We'll be back in a few hours, Ross. See you soon."

He nods, happy enough to move on from the subject, and sinks back into his chair.

Lucas is staring at me, and I bite back a laugh. After we leave and close the door behind us, he asks, "Shouldn't we tell him I don't work at the circus?"

"But it seems to have really tickled him," I say, laughing. "And it's his own fault for choosing the slowest possible shipping speed for his hearing aid."

Lucas rubs the back of his head. "Is it coming soon?"

"Tomorrow, thank goodness. Believe me when I say this isn't the first small misunderstanding it's created."

"Just tell me I don't have to buy a tiger, Sunshine."

I take his hand as we make the short walk to the car. "Thank you for being sweet with him."

He pulls me to him for a kiss. "He's good to you. That's all I need to know. Now, are you ready to go transform the fish room?"

"Yes. Let's help Constance put this whole sorry episode behind her."

"You look cute together."

I jump, then turn to see Shauna regarding me with an expression of amusement. She's wearing some kind of apron covered in smudges, and her lilac hair is mussed.

"Sorry," she says. "I needed to grab some water. I thought you heard me."

Lucas, Leonard, Constance, and I have all been working on the room downstairs. Honestly, it's too many people for a room so small, but the benefit is that we're almost done. The shelving has been removed, the walls sanded and prepped and painted.

Constance bought blue paint in honor of the fish who died there. She said it with a snort, but I think she may have partially meant it. She's sentimental, Constance, although she wants people to know that no more than Lucas wants to broadcast that he likes helping people.

I came upstairs to use the restroom. One of the old house's many flaws, according to Constance, is that there are only two bathrooms, one attached to the main bedroom and the other positioned next to the kitchen. Shauna must have returned home from work while I was in there, because there was no sign of her a few minutes ago. In addition to being a sculptor, she's part of a new art collective, The Waiting Place, that Sinclair Jones is opening with her fiancé. It's going to offer various workshops for beginners and also display and sell local art. Sinclair, of course, has been busy filming the movie, but preparations are still underway.

I'm reminded of Shauna's comment—*you look cute together.* "Were you talking about Lucas and me?"

"Yes, you and Lucas," Shauna says, capturing my attention. "I sure as hell wasn't referring to Leonard." She rolls her eyes as she takes a sip from her water cup. Reaching over with her leg, she rubs Bertie's belly with her foot. He's reclined on a bed on the floor, his tummy lifted for love. From what I've witnessed, Bertie has at least four different dog beds spread across the house, each plusher than any blanket in my collection. "Do you have any idea how many people have asked me about those Facebook photos? One of my father's best friends called me up this morning and asked if Nana was 'having relations with that young man.' I mean, gouge out my ears, right? Did Leonard have to ham it up so much?"

"I don't know if this will make you feel any better, but I'm pretty sure he couldn't help himself. What have you told them?"

"The same thing I've told Grandpa Frank—to ask Nana. I'm sure she's in seventh heaven coming up with ridiculous shit to impress the busybodies. It's always been a favorite pastime of hers, and now she has dozens of photos with a hot young thang to fuel the fire."

"You think he's hot?" I blurt, surprised. She didn't seem to admire him very much the other day, although it's hard to imagine anyone would find his appearance genuinely distasteful. A little weathered, maybe. He has the kind of look that comes from hard living, one of my clients would say. But it only adds to his charm.

She rolls her eyes. "And doesn't he know it. I've got no use for bullshit. Or bullshit purveyors."

"He's a pretty nice guy," I say with a shrug, because she's not wrong, but I still like Leonard. There's something inherently likable about him.

"He's nice now. Wait until he steals your wallet."

"I think you've got him wrong," I say. "He'll be the first person to tell you he's no saint." I know this because he's said it in front of me several times. "But he's loyal to the people who matter to him."

She snorts. "We'll see. But I don't want to talk about my step-grandfather. I was wondering if I could buy you a drink sometime to thank you for helping Nana. I feel like a real asshole for not taking care of the fish room on my own, but I've got, like, five hundred irons in the proverbial fire right now. I lost sight of it."

"You don't have to do that," I say. "I seriously love your grandmother."

"Which only makes me want to get to know you more," she says with a genuine-seeming smile. "Besides, my male best friend's marrying a movie star, and my former female best friend is marrying my ex-boyfriend in, oh, forty-five days, so I wouldn't mind making more friends." She flutters her eyelashes dramatically. "Don't make me beg."

I can't help but smile. She reminds me of Constance, and being reminded of Constance can only be good thing. "I'm told it's strange that I have mostly senior citizen friends, so it's probably not a bad idea for me to branch out too. When are you free?"

Shauna says she has time tomorrow night, and we make plans to meet at Glitterati. It could be argued I'm not doing much branching out if we're going to my sister's bar, but I want to introduce her to Mira. Something tells me they'll get along too.

"So what's going on between you and Snow White?" Shauna asks, wiggling her eyebrows.

A laugh escapes me. "Your grandmother told you about his nickname, huh?"

"She talks way too much. I blame her for my own inability to shut up. So...?"

"He's incredible," I admit, feeling myself blushing. I'll never look at a picnic blanket again without thinking of him burying his head between my legs, telling me to eat strawberries and drink champagne while he went down on me. "But the timing isn't great. He's going through something really heavy."

"I heard," she says. "And not just from Nana this time. We have some mutuals in common."

"Sinclair Jones."

She nods. "She's the aforementioned movie star in my sphere. I wish I had useful advice for you, but like I said, my former best friend is marrying my ex-boyfriend, so clearly I'm terrible at life and relationships."

"Or maybe they are."

"Yes," she says with a broad grin. "Let's go with that."

"Your grandmother mentioned you're going to be a bridesmaid in their wedding?"

She looks a little annoyed, so I apologize. "Oh, please," she says, "it's not your fault. She's been telling everyone and their brother, brother-in-law, and brother-in-law's cousin about it. And I don't blame her. It really was an instance of terrible decision-making. The only reason I said yes is because I didn't want them to think it bothers me. But it *does* bother me. So the only person I'm hurting is myself."

"When is it?"

"End of September. So I have some time to regret my life decisions."

"Do I hear the love of my life up there?" someone calls up the stairs, and a few seconds later, Leonard comes out with a shit-eating grin on his face. Bertie instantly rises from his stupor, suddenly with grand notions of being a guard dog, and barks at him.

"Nope," Shauna says, making a dismissive gesture. She bends to pick up Bertie, who's still barking but settles in her arms. "That's a big nope. I'll see you tomorrow, Delia."

"You don't want to see the de-fished fish room, Bright Star?" Leonard asks her. "Lucas sent me up to get Delia."

I'm surprised Lucas didn't come up himself, only he's a perfectionist, something I saw signs of in the perfectly turned-out flip house. I wouldn't be surprised if he's still fixing the trimming.

"I'm sure she'll show me later. No need to rush down." She disappears into the back hallway, and I catch Leonard watching her butt as she walks away.

He lifts his hands. "A man can look," he murmurs, then makes a grand gesture toward the stairs. "You ready?"

When we get downstairs, Lucas and Constance are standing outside of the closed door of the former fish room. There's a splash of blue paint on his shirt, a few tiny freckles of it on his face. He looks far from immaculate, but he's perfect like this. I remember what he said about feeling more alive when he's working with his hands. He may have been raised to rule boardrooms, but he was born to love *this*.

"Are you ready to see the space formerly known as the fish room?" he asks with a smile, reaching for my hand. I give it to him, and the joy of touching him fizzes within me. "You might have seen it a few minutes ago, but I figured you'd appreciate a grand unveiling. You're the kind of woman who requires one."

"If only we had a red ribbon to cut," Constance says with a touch of sarcasm, but just a touch, because she seems genuinely thrilled. There's not a shadow of the self-consciousness she showed the day she brought me down here the first time. I'm grateful to Lucas and Leonard for that.

Lucas flings the door open ta-da style, and we all step in together. It's like a form of alchemy. Even though I saw it nearly complete a few minutes ago, there's something magical about those last steps. They've transformed the room into a place of possibilities. The light, frothy blue on the walls feels like it's brimming with them.

"What are you going to do in here?" I ask Constance, lifting a hand to my throat.

"It looks like it could use a few fish tanks," she says, then grins. "Too soon?" She pauses, taking in the different angles of the room. "I don't know, but I feel like it's going to be fabulous. I'm ready for something fabulous, kids."

I look up at Lucas, his eyes nearly the same color as this room, and I think that maybe I'm ready for something fabulous too.

"Should we name the room?" he asks me, his smile catching.

"We're naming rooms now?" Leonard asks. "Did you pass out psychedelics earlier and skip me?"

"Yes, bud, but we'll get you ice cream as a consolation prize," Lucas says. Grinning at me, he says, "What do you say, Sunshine? Want some ice cream? Strawberry, maybe?"

I can feel myself flushing. Lucas puts his arm around me and pulls me close. Whispers in my ear, "I've been thinking about you and those strawberries."

It strikes me that I didn't know any of these wonderful people two weeks ago. It's hard to believe, but I remember that moment with my birthday cake, when I wished for something in my life to change, and it feels like someone listened.

We invite Shauna to join us for ice cream, and she makes her excuses. She looks upset, presumably by something other than Leonard's presence in her house, and none of us push her.

Lucas and I take turns ducking into the bathroom by the kitchen to change for dinner. He goes first, changing into a clean button-down shirt and khaki pants, then I change into my outfit—a short-sleeved blouse secured by a pink ribbon, an unintentional nod to Constance's ribbon-cutting comment, and one of my favorite flowy skirts with rainbow stripes.

When I come out, I can feel Lucas's hot perusal as he takes me in.

"You look like a piece of candy," he says with a wolfish grin.

"Yes, and we all know you'd like to eat her," Shauna says. Bertie, at her feet, wags his tail tentatively, as if he's hoping she's not mad at him too. She picks him up, sighing, and says, "Sorry, guys. Bad mood. Have a fun ice cream social."

She heads deeper into the house with Bertie while we head outside, Constance closing the door behind us. I don't miss the worried look she casts at the door.

"It's that damn boy who left her," she says as we pile into Lucas's car. He offers her the front seat, then me, but we both turn him down on account of Leonard being significantly taller than us. "Between him and Frank the Fuck, I can't decide which one's worse."

"What'd he do?" Leonard asks, turning back to look at us. "Do we need to kill him? Or how about some maiming? There'd be less legal trouble for Shane to bail us out of."

While Lucas drives, Constance tells them about the wedding, and Leonard listens intently, a muscle in his forehead twitching. Then he says, "This joker is definitely worse. At least Frank is straightforward about being worthless. This guy wants to come off like he's a saint. She going to screw up the wedding?"

Constance lets out a huff of air. "No, but I wish she would. I keep trying to encourage it."

"I'm going to give this some thought," he says.

who smiles and angles her head at it. *See*, she seems to be saying, *it's his one likable thing.*

Only I think I've developed a sudden aversion to orange.

I don't like this guy. Didn't like the way he was looking Delia up that first day; *definitely* didn't like the way he touched her. In fact, I'm less than partial to the way he's looking at her now, like he's fooled himself into thinking he has a claim on her. Like he's miffed she didn't show up in an orange dress and throw herself at him.

"Oh," Thomas says, narrowing in on me. "You came. Doris mentioned you might." He waves a hand between us. "Is this method acting, or are you two fu—involved now?"

His tone is as ugly as his shirt, in my humble opinion, and it's obvious the only reason he didn't go for "fucking" is because his great-aunt is standing next to him. He's under the impression she has a good opinion of him, and he doesn't want to ruin that. Really, if he were half as smart as he thinks he is, he'd stay permanently away from her and only converse in letters written by other people. Because that's the only way he'd get and keep her good opinion.

"Wasn't that obvious?" I ask, lifting my eyebrows as I wrap an arm around Delia. "We made the power short on set."

"I don't think you can take credit for an electricity malfunction," he scoffs.

"It did happen right next to us," Delia says, smiling at me. "We'll have to be careful with our superpower."

Thomas makes a sound of disgust, or maybe annoyance. "You want the producers to send you the bills? The shooting schedule's off by another two days. This whole production is cursed."

We'd already gotten that email. Some important circuits blew, and since the house is old and requires a special electrician, we won't be going back on set until Monday.

"I don't know about that," Delia says, squeezing my hand. "I met Lucas and Constance on set, and we were meant to know each other."

"Not Leonard?" I ask, teasing.

"Leonard too, but especially you and Constance. It was like the universe was insisting on it."

It's not the first time she's said something like that. I feel behooved to tell her the universe isn't a teenage girl playing matchmaker, but at the same time, it's charming that she believes it. It's Delia.

"Who are we to deny the universe?" I ask with a grin.

"Who indeed?"

"Come on," Thomas says flatly as he shifts on his feet. "It's bad enough that I got backed into filming a movie that makes saccharine seem sour."

"You hungry?" Ross says, clapping him on the back. "When it hits five-thirty, my blood tells me it's in need of some sugar. Well, let's get you in there, and you can tell me all about your back pain."

Thomas gives him a strange look. "I don't usually make a habit of eating at five-thirty."

"I don't have the slightest idea what you just said, but I'm sure it was as fascinating as ever. Now, how about we get in there?" Ross says. "God knows I'd love for this evening to last forever, but we gotta get some food into you."

"You know, just because you can't hear us, doesn't mean we have the privilege of not hearing you," Doris retorts.

"Shall we?" I say with a grin at Delia.

"Yes, please," she says.

Ross accidentally orders the special despite not liking rockfish. He thought the server was talking about Roquefort, a mistake that makes me think of Leonard and his ongoing cheese conversation with Constance. When he explains his error to us, Doris gets into a huff because he's actually supposed to be eating more fish, so she finally thought he was taking his heart-healthy diet seriously, "the infernal man."

Thomas has been sulky and quiet since we sat down, but I couldn't care less whether he's having fun, because Delia's clearly enjoying herself, and so am I. I like seeing this slice of her life. Now that I've seen them together, it's obvious that Ross and Doris see Delia as family, and she clearly sees them the same way.

I feel like I'm on the edge of some kind of important revelation, when a middle-aged woman approaches our table. She has dark eyes and dark curly hair with plenty of gray sprinkled in. She looks familiar, but I couldn't say how. "Delia?" she says.

Delia turns in her chair to look at her, and her face instantly loses color. "May."

The woman's eyes flick to me, to my hand wrapped around Delia's. There's confusion in them, followed by recognition.

Then horror.

Well, shit. It's been a while since this has happened. After my family started to hit the news cycle, I got recognized a few times. A few people directly confronted me. I probably got some spit in my to-go coffee. So I started wearing more casual clothes and let my hair grow out beyond the length a Burke male has probably had it in a hundred years—in other words, longer than an inch and a half—hoping that would help. It did, mostly, although Leonard says it's partly because people forget. Other shit happens, and your infamy stops being as important. The public moves on. But it's clear this woman hasn't moved on. There's the glint of hatred in her eyes, in the purse of her lips.

I grit my teeth. I know what's coming.

"*You*," she says.

Delia releases my hand. I'm surprised. I'm a little hurt. She knows this woman, and she'd clearly prefer not to advertise that there's anything between us.

"You were holding his hand," the woman says in horror. "Do you know this man is a Burke? That he's the son of *those people?*"

"Huh, what'd he do?" Thomas asks, interested for the first time since we sat down. It's like someone flicked the switch on his battery pack.

The woman, May, glances at him and then dismisses him. "Delia, tell me you didn't know."

"I knew," Delia says, but she looks small, shrunken. "But Lucas didn't have anything to do with it."

"Here's the rockfish for you," the server says, setting a plate down in front of Ross, who eyes it without any enthusiasm.

The rest of us have plates slid in front of us, all while May stands next to Delia, the tension between them, between *us*, enough to have blown the electricity twice. But no one else seems to notice or care. Life has this insistence on rolling along, no matter what's happening to you. The worst moments of your life are someone else's humdrum day.

Finally, the server walks away, and May shifts her attention toward me. She points an accusatory finger at me. There are tears in her eyes, and there's a feeling of growing horror in my gut, because this isn't the reaction of someone who saw my name in the news and decided I'm a piece of shit and she'd like to tell me so. No, this is the reaction of someone who takes what she thinks I did personally, because to her it *is* personal.

"You and your family killed my daughter, and you're sitting here eating your dinner like nothing happened. You're with her *best friend.*"

The truth deals me a knockout punch. This is Natalie Reiter's mother.

Her gaze slides back to Delia, who looks like she feels guilty too. Like maybe she regrets her certainty that fate put me in her path. "He didn't have anything to do with it," Delia repeats, but her tone seems to lack conviction.

"*She* should be the one who's sitting here," the woman continues.

I feel numb one second, and the next I feel every single hairline fracture inside of me.

"You're right," I say, getting to my feet. Then I realize it was a mistake—she's so much smaller than me, so breakable looking. The last thing I want to do is intimidate her. So I sit abruptly, feeling miserable and wrong-footed. "I would do anything to trade places with her."

"But you can't," she says, her voice hard. "She's gone forever. I'll never be able to hold her again. *Never.*"

I hear Delia get up, see her put an arm around May, then I sense them walking away. But it's all through a haze, almost like I'm watching it on a screen rather than here in front of me.

I stumble back to my feet.

"Lucas," I hear Doris says. "*Lucas.*"

I slip a couple of hundred-dollar bills out of my wallet and set them on the table. The least I can do is buy everyone the dinner I ruined. "I'm sorry," I say, although I'm not sure who I'm telling. Delia and May have left the table. It's just—

I've been so selfish, letting Delia lift me up. Letting myself soak in her sunshine and believe that I'm worthy of her forgiveness. Her affection.

As I walk away, I notice Thomas digging into his food. I'm tempted to kick his chair but don't. With my luck, he'd probably choke, and I'd have another sin to add to my list. People are staring, their gazes beating into me. *The bloody Burkes.*

I stagger outside in a daze, which is when I remember I'm the one who brought everyone here. I'll have to call them a car. It's such a simple thing, but it seems like an impossible task. I circle around to the back of the restaurant and lean against the alley wall, sucking in the hot air, but it doesn't soothe me. I feel like the alley is collapsing in on me, stealing my breath. Is this what they felt like before it happened? Only for them there was no escape, no end in sight. No rescue. There was no—

"Lucas." Her soft vanilla and sea salt smell surrounds me. I don't want to be comforted. I don't deserve it, but it already feels like some of the weight has been lifted. I hate myself for that, too, because May is right—no amount of wishing will bring her daughter back.

I keep my eyes fixed on the ground. "I shouldn't have come out with you. Sometimes it's like this when I'm in public places. But I didn't think..." I feel my jaw flexing, as if it's trying to break itself. "It didn't occur to me that Natalie's mother might be here."

"Why would it?" she asks softly. "It didn't occur to me either. May lives in Hendersonville. She's visiting a friend."

And they just so happened to go to the same restaurant as us. There's a weird feeling of déjà vu, of fate fucking with me again, but I guess you can't say you don't believe in fate and then turn around and accuse it of being an asshole.

"I'm sorry to have put you, and her, through that."

She takes my hand and presses our clasped hands to my heart. "I'm going to take you home now. Can I have your keys?"

"Doris and Ross..."

"Let's let Thomas feel useful for a change."

I glance up at her in surprise.

"I explained the situation to May," she says, holding my gaze. "She didn't know you were the whistleblower. She doesn't blame you, Lucas. She doesn't blame you because it's not your fault."

"I—"

She presses a finger to my lips. "The keys."

I take them out of my pocket, my hand shaking slightly. Embarrassment makes my skin heat. My father has always looked down on weakness—on men who let themselves have tells—and even though I despise him, I can't help but agree. Leonard called me strong, a rock, but I don't feel that way.

She lifts my hand to her mouth and presses a kiss to it before taking the keys, and it's steadier as I tuck it back into my pocket. I'm still ashamed, still shaken, but I can't deny her. I follow her to the car and get into the passenger seat like the weak man I am. I'm silent, wrapped in my own mind and not even trying to escape. She's silent too, and although she turns on the car, she doesn't back up or leave the spot.

She looks at me, and I try to prepare myself for whatever she has to say. I tell myself I can take it, whatever it is, even if she's about to tell me that we're through.

"What is it, Delia?" I ask, my voice like sandpaper.

"I've never been to your apartment before. You're going to have to tell me where to go."

A laugh escapes me for half a second before it dries up. "Just tell the car to direct you home. She knows the way. The key card for the garage is hanging from the mirror."

Delia's eyebrows lift, but she tentatively says, "Take us home, car." Then her eyes light up as the car's virtual A.I. assistant starts telling her where to go.

"This is amazing," she says with shining eyes, some of her enthusiasm genuine. Like most things about her, it's adorable.

"Money can buy a lot of things," I say, "but most of them aren't very important." I sound bitter and whiney as fuck, which makes me dislike myself that much more, so I make a pledge to stay quiet for the rest of the ride and lean back in my seat.

I space out until she pulls into the garage, then into my space.

"It has your name on it," she says, bemused.

"And we're back to what I said about money," I tell her.

"Everyone thanked you for dinner, by the way," she says, not getting out. She scrunches her nose. "Not Thomas, actually, but he doesn't strike me as a person who feels gratitude."

I swear under my breath. "You didn't eat anything. You must be starving."

227

"Neither did you, and it's only six-thirty. I'm barely even peckish yet."

Her word choice makes me smile. I'm not sure she knows it, but she has the vocabulary of a person from a different era. Not surprising considering who she spends her time with. But the smile drops from my face, because I'm not convinced she's not just saying that to preserve my feelings. I might not be famished at six-thirty, but she's used to a different schedule. That's something I should have thought of before I let her bring me here, like I'm some lost dog that needed to be led home.

"I'll order something for you. Or have something brought to the house."

"Trust me, Doris and Ross don't waste food." She tucks hair behind her ear. I'd prefer to do that. I want to feel her silky hair beneath my fingertips. To fist it and lose myself in her, but that's a selfish thought, the thought of someone who takes what he wants and leaves everyone else to burn.

She said something, and I missed it, so I ask her to repeat herself.

"They'll get both of our meals to go. My guess is that Ross will be eating one of our meals at four in the morning."

"He sleep-eats?"

"He wakes up at four in the morning."

"I like him," I say, my hand playing with the door handle. I know I should get out, but then what? I wasn't thinking when I agreed to let her drive me here. I'll have to call her a car.

"And he likes you, although he's stubbornly fixed on you working at the circus."

I try to smile and fail. "You didn't need to bring me back here."

"Yes, I did, and I'm bringing you upstairs too."

She opens her door, then circles around to mine. For half a second, I have images of locking myself inside like I'm a naughty toddler, but I'm in my mid-thirties, for Christ's sake. It's time for me to face up to my shit like a man.

I get out, and she takes my hand and leads me to the elevator, as if she's the one who knows where we're going. There's something about the way she does it that makes me want to get on my knees and worship her.

The doors ding and open, and Delia herds me into the empty interior. "Which floor?"

"Top."

She presses the button and then turns to me, wrapping her arms around me like it's the most natural thing in the world. I let her, because I need her. And isn't that the weakest thing of all? To let yourself need another person, to depend on them, to take what they have to give you.

I swallow the feelings down as the doors once again ding and then open, depositing us out onto my floor. There's only one unit up here, one door, which Delia notices with a look of surprise. Or at least I think that's what she's reacting to.

"Money," I say again, bitterly.

She still has the keys, so she opens the door. I step inside. Delia follows me and shuts the door behind us, her gaze curious as she glances around the main room. I try to see it through her eyes, and it looks expensive and blank. A space free of personality, of color. Of all the things Delia thinks make life worth living. That's because my parents hired an interior decorator to choose everything inside of it before I even learned they'd bought this place. It's still like that, still sterile and cold and devoid of personality. Then she wraps her arms around me again, her smell weaving around me, her touch burning into my consciousness.

"You should pick someone else to care about," I say into her soft hair. It comes out in a whisper, because I don't want her to pick someone else. In fact, the only thing I'm capable of wanting right now is her. I want to carry her into my room and lose myself in her. I want to pretend that nothing exists except for Delia Evans. But I've spent my whole life being selfish, and I don't want to be selfish anymore. Especially not when it comes to her. "You were right about me. I'm a mess, and I don't know how to fix it. Maybe it's too late."

She smooths a hand up and down my back. "You're already fixing it. You've *been* fixing it. You need to give yourself some grace, Lucas. So, today wasn't the greatest. There are going to be days like that and then there are going to be strawberry ice cream days. And sometimes they're the same day, Lucas, and that's okay. That's life."

I reach down and lift her chin, and the earnestness in her eyes twines around me, wrapping me into knots. "You're something else."

"I'm *yours*," she says.

And the final ropes holding me back from her snap.

twenty-five
DELIA

I FELT guilty when I saw May.

I felt like I'd done something wrong, and not just because I was at the restaurant with Lucas. It had been too long since I'd last reached out to her. Being around her was painful. I always noticed the ways she was like Nat—and all the ways she wasn't—and it didn't feel right to judge a person for what they weren't. To find them lacking just because they were an echo of the person you really wanted to see. So I'd fallen away from her over the years, and it hadn't even occurred to me to call her to let her know that the media had it wrong about one Burke.

But then I noticed the look in Lucas's eyes, like he was a whipped dog who thought he deserved it, and I snapped out of it and hustled her away to explain.

Although she wasn't quite as understanding as I'd conveyed to Lucas, I know she *will* understand. She left me with a hug, and I promised to call soon, and I meant it. I owe it to Nat to keep an eye on her mother, and I'm feeling stronger and more capable these days —more able to recognize and honor May's good qualities without comparing her unfavorably to Nat.

By the time we stopped talking, he was gone, and my heart felt like a scared rabbit's. I asked Doris where he'd gone, and she told me he'd paid for dinner, bless him, and staggered out. So I asked Thomas to take Doris and Ross home, he agreed after getting *that look* from Doris, and I left to find Lucas.

When I saw him in that alleyway, his beautiful face a mask of pain, I nearly started crying. I've always been a mirror to other people's pain, but it's stronger with people I care about. All I could think about was getting him home and making him feel better, but that's not what I'm not thinking about anymore.

Now, I'm thinking about the other day, on that deck, when he made me come out in the open, with a warm breeze pushing at my skin. I'm thinking about all the things I've imagined him doing to me, and me to him.

He looks down at me with a hunger in his eyes that lights up all of my nerve endings. I feel like a prey animal who's noticed, too late, the presence of a predator. Only I'm happy to be caught. There's still work for both of us to do before we'll feel completely comfortable in our skins. But that doesn't mean we have to go through life broken and alone, not when fate has gone out of its way to bring us together.

He puts his large hand around my jaw, lifting my face to him as if it's a flower tipping upward. He's a big man, and that presence he has only makes him seem bigger and more imposing. But his strength is a protector's strength—to be used with a vengeance only against the people who would hurt others. "You're mine?" he asks. Pleads.

"Yes. If you want me."

"Oh, I fucking want you," he says, his blue eyes hooded as he stares at my mouth.

He brushes his thumb over my lips, and the nerve endings bloom, crying out for more. Then he lowers his head and kisses me, and the ferocity he's radiating, his hand almost brutal as he lifts me to his kiss, fills me with frantic need. I want him inside of me, everywhere, and it still might not be enough.

I pull his shirt out of his pants and slide my hands under both the button down and his undershirt, wanting to feel his heat, and he groans into my mouth and then pushes down my skirt and underwear. I barely have time to step out of them before he's backing me into the wall, his mouth still on mine, his hand against my jaw. I gasp as the fingers of his other hand dip between my legs, finding my clit. He does it so quickly, so efficiently, as if he's dedicated his life to the pursuit of making me a *very* pleased woman. Then he thrusts a finger into me, hissing at the sensation, probably because I'm liquid with need. Another finger, and they curl inside of me, finding a spot that radiates pleasure to every other point in my body, making my joints want to buckle from it. They can't, though, because he's pinning me to that wall, his mouth and hands on me, his hard cock pressed against me—a promise I'm really hoping he'll fulfill tonight.

He lifts his mouth from mine, his eyes engulfing me as his clever fingers continue their work, his palm pressing against my clit. My body is quivering, needy and in no mood to hide it. My hands grasp at his shirt, because I want it to come off. I want all of him to be revealed to me.

"I want to watch your face while you come," he says. "You're so beautiful, Delia. So impossibly beautiful."

He makes me feel that way. It's in the way he watches me, his eyes soaking in the details and saving them for later.

"Your shirt. Your pants," I say, as if I'm a person no longer capable of full sentences.

"What about your shirt?" he says, lowering his hand from my jaw to brush over the ribbon holding my shirt to my chest. "This has been driving me crazy all night. I've been thinking about pulling it." He plays with the end of the ribbon and tugs it, hard, his other hand still toying with me, sending pulses of pleasure rolling through me.

I lift the bottom of his shirt more insistently. "I need to feel your skin against me, Lucas. I want to see you too."

"I don't want to stop touching you," he says, his hand stroking,

233

coaxing, as his other hand works the ribbon looser, reaching for my breasts underneath it. "I'm not ready to stop." His hand feels hot against my skin as it dips beneath my bra and caresses me there, sensation shooting from my nipple down between my legs. Then his head is dipping to me, his lips kissing the place where my shoulder joins my neck, his five o'clock shadow sending zips of sensation through me, and the combination of the three things he's doing to me...

"Lucas, if you want to watch me come, you'll need to look now," I gasp out, my voice barely recognizable to my own ears.

He places one more soft kiss, then shifts so his eyes are on me as he continues to play with me, his hands all over me, my body pinned to the wall, and it's so much, so good, that it pushes me over the edge. A sound of pure pleasure escapes me, and my eyes flutter shut. I haven't fully come down from it when I feel him picking me up. My eyes open, and he's carrying me like I'm a princess, my shirt open enough that my breasts are bared, my skirt and underwear left behind in the other room. One of my shoes falls, and I kick the other off before I remember.

"Don't you have a roommate?" I ask, horrified.

His grin is like the big bad wolf's. "He said he'd be home late."

"Oh, thank goodness."

He reaches a door that's a sliver open and kicks it, revealing a stark bedroom with a huge king-sized bed, the comforter an understated gray, the sheets crisp white. There are two nightstands beside it, sleek and modern, and a desk in the far corner, along with a reading chair that doesn't look comfortable enough that a person would want to lounge on it.

His whole apartment is like that—crisp and masculine and a little...boring. Or at least it would be boring under less stimulating circumstances.

My gaze flits back to the bed as we approach it. I've always wanted...

I look up at him. "Will you throw me onto the bed?"

I have a second to take in his smirk, the bright lust in his eyes, and then I'm airborne. Landing hurts a little, to be honest, but it's a good kind of hurt—one that's edged with anticipation for the pleasure that's to come. I settle into the soft mattress and watch as he unbuttons his shirt and shrugs it off, then his undershirt. He's so beautiful like this, poised over the bed, his hair a mess, his chest bared for me.

"Your pants," I say again.

There's a ripple of amusement across his features—pleased amusement—and then he does as I asked, pausing first to take off his shoes and socks.

I edge to the end of the bed, because to see Lucas Burke's cock is to want to touch it, and I wrap my hand around him, reveling in how hard he is for me, how much he wants me. I stroke my hand up and down, watching the way his jaw tics as he leans in and finishes unfastening my shirt, then my bra. I need to shrug them off, but I don't want to take my hands off him.

"Delia," he says, his voice strained, "you keep doing that, and I'm not going to last very long. I need to come inside of you."

"Does this mean you have condoms?" I ask.

"I bought a multipack after last time," he says, amusement curling his lips.

"So what are you waiting for?"

He sucks in air audibly, then reaches into the nightstand by the bed and pulls one out. I take it from him and remove it from its metallic package, slowly rolling it over him while I look up at him. His eyes are closed, as if he's just barely hanging on.

I take his hands and pull him down to me, and suddenly his mouth is on me again. He's kissing me like he doesn't know how to stop. Then he lifts my arms over my head, capturing them in his hand, and lowers his head to my breast. Sucking on my nipple, he moves his hips on top of me, his hardness pressed between us.

"Now," I say, my voice breathy and strange. "I need you *now*."

He moves on to the other breast, sucking, then releases my hands and props himself up on one elbow as he reaches down to align himself.

He captures my mouth as he slowly thrusts inside, giving me time to get used to him. It feels so impossibly good to have this man filling me, stretching all of the places he made quiver with pleasure just minutes ago. I already feel new sensations unfurling inside of me. New joy wanting to bloom.

His mouth leaves mine and finds my neck, kissing me softly there, his cock still buried inside me. Then he looks at me. "Is this okay? Tell me when you're ready—"

I rock my hips against him, needing him to move, to take me. "I need everything, Lucas. Don't hold back."

He groans as he starts moving, pulling nearly all the way out before he thrusts back in. Then he captures my hands again and pins them above me. "I might not have a lanyard, but I can still do this," he says in my ear before kissing my neck, his cock and his hands holding me to the mattress, his body in complete command over mine.

His comment is funny enough that I nearly laugh, but there's no room for laughter in me right now as my hips rise to meet his thrusts. I feel an instinctive need to be closer, even though there's not much closer we could get, so I wrap my legs around his hips. But after a few minutes I need more. When I buck my hands, he lets them go, and I wrap them around his muscular back, his butt, driving him in even deeper.

"You feel good, Delia," he says with a groan. "So damn good."

Then he surprises me by rolling onto his back, still inside of me, and positioning me on top. His hand reaches for my clit as I ride him, and when his mouth finds my nipple, I can't take it anymore— the waves of pleasure are pulling me under again, insisting that I ride them out. My mouth falls open, and the look of determination, of almost greed on Lucas's face says he knows it's happening again. This time, instead of watching me, he captures my lips with his mouth, kissing me hard as he plays with me. Pleasure weaves around me and through me, flooding out everything except for him. My ears ring from it, my toes flex with it, and I can feel him falling apart with me, his mouth shuddering against mine, his body going rigid.

I lower onto him, my breasts pressed to his chest, his cock still inside of me. We lay like that for a long moment, Lucas caressing my back even though it has to be sweaty.

"I must be sweaty," I say like an idiot.

"That's because I worked you hard," he says, and when I look at him, there's a pleased smile on his face. I'm happy to have put it there. "I'll bet you're hungry now."

He pulls out, and I feel the loss of him. "You're offering to feed me?"

He makes a face. "I'm a terrible cook. I can't even make decent toast."

"That picnic you brought the other day was pretty memorable."

"I told you, Danny made most of it." His expression wry, he says, "If I tried to make you something, you'd never want to come back. I refuse to risk it."

I feel a grin stealing across my face. "So what you're saying is that you want me to come back?"

He reaches for my cheek, runs a finger over it. "Of course I fucking want you to come back. Did you somehow miss the past hour?"

"It was more like half an hour."

He laughs, his blue eyes sparkling. "Sure, but if anyone else asks, tell them it was an hour."

I smile at him. "While I'd prefer not to discuss my sex life in such detail with inquisitive strangers, I promise I'll tell them it was two. *If* we can make some food."

"Give me a second to clean up," he says, waving to the door that presumably leads to a bathroom. "We'll order food."

We'll be cooking, but I decide not to tell him that yet. While it's perfectly fine for him to rely on Danny—and his money—for sustenance, every person should know how to make at least one meal. Mine is eggplant parmesan. Lucas's, I decide, will be eggs and toast.

twenty-six

LUCAS

"ARE YOU COOKING?" Danny asks, dropping his keys.

He just walked into the apartment, and apparently the sight of me in the kitchen was shocking enough for him to temporarily lose his grasp on reality. Delia is with me, of course, the only thing standing between me and a kitchen disaster. She's wearing one of my T-shirts because I accidentally ripped her ribbon shirt. Although she insisted it wasn't a big deal, I ordered a replacement for her while she was in the bathroom. I can't say I regret ripping it, to be honest, because I really like seeing her in my shirt. My primal side is preening over it.

"Had to happen eventually," I say in response to Danny's continued gaping over the unusual sight of me in the kitchen. That's not quite true, though. I'm pretty damn sure my father's never poured himself a bowl of cereal in his whole life.

We're not doing much—scrambled eggs and some toast—but it feels surprisingly good. Like maybe I shouldn't have let thirty-three years pass me by without putting in more than a token effort.

When I insisted, yet again, that I was bad at cooking before we walked into the kitchen, Delia gave me a flat look and said, "You're afraid to fail at anything, aren't you?"

She's the only woman who's ever been able to cut me to the quick like that. See through my bullshit so utterly.

She was right, obviously. I've never really tried, because I felt certain I would fail—and I categorically do not like failing.

Danny picks up the keys and approaches us tentatively, as if he's afraid the oven will explode.

I put my arm around Delia. "Danny, this is Delia. Delia, Danny."

He shoots me a semi-annoyed look. "Or Daniel, to people who haven't known me since I was seven." But he's a man who knows a losing battle when he sees one, so he smiles and shakes his head. "But fine. Yes. You can be grandfathered in."

"Hi, Danny-slash-Daniel" she says, then gives him the second potentially fatal shock of the evening when she leaves the kitchen and hugs him. "I've heard so much about you."

"You have?" he asks, openly gawking now.

"Of course. And thank you for the picnic you helped Lucas prepare the other day. We're going for something a bit simpler for his signature dish, but we'd love it if you'd join us for dinner. If you haven't already eaten."

I'm guessing he hasn't, but he pauses as if trying to think of an excuse to say no. I'm guessing he wants to refuse for my sake, or because he's uncomfortable around strangers. The polite thing to do would be to give him an out, but I want him and Delia to know each other. It feels wrong that they don't.

"Stay," I tell him. "If it's terrible, you'll have something else to give me shit about with the guys."

"It's hard to refuse an offer like that," he says with a half-smile. "Can I help?"

"You can set the table," Delia says. "Lucas is going to be one hundred percent responsible for the food."

"You're the surprising kind of ball buster," I say. "You come off as sweet and innocent, but really—"

She hip-checks me. "Less talking, more cooking." But there's a smile hiding at the corners of her mouth, and I'm the lucky guy who put it there.

"So I take it dinner didn't happen?" Danny says, grabbing some plates from the cupboard. He's always been reliable like that. Give him a task, and he'll do it. He's not going to try to wait long enough that you might forget you asked.

Delia gives me a worried glance, like she's concerned the reminder will toss me into another existential crisis.

"It was at five-thirty," I say. "How do you know we're not just hungry again?"

He pauses in collecting the table settings and takes in the state of us—my messy hair, the glory of Delia in my shirt—and shrugs. "None of my business."

"Nope," I agree. I have no problem with telling him why the dinner ended early, but I'd prefer to do it later, because this moment has all the marks of a memory that shouldn't be tarnished.

"Eggs," Delia says, pointing to the bowl. I've already cracked them and added the other ingredients she recommended, a little cream and salt and pepper.

"What about cheese?" I ask. "Everybody likes cheese."

"You're making it your own," she says with a grin, as if I reinvented the fucking wheel. Hearing her say it, I feel like I did. "Cheese is a great idea."

While Danny continues to set the table, I get out a bag of cheese and add some in, looking up at Delia for her "when."

She starts laughing. "Are you going to add the whole bag?"

"Would you recommend that?"

"No, dude," Danny says, looking up from the table as he finishes. "That would be like putting a whole stick of butter on a piece of toast."

"You're already insulting my toast? This is a new low. It hasn't even gone in the toaster yet."

He smiles and shakes his head. "Just don't give it all up to open a food truck. We'd all feel obligated to go, and no good could come of that."

"A food truck, huh?"

"Shit," he says. "I'm giving you ideas."

"Let's see if we can get through making scrambled eggs before we start talking food trucks," Delia says, giving me a fond look, like she knows I'm exactly the kind of asshole who'd jump from making eggs and grilled cheese to forming a business out of it.

I turn the burner on, and Delia gives me a little nudge. "I thought you knew how to start a fire with a stick and prayer," she says in an undertone meant just for me. Warmth settles inside of me, like I just downed a whiskey.

"Sure, but why bother when you have a burner?"

"You raise a practical point, Bappy."

I follow her instructions, and to my delight, I don't burn a single thing, although I suppose the toaster is owed most of the credit for the crisp bread. We carry the food to the table, and we all help ourselves.

"Is this where we beg a higher power to save us from food poisoning?" Danny asks wryly.

"Let's just send up a blessing," Delia says, pressing a palm to her heart and then mine. "Because we're here and eating with friends."

Danny looks vaguely guilty, and although it clearly costs him plenty of awkwardness to do so, he presses a palm to his own heart and looks skyward.

"The sad thing is that you're actually trying, and it still comes off as sarcastic," I say, laughing.

"I am genuinely thankful," Danny says. "Don't listen to him, Delia."

"If you want to express your thanks a different way," Delia says, almost slyly, glancing up at me through her lashes, "then I'd love to hear embarrassing stories about Lucas."

"There are none," he tells her, definitely sarcastic this time. "Lucas is perfect in every single way."

"No," she says, and before I can pretend she just stir-fried my ego, she says, "And thank goodness for that. There's nothing more boring than perfect."

Danny lifts his water glass into the air. "I'll drink to that." He does and then takes a big forkful of eggs and immediately makes a face.

"What?" I ask. "Is it the best thing you've ever tried in your whole life? You can't hold in all of your relentless positivity over what I've created?"

"Eggshell." Casting a glance at Delia, he says, "I correct my earlier statement. Lucas is perfect in every way except he's a shit cook. Incurable."

She takes a big bite of her own eggs.

"Isn't that overconfident?" Danny asks.

She gives him the smile a winner gives to the losing team. "Nope. I watched him make it. Only one piece of eggshell fell in." Turning toward me, she says, "They're generally delicious. I knew you could do it."

Damn... I've been told I could do world-changing things. Move mountains, sell buildings, change the city I live in. But none of it felt nearly as gratifying to hearing Delia tell me I can make some eggs that won't kill a person.

"I'm not sure I would have, without you," I say, moving my chair slightly so our legs are pressed together.

"Aren't you going to taste them?" she asks with a smile as she reaches her hand over to touch my thigh.

"After all of this buildup, I'm almost afraid to."

"They're not so bad now that I've gotten through the eggshell," Danny comments. "I'm ready to chalk it up to extra calcium."

I shake my hands out dramatically, like I'm an athlete ready to take a big jump, then I grab my fork and scoop up a bite. Shove it in my mouth.

I'll be honest, it's far from the best thing I've ever eaten, but it's also not the worst.

"Thank you, Delia," I say. "I feel confident that I could take care of myself now if anything ever happened to Danny."

"Well, shit," he says. "There goes my usefulness."

Delia asks him about his day job—debugging code for a local startup—and his game, about which he is much more enthusiastic. We all clear the table, but Delia insists the cook can't help with the dishes, so I stand by and watch as she and Danny take care of them. Then we grab drinks and go sit in the living room to chat, Delia and me on the couch and Danny lounging on the chair across from us.

After a while, he brings up the brick that almost brained me.

"Did you see it happen?" he asks her.

She gives a little full-body shake next to me. "Sorry, a goose just walked over my grave. I didn't see it happen, no, but I heard it crash."

Danny glances at me. I try to silently shut him up, but apparently it's not working, because he says, "You give any more thought to what I said about it not being an accident?"

Delia looks like a whole gaggle of geese just attacked her grave. "You don't think it was an accident? But the movie did a thorough investigation." She bites her bottom lip. "Lucas, is this why you hired that private investigator?"

"You hired someone?" Danny asks, lifting his eyebrows. "Why didn't you tell me and the rest of the guys?"

Busted.

"Shane knows. It's someone he recommended." He looks downcast, so I don't point out that Leonard is also in the know. "I didn't tell you because I didn't want to make it seem like a bigger deal than it is. You always jump to thinking everything is some well-thought-out conspiracy. And Drew...he wouldn't be able to do anything. He already feels like he's disconnected from everything here, so I didn't want to worry him."

He shrugs. "Still wish you'd told me. And you should tell Drew. It makes him feel more isolated when we don't keep him up to date." Turning to Delia, he says, "I do think it's too on point, what happened to Lucas."

Did he really need to pick this moment to turn into Mr. Fucking Chatty Pants?

I'm glad he doesn't know about the magically reappearing equipment or the power outage. I mentally pat myself on the back for not telling him.

"I'm assuming he's told you about his parents," he hedges, glancing at Delia.

"I know why they're unhappy with him," she says.

"We don't actually know that they're unhappy with me," I point out. "Maybe my dear mother asked me to tea this weekend because she misses me. She did text me yesterday asking for an RSVP, so I guess they're getting jumpy about me not coming."

"Did you tell her no?" Danny asks.

"The P.I. agrees it might be better if I drop in on them sometime. If I let them summon me, they'll be in control. They'll have a plan."

Delia captures her bottom lip between her teeth. "What about the other things that have happened on set? Do you think..."

I'm less worried by what seems to be a series of disconnected events than I am by that car I saw idling on the road beneath the flip house, but I don't want to tell her so.

"Clancy, the costume guy, says the movie's cursed. He might be on to something. I mean, look at Jeremy. He's a stain on humanity. I wouldn't put it past him to curse the movie with his mere presence."

"You're really going to see your parents?" Danny asks.

"I said I'd consider it," I tell him. This is the last thing I want to think about, especially after tonight. It's been a day of severe highs and lows, enough to give a man whiplash, but I'd prefer not to go out on a discussion of Lucas Burke the III and his lovely wife, who's always gone by Mrs. Lucas Burke the III because she doesn't think Marjorie Lee Burke has quite the same ring to it.

"Should you get in touch with the police?" Delia asks. "Did the P.I. say anything about that?"

Laughter escapes me. "Deacon says his gut tells him it's nothing, but even if it weren't, my father's made sure to make nice with the chief. Sends him a gift basket every Christmas. Lends him the use of his accountant to make sure he gets all the nice tax breaks." I take her hand, because I can tell she's genuinely worried about me. "Deacon says it would be against their self-interest to be anything but sweet to me, and he's right. All they've ever cared about is themselves."

Danny nods as if to accede the point, but Delia still looks troubled.

"What if something else happens?"

"The P.I. is keeping an eye on them. For now, let's just let this lie."

She squeezes my hand as if she's afraid to let it go. "Are you sure we shouldn't go talk to your parents on Sunday? Show up for that tea?"

"And miss your mermaid storytelling? No way. They don't get to plot and plan and ruin my day. They can write me a strongly worded note if they feel the need to get in touch. I'd very much enjoy setting it on fire. Or reporting their emails as spam. If Deacon thinks I need to go over there at some point, I will. But I'm doing it on my terms."

Danny makes his excuses not long after, grimacing at me to acknowledge he shouldn't have brought up the Brick-cident.

Delia's quiet as she watches him leave. Then, just when I'm starting to hope she'll let it go, she turns to look at me and says, "Does Leonard think all the accidents on set are linked?"

Sighing, I lean back on the couch and pull her onto my lap. She lets me, but she glances at me over her shoulder, giving me a look that demands answers.

"He's concerned too, but you've got to understand... Leonard has history with my parents."

"Oh?" Interest glints in her eyes. "I've been wondering how you two became friends. On the surface, you're so different, but you're also not."

"Kind of like us," I say, putting my arms around her.

"Kind of like us," she agrees and snuggles back against me.

It makes my dick half hard, but I don't feel inclined to do anything about it. Yet. It feels good just to hold her, like I can't be half as aggravated about anything with her in my arms.

I take in a deep breath and slowly blow it out. "So, this is kind of a crazy story."

"The best ones begin that way," she says with a small smile that I can see looking down at her.

"I wouldn't say this is one of them. The guys and I met Leonard after college. I knew he was a good salesman, had an eye for real estate too, so I helped him get a job with my parents. He's the one who figured out what happened with the Newton Building, only he didn't tell me at the time." I run a hand over my jaw. "He wasn't sure he could trust me, which was fair. I had my head up my ass, because I missed all of this, but I guess my parents made it clear they would ruin his life if he tried to take a stand against them. They, of course, insisted I'd take their side—that being a Burke was more important to me than life itself. Specifically the lives of other people."

She's looking up at me with wide eyes, the corners of her mouth twitching, and I know what she's thinking: *He knew all this time. He could have said or done something.* "Now, I don't know many details, but there's bad shit in Leonard's past. He figured my parents were right. No one would believe someone like him over a couple of 'upstanding citizens' like them, and he had no definitive proof. So he cut a deal with them. But afterward, he noticed someone following him around town. He figured they may have decided to protect themselves by getting rid of him. So he took off." My heart thumps in my chest, because it's this part that kills me. That he didn't think he could trust me. That he thought I was more of a Burke than a friend. "We all thought he was dead, because he figured he'd be safer that way. It was only recently we found all of this out."

"How?" she asks, half turned in my lap. She turns all the way so she's facing me. It's the same way she was riding me earlier. My hard-on has to be incredibly obvious, but she doesn't comment on it, just rocks against me slightly in acknowledgement. My ego would like to believe she can't help herself.

I wrap my arms around her.

"My buddy Drew. His girlfriend was working with a couple of private investigators, and she got it into her head that something was off about Leonard's disappearance. They're the ones who found him, and they helped us get proof about what my parents did. They're out of town now, or they're the people I would have called to keep an eye on things."

"But you're the one who had to get the proof," she says, holding my gaze.

"Most of it. I still worked at the office, so I had access. I couldn't quit until we got what we needed."

"It must have killed you to lie," she says and rocks against me again. "You're a man who likes to be direct. You're not a liar."

"I had to smile at them," I tell her, feeling the undercurrent of unease I carried around all those weeks, the feelings of disgust. Disgust with them, of course, but with myself too. Because she's wrong about one thing—it was easy to lie to them. "I had to go to Sunday dinner and make small talk and cheerfully field my mother's attempts to marry me off to debutants."

"I'm sure they're all very lovely, but they can't have you," she says, rocking forward again. This time she grabs the top of my shirt and kisses me. Pulling back slightly, she says, "Your mother would think I'm messy and cheap. A loser."

"Maybe. That's what they think of all of my friends," I say with a hard exhale. "Doesn't matter to them that Danny is certifiably a genius, or that Leonard's got a better sense for real estate than every surviving Burke combined. Or that Drew has a big heart. Or that Shane's more loyal than they've ever been to anything besides money."

"Danny, Leonard, Drew, and Shane...they're more than your friends," she says, cupping my jaw. "They're your family. You made a family for yourself because you never had a real one."

Her words stab at first, but then something beautiful blooms from them, because she's right, dammit, and it means I've been looking at this the wrong way. I haven't lost my family. They've been around me the whole time, supporting me, cushioning my fall.

I kiss her softly, because I need to feel her lips on mine to prove to myself that she's real, and she's here, and she wants to be part of this circle I've created. For however long I get to have her. I pull away slightly, taking her in. "You're right. And Doris and Ross are your family too. I'm sorry if I didn't see the way of things at first. I understood as soon as they met them."

Her smile is soft and sweet and so very Delia. "I'm not very close to my mother, as I'm sure you've realized. My dad's great, but he's off living his own life. He and my mom got divorced after Mira and I graduated high school. Now, he's retired and he travels around with his Appalachian rock band, the Blue Ridge Bandits. They're in Georgia right now, or maybe Tennessee. I lose track. Guess who people think I take after?"

I wrap a hand around her hip. "Does he have ginger hair?"

"My mother certainly doesn't. She has dark brown hair like Mira, and the second she found her first gray, she started dying it black."

Another reason Delia dyed it in high school, maybe. I hope her mother didn't back her into it, but from what she's said, I wouldn't be surprised.

"Not everyone can pull off the sunrise look," I say.

Her smile makes that strange warmth that's developed inside of my pulse, almost as if it's growing with each beat of my heart. Damn, I *do* have the Drew Affliction, no doubt about it. I make a mental note to call him to catch up.

"Stay with me tonight," I tell her. Then, realizing it sounds like an order, I add, "Please."

She smiles at me. "I was starting to worry you wouldn't ask."

twenty-seven

DELIA

LAST NIGHT WAS...

I don't have words for it, or for the connection I feel with Lucas. On the surface, we're such different people, but we have a deep understanding of each other, as if the kernels of our being are the same. If I told him, I'm pretty sure he'd remind me that people don't have any deep kernels hidden within them unless they've been eating popcorn by the handfuls. At the same time, I think he'd understand what I mean. After he carried me back to his bedroom, he slowly made love to me, and it went on for longer than half an hour. Then we lay in each other's arms and talked for hours, as if we haven't already spent the last two weeks talking—sharing intimate things with each other without meaning to.

Even in the beginning, when I thought I should hate him, I felt this draw. This *connection*.

I told him about Mira and the bar, and he admitted that he'd come in several weeks ago with his buddies and noticed the décor. I accused him of hating it, and he demurred, of course.

In the back of my mind, I had to wonder...

Weeks ago, it was my birthday.

Weeks ago, I made that wish for something wonderful to come into my life.

Is that the day he came in?

I want to ask, and I also don't, because I want to *believe*.

It's Saturday morning, and we're lying in bed—me in nothing but Lucas's T-shirt, and him in his boxer briefs—doing Lucas's typical Saturday morning activity. Which is apparently funding Kickstarters, GoFundMes, and various micro investments sent to him by his accountant. I asked him how long he thinks he can afford to do this, and he insisted that was what the investments are for—making sure he has more money to flow back in if he ever runs out.

"What about this one?" I ask, brandishing his phone at him. "She wants to make sweaters for puppies. Constance would love this. And look, we could get one for Bertie if we put in a big enough donation."

"Constance could *do* this," Lucas says as he reclaims his phone. "I know I talked shit about her sweaters, but they're way better than these. Maybe we can convince her to start a rival Kickstarter."

"Is that moral?"

"Of course not," he says with a grin. "It's business."

He sets the phone on his bedside table and then turns on his side, angled toward me, his head propped on one hand. The other reaches out to smooth my hair.

"I'd like to do something for May," he says, almost shyly. "Do you think she'd let me?"

No. But he doesn't need it put to him so baldly.

"I don't know, Lucas. What did you have in mind?"

"I know she wouldn't take money from me. She wouldn't want *their* money."

I'm starting to realize he doesn't want it either, at least not until it's cycled through the businesses he's funding. He'd like to create something of his own, something that's his—and he's doing it.

"You're right about that," I say thoughtfully.

"Was there something Nat really loved?" he asks. "I mean, other than old people. I was thinking I could start up a scholarship fund in her name. Maybe for business school students? You said she was business savvy."

Emotion forms a solid ball in my throat, and tears well in my eyes.

"Shit," he says. "Is it a horrible idea?"

"No." I reach for him as he starts to sit up. "No, it's the perfect idea. Maybe Danny was right about you after all."

The corner of his mouth hitches up. "He was definitely being sarcastic when he said I was perfect."

"And yet he got it right. May would love that, Lucas. *Nat* would love it."

He seems embarrassed again, and he says, "I was thinking I could do something like that for the families of each of the people who died. If they'll let me. I mean, it wouldn't be a business scholarship for each of them. It would honor something special to them."

I reach for the back of his head and tug him to me.

Kissing him feels as natural as drinking water or soaking in sunshine. It feels like it's something my body needs, which is a crazy thought since we've only been doing this for a matter of days. But there's no denying that I already feel more for Lucas Burke than I ever have for another man. That's a frightening thought, but some beautiful things are frightening too.

I pull away slightly and say, "I'm going to need you inside of me. Immediately."

"I'm not about to object," he tells me with that self-confident grin. His big hand sweeps under the shirt I'm wearing, finding its way between my legs. He swears under his breath. "You're always so wet for me."

"Yes, you'd better take advantage of that."

And, like a man who knows how to listen, he does.

After we get dressed, we migrate into the kitchen. Lucas makes some coffee, which was as far as his culinary skills extended before last night, and says, "Well, what will it be? Eggs and toast, or eggs and toast?"

"Getting cocky, huh?"

"Making love to a beautiful woman will do that for a man."

I kiss him on the nose. "Eggs and toast. And I'm not even going to observe you this time. I have to text Shauna to see if she's still up for getting drinks tonight. She asked me to hang out because she's grateful we've been helping Constance."

He lifts his eyebrows. "Leonard's and my invitations get lost in the mail?"

He's clearly teasing, but I say, "Do you want to come? We're going to Glitterati."

"No," he says, rubbing a hand over my arm. "I think it's great that you're getting to know her. She seems like a real spark plug. A Constance reborn."

"I think so too," I admit. "It makes me feel like we're already friends."

"Ask her why she hates Leonard so much, will you?"

I laugh. "It really bothers him, doesn't it?"

"Yes. I think he's got a thing for her."

"I'm not much of a spy," I say, which is probably putting it mildly, "but I'll talk to her."

"Thanks. Now, I'm going to have to insist that you at least be in the kitchen," he says. "Bad things will happen if you're not in here with me."

So I stay, and he burns the eggs because he was kissing me, and we eat them anyway, laughing.

Danny comes out of his room while we're eating. He doesn't seem all that surprised to see me, and I can't find it in myself to be embarrassed. "You got him to cook a second time?" he asks in feigned shock. Or at least I think it's feigned. "You're a miracle worker, Delia."

"She is," Lucas says with a grin.

He grabs his helmet, hanging by the door. "I'm gonna go for a bike ride. I'll see you guys later."

"Wait a sec," Lucas says, setting down his fork. "There's something I wanted to ask you."

"Nope, don't want any eggs." Danny makes a face. "While I'm thrilled that you made them, I smell a distinct burnt scent, and I'm in a no-burnt-eggs kind of mood."

"Not what I was going to ask. Would you have any objection if I made some changes around here?" My heart leaps with excitement when he waves a hand around at the lackluster décor.

"Absolutely not," Danny says, looking like he's holding back a smile—with a lot of effort. "This place has looked boring for years, but I wasn't about to complain. Free rent and all that."

"It's not free, you—"

"Yes, I'm your indentured servant." He rolls his eyes, then glances at me. "Good luck thanking him for anything, Delia. He's impossible."

"In addition to being perfect?" I ask, because that's actually the most spot-on description of Lucas I can think of. Perfect and impossible.

"Yes," he says with a chuckle. "Yes, exactly."

Then he leaves, humming a tune under his breath.

I turn to look at Lucas, feeling excitement humming beneath my skin. "Did you mean it?"

He grins. "You're the one who said I don't make a habit of saying things I don't mean. My parents had this place professionally decorated before they handed over the keys. I've never really liked it, but I haven't felt moved to do anything about it. But when I brought you here last night, I saw it with new eyes."

ANGELA CASELLA

"This is probably the best news I've ever gotten in my life," I say, pushing my eggs away.

"Good enough that you don't want to finish breakfast?"

I grimace. "Sorry, Danny's right. There's something about burnt eggs."

"Thank God you said so. Can we get breakfast burritos?"

"You can. I'm getting a pink donut with sprinkles. I need to get inspired."

He laughs and reaches over to tuck hair behind my ear, the gesture so casual, so sweet, I feel a swelling in my chest. "Don't get too inspired, Sunshine. There will be no pink, no sparkles, and absolutely no bedazzling of any kind."

"Hey," I say, swatting his hand, "I can read a room." I wave around. "Like this room, bereft of personality. Let's make it look like Lucas and Danny, okay?"

His grin is positively vulgar. "Ridiculously handsome and full of charm?"

"Yes, that's obviously what I meant. I can work within someone's style. I'm good at helping people redecorate. It's one of the things I do for Granddaughter for Rent."

"Really?" he asks, getting up and grabbing my plate. "There's nothing about it on your website." He empties both of them into the trash, then rinses them and puts them in the dishwasher.

"Stalking me?" I tease.

"Unabashedly." He pauses in what he's doing, then turns to face me. "I meant what I said the other day. I'd like to help you with your business, but I don't want you to think I'm doing it because it's not good enough or *you're* not good enough. It's just... I like—"

"Using your powers of good and evil for the people you care about," I say with a nod. I make the Boy Scout sign, or at least I try—I hadn't seen it for years before the other day, and now I only half-heartedly remember it. "I get it. I'm okay with taking your advice, Lucas. I know you're good at what you do."

256

"All of it?" he asks with a smirk.

"All of it," I confirm. Mira would be proud of the innuendo I pour into my voice.

"You do want to leave the apartment, don't you?" he says, stalking over and sweeping me out of my chair. I squeal as he lifts me out of my seat and twirls me through the air. "Because you're not talking like someone who wants to spend a minute out of my bed today."

"I don't want to," I admit. "But I'm at an impasse, because I also really, really want to help you redecorate your apartment."

"I guess we can arrange that," he says, dipping his head to kiss me. "Are you going to wear my shirt?"

"I'll tie the bottom up so it doesn't look like I'm swimming in it."

"I like that. I like that people are going to look at you and know whose shirt it is." He gazes at me through hooded eyes that make me second-guess the whole leaving this apartment plan, until I take another look at the apartment. There's nothing here that marks it as his—or as a home. I want to help him with that.

"Now let's go spend your money."

We do just that. And because we're spending it on him, I don't feel self-conscious about it. We go to four different furniture stores and spend the day laughing as we lounge on sofas and pretend we're Roberta and Bappy, Constance and her fictionalized version of Leonard, and several other characters we make up on the spot. A man with chronic fatigue syndrome and his insomniac soulmate, a butcher and her vegetarian love.

He chooses a red sofa and a checkered chair, a fluffy white rug that looks positively ideal for some fireside fun, and curtains with a geometric design. He's pretty sure Danny will love them, and if I hadn't already melted inside, I'd be like a popsicle left out in the sun.

We're in one last store to look for some things for the bathroom— a shower curtain and a few knickknacks that don't look like they were purchased wholesale from a manufacturer of beachside bath-rooms—when Lucas's eyes catch on something behind me.

"You need that," he says, grinning.

I turn, and a sound of surprised delight escapes me, because he's right—my instinctive response is that my soul needs the quilt on display. It's designed to look like mermaid scales, some of them rendered in shiny fabric. I glance at the price tag and flinch. It's over three hundred dollars.

"No, I don't need it," I say, but I let myself edge close enough to reach out and touch it. The fabric feels lush under my fingertips, surprisingly soft, even in the metallic parts. "It's lovely, though. It's going to make some mermaid very happy."

"This one," he insists, gathering it up into his arms.

"Lucas."

He pauses, studying me. "Delia, you told me you don't want me to buy you things because you're worried you'll send the message that all I have to offer is my money." He smiles. "And, obviously, my resemblance to Snow White. But I don't want to buy this to impress you. I want to do it because it would be a travesty if you don't have this blanket. I'm in a position to do things for you, and sometimes I'm going to have to insist on it. Like after you spent all morning helping me redecorate my apartment."

I raise my eyebrows. "So you're saying it's an exchange?" It's hard not to think back to the way he showed up to Constance's house with those wrapped gifts, wanting to be forgiven and presenting a package.

"No." He meets my gazing, unflinching. "I'm saying if you get to be good to me, then I damn well get to be good to you too. So you can expect more of it." Neither of us say anything for a beat, and then he adds, "I have this money. I might not have done anything for it, but I have it. And I need to use it in ways that don't make me feel like shit. Helping people, like we were doing earlier. Investing in businesses that wouldn't make it otherwise. Doing things for the people I care about." He pounds a hand on his chest. "That feels good to me, Delia. It feels right."

I can't argue with that, and I'll be honest, I don't want to.

I nod, then swallow the lump in my throat and admit, "I have a hard time letting people take care of me."

Smiling softly, almost sadly, he lifts a hand to my cheek and kisses me. "So do I. Let's change that, shall we?"

twenty-eight

DELIA

I CALL Mira after I get home from the furniture shopping spree so I can fill her in on the past few days.

She waits until I run out of words, then says, "I revoke my earlier comments about Jeremy. It was clearly Lucas's pogo stick you were destined to ride." I thank her for her always stellar advice, then tell her that Shauna and I will be coming to the bar tonight. It's her busiest night, something I should have thought of but didn't, but she promises to pop by sporadically to talk to us.

When I get off the phone, I tell Doris everything, except for all of the sex, of course. I let her infer that from the rosy glow she keeps mentioning.

She beams at me and pats me on the back. "I had my doubts at first, but he's a very fine boy." That's a real upgrade from Thomas being an "okay boy," but I don't point that out. She's already cross with Thomas for complaining so much about having to drop them off last night.

Ross's hearing aid arrives soon after that, and Doris and I are so excited we insist on doing an unboxing video, which he barely tolerates. "I'm so thrilled I'll be able to hear everyone now," he says flatly for my phone camera. "Really feel like I've been missing out."

"I mean, you did think Lucas was a circus performer," I say. "So at least you won't walk around misconstruing everything that's said to you."

He shrugs, but I can tell he's holding back a laugh. "The world's a more interesting place when you hear what you want to."

Doris calls him a curmudgeon and kisses him, and I feel a warm, gooey feeling in my chest. I've always wanted to find a love like theirs —the kind that lasts for decades—but I'd started to think it wasn't possible for me. Maybe I was looking in all the wrong places, though, or not really looking at all. Maybe—

I'm getting ahead of myself again, miles ahead, something that's reflected back at me a few hours later when I'm sitting at the bar at Glitterati with Shauna.

"You're falling for him," she says. "I can always tell." From her tone, I can't decide whether she's pleased by this power of hers or upset with me for being foolish enough to fall for a man's bullshit.

"Fast and hard," I admit.

She mimes fanning herself. "It's been a long time since I've fallen fast and hard."

I have to laugh. Shauna's the kind of person who immediately sets the people around her at ease just by virtue of being herself. It's her likable thing, although she has many. She stares at me with a knowing look as she stirs her In a Mermaid Mood with the mermaid swizzle stick. Mira named and designed that cocktail after me, and she poured one for each of us when we first arrived. "He's a looker," she says. "I'll give you that."

"He's more than just a looker." My voice is dreamy, and I pinch the side of my thigh, because I really *do* need to wake up.

"Good," Shauna says with a wicked glint in her eyes. "The last thing you want is one of those guys who just likes to watch."

She surprises laughter out of me. "True. That would be anti-climactic."

"In every sense of the word, my friend. Now, I heard through the grapevine that my grandfather got pantsed in water aerobics yesterday. Would you happen to know anything about that?"

"What?" I ask, my mouth falling open.

"My grandmother told me your landlady was going to be our inside person. There were lots of winks and nudges, so I figured something would be going down, and when I found out about this..."

Would Doris have forgotten to mention such a pivotal thing? Then again, I was away from home for most of the day and all of last night, and our dinner was interrupted.

"Can I text Doris?" I ask. "I don't know if I can go much longer without getting every last detail possible."

Shauna laughs. "Of course. I was hoping you would. And if she is behind this, I'm guessing Nana will want to buy her a drink."

"Doris only drinks one Manhattan a week."

"Then Nana will buy her a truly fantastic one to make it count."

> Doris, did you pants Frank at water aerobics? Why didn't I know about this? Constance's granddaughter and I require all the details.

Looking up, I ask, "Did your grandfather tell you what happened?"

She appears slightly amused, slightly sad, when she says, "Nah, Phoenix—that's the instructor's name—livestreams the class. As you can imagine, it got a lot of interest today. I saw a clip in one of those local social media groups that has nothing better to do than create drama. Of course, I love the drama, but I don't usually take part in it. Or see my family members in it. I'm not really talking to Grandpa Frank right now. He seems to represent everything that's bad about men. I mean, seriously, talk about walking stereotype."

"Is there a stereotype about water aerobics instructors and fish rooms?"

She twirls a finger through the air. "I was thinking on a broader scale, but maybe there should be. Does anything say late-in-life crisis like buying a room full of fish? I mean, that used to be Nana's art room."

"I didn't know Constance did art," I say, perking up.

"Yeah, she mostly draws and paints, but she does some sculpture too. She's the one who got me into clay. I definitely didn't get the art bug from Grandpa Frank. His idea of art is a bottle of beer with the cap off."

"How long have you lived with them?" I ask, because this is something I've wondered about. She seems so comfortable there, so settled in.

"Since I was eleven," she says as she plays with the swizzle stick again. "My parents died in a car crash when I was a kid, so they finished raising me. Mostly Nana, but Grandpa Frank used to bring me to taekwondo matches before he turned into an asshole."

"I'm sorry," I say, but it doesn't feel like nearly enough.

"That he's an asshole or that my parents died?" she asks, her mouth lifting in wry amusement. It's funny, because she's made her dislike for Leonard obvious, but she reminds me a little of him. They both find humor in dark places, or everywhere, really. That's another likable thing. The world is so full of dark and light, and if you can find places to smile when you're in the thick of both, then you're automatically ahead of the pack.

"I'm sorry for both things."

She takes a sip of her drink, nods in approval, then says, "Thanks. It was a long time ago—my parents, not Grandpa Frank's assholery."

I think about what Constance said about him giving her chlamydia. I'm guessing he's been a bit of a jerk for a while now, but Shauna doesn't need to hear that. He might be a terrible husband but a perfectly adequate grandfather.

My sister hurries down the bar toward us, nearly tripping in her heels. "What did I miss?"

"My dead parents," Shauna says, putting up a finger. "My grandfather getting pantsed." Another finger. "And your sister being positively *gooey* for Lucas Burke."

She knows who he is now, on account of Constance having told her. This came as a surprise to me, because I wasn't aware that Constance knew. Then again, she's been buddy-buddy with Leonard from the first day of shooting, and it doesn't surprise me that he chose to tell her rather than let her make the discovery on her own. He may not have trusted Lucas enough to stay in Asheville all those years ago, but it's obvious he trusts him now. He's protective of him, and also of the narrative of what happened. Understandably so.

Mira whistles, then flinches, probably realizing it's a no-go to whistle for someone's dead parents. "Sorry, new friend of Delia's. But seriously. All of that went down in five minutes?"

"We're efficient chatters," Shauna says.

"Of course, I already knew about Lucas," Mira tells her. "You can tell just by looking at her. She has that look of a woman who's been satisfied by a—"

"Can we get some help over here?" grumbles a man standing a few people down from us. "Your friends already have drinks. *I've* been waiting for five minutes." His date glances around, bored or embarrassed. Maybe he's hoping he can reclaim her interest by being difficult, because he says, "I'd like to talk to your manager about this. Now."

"Of course, sir," Mira says as sweetly as if sugar wouldn't melt in her mouth. "And what would you like to say to them?"

"To lodge a complaint about you," he sputters, his cheeks getting redder. He has that ruddy appearance of one who's quick to anger and dissatisfaction. Doris says it's the shade of a man who lacks decorum. "He should have better control over his staff."

"I'll have a very strongly worded conversation with myself about it later, *sir*," Mira says. "I'll laugh, I'll cry. It'll be a whole production. In the meantime, is there anything I can do for you?"

It takes him a solid five seconds for him to realize this means *she's* the manger, and when he does, he mutters something about bad reviews and hustles his poor date out of the place.

"There goes your online review ranking," I say worriedly, then take a sip of my drink, needing some of the mermaid goodness to wash down the encounter.

I've already written Mira a five-star review, obviously.

"I don't know about that," Shauna says. "If you ask me, one-star reviews are the most compelling feedback out there. I mean, you look at that dude"—she waves at his retreating back—"and you just know he's going to write the kind of review that will drive sensible people here in droves. I mean, would you go to a place that guy reviewed well? He was wearing a *tie*." Here she waves a hand at Mira. "No offense, but this is not a tie kind of bar."

"I'd have been offended if you'd said it was," Mira replies with a straight face.

"So, yeah, he'll rant and rave about how the manager has a sense of humor and friends, and the drinks look so fucking delicious but he never got to lift one to his withered lips, which have never known the touch of a woman, and yeah...presto, you've got yourself some new customers."

Mira brightens. "I like the way you think. My sister showed me a few pictures of your art. Do you have a website? I think your aesthetic vibes with mine. I'd love to get some of your stuff displayed in here."

"Sounds like you're dropping me a line, but I'm not about to object," Shauna says with a laugh, but she seems delighted. I'm delighted too. It's wonderful to see my worlds crossing over, and Mira's right—Shauna's aesthetic vibes with ours.

She gives Mira her information and then my sister hurries off to help half a dozen of the more patient patrons on this side of the bar. Her backup bartender is seeing to the rest.

Shauna smiles at me. "I'm glad you brought me here. I like this place. It's exactly the kind of place I enjoy and my ex *hated* going to. All the more reason to be single, huh?" She gives a conciliatory shrug. "Or to date a hottie with a body who's good in the sack and lets you go wherever you want. Of course, even if you find said hottie, he might eventually leave you for a water aerobics teacher who's thirty years younger than you."

"Are we sure she's actually in her fifties?" I ask. "Doris said she looks like she's had a bunch of work done. Maybe it's not as big of an age difference as we're thinking."

She makes a thinking face. "Actually, now that you mention it... I mean, she *says* she's in her fifties, and everyone knows people don't lie on social media. I mean, perish the thought."

"Doesn't matter, I guess," I say. "He thinks she's in her fifties, and it's that perception he likes, I'm guessing. Or maybe the whole water connection, although you'd think she would have wanted to rescue those fish if she were so in tune with the water."

As if on cue, my phone buzzes on the bar, and I straighten. "It's Doris. And she wrote a paragraph."

It's her typical texting style. Once she sent me something so long my phone cut it off.

I tap into the message, Shauna crowds in close, and we read it together:

I'll admit that it didn't quite go as planned. We thought it would be quite funny to accidentally pull off Frank's swimming trousers on camera so everyone could see his shriveled noodle, but it wasn't nearly as shriveled as it should have been after being in the cold water. You know my vision isn't what it once was, but we both got an eyeful. You can imagine our surprise! He didn't seem to mind a bit until I told him I'd seen a strange growth to the right of his ballsack. There wasn't one, mind you, but I didn't like that self-satisfied smile of his, especially after what you told me about your friend Constance. He tried to show it to another classmate, a doctor, who didn't take kindly to being flashed. The man splashed him to get him to stand down—and he splashed back, and before we knew what had occurred it was like a hurricane had broken out across the pool. Very immature. The children's aquatics coach had to intervene. I don't think she was at all pleased with Phoenix. She accused her of making the YMCA a brothel. Then Phoenix pulled down the front of her swimsuit, and said, "There's nothing wrong with nudity, Sharon. It's much worse to be a prude." I think she's going to get fired, to be honest. Which is a pity, really. She may be a hussy, but she's a VERY good instructor. Not afraid of turning on some good, fast rhythms.

Shauna looks up at me with shining eyes, and I see it again—that similarity to Leonard she would never acknowledge. "Can you please screenshot that and send it to me? We're about to make Nana's night."

"I would be thrilled to make Constance's night." I send it to her, then send the screenshot to Lucas and Leonard too, because I'm absolutely sure they'll want to know. "But I have to say I'm shocked that Doris didn't mention any of this before now. I mean, that's not the kind of story you keep to yourself."

"Maybe she didn't want to tell you Grandpa Frank has a nice dingdong in front of her husband."

I nod, although there's a very minimal chance Ross would have even heard her prior to this afternoon. "That's possible. Does it bother you to hear that about your grandfather's sizable...appendage?"

I can't bring myself to say or think of it as his dick or cock. It would be like admitting that Ross has one.

She gives me a dubious look. "You really think my grandmother hasn't mentioned it dozens of times within my earshot?"

Fair point.

I study her for a moment. "Can I ask you something?"

"You can ask. Doesn't mean I'm going to respond."

Also a fair point.

"Why are you so convinced Leonard's bad news? I mean, he's been helpful with the fish room, and he's always really nice to you. Constance seems to think the world of him."

Her face hardens. "And for more than fifty years she thought the world of my grandfather, and here he is flopping his dick around at the YMCA and pursuing a woman who may or may not be lying about being thirty years younger than him. No one's going to tell you she has great taste in men, herself included."

"Maybe she just made one mistake," I suggest.

Her eyes drill into me, making me slightly uncomfortable. "Delia, one mistake is all you need to make."

There's no denying it's true. A week ago, I felt the same way about Lucas, and yet...

"But if you don't try at all, you fail anyway."

"There's no failing at love if you have a good vibrator," she says with a grin that hides more than it shows. "Self-love is the best kind there is."

"Are you still in love with your ex?" I decide to ask.

"No," she says flatly. "But I'm not over what happened. If anyone screwed with my self-love, it was those two."

"Are you sure you should go through with being involved in the wedding?"

"I absolutely should not, but I'm going to anyway," she says, as stubborn as any granddaughter of Constance's would be. "Because fuck them. They don't get to make me feel this way."

I could point out that they did—and are—making her feel this way, and that being involved in the wedding is sure to make her feel worse, but I don't. Sometimes being a friend is waiting to give advice until it's ready to be received, and it's obvious she'll close down if I push.

My phone buzzes, and I laugh as a I glance down at the screen.

Lucas: *There's video footage of the whole thing.*
Lucas: [*Video link.*]
Lucas: *Don't worry. Someone put an eggplant emoji over his dick, and two mangoes over the instructor's tits.*
Lucas: *Breasts. I meant breasts.*
Leonard: *Fuuuck. If I'd known about this plan, I could have stormed in at the end of class and demanded revenge for what he did to my woman. Or thrown a fish at him.*
Leonard: *Actually, that's what I would have done. I would have gone in, thrown a fish at him, and left without any explanation. That would have really fucked with his subconscious.*
Leonard: *You're with Shauna? Tell Shauna that.*

I show Shauna, and she rolls her eyes. "Child."

"Maybe," I admit. "But he's a funny child."

"Yes, he's capable of being moderately amusing. Not nearly as amusing as he thinks he is, mind you."

"And you *did* admit you find him attractive."

She blows out a breath, making the ends of her purple hair sway. "I find John Mayer attractive too, despite the deep disappointment it makes me feel in myself. I certainly won't be sending him my panties."

"So are we going to watch the video?" I ask.

She grins back at me. "Obviously."

Before we can, my phone buzzes again, this time with a message directly from Lucas.

> Text me when you're ready to leave. I'll give you both a ride home.

Shauna reads it and meets my gaze. "Does this mean you got the one man in the world who looks like that and *isn't* a raging asshole? I'm bringing you the next time I buy scratch-offs."

I don't answer her, because I'm still looking at the message. I run a finger over it, because it's a dear thing that deserves some love.

Then I answer:

> I will.

We stay for another hour, then two, Mira stopping by at increasingly short intervals as the bar gets ever busier. By the time we step outside to meet Lucas, we're a little unsteady on our feet.

"Delia..." Shauna says, "I think this is the beginning of a beautiful friendship."

I burst out laughing.

"What?" she asks, propping a hand on her hip. "Not a fan of classic cinema?"

"No, it's your grandmother. She said the exact same thing to me last week."

She starts laughing, harder and harder until her whole body's bobbing with it. "Of course she did. What can I say? When the woman's right, she's right."

"She is, and you're both my friends."

It's true, and I feel fantastic. Without meaning to, I've held back from making connections with other women my age—from doing anything that might make it feel like I'm replacing Nat. But if I know one thing about Nat, it's that she wouldn't want me to be alone.

There's a car at the curb, idling, and I can see the driver watching us through its tinted windows. They're dark enough to mask their features except for their general shape, which is that of a man. There's no reason to believe this person has anything to do with us, but a chill runs down my spine. It's in the angle of the person's head, the scrutiny that I can feel pounding into us. The window starts to inch down, and I suck in a breath, waiting.

Before I can do or say anything, Lucas pulls up behind the mystery person and opens his driver's side door. When he gets out, the other car instantly speeds away, the window still slightly open, driving way too fast for a downtown street full of pedestrians.

"You animal!" Shauna shouts. "Go back to Great Falls!"

"Where's Great Falls?" I ask through the buzz of *not right* in my brain.

"I don't know. But we both know it was a tourist from some-where. They always drive like they don't realize rules apply to them."

That buzzing in my head gets louder.

"Hey, are you okay?" Lucas asks, approaching us and wrapping his arms around me.

I let myself sink into his hold for a second before going with my gut. "Yes, but something wasn't right about that car. The person inside was watching us. I think it was a man."

His expression hardens, and I know he believes me. There's relief in that, in being believed without any questions or buts.

"Did you see what kind of car it was? I was looking at you."

"It was dark, black or navy blue. The shape looked a little bit like your car."

"What, you think he was some kind of perv?" Shauna asks, squinting in the direction of the car.

"Or someone my parents sent to spy on her," Lucas says bitterly.

twenty-nine

LUCAS

IF MY PARENTS are trying to hurt me, they're doing it through surrogates, the same way they do everything in life. I was even born to a surrogate. When I was a little kid, I thought that meant I'd been adopted. It took me a while to realize there's one set of rules for regular people, and another for those who were born rich. Why go through a pregnancy when you can hire someone to do it for you? It was a disappointing day when I got my genome tested and found out that I am, without a doubt, related to both of my parents.

I call Deacon the second we get into my Range Rover, Delia in front and Shauna in the back. He says he hasn't been able to find any connections between my parents and anyone on the movie set or find firm evidence that anyone was hired to follow me. Both pieces of news are a relief, although assuredly not a guarantee. I give him the description of the car, but I don't know much beyond that it had tinted windows—darker, based on Delia's description, than the allowable amount in North Carolina—and looks slightly like mine.

I'm tempted to text my parents, or maybe drive over to their mansion and tell them point blank that they have to stop or I will stop them. But if they're really tracking Delia and me, that's probably what they want—a knee-jerk reaction. The sensible thing to do is to have Deacon keep working the case and to spend as much time around Delia as I can. I know I won't feel assured of her safety unless I'm personally around to protect her.

It's not logical, maybe. I'm no bodyguard. But no one could be more motivated than me.

Silence descends on the car after I drop off Shauna. I cast a glance at Delia as I drive back in the direction of her house—and my apartment.

"I'd like you to stay at the apartment tonight. I know you have your reading tomorrow morning, but there'll be plenty of time to pick up your costume beforehand. We'll bring Ross and Doris breakfast." My brain is urging me to insist, not ask, but I know Delia wouldn't like it.

"Thank you, Lucas," she says, and I can hear the "but" from a mile away. "But I'd be worried about leaving Ross and Doris. If someone is following me, then they know I live with them."

I can't begin to guess what messing with Ross and Doris would do for my parents—it would be an extremely roundabout way of fucking with me. But I don't say so. She's worried, and she has every right to be worried. At the same time—

"What would you do if someone *did* show up?" I ask, my brow furrowed, my hands white-knuckled on the wheel. "Throw a can of beans at their head?"

I can feel her considering it.

"That wouldn't do much, Delia. I saw you throw that fish filter to Leonard the other day. He was two feet away and you missed."

"He moved at the last second."

"And you think some asshole home invader would stand still?"

She's quiet for a second, then says, "You really think there's someone following us?"

"Probably not," I say, tapping the wheel, the pressure in my head suddenly unbearable. "But I'm not going to take chances with you. If something happened to you..." Suddenly my throat feels too tight, as if it's not working the way it has for the past three or so decades. "And if it was my fault? It would break me."

I feel her hand lower onto my thigh. It anchors me. It pulls me back. "You can stay," she says. "But be aware that Ross snores so loudly it can be heard in my basement apartment, and you're probably going to get asked two dozen questions, to put it conservatively. And there will be no funny business of any kind. If either of them walked in—"

"No funny business," I pledge, lifting a hand off the wheel. My throat is working again, probably because a thousand pounds have been lifted off my shoulders. "I don't want Doris or Ross walking in on us. Something tells me we'd be hearing about it for the next ten years."

She gives me a sidelong look, and I realize what I said.

Ten years, like we'd still be together in a decade.

I wait for the thought to terrify me.

I wait for the sensation of being trapped.

It doesn't come.

We're both quiet for a few minutes as I navigate the traffic and then turn onto her road.

"They'll be asleep when we get there, right?" I ask.

She looks at the clock embedded in the dashboard and laughs. "For about two hours now, yes. We'll have to be really quiet when we go in. Ross might be asleep in front of the TV."

"So his own house-shaking snoring doesn't wake him up, but the sound of my footsteps might?"

"Yes," she says, very seriously. "It's like what they said at the Rolf Estate. We need to be gentle with the floor."

"I think we can manage it, Sunshine. We haven't gotten kicked off set yet."

"We've only been on set two days."

I park the car on the road beside the house and reach over to touch her cheek. "So maybe Monday will be our lucky day." I run my fingers across her jaw, letting myself acknowledge how much she means to me. I can't deny it feels as if something has been pulling us together. Insisting. And I've never had the slightest desire to push back or say no.

I lean in and kiss her softly. "Thank you for letting me stay."

"I've never brought a man here before," she says in a burst of words.

"Never?" I ask, liking that I'm the one she decided to bring, even if I did back her into it.

"Never. They really are going to interrogate us. But the good news—or at least I think it's good news—is that Ross has his new hearing aid."

"I'm going for not good news." I tuck her hair behind her ear, then reach over to unbuckle her seat belt. "He seemed pretty impressed by me when he thought I was in the circus."

"He'll be much more impressed when he knows you know how to fix things."

We get out and make our way to the front door, where she pauses. "I think we should take our shoes off."

"Really?"

The look on her face is my answer. I won't deny her this, not when she's stretching her comfort zone to let me stay, so I do it.

When we walk through the front door, shoes in hand, the TV is blaring with some Ken Burns war documentary, and sure enough, Ross is splayed out on the couch, snoring.

Delia lifts a finger to her lips in the universal *shh* signal, which is so laughable I almost do the opposite of *shh*-ing. I doubt he'd hear us if we decided to run laps around the room. But I said I'd follow her rules, and that's exactly what I intend to do. We set our shoes beside the front door, and I try to focus on soft footfalls as I follow her to the door that presumably leads to the basement.

When she opens the door to the stairs, I have to smile. There are fairy lights threaded all over the ceiling and side of the walls, and we head downward into the soft, magical glow.

The small finished space at the bottom is all Delia—a big, plush rug in turquoise, pink, and orange, a large bed with a shimmering canopy and the blanket we got this afternoon. Colorful paintings and prints cover all of the walls.

"It's like we stepped into your head," I say in an undertone.

She looks slightly self-conscious, her hands wrapped around her arms. "And do you like it in there?"

I pull her close, tucking her under my chin. "Nowhere else I'd rather be."

She turns and wraps her arms around me, getting on her tiptoes. "I know what I just said, Lucas," she whispers into my hair, "but would you like to take a shower with me? I'm reasonably sure neither of them would walk into a room that has a running shower."

"Of course," I say. "I've been wanting to see my mermaid in the water."

She kisses my neck, and just like that, I'm an impatient man. I lift her into my arms and carry her to the bathroom.

"Are you doing this again just because I said I'd be too heavy for you that one time?" she asks, laughing lightly.

"No. I'm doing it because I like feeling you in my arms. But if you're asking if the challenge would have been enough motivation, sure."

When we get to the bathroom, I flick on the light, Delia still in my arms. I smile as I set her on her feet, because there's a collection of seashells arranged on top of the bathroom cabinet. I like the image of her collecting them at the beach, preferably wearing a bikini.

"You like the beach, Sunshine?"

"Love it," she says, reaching for the bottom of my shirt. I let her pull it off me.

"I'm going to take you someday. Next summer, maybe."

There's a glimmer in her eyes, and I know she's noticed it again.

Next summer. This time I meant for her to. Because I want her to know this is no fling for me.

"I'd like that."

She reaches for the hem of her dress, but I stop her. "Let me do that."

I lift the silky fabric over her soft curves. I'm hard by the time it's pooled on the floor at my feet, my mermaid girl in a yellow bra and panties. She's so beautiful it hurts to look at her, but it's a pain I'm more than grateful for.

"You're exquisite."

"You're full of flattery."

I trace her side, stopping at the bra so I can take it off. The panties follow. They're pretty, but she's even prettier without them.

"No, that was purely factual."

I reach over to turn on the shower, and she starts in on my belt, slowly unfastening it. She does it so purposefully, so carefully, that I'm half crazed by the time she has it undone. When she unfastens the button of my pants, it's hard for me to remember my own name.

Glancing up at me, she pushes down my pants and boxer briefs. I toe them off, remove my socks, and tug her to me for a kiss. Her scent surrounds me, both familiar and alluring.

Breaking away, she takes a step toward the shower and pulls me with her.

"Delia," I say. "I need to get a condom."

"No, you don't. I'm on birth control, and I'm guessing you've been tested since the last time—"

"I have." I don't want her to have to spend any more time thinking about the way it used to be with me. I don't want to think about it either. I was desperate to prove something to myself, although I'm still not sure what it was. And, fuck, I'd be lying if I didn't admit it was fun. Enjoying the money. The status. The *admiration.* Not feeling like I had any debts to be paid. But it was the kind of enjoyment that gutters out quickly, and it couldn't compare to the way I feel now. These last weeks, I've been finding the kind of meaning that really matters, even if at times it has felt like a one step forward, two steps back process—and to have Delia offer herself to me like this...

To know she wants to find a way to be even closer to me...

Fucking bliss.

"Are you sure?" I ask, running my hands over her, because I know I'll never get sick of learning her shape.

Her answer is to kiss me.

Well, all right then.

I reach my hand into the shower to check the temperature, adjust it, then pull the curtain back for her to step inside. She does, arching her head back into the hot spray with a look of satisfaction on her face as it soaks her long hair, turning it a deeper red. Her eyes are shut, her mouth lifted into a small smile of pure contentment. That warm feeling that's been hanging around in my chest stokes.

I step in after her, crowding her, because the bath tub really isn't big enough for both of us, but where there's a will there's a way is an old saying for a reason. When I put my hand on her hip, she makes a sound of happiness deep in her throat.

There's one of those frou-frou bath poofs hanging from a hook on the wall, and I get it down and froth some soap into it. Delia's still got her eyes closed as she finishes soaking her hair, water droplets running over her body, coursing between her tits and her legs.

"If I died looking at you like this, I'd die a happy man."

Her eyes pop open. "Please don't. I'd much prefer it if you didn't die."

So I start running the poof over her body, using my palm to glide the suds over her breasts, under her hair, and between her legs. She closes her eyes again, humming with pleasure, as the water rinses the soap off her.

"Your turn," she says, taking the poof from me. She gives me a perplexed look, probably trying to figure out the logistics of switching places in the shower, so I eliminate the need for guesswork by picking her up, lifting her above the edge of the bathtub, and whirling around.

She's laughing as I set her on her feet. So am I, but I don't laugh long, because she starts gliding that poof over me with purpose. Then her hand is on my hard cock, firmly fisting it up and down. That sensation, paired with the water pounding on my back, is almost enough to make me come. But I'll be damned if I miss out on taking her like this, in the shower, her hair plastered to her shoulders and back, droplets of water coursing over her.

"Stop," I say, putting my hand over hers. "I want to fuck you against the wall, without anything between us. I want to come inside you."

The look of raw need on her face puts me over the edge. I step back into the water, rinsing the soap off, and then prowl the two steps to her, claiming her wet lips. My hands roam over her body, seeing what it feels like under the water, slick and hot.

I dip my fingers between her legs, searching for the spot that will make her moan into my mouth, and I play with her there, the water pounding into my back. My cock is desperate with need, especially now that it's been given free rein, and I edge back. "Put your hands on the wall for me, Sunshine."

She turns around, her hands trembling a little as she presses them to the wall.

"Get on your toes."

"Aren't you too tall to do it this way?" she asks, her voice thick with desire. Good.

"I'd break my back to fuck you in the shower," I say, palming her ass. She's lifted it toward me, as if presenting herself to my cock, and it's the most beautiful sight I've seen in my life.

"That's not very...practical," she says, pausing to inhale as my fingers dip into her, making sure she's ready for me.

She's wet all over, but especially there.

"When it comes to you, I couldn't care less about what's practical," I say, lowering enough to line myself up. I press in slightly, enough that I know it's at the right angle, then grab her hips and stroke in.

Being inside her without anything between us...the feeling is indescribable.

"You feel incredible," I say, my lips pressed to her ear. I bite the lobe softly. "Actually, incredible is a small word for it, but my brain's not working anymore."

She laughs, but as I pull out and thrust in again, giving her clit the attention it deserves with one hand and holding her hip in the other, it cuts off. When she rocks back against me, her hands still pressed to the wall, it's a challenge to hold on to my sanity. Even more so when she looks back over her shoulder, watching as I fuck her, her hair a beautiful mess around her face, her lips and face wet from the water. My legs are probably going to resent me for this position tomorrow, but I meant what I said—pain is a small price to pay.

I can feel her tightening around me, the water driving down on us.

"Lucas, I'm close," she says.

And I thank all that's holy, because I wasn't going to last much longer, no matter how iron my will.

"Come for me, Sunshine," I say, my hand giving her another stroke as I pound harder into her. "Come for me."

She does—and the clutching feeling around my cock drives me over the edge. I come hard enough that I'm seeing stars, and I hold her body to me with one arm while I press the other against the wall next to hers.

She tilts her head to the side and kisses me. It's wet from the water, and it's perfect, and I'm falling for this woman much faster than I'd ever believed possible.

We get out and dry off. I don't have a change of clothes, so I wear boxer briefs to bed. I'd go without them, but there's a chance someone might come downstairs in the morning to get Delia, and I don't want to go full frontal in front of Doris or Ross. She puts on an oversized T-shirt from her dresser drawer.

"What?" she asks, catching me watching.

"I like looking at you."

"It's not that kind of look," she says accusatorially.

She's right. "I like seeing you in a T-shirt, but I figured you'd have some kind of elaborate Victorian nightgown."

Her eyes alight, she searches through the top drawer of her dresser and pulls out a pink nightgown with lots of ribbons and lace. "Like this one?"

"Yes, Sunshine, like that one."

Smiling, she puts it back. "Sometimes I just like to be comfortable."

I pull her to me and kiss the top of her head. "I'm glad you feel you can be comfortable with me."

Pulling away enough to look at me, she says, "Do you feel it, too, Lucas? It's like we know each other better than we should be able to. Like we were destined to find each other."

"You know I don't believe in that kind of thing," I say, caressing her cheek to take away any sting that might cause her.

"You don't have to believe it for it to be true. You said you and your friends came to Glitterati before, earlier in the summer. Do you remember what day it was?"

"No," I say, because I'm not a walking calendar app. But it seems important to her, so I pull out my phone. I remember that day, in particular, because we'd helped Drew do some work on his girl-friend's grandmother's house. I find it on the calendar, then toss the phone onto the bed.

"June 3rd," I say.

Her smile makes that warmth inside me give an answering pulse.

"June 3rd was my birthday. I made a wish that the universe would bring something wonderful into my life."

"But wouldn't you have made the wish that night?" I say, my practical side forcing me to say it, even though I immediately feel like an asshole.

"We celebrated at lunch because Mira was going to have to work at night."

There's a ringing in my ears. Everything I was raised to believe revolts against the idea that there might be something larger at work here, that she might be—what, my soul mate? But I don't disbelieve it either. It feels like more than a coincidence, and this connection we have is undeniable.

So all I say is, "I have trouble believing it on a conceptual level, but yes, I feel it too."

Her expression is as if pure light has filled her to bursting, and it's impossible not to smile back at her. "Yes, you've gotten me to partially admit to feeling the presence of the universe. Are you proud of yourself?"

"Epically. Let's go to bed, Lucas."

We lie together, curled around each other, and I sleep better than I have in months. I feel a sense of deep peace—of being comfortable, again, in my own skin.

In the morning, I check my phone, and there's a message from my mother:

> We haven't heard from you, but I'm going to be ready for you, Burke. You're our only child.

thirty

DELIA

FOR THE SECOND TIME EVER, there are more adults than children at my mermaid reading. The first time it happened was after someone who worked at the community center hosting the event put posters up at a bar. The wrong message was conveyed, either from context or alcohol. Several horny men showed up expecting to see some kind of strip show and were sent away disappointed and without goody bags.

Today, I'm in an events room at a local bookstore, and the adults in question are all people I'm happy to see. Lucas, Danny, Leonard, and a man with dark brown hair and brown eyes, whom I'm guessing is the elusive Shane. He's dressed in a smart button-up shirt, rolled at the sleeves, and dark pants, as if he was in a suit and just took off his jacket and tie. Constance and Shauna also came, and so did Doris and Ross, primarily to meet the famous Constance. Mira's standing next to Shauna, wearing the My Sister is a Mermaid shirt she bought herself.

I came with Lucas, Doris, and Ross, and the others arrived after I'd gotten settled on my ocean—a soft blue blanket studded with seashells, starfish, and sparkles. My tail is fanned out to one side, and my hair is teased into elaborate waves with braids and seashells woven in. Lucas helped me fix it this morning, and even though he was clumsy at first, his big hands unsure of what to do, he insisted he wanted to help me. The sweetness made my heart swell. So does this gesture—because he must have invited them all.

They're hanging back while I do the reading, letting the little kids cluster in close, including one little girl, maybe four or five, who keeps reaching out to touch the gorgeous sunrise tail that Lucas got for me. I can't blame her.

Whenever she reaches for it, her mother pulls her back, her expression worried, but I pause in my storytelling to tell her it's okay.

"I like touching it too," I say.

The little girl's eyes light up, and she runs a hand over it reverently. "It's magical, Miss Delia."

That's exactly why I do this—it *is* magical.

At least for me. My friends must be bored, unless they're out of their minds with curiosity about what will happen next for Harmony and Echo, the best friends preparing for the Mermaid Ballet. It *is* a good book, but I have my doubts.

Doris and Constance have stepped away from the others. They appear to be in deep conversation, and Ross is standing beside them on his phone, probably playing Candy Crush. He'll grumble about it later, calling it "that damn game," but he can't seem to help himself. The guy who must be Shane keeps tapping his foot. Danny, beside him, has his phone out, and is either filming the reading or entertaining himself on YouTube. Lucas, though...

Lucas is grinning at me like he honestly couldn't think of anything he'd rather do.

I finish the books I brought to read, and my little friends line up to be photographed with me and receive a goody bag. The girl who touched my tail wraps both arms around my neck, and we're both laughing as the photographer takes our photo.

The children leave, ushered out by the events director, since no one wants to see a mermaid lose her tail, and she grins at me and gives a thumbs up as she shuts the curtain behind the last of them.

Lucas approaches me, bending to kiss my forehead. "Do I get a photo with you too, *Miss Delia*?"

The photographer, Madge, who does all of these events with me, grins. "Want a photo with your boyfriend?" She's said that word at least ten times since I introduced them an hour ago.

"Yes, please."

She has Lucas sit beside me, and Constance catcalls us just as Madge takes the shot.

"Didn't know this was going to be a photo shoot," Leonard says. "I would have worn my best clothes."

"Aren't *those* your best clothes?" Shauna shoots back. He's wearing an old rock band T-shirt and torn jeans.

"No," he says with a wink. "I'm saving those for our first date."

"Did you figure out why she hates him?" Lucas asks in an undertone as Madge takes a couple of candid shots.

I glance at them, making sure they're far enough away that they won't hear. They seem to be busy sniping at each other, so I reply, "I don't think she does hate him. I think she's attracted to him but doesn't want to be."

He makes a speculative face, and I nudge him. "Leonard might be a good guy, but I'm not sure we should push it. Give them some time to figure it out."

"You're right. Neither of them would respond well to pushing." He angles his head to the side, eyeing my tail. "Time to unzip you, or do you want me to carry you out of here?"

"Don't get any designs on this tail, Lucas. I refuse to let anything happen to it. If you want to make that particular fantasy come to pass, it'll have to be with the old one."

He presses a hand to his chest in mock offense. "Wouldn't dream of it."

Madge starts packing up her equipment, a self-satisfied look on her face.

"Can I get your card so I can order one?" Lucas asks her.

"Oh, I'll be sending them to Delia, don't you worry." She winks. "Free of charge this time, but if you start bringing around a new boyfriend each week, we'll have to revisit this conversation."

"I won't be," I say, looking at him, taking in all the ways he's changed over the last couple of weeks. When I met him, he looked like he had the weight of his world on his shoulders. Maybe he still does, but it's not so heavy when you have friends carrying it with you. "I think I'll keep this one around for a while."

"That's what I like to hear," he says. He unzips my tail, and I step out in my leggings.

"That just killed my mermaid fantasies," Leonard comments, nodding to the tail lying on the floor. "Looks like someone made sushi out of Ariel."

"Gross," Shauna says, rolling her eyes.

Mira clearly finds it funny, but she waves a hand at the "ocean" and says, "Why don't you make yourself useful, hotshot, and fold up the blanket."

He does it without any hesitation, because even if he'd like to come off as otherwise, Leonard is helpful.

"Did you introduce everyone?" I ask Lucas.

He nods. "I'm starting to doubt that Doris and Constance will ever stop talking." I glance over, and sure enough, they're still in the middle of an animated conversation—no longer hushed. Ross is nodding along beside them, pretending to listen but engrossed in his phone.

I glance back, and Lucas startles. "Oh, come meet Shane and Drew." He leads me over to the back of the room, where Shane's talking to Danny, who's still got his phone out.

I point to it as we make our approach. "Is Drew on the phone?"

"Yeah. Danny made me think the other day. I don't want to make

Drew feel left out just because he's not here. So we agreed to call him, and Danny volunteered as tribute."

Shane steps forward and shakes my hand. "Good to meet you, Delia. We've all been curious about the woman who slayed the player."

"Is that a Dungeons & Dragons reference?" I ask.

Shane whistles. "Told her about our old D&D games, huh? You *do* like her."

"Don't talk about them like they're past tense," comes a voice from the phone. Drew, presumably. "As soon as I'm back, they're on."

"Yeah, but who knows when that's going to happen," Danny says, his tone a little wistful. "I really need you back before we launch the game, man. I don't think I can go through that alone. You know I'm not much of a front man. Speaking of..." He lifts the phone so I can see the face on it.

Drew looks a little familiar, but then again, I've met his sister a couple of times. Also, while Asheville is a legitimate city, with around a hundred thousand people to its name, it can feel positively small. There are a few places where locals like to go, and if you go to them, you'll probably see the same people more than once. So sometimes I recognize people I don't know.

I wave, feeling an old self-consciousness rise up, but maybe that's because I'm wearing a giant shell bra and over-the-top mermaid makeup. "Good to meet you, Drew. I've heard a lot about you."

"And me?" Shane asks with a smirk.

"I guess I've heard a few things about you," I tease, because these guys like to mess with each other, and I remember Danny's word for him. He mentioned it at dinner the other night.

I'm grateful when Shane laughs, tipping his head back. It makes me feel like even if he's braggadocious, he's still one of them—part of this friend family Lucas has built for himself.

Leonard comes over to us, the ocean slung over his arms. "We going?"

"Where are we going?" I ask, taken aback.

"Romeo here is taking the whole gang to lunch," he says with a snort. "At the Biltmore. His treat, he says. His funeral, I say."

I look up at Lucas, a sense of wonder unfurling in me. When did he make these arrangements? We were together for most of the morning, except for an hour or so that I spent helping Doris out in the garden.

He tips my chin up, his touch sending pleasure tickling through my veins. "I thought we could both use some fun today, Sunshine. Mira brought you a shirt to change into." He smirks and eyes my seashell bra. "Or, if we're all very lucky, wear over your outfit."

I glance at my sister, and when she notices I'm looking, she pulls a shirt out of her purse and dances it around in the air. Shauna snort-laughs. It says "Mermaid," of course. We'll look ridiculous wearing our matching mermaid shirts, and I love the thought so much I instantly have tears in my eyes.

To be honest, this whole thing is putting tears in my eyes.

"We're really going to the Biltmore?" I ask, looking up at him. Trying to calculate how expensive it would be for him to get so many people through the gates.

Very expensive.

I know if I said something, he'd tell me he doesn't care, that he wants to be able to take care of his friends and me.

"I figure we've been spending time at the Rolf Estate. Might as well check out the competition."

"You know there's no competition. The Biltmore's at least two or three times bigger."

"No, but it's a beautiful day, and we might as well spend it in a beautiful place with our friends. Taste some subpar wine and complain about it. Check out the gardens. Maybe walk through the house and name all the rooms."

"Who are you, and what you have you done to Lucas Burke?"

Drew asks from the phone.

"You think he got pod-peopled?" Shane asks, scratching behind his ear. "He looks like Lucas, but he doesn't sound like him."

"Nah," Leonard says. "I've already discussed this with our buddy here. It's the Drew Affliction."

"There's a disease named after me now? Stellar," Drew says from the phone. Then, abruptly, he adds, "Gotta go, guys. Andy and I are going to the beach."

"*Drew Affliction*," Leonard mouths, and I find myself laughing even though I'm not totally sure why. In a conspiratorial undertone, Leonard adds, "What do you wanna bet his fiancée just walked out in a bikini?"

"What a hard life you lead," Danny says to Drew, lifting the phone and turning it back toward himself. "What a struggle."

"Uh-huh," I hear him say. "We still on for later?"

"Yeah. Goodbye, old friend."

"What's happening later?" I ask as he pockets his phone. It's truly none of my business, but I haven't met a question I didn't like.

"We're fixing some bugs on our game." He gives me a half smile. "Almost there."

But he doesn't seem joyful about the prospect, and I remember what he said about being a front man for the game. I can see why he wouldn't like that. He's perfectly personable, Danny, but he's no schmoozer. Probably not much of an extrovert either.

Maybe Lucas and I can talk it through later, come up with a solution for him.

In the meantime, I have a house full of rooms to name.

"We're going?" Ross says hopefully when he sees us walking toward the curtain.

"Yes, you old boot," Doris says fondly, although she clearly hasn't been paying attention to us until now. "Get with the program."

He releases a sigh. "There are only so many times I can hear about Frank's dick before I lose interest. Sue me, woman."

thirty-one

LUCAS

YESTERDAY WAS EASILY the best day of my life. Delia and I spent the afternoon and evening with the people who are important to us in an estate much grander than the Rolf Estate. We made a game of naming each of the rooms, and with so many people in our group, we actually managed it. Leonard won the unofficial contest by naming the library the Beast's Boner. Listening to him explain to Ross why he'd named it that would have been the highlight of my day if I hadn't also watched Delia dance around the rose garden.

Yes, she asked me to do it with her, and yes, I fucking did it. Shane took a video, of course, to document the day I finally lost both of my balls. I warned him he was in danger of losing his in a different way, and he wouldn't enjoy it nearly as much.

At the same time, I couldn't banish the memory of that car Delia saw, or the one idling on the road by Peggy. And I kept thinking about my mother glancing at the clock, wondering if I'd come. Or my father, tapping his fingers impatiently. How long did it take them to realize I wasn't coming? Did it hurt them?

Am I wrong for wanting it to?

When I finally checked my phone at around seven, right before we headed to Cedric's Tavern for our second meal on the estate, out in the garden behind the restaurant, there was a message from my mother.

> We raised you to show more civility than this, Burke. Cook made tea for three, and all her hard work went to waste. Your father and I miss you, though, and when you're ready, we'd like to have a talk. You owe us that, at the very least.

I tapped out a response and let *I owe you nothing* sit on the phone for a solid beat before erasing it and pocketing my phone. Responding would have given her satisfaction. Responding would have fed their need to control me—to get something out of me, even if it's not what they want.

Instead, I wrote a message to Deacon, asking him if he had any updates.

No go.

So I had dinner with my friends—my *family*—and my girl, and I let myself forget everything for one night. Sure, I caught a few people looking at me. Whispering. But no one approached us. They probably didn't dare with such a large group of people wrapped around me, supporting me, letting me know that even though I'd let myself feel alone, I never really had been.

Then I went home with Delia, because she still didn't want to leave Doris and Ross, and I still didn't want to leave her. This morning I made breakfast for everyone—eggs of course—and Ross asked me, "We gonna have to start charging you rent, bucko?" and then clapped me on the back. "Just kidding. Don't make any more eggs, and we'll call it even."

I haven't gotten the making eggs without burning them part quite right unless I have direct supervision by Delia. I'm all right with that.

When we reached the Rolf Estate this morning, Christian gave us a rah-rah speech about rising above adversity, as if we were a persecuted minority rather than poorly paid 1099 employees. He also gave out snack cakes from Starbucks, giving us the beneficent smile of a generous overlord.

Now we're on set, setting up a shot, and Thomas just positioned me next to a potted plant—fake, of course—and some sound equipment, closer to the principal actors than Delia and I have been before. Sinclair winks at me. Jeremy looks like he wants to hustle over and sweet-talk me, but a glance from the director keeps him pinned in place, thank God. According to Sinclair, the powers that be remain less than pleased with him for alienating the Rolfs.

Delia is at the edge of the set, getting her look touched up by hair and makeup, because Leonard cracked a joke that made her laugh so hard she cried. She's wearing something else from Doris's closet—a dark gray dress with a white tie at the throat. I know because I helped her pick it out this morning. The scene we're filming takes place on a different day than the other two we've filmed, but we were told that we'll need to wear our Day One outfits again tomorrow.

Leonard and Constance are on the other side of the set, so far off-camera they may not be seen, which is probably the way they prefer it, since they can talk in whispers as long as they're subtle about it. Of course, we've never let that stop us.

"Hey, I meant to thank you for dinner the other night, man," Thomas says, nodding several times, presumably because he agrees with himself.

"Yeah, no problem."

"I hope you don't mind that Doris let me take your meal. She's always looking out for me, you know. That's what family's like. I don't get to see them much, but there's a deep bond there."

"Sure, man. I don't care about the food."

His eyes are beady under his caterpillar eyebrows as he stares me down. "Because you got something a lot better, huh?"

His gaze shifts to Delia, who's smiling at the woman who just poked her in the eye with a mascara wand.

"I don't care for the implication," I tell Thomas, letting menace flow into my voice. Doris's great-nephew or not, I'm not okay with him openly lusting over Delia. I've had enough of his bullshit.

He raises his hands, palms out, a crude smile on his face. "Hey, man, I'm not after your girl. She's practically family."

That's a bit rich, considering he first met her on this movie set, but I refuse to get into an argument about semantics with a man whose only good quality is his affection for a bright color. He's wearing a bright orange shirt today, that orange juice lanyard over top of it.

"Then you'll agree she should only be talked about respectfully," I add.

"Got it bad, huh?" he says with a grin.

"Got it good," I say pointedly, then shift my gaze. Delia's coming over, which will hopefully put this conversation to an end.

"Heya, cuz," Thomas says to her, his tone jovial. The corners of her mouth turn down before she recovers.

"Good to see you, Thomas. I like your shirt."

Of course she does.

He peers down at it and grins. "Never met an orange I didn't care for."

Delia's glance at me is sly—*see, I told you.*

I wrap my arms around her. She's adorable, and the dress is chaste in a way that makes me want to see it on my floor.

"Good, good," Thomas says. "That's exactly what we need. The only wood should be in your pants, not in your acting."

I give him a hard look. "We're good here. Maybe you can go give Leonard instructions on pointing at that potted plant."

He gives us a double thumbs up and backs away as the director calls, "Background!"

"There's something wrong with that guy," I murmur to Delia, pulling her closer.

She leans into my ear. "Maybe it's just film people in general who are peculiar. You saw Christian this morning. He must know the bird story is fake, but he had that photo of the birds' nest made into a poster, and he wants to call us his 'Vermillion Flycatcher' extras."

My body shakes slightly with silent laughter.

"Action!"

I'm still silently laughing as Jeremy's character, whose name I can't remember for the life of me, challenges Sinclair to a design-off. They're going to come up with new designs for the entrance hall, and the guests at the house—us, presumably—are going to vote on which one they like best. Based on the hint of flirtation in their voices, I'm guessing this is one of the scenes leading up to the shift from enemies to lovers, but Leonard's right. There's about as much chemistry going on between them as there is in inert gas.

Delia kisses beneath my ear, and I'm no longer laughing. "Dirty trick," I murmur.

"I don't want to get in trouble," she whispers back.

"So don't tempt me to carry you off into an empty room."

She shifts closer. "We'd be banned for life."

"I don't think I'd mind."

"Cut!" the director calls. Or at least I think it's him. There's a chain around his neck, but the pendant is tucked into his shirt today.

The scene is filmed again, then again, then again. Then *again*. It's obvious the director senses the inert quality too, and he continues to have them do it differently—Sinclair leaning into Jeremy; Jeremy putting a hand on her arm, just so. None of it seems to satisfy, though, and he finally calls for a scene break.

Jeremy instantly hustles over to us. Fuck.

"Hi, friends!" he says brightly.

"Hi, Jeremy." I keep my arms around Delia, making sure he knows what'll happen if he looks at her the wrong way.

"Oh, so you two are a thing now." He nods repeatedly, as if he's been taking lessons from Thomas. "I figured you and Leonard were... Well, good for you. You know, Lucas, I've been thinking about what Leonard said about the bird. Let's do it. He's right, those damn birds are really something else. Something special. And with the story of what happened here...we're going to be changing hearts and minds, man. People will be talking birds, walking birds. They'll want nothing else."

I have no idea what he's talking about, and the look on his face says he's not too sure either. Did he get more than a slap on the wrist for the whole Rolf mess? Maybe he's burned some bridges and he's trying to piece some new ones together with popsicle sticks.

With unwarranted confidence, he adds, "We can change the title to *Bawk-Chicka-Bawk-Bawk*."

"That's an interesting idea, man," I say. "But I'm starting to think the film world isn't for me."

His expression turns hard. "Seems like you've gotten a lot out of the experience," he says pointedly, looking at Delia.

"I have," I say. "Everything I need, really."

She smiles sweetly at me, while Jeremy glowers. "I don't like time wasters."

"I don't think anyone does," Delia comments. "Waste has pretty negative connotations."

He ignores her, his gaze on me. "You're going to regret this when *Bawk-Chicka-Bawk-Bawk* is a hit."

"I think we both know that's not going to happen."

He looks like he wants to say something else, but the assistant director, who's been deep in conversation with his doppelgänger, storms over to him. "Jeremy, we're doing it again. It's a goddamn embarrassment when a couple of nobodies off the street have more heat than the lead actors." He's speaking loudly enough for all of the people around us to hear, and Jeremy's ears turn red. It's obvious he wants to unleash on the guy and is holding back—barely.

"Are we the nobodies?" I ask.

The assistant director ignores me.

"I need to take a leak," Jeremy says, storming off.

The AD stares at his retreating back for a second and then gives it the finger before making his way back to Sinclair. Based on the fact that I can only hear three out of five words, I'm guessing he's talking to her in a whole different way.

"Still think Jeremy's special?" I ask Delia, rubbing her back.

"Very funny."

Then the director's pointing at us. "Them! Move them farther back. They're too close to the principals."

"I think we're making them look bad," I whisper to Delia, leaning forward to give her a quick kiss.

That's when it happens. One second, we're standing there, huddled together, and the next Delia is shoving me with all her might. Which isn't much, to be honest, but I was leaning forward, and she catches me off balance. I stagger a couple of feet and fall, and she falls on top of me.

An "oof" escapes me and then the sound equipment that was just overhead crashes down to where we were standing. Someone screams, someone *else* screams, and glass and debris are flung at us.

Terror rips through me as I look at Delia, running my hands up and down her body to ensure myself that what my eyes are seeing is true and she's okay.

"I'm okay," she says through tears. "I'm okay. It's only my leg..."

I look down and see a bloody slice in it, and my heart speeds into panic mood.

Deacon told me that my parents might retaliate if they really were responsible for all the shit that had been happening around me and on set.

And this is their way of retaliating.

thirty-two

LUCAS

MY HEART RACES as I watch the on-set med tech patch up Delia's leg.

I keep seeing flashes of those photos from the Newton Building collapse. People crying. A bleeding cut. The devastation on their faces...

She could have died.

I could have died, too, obviously. Would have. But she could have died trying to save me, which is an unacceptable fucking risk.

Leonard's standing next to me, and Constance is shouting at someone, and it's all a buzz in my ears. I vaguely remember Sinclair running up to me after it happened. She said something, but I don't remember what, and now she's not here anymore. As soon as the med tech finishes, I put a hand on Delia's shoulder. "I need to get you out of here. *Now.*"

She looks up at me, her pupils dilated with shock. "They said they have to take a statement. I don't think we can just leave."

There's going to be an investigation, I guess, like there was with the brick, but I couldn't give a fuck. I want to get her out of here—for good.

"Then they can call you on the damn phone."

I look up at Leonard. "Will you wait at Ross and Doris's house with her? I think they said they were going to be at some community center thing for the day, right, Delia? I don't want you to be alone."

Or for Doris and Ross to be alone, for that matter.

"Why won't you be there?" Delia asks, her voice shaking a little.

"I'm going to see my parents. It's past time. I'm not going to..." I swallow, regaining my composure. "I'm not going to let them keep pulling this shit. Deacon seemed to think he could figure out their connection to the film crew if we could grab one of their phones. Or he thought that I might be able to find something in the house. So I'm going to do that."

"I don't think that's a good idea, man," Leonard says, scrubbing a hand through his hair. "Think logically. If you really believe they just tried to kill you, do you want to go over there for tea and poisoned crumpets? I'm the don of bad ideas, so I can tell you with authority that this one's crap."

Delia grabs the collar of my shirt. Her eyes are big, and right now they look more blue than green, like an ocean I could drown in. *She almost died.* "He's right, Lucas. You can't just go over there. Call the P.I. Let him know what happened. We can all leave."

"I have to do this," I assert, because everything inside of me is insisting on it. I feel like a coward for having waited so long. "I'm going over there to talk to them face-to-face, like a man. I've been avoiding them, letting myself think I was getting the upper hand, but they've been conniving all along. I'm not going to let this go on. I'm taking control."

"You can't go alone," Delia insists. She gets to her feet, wincing, and the look of pain on her face drives a knife through me. This is my fault.

"You're not coming," I snap. "I'm not letting them anywhere near you."

"Buddy, I don't know how to break this to you," Leonard tells me. "But if they're behind this, then they've already gotten close to her—even if they did it from behind the gates of their pretty house."

"That's why I need to go see them," I state. "I've let them think I'm weak."

"I'll go with you," he says, though it obviously pains him to make the offer.

"No, man. I need you to be with Delia."

Emotion glints in his eyes, and his jaw flexes. "You'd really trust me to watch over her?"

"Yeah," I say, swallowing, "yeah, I would."

"Who says I need anyone to watch me?" she asks, looking pissed. "I'm not a child or a lost goat. You don't get to control me, Lucas. You can't lock me away in a room and throw away the key."

I tip my head. "Why a goat?"

"Stop trying to distract me." She puts her hand on her hip. "The goat was an example, and it's beside the point."

Constance hustles up to us, having put someone or other in their place. "What's happening over here?"

"Lucas is being stubborn," Delia says.

"He's a man, dear," Constance says. "That's like saying Christian smells like cigarette smoke and cheap cologne. We all know. Now, how's that cut on your leg? Did you take photos of it?"

"I did," I say.

"Why?" Delia asks, her eyes wide.

"Because if my parents are behind this, it's a crime scene."

Constance shrugs. "And if not, the movie is guilty of gross negligence and you should sue."

"Sue?" she repeats as she lifts a hand to her throat. "I'm not going to sue anyone. That's absurd."

Constance makes a hum in her throat as if she agrees to disagree. "Now, what is this stubborn man insisting on?"

"He wants to go see his parents. Alone. And tuck me away in Ross and Doris's house."

"With me," Leonard says, lifting a hand. "Want to come along and make it a party?"

"Of course."

"Delia," I say, pleading. I run my hands down her arms, reassuring myself that she's okay. "I need to know you're safe. If something happened to you because of me, I'd never be able to forgive myself."

"You think I want something to happen to *you*?"

"Nothing's going to happen to me. If they're behind this, it's because they want to get me out of the way and make it look like an accident. It's not going to look like an accident if someone shoots me in the head at their house."

"What if they push you down a flight of stairs?" she asks, her lips trembling slightly. "Give you an untraceable poison? They could still make it look like an accident."

My laughter is bitter. "They'd never let anything dirty happen in their own home. Much better to have someone else take care of the problem and keep their hands clean."

"Don't go alone," she repeats.

I glance at Leonard, helplessly, and he nods. "She's right, man. See if Shane will go as your lawyer."

It's not a half-bad idea, and I shift to look at Delia to see what she makes of it. She gives a slight nod, and something eases in my chest. I didn't like having her upset with me, especially not right now.

"Can you guys give us a moment?" I ask them.

"Yeah," Leonard says, patting me on the back. "Come on, Constance, let's continue our conversation about cheese."

I'm ninety percent sure he's joking, but with Leonard there's no knowing.

"Please stay with them," I say to Delia. "There's a chance this means nothing. That it's just one more accident, but—"

"But you don't believe that," she says.

I think of that missing equipment miraculously turning up,

leading to the power outrage and then the malfunction of the sound equipment. "No, I don't. I...I really didn't think they'd stoop to something like this. They've always valued their reputation at the cost of everything else, but I guess I've already ruined that for them. Maybe they're so desperate to get rid of me, they're willing to risk it all to see it happen." A corner of my mouth hitches up. "They may even figure they can get some public sympathy out of it."

She puts her hand flat on my chest, pushing me a little. "Don't make a joke about your theoretical death, Lucas. It's not funny. You need to be careful. Don't go unless you can get Shane or Deacon to go with you."

"I won't," I promise. They're right. It would have been a foolish, knee-jerk reaction to storm over there alone. "But please promise me to stay with Leonard and Constance. Just in case."

"I will."

I kiss her softly, not wanting to hurt her. Logically, I know it's her leg that got injured, not her lips, but I'm still firmly in danger mode.

"I need you to be okay," I tell her. "If anything happens to you—"

She kisses her hand, then presses it to my heart. "Same."

I look over at Leonard and nod to him. He nods back. "Call us as soon as you have an update."

"And you'll drive them to the house?"

"What am I, geriatric?" Constance complains. "I can drive my own damn car."

I nod, because I'm not about to tell Constance what to do. Then I squeeze Delia's hand one last time. "I'll see you soon. This will be over before you know it."

But as I hurry off to my car, ignoring Christian, who shouts something about team spirit and the Vermillion Flycatchers to me, I have to wonder if I was being honest with her. Or myself.

If it's them, they're not just going to stop, but if I can find something at their house or get them to confess to wrongdoing, then maybe I can force the issue.

When I get to the car, I text Shane, explaining what I need and asking if he can take a break from work, then call Deacon.

"Still haven't found any connection to your folks," he says as soon as I pick up. No greeting or empty niceties. I appreciate the efficiency. "The only cars that have come or gone from their property over the weekend were for people who are confirmed to work there. And none of the P.I.s I know of around town have a make or model car similar to the one you described. I put together a short list of what we might be looking at, though, and I have to wonder if the Kia you saw idling on the road outside the house is the same one your girlfriend saw outside the bar. To someone who doesn't know much about cars, it might look like a Range Rover."

I swear under my breath, then quickly tell him about what happened on set, ending with my plan to pop in on my parents.

"You're bringing someone?" he says ruminatively. "That's good. Because if they've set this all in motion, they're expecting you. Run a recording on your phone in case they give up anything good, but I have my doubts. They've covered their asses if they're behind this. Might even be another layer of connection we're missing."

"Like if they hired someone who then hired someone else?"

"Could be. But there's a risk involved there too. More people who might potentially get caught. I have to admit, I still don't know if I like them for this."

"You think all of this shit happened by coincidence?" I ask, incredulous.

"Didn't say that. Could anyone else on set have it out for you?"

I nearly laugh. Probably a good portion of the city has it out for me. People don't much like the bloody Burkes these days, and according to Clancy the costume guy, everyone on set knows who I am. I feel like an idiot for not giving it more consideration before now. "Yeah," I admit, tapping the steering wheel. "I guess it's possible."

"Any reason you didn't come out publicly against your parents?"

My heart thumps uncomfortably in my chest. "There are legal reasons related to my employment contact. But it's not just that. I didn't want to look like I was excusing myself."

"It's an avenue for us to look at, kid, if your folks aren't involved. See what you can find out from them, but don't take any stupid chances. We don't have an in in the house, so don't try to grab a phone to clone. We'd have no way of getting the original back."

"Okay," I say, rubbing my forehead, my mind whirring. "Thanks, Deacon."

"Thank me later."

He hangs up without a goodbye or any flowery promises, and I smile despite my shit mood. I like the guy. I'll like him even better if he can help me put a stop to this.

There's a text from Shane confirming that he'll come, so I drive to his office to pick him up. When he emerges from the building, he's wearing a pinstriped suit that reminds me that I still have on that dumb golden belt. I guess Clancy decided it's my signature look, because he's handed it over every day, even though Delia hasn't been wearing hers. Either that or he's fucking with me. I consider taking it off, then decide that I like the thought of horrifying my mother.

"You all right?" Shane asks, climbing into the passenger seat. His gaze catches on the belt and he grins.

"Yeah, yeah. It's part of my costume." I start driving, the way burned into me.

"Do you really think your parents are trying to have you killed?" he asks after a moment of silence.

"I don't know," I say. "But I don't think I can go on much longer without knowing."

He gives me a sidelong look. "I'm not sure how to say this in a sensitive way."

I let out an amused huff of air. "Since when have either of us cared about being sensitive?"

"Okay, so I'll just come out with it. They're not going to break. They're not going to take one look at you and have guilty consciences and tell you they've been trying to snuff you out. People only do that in the movies." He shrugs. "And they're definitely not going to do it in front of a lawyer."

"So you think I should go in there alone?" I ask as I take the car around a sharp turn.

"Didn't say that. They need to be reminded that you have people on your side. Powerful people."

A grin sneaks across my face. "Are you one such powerful person?"

"Bet your ass I am." He pauses before adding, "Besides, even if they don't admit to anything, you might need this. You never got a chance to tell them to fuck off up close and personal."

I take a quick glance at him before returning my gaze to the windshield. "Thanks for coming with me."

"You got it. Now, let's see how many people we can offend."

"Wouldn't it just be the two?"

Humor lacing his voice, he says, "They've got like five hundred people working for them. We can do better than that."

thirty-three

LUCAS

WHEN WE GET to the gate, I announce myself as "the prodigal son," making Shane laugh under his breath. The gate creaks open, and I don't like that it instantly creaks shut behind us. Logically, I know they can't keep us here and wouldn't try, but it reminds me of being a little kid, shut behind those bars. It makes my skin feel itchy, my feet want to turn the car right back around and slam my way free. Instead, I drive up to the roundabout in front of the house and park beside the door.

"You ready for this?" Shane asks.

I bark out a laugh as I get out my phone. "Fuck no."

I frown when I see a text from Delia.

> I gave my statement to the police. I guess it's procedure for the police to be called whenever something like this happens, but it does look like the equipment that fell is part of what disappeared the other day. We're on our way home now, but the police will want a statement from you too.

Sure enough, there's a voice message on my phone from an unknown number. A problem for a different time.

I tell Shane what's going on, then start the camera recording and stick my phone back into my shirt pocket. "I need to get back to her. Let's make this fast."

"I'm on board with that," he says wryly.

My parents' housekeeper, whose name escapes me since she's only worked here for something like six months, opens the door for us. There's a solemn, disapproving look on her face, like she wants to give me a scolding for being the kind of son who doesn't check on his parents after they were arrested.

"I'll show you to the sitting room," she says.

"Thank you, but I know where it is."

She leads the way regardless, probably because my parents don't want me wandering around the house. It occurs to me that we're not going to be left alone while we're here. Even if one of us tries to go to the restroom, there'll probably be an escort waiting in the wings to take us there. It makes it less likely that anything useful will come out of this visit. But part of me wants to believe that I'll be able to read the truth on their faces. It's flawed logic, obviously—if I'd been able to read them that well, I'd have known about all of this years ago.

Shane claps his hand to my arm right before we follow the housekeeper into the sitting room.

They knew I was here, obviously. They must have been alerted the instant my car drove up to the gate. But my parents both look up with affected surprise. They're sitting at the table by the window, my mother with a cup of tea and my father with the paper open in front of him. I wonder if he's reading about himself.

"You're a day late," my father says with an aggrieved sniff. He's had snow-white hair for as long as I can remember, even in his late thirties, so it's not like his hair has gone white overnight. His faces is older, though, with more pronounced lines around his eyes. My mother is put together as always, wearing a dress that wouldn't look out of place in *Southern Belle* magazine, but she looks like she's two weeks late on her usual beauty treatments.

Good. If you do to people out of greed what they did to Nat and her mother and Delia and so many others, you *should* pay a price.

"I don't recall saying I was coming."

"You're here now...and you've brought a friend," my mother adds, setting her tea cup down in its saucer.

"Yes, we've met before. Multiple times," Shane says, not bothering to drop his name.

Neither of them comment on that. "You're welcome to sit," my mother says. "We've already asked Hilda to bring more tea."

Which neither of us will be drinking. Again, they'd be foolish to poison us, but it's a pretty solid rule never to eat in your enemy's house.

I'd prefer not to sit with them at a table so small, so I nod toward the love seat across from it, angled to get sun from the big window they're next to. Both Shane and I sit.

"You might wonder how your father and I are doing," my mother says primly, "after the anguishing experiences of the last month or so."

"No," I say flatly while Shane fights a smile, crossing one leg over his knee. I'm surprised he doesn't fold his hands behind his head so he can really enjoy the show.

My mother flinches. My father's gaze lifts from the paper, narrowed at me.

"No," I repeat. "I haven't wondered. You know I'm the person who helped the FBI form a case against you. I know what you did, and you deserve to pay for it."

"You'd ruin your own family?" my father says, his voice cold. "You'd ruin your name?"

"I'm not the one who ruined it. It's bad enough that you consciously made a decision to risk human lives because you didn't want to lose money, but when it did hurt people—when people *died* —you ruined another man's life because you refused to take responsibility for what you'd done. That's corruption. It's..."

"Evil," Shane offers.

"Evil," I repeat. "And you drove Leonard out of town. He thought you were going to kill him to keep him quiet. I—" My voice breaks, and I swallow. "I wouldn't put it past you. Do you have any idea how much devastation you caused?"

My mind conjures an image of Delia, of May, and of Natalie Reiter with her crooked smile. And she wasn't the only one. For each of the other lives lost, there's a web of connectivity, of hurts.

My father pushes the paper aside and gets to his feet. "Your friend is an unreliable fop. An idiot. We only hired him as a favor to you—one we *deeply* regretted."

"Did you also regret the payout you gave him?"

"You mean the severance pay we offered as a courtesy to you? Yes." He casts a spiteful glance at Shane, as if to say he's no better. "Now, I won't let you sit here in my own home and accuse me of such things. You weren't raised to be like this. I'd hoped you were capable of loyalty, of having some family feeling."

Yes," I say wryly, "I got the book. Thanks for that."

"So did I," he snipes. "*Simple Tips On How To Be a Good Fucking Person.* Very funny. Maybe you should have kept it."

I didn't send him any books, but I have a feeling Leonard might have taken liberties. Not that I'm going to tell my father that. "Figured we'd start a book club," I say, getting to my feet too.

Shane stays sitting in his casual pose, but I can tell he's ready to get to his feet too. My mother starts fidgeting with the saucer of her tea cup. She never fidgets. "I know plenty about loyalty, by the way," I say, "but you've done nothing to deserve any. I don't need you." I glance from him to my mother, still fidgeting. "Either of you. I've made my own family."

He laughs, the sound empty of any feeling. "Of deadbeats and losers? Glory, if my father and grandfather could see what's become of their name. I thank the lord for taking them too soon so they couldn't. What a waste of time and money and effort you turned out to be. You've always been a disappointment, but I never thought you'd be so worthless."

Those words would have hurt once. Years ago, they would have devastated me and cut me to the quick. Because I had been raised to care about our family legacy, of the meaning behind "Burke." Of the years of work and toil our family had put in to earn their place in Asheville history. But I know better now. "Here's the thing, Dad. Kids aren't like any old investment. You don't get any say in what happens to them after they turn eighteen."

"We asked you to tea yesterday in the hopes that you'd have a discussion with us like an adult," he snaps, "but I can see there'll be no reasoning with you. How you can throw away your family legacy —the legacy our family has spent over a century developing—is beyond me."

"I'm not the one who threw it away," I say, my voice booming.

He sniffs. "Temper tantrums like a child. I can see not much has changed. You don't have the ability to talk man to man, to have a real discussion."

"What did you *think* was going to happen?" I ask.

He doesn't answer, so I shift my gaze to my mother. "Mom?"

"We were hoping that you would be willing to stand with us publicly, Lucas. To minimize the damage you've done to us. We were hoping we could come together as a family. You're our only child."

In my head, I can hear Leonard saying, *Yeah, sucks to be you.* And it nearly makes me smile. Nearly.

"We're not going to jail," my father sneers at me, like I'm still a seven-year-old who doesn't adequately grasp a pivotal concept of real estate. "I should hope you're not naïve enough to think otherwise."

"I figured," I say. "Your lawyers are too good for anything major to stick. But there are going to be fines. Payouts. You *will* lose the company. I heard Jeff is already running it. He might idolize the Burkes, but he doesn't lack business sense. I'm guessing he's going to want to change the name. Even then, I don't know if it will survive."

His face is red, and he takes a couple of steps toward me. It's obvious he'd love to hit me—to beat me down with his fists—but he's logical enough to know it isn't a fight he'd win. "I've never seen someone so willfully self-destruct."

"Did you hire someone to follow my girlfriend? To mess with me on the movie set?"

My father's face crinkles. "Movie set? What on earth are you talking about?"

"You're seeing someone, Lucas?" my mother adds.

They could be lying. They lie so well. But I don't think they are. There's a note of confusion in their voices that's been completely absent from the rest of our discussion—because even though my father admitted to nothing, it's obvious he wasn't confused about what I was accusing him of.

"You know what I'm talking about," I insist, doubling down, but that confusion is still there—until spite overtakes it.

"There's one of your other weaknesses, boy," my father says.

Hilda opens the door with the tea service, takes one look at my father, and retreats.

"You always think everything's about you," he continues, unabashed. "Do you honestly believe we've had any interest in following what's happening in your life while you've sat back on my parents' money and enjoyed yourself? You can burn, for all I care, but I won't be setting the fire. If you persist on this path, you're dead to me."

Shane gets to his feet. "Well, this has been fun. Ready to go, Lucas?"

But it takes me a second to respond, because my mind is caught on what my father said—

You always think everything is about you.

Fuck. Fuck. Fuck, fuck, fuck.

I grab Shane's arm. "We have to get to Delia."

thirty-four

DELIA

THE POLICE OFFICER who interviews me is very cross—not at all the type of person who accepts "I just had a feeling" as an explanation. Only, it's true. I felt the need to push Lucas, so I did, and then the sound equipment fell right where we'd been standing. The officer insists that I must have sensed something. He may be right, but if I did, my subconscious mind was at the wheel. When he releases me, there's a look of pinched disapproval on his face.

Leonard and Constance are waiting at the door. I'm surprised Sinclair's not with them. She's been babysitting us on set for the last half hour or so, ever since she came looking for Lucas and found us instead. She immediately pulled me into a hug, surprising me, since it's not every day you're hugged by a movie star. "You have personally salvaged my relationship with my brother, you divine woman. He would never have forgiven me if something had happened to Lucas on set."

"But it wouldn't have been your fault," I insisted, flustered. "I'm sure he would have forgiven you."

She gave a shrug. "Either way, I'm glad we won't be testing it."

It's obvious she feels personally responsible for us. She even insisted on scheduling a takeout delivery for us so no one has to cook when we get back to Ross and Doris's. When I protested—I barely know Sinclair, and goodness, I can do some things for myself—she insisted the production would be paying for it.

"Can't say no to that," Leonard had said, deciding for us. "They fed us on lettuce leaves and hopes and prayers the first night. I'd say we're owed a good meal."

Now, waiting next to the door, Leonard and Constance look neither happy nor sad, maybe a little bored, so I'm guessing they don't have any news for me. Still, I ask about Lucas.

"We haven't heard from him," Leonard confirms.

"Sinclair was with us, but she had to leave to meet her fiancé," Constance says thoughtfully. "Nice boy. Very big muscles. I used to wonder why Shauna wasn't interested in him, but she's always insisted they're just friends."

"She was waiting for *me* to show up," Leonard says with a straight face.

She gives his arm a little shove. "Oh, you are wicked."

I take out my phone, but there aren't any new messages from Lucas. My mind suggests dozens of possible scenarios, none of them good.

"Can we go home now?" I ask, because I'd prefer to worry somewhere where all the chairs are comfortable and we know we have delivery food coming. Lucas is also about forty-five minutes away from us while we're here, and that forty-five minutes seems pretty unacceptable right now.

"Please, for the love of God," Leonard says. "I've never wanted to leave a place more. Someone sent in a trauma counselor, and they're holding a group healing session out on the floor. I mean, isn't Delia the only one who got hurt? What are they up in arms about, not being the center of attention?"

"What are they doing?" I ask curiously.

"Holding hands and singing Kumbaya," he says.

Constance snorts laughter. "I left when I saw someone pull out a crystal."

"Sounds interesting," I say with a shrug, "but I'd rather go home."

We head to the door, walking around the group circle. Clancy is once again manning his collection station, and when I hand over my accessories, he clucks his tongue and says, "Your boyfriend still has that belt."

"He also almost got his head caved in twice on this set," Leonard says in a wry tone. "Wouldn't you say it evens out?"

"I'll get it back for you," I amend, because none of this is Clancy's fault. Or at least I don't think it is. I guess any of the people we've dealt with on set could be working for Lucas's parents, a thought that makes my skin crawl. "I'm pretty sure he doesn't want it."

"Thanks, doll."

"I guess this means you're going to make me give the fedora back," Leonard says with a sigh, doffing it.

Smiling, Clancy says, "Naw, you keep it. Suits you better than it has anyone else, and I can't think of any reason we need hats anyway. Damn near the entire production has filmed indoors."

Leonard brightens as he returns it to his head, setting it at a jaunty angle. "Thanks, man. You made my day."

"Glad to make somebody's day." He shifts on his chair and looks mournfully toward the trees hiding the parking area. "I'd like to get moving, myself. This movie really is cursed. Has been from day one."

"You take a listen to the script, buddy?" Leonard asks with a whistle. "I'm gonna go ahead and say it was cursed from inception."

That gets us another laugh from Clancy, and Leonard tips his hat to him before we walk out the door.

"Y'all be careful now," Clancy calls out, which gives me the goose-on-my-grave feeling.

When we get close to Constance's car, which barely looks big enough to hold all three of us, Leonard nods to her. "What do you say we play rock, paper, scissors for who gets to drive? May the best man win."

She puts a hand to her hip and walks backward a couple of steps.

"Careful, Constance," I say.

She scowls at me. "Don't age me, child."

A broken hip would age anyone—I've seen that firsthand with one of my clients—but I suspect she wouldn't thank me for saying so.

"And you," she says, pointing at Leonard. "The best man is always going to be a *wo*-man, you ingrate."

"I don't think that sounds the way you thought it would sound, hotshot," he says with one of his dozens of grins. "Come on, quick draw. You can count for us, Delia."

I do, and Constance chooses scissors. Leonard goes for paper.

She hoots, and he grumbles something about paper being statistically the best bet for the game.

"There's nothing predictable about me, you hooligan. Want to ride in front, Delia?" she adds, her tone saucy. "The driver gets to choose who gets shotgun."

Leonard gives her the stink-eye. "It's not enough that you won, huh? You want to grind your victory into me by packing me in there like a sardine."

"No, of course I'll go in back," I say quickly, because the backseat looks like it would barely hold him. He opens the door and folds down the seat, and I climb in mechanically, barely paying attention.

Constance takes off after we all put on our belts, almost certainly speeding. While she drives, Leonard launches into stories about Lucas and their friends. It's obvious he's trying to keep my mind off whatever's happening to Lucas right now, but it's not working. We lapse into an uncomfortable silence that not even Constance attempts to break. There's still nothing from Lucas, so I tap out a text letting him know that I spoke with a police officer and we're almost at the house.

No response. Is he sitting with his parents now?
I tap out another text.

> Don't eat or drink anything. And I meant it about the stairs. In books, they always push someone down a flight of stairs if they want it to look like an accident.

"Texting Lucas?" Leonard asks, glancing over his shoulder.

"Yes," I admit.

"Tell him he's not allowed to croak until we have L&L business cards made."

I don't particularly care for the wording, but I send it anyway, because I suspect it's Leonard's way of showing his support.

"L&L?"

"He wants to start a house flipping company with me. Lucas and Leonard Restoration. He says it's not just for my sake, but we both know he could do whatever he wants."

"But he likes working on houses with you most of all." I reach up to touch his arm. "He told me so. I think getting Peggy up to date gave him a purpose when he needed it most."

"Peggy?" he asks, waggling his brows as he glances back. "You two got some group action going on?"

It's obvious we have no real misunderstanding, so I roll my eyes and say, "The house."

"You named my house Peggy?"

"Doesn't she strike you as one?"

"Now that you mention it, she does remind me a bit of this broad I once—"

"Oh, please," Constance says as she pulls into view of the house. "Let's have none of that. No one wants to hear a man droning on about his conquests. Now, I understand talking up a victory. I've never met a challenge I didn't dominate, but—"

"Frank learned that," I interject.

317

Constance parks on the curb, leaving the driveway free for Doris and Ross. "Oh, I'll give credit where it's due," she says as Leonard gets out and cranks the front passenger seat down for me. "Doris and Jane took care of that old dolt."

"With a little help from those photos with Leonard," I say, climbing out. "Shauna says she's been hearing from a lot of your mutual friends about them."

"So have I. I haven't answered anyone." Constance cackles as she leaves the car, both of us shutting the doors. "Let them assume and spread misinformation. I'm all for it."

Or maybe she doesn't like flat out lying to her friends. I'll bet that's part of it.

I lead the way to the house and open the door, sighing when I smell something baked.

"Did she make muffins again?" Leonard says, sniffing dramatically. "I volunteer as taste tester. She may have put in the correct measurements this time, and the takeout's not getting here for another hour."

Suddenly, I'm exhausted. It's as if everything just crashed down on me—a thought that makes me shudder. I can barely stand on my noodle legs. "You two test them out. I'm going downstairs to take a nap. Come and get me if you hear from Lucas."

Leonard gives me an incredulous look. "Something tells me you're going to hear from him first."

I take out my phone and turn all the alerts up to high.

"He'll be okay, Delia," he says. "Shane's with him, and his parents aren't mobsters. They're not going to gun them down in their house and then ask the staff to dispose of the bodies."

"You're giving her new things to worry about," Constance says, shoving his arm.

"Shit, you're right." Looking at me, he continues, "My point is, he's going to be fine. Go get some rest. You're probably in shock."

I force myself to smile at them, then head downstairs, shutting the door behind me. I make a face. It's too warm down here. It's always cool in the basement, even at the end of summer like now, unless—

The curtain in the far window is fluttering, the window a few inches open. I frown, crossing the room toward it, and someone grabs me from behind, one arm around my neck in a chokehold, the other shoving something into my mouth that makes me gag as I try to scream. Tape goes over it, getting caught in my hair, and then he has my arms pinned too.

The tape is orange.

Orange.

I'm still trying to scream through the cloth he stuffed in my mouth, but the sound comes out muffled and quiet.

"Shut the fuck up," Thomas says in a harsh undertone. Disbelief is followed by horror. Did Lucas's parents send him after me, or—

It doesn't matter. Do something, Delia.

I kick backward as hard as I can, but he just grunts and curses. His hold doesn't waver, and he moves another arm across my middle, his touch making me shudder with revulsion. "Behave, or I'll break your neck."

His words make me still for a second. Only...isn't that exactly what he plans to do? There's no point in standing here like a good girl and letting him kill me. I have to fight, or at least make a fuss loud enough that Constance and Leonard stop eating their muffins.

"It's not going to hurt," he whispers, whether to me or himself, I don't know. "It'll be over in a minute, and no one needs to know. Plenty of healthy young people die from heart attacks."

He's nervous, I realize. His plan has gone off the rails and then put on roller skates. He must know there are people upstairs. We weren't making any effort to be quiet, and he would have heard us. I can't hear Leonard and Constance now, but maybe that's because they're in the kitchen, far enough from the doorway that I can't hear them and they can't hear me.

Thomas clearly didn't intend to kill me this way. It was supposed to be hands-off—an unfortunate accident. Now, he'll have to do it himself, and I'm going to be found dead in my apartment hours after I was almost crushed by falling production equipment.

He may just be an *okay boy*, certainly not the sharpest tool in the shed, but he isn't completely naïve. The scenario is studded with red flags. He has to know there's a good chance he'll be found out.

I think I could talk him down if he hadn't taken away my ability to speak. Maybe he did it on purpose because he felt his will lagging.

He pulls me backward, and I know he's going to push me down on the bed so he can force me to consume whatever drug he brought with him. Will I have time to scream? Or maybe he'll inject me with it, and I won't even get the opportunity to do that. I pound the floor with my feet, trying desperately to be heard, and wriggle against his hold. It's surprisingly firm, though, and he tightens his arm around my neck to a punishing grip. Again, if I didn't have the gag, I could point out that it's not the best idea to leave a ring of bruises around someone's neck if you want it to look like they died of natural causes. Or I could if he weren't choking me.

Desperate, I throw my head back against his as hard as I can. There's a burst of pain as my head collides with his, but from the way he shouts, it hurts more for him. His arm loosens a little, giving me air, and I suck it in greedily as I try to push free.

There's the sound of flesh hitting flesh, hard, and for a split second, I think Thomas must have hit me, but then he drops me, my body suddenly a deadweight, and I fall, hard.

"You didn't say you were dropping by, fuckface," Leonard says. I use my remaining strength to force my body to turn around so I can see them. Leonard and Thomas are facing off, their fists in the air. From the red spot on Thomas's face, it's obvious Leonard hit him in the side of the head.

"This isn't what it looks like, man," Thomas says, edging back as Leonard advances on him.

"So you weren't waiting down here for Delia, and you didn't have her in a chokehold? I'd be mighty interested to find out what actually happened."

Thomas takes a swing at him, but he easily avoids it. "I have every right to be here. This is my great-aunt's house. It's going to be mine someday."

"Doubt it," Leonard says as he ducks another swing.

"They just met this girl a few years ago. They don't know shit about her."

"They know they don't want her to die," Leonard responds as he ducks another hit. Thomas looks frustrated, sweaty, and he tries again, then again. He's getting sloppier, so he's wide open when Leonard steps in at an angle and punches him just to the right of his forehead. The air whooshes out of him, and he goes down as heavily as that audio equipment did earlier.

His body lands too close to me, and I struggle to get up, horrified that he's going to grab me again.

Leonard lifts me up. There's no humor on his face now, just deep concern. "This is gonna hurt, Delia," he says, "no way around it." And he rips the orange tape off my mouth. It does hurt, but it feels so good to spit out that cloth. My mouth is left dry, every bit of moisture wicked from it.

"Are you okay? You're pale as fuck. Talk to me, Delia."

"We need to call the police," I choke out.

Relief warms his face. "Constance is already on the phone with them, honey, and Lucas is on his way over." He rubs the back of his neck. "He called me to say he figured someone was going to attack you. Something tells me he's speeding."

"You saved me," I say, feeling tears in my eyes. Then I realize how close I still am to Thomas, within reach of a grabbing hand, so I back away.

"He's unconscious," Leonard says. "I got him in the temple. That's usually a knockout hit if you land it right. I'm going to level with you. I didn't get it right the first time because I was nervous. And I'll have to share the credit for saving you with Lucas, though you were doing a pretty damn good job trying to get away when I got down here."

"You said Constance is already calling the police..."

"I heard something when I got to the basement door to check on you. Figured we'd rather waste their time than wait until we were sure." He lifts a hand to scratch his forehead, and I almost laugh when I register that he's still wearing the fedora. "I thought you were safe, dammit. I'm guessing he parked a couple of streets away. Does he have a key?"

"I don't think so. The window was open," I say. "I guess he must have unlocked it the night he dropped Doris and Ross off after dinner. I just... I don't know why he'd want to kill me. Do you think Lucas's parents are paying him?"

I edge further away from Thomas. He certainly looks unconscious, but I'm not taking chances.

Leonard notices and asks, "You got any robes? Anything else with a tie?"

"Yes." I pep up and hurry over to my closet. I grab a couple of neckties and a tie from a robe and come back and hand them over.

Leonard starts securing Thomas's hands and feet. "Doris and Ross have any other younger relatives?"

"Thomas's mother," I say. "But Ross doesn't have any family left."

"Any family but *you*."

That's when his meaning hits me. "We've never spoken about it. I don't think they'd leave anything to me. That's never been my expectation."

He gives me a small smile. "And that's probably exactly why they would."

"But they're not wealthy."

He makes a sound that's nearly a laugh but not quite. "They

don't have to be." He gives Thomas a nudge with his foot. "He thought you were getting something that should have been his. My guess is that he called up his great-aunt, hoping to put in a little face time, and she wouldn't stop talking about her pretty lodger. Just like a granddaughter to her. He probably asked for that dinner so he could see you together. Wrap his head around how they feel about you." He purses his lips to one side and shrugs his shoulder. "You'd be surprised about the financial angle. Retirement savings. This house that he already thinks of as his. It adds up. Maybe this guy's a gambler. Or he took out a loan he couldn't pay to live a lifestyle above his means. He might be in a bad place, where five hundred thou might sound like it's worth killing for. I've known people like that before."

He's finished with his knots. They look secure, like Boy Scout knots. I tell him so, and he laughs. "I'm no Boy Scout."

Then there's the chorus of running feet overhead, and he grins. "Looks like our Boy Scout is home."

My heart thumps in response, in welcome, and then Lucas comes racing down the stairs. There's raw terror on his face, but when he sees me standing—alive and mostly well—relief overtakes it. He runs to me, not even seeming to notice Thomas trussed up on the floor. "Oh, thank God," he says. "Thank God." And he takes me into his arms, lifting me off the floor, and kisses me. Suddenly, the shock breaks enough for tears to escape my eyes. Tears of relief, because somehow we're both okay. Then he sets me back on my feet to examine me, his eyes lingering on the bruises that must already be forming on my throat.

Anger pulses in his eyes. His gaze dips to Thomas and he swears loudly. Possibly because it's Thomas. Possibly because he's already unconscious and Lucas didn't get to be the one who made him that way.

"Do I get a greeting too, Cupcake?" Leonard asks with a grin.

Lucas frees one of his arms to pound him on the back. "You did good, Leonard." He swallows and then pulls Leonard into a hug. "You did great, man. And I see you stole the hat."

"Nah, Clancy gave it to me. You're the one who stole that belt."

Turning to me, Lucas pulls me back into his arms. "He tried to kill you?" he asks, his voice tight.

"Are we congregating down here?" Constance calls from the stairway. "I take it the danger is at an end? The authorities are on their way."

"Affirmative, Hot Rod," Leonard calls out. "Come join us."

Tears are still rolling down my cheeks, but I find it in me to laugh.

"It feels good to hear you laugh, Sunshine," Lucas says, wiping the tears off my cheeks. "Can you tell me what happened?"

"Do you promise you won't kill him? I don't want you to go to jail."

Leonard glances around the open space. "Maybe it would be best if we move the"—his gaze lingers on the divan against the far wall—"whatever the fuck that is so it's facing him, and we can go sit over there. Don't think this sucker's going anywhere, but it's never a good idea to let a desperate man out of your sight."

Constance comes into the room with the tray of muffins and a big glass of what looks like sweet tea. Shane's with her, and he lifts his hand in a wave.

"You want to eat muffins around an unconscious man?" Leonard asks with a whistle. "Cold. I like it."

She clucks her tongue. "Our girl's in shock. I thought she might need some refreshments. They're actually quite good."

I'm weak, trembling, but I'm so, so thirsty, as if I haven't had a drink in days rather than maybe an hour. I take the cup from her and drain it. Then Lucas picks me up without commentary and carries me over to the divan. It's still facing away from Thomas.

"Sit down, Sunshine," he says. "I-I can't sit yet."

"Can you move it so I can see him?" I ask, my voice small. "I don't want to have my back to him."

He bristles but does it while Leonard, Constance, and Shane join us, everyone else standing.

"Now, tell us what happened, Delia," Lucas says as he gets me settled, grabbing the mermaid blanket from the bed and putting it over me. "If you can."

"I will. Was it okay with your parents?"

He gives a nod, a half-smile. "You almost got killed, and you want to know how it went with my parents? They're terrible, obviously, but it became pretty clear to me that they weren't behind this. That I was looking at things the wrong way, and the issues on set... the car...none of it was about me."

"What about the brick?" I ask. "I wasn't all that close to you when it fell."

"Maybe he has bad aim. Or it could have been an accident."

I nod, swallowing. He's pacing a little, his movements angry, and I can feel how much he wants to hurt Thomas. It's making me twitchy, because I can't let that happen. "Come sit with me, Lucas. Please."

Something shifts on his face, and he sits next to me on the divan, which suddenly feels tiny, pulling me onto his lap.

"I'm not going to tell you now," I say. "I'll tell you after the police get here. That way I only have to say it once."

That's not the real reason. The real reason is that I'm afraid he'll get mad enough that he'll storm across the room before anyone can stop him. So I don't feel at all guilty for telling what Doris would call an acceptable white lie.

I wince, thinking of Doris. This is going to upset her and Ross. Not nearly as much as if Thomas had murdered me in their basement, but even if they didn't have the highest opinion of him, I'm sure they're not going to be happy to learn he's attempted murder. More than once, probably.

"We need to call them," I say. Mira will want to hear everything from me, but I don't have the energy to call her right now.

"I'll do it," Lucas says. "Do you have your phone?"

"Upstairs," I say. "In my purse."

"I'll go get it." Shane makes a move toward the stairs.

"Oh, don't you worry about that," Constance says, pulling out hers. "I'll make the call to Doris."

She goes upstairs, and Leonard takes a glance at us before announcing, "I'm going to go make sure that asshole's still unconscious," and stepping away.

"Actually," Shane says, his foot tapping the floor, "I have a deposition in half an hour, and if I don't leave now, I'm going to be late."

"Seriously?" Lucas says. "You didn't say anything."

He gives him a half grin, half grimace. "You needed me, man, and this situation is obviously more important, but now that everything seems to be settling down... The police probably won't need to question me because I wasn't here. But if I'm here when they show up, I'll get caught up in it."

"Go," Lucas says, grabbing a key out of his pocket and throwing it to him. "*Thank you.* I'm not sure if I could have done that without you."

He nods to us, then gets up and goes.

Leonard's still on the other side of the bed, presumably watching Thomas be unconscious. It's obvious that he's trying to give us some time alone, and I'm grateful for it.

Lucas draws me closer, tucking me into him. "I was so damn worried," he murmurs, hugging me close. "I thought I was going to be too late. If Leonard hadn't been here..."

"But he was," I say, turning to face him. "And he knew I might be in trouble because you called him. You helped me, Lucas. I...I still can't really believe it. Leonard thinks Thomas did it because he was worried Ross and Doris would leave me something in their will, and he thinks it should all go to him. Can you imagine? They're not... I hope they're here for many more years, Lucas. Do you think he would he have hurt them if he got me out of the way?"

"There's no point in thinking about that now, Sunshine. He's not going to get anywhere near you ever again."

"After today, obviously," Leonard adds from behind the bed. "He's still out cold, by the way."

Lucas gives his head a shake, smiling slightly, then leans in to kiss me softly, as if I'm something precious. He pulls away, his face still achingly close. "I love you, Delia. Maybe it's crazy to say that, but I don't much care anymore. I wanted to say it last night, when you told me about your birthday wish. But it felt like it was too soon. On the way over here, I couldn't stop thinking about how I might have missed my chance. How I might not—" He cuts off, his jaw working, and there's that fire in his eyes again that tells me he wants to pound Thomas into the ground.

I touch his jaw, then press a kiss to it. "Don't think about him. Think about us. I love you too, Lucas. We're going to have a future together. We'll paint Peggy this weekend."

"Oh yeah?"

"Yeah. And we're going to bring Doris for another visit to the ophthalmologist, whether she likes it or not."

"A world where Doris can see and Ross can hear," he teases. "Are we ready?"

"They'll take it by storm," I say, running a finger over his lips. They part slightly, and I lean in to kiss them again.

He pulls back an inch. "If you don't feel the same way, I'll suffer through it, but I'm done with that fucking movie."

"Amen," Leonard adds.

"Yes," I agree. "I can't imagine going back after what happened today. I wonder if there'll even be a movie to go back to. Everyone seemed so upset."

"Don't get me started about that trauma circle," Leonard interjects.

"Leonard, if you went over there to give us some space, it's not working," Lucas says.

"Fair. I'm taking out my phone. Consider me distracted."

"We'll have to go back to return your belt, though," I tell Lucas. "I promised Clancy."

"You'll get no argument from me. I don't like letting Sinclair down, but I think she'll understand given the circumstances."

"So do I. She was very sweet to us this afternoon." I gasp. "We'll need to let her know what happened too."

He kisses the side of my head. "Honey, I have a feeling everyone's going to know. It'll either make this movie very popular when it releases or non-existent."

I hadn't thought of it that way, but he has a point. This will likely be on the news—perhaps even the national news. That means the movie and the Rolf Estate will be infamous.

There's the sound of a door opening upstairs.

The police.

A sigh escapes me. Although Thomas is no criminal mastermind, I realize I've been waiting for him to spring to his feet and mass-murder us all, like what happens at the end of a horror movie.

"A secondary reason I want to skip the rest of the movie is that I think we should go to the beach now," Lucas tells me, his eyes glinting. "Let's go this weekend. Stay for a while."

Hearing him say it, I can imagine what it'll feel like, having the sun on my skin, my hair loose in the wind. Maybe we can get a kite and fly it along the water. Drink margaritas and eat seafood. It'll be a break from all of this, a chance to reset.

"*Yes*. We'll spend your birthday there."

A surprised laugh escapes him, but he doesn't look shocked. "I don't think I told you that."

"No, Google told me."

"Sleeping Beauty's up," Leonard announces as footsteps start moving down the stairs.

"This has all been a misunderstanding," Thomas blathers in slurred voice. "I told you, I have a standing invitation at this house. I just stopped by to see my great-aunt and uncle. That's no crime. And—"

"Naw, man, you're right. It's the attempted murder they'll be interested in. Not the whole drop-in thing."

The officers reach the bottom of the steps.

"He's over there," Lucas says gruffly, still holding me. I think it's maybe the only thing keeping him from storming over there. "Our friend was able to restrain him."

I can just imagine the look of satisfaction on Leonard's face.

epilogue

BURKE

"ARE YOU READY?" Delia asks. "Leonard texted to say he's downstairs." We're in my apartment, newly decorated to look less like a model unit and more like a home. *My* home. Danny's home. Hers too, when she agrees to stay away from Ross and Doris for a night.

She looks like a goddess in her golden dress. My sunrise girl. Even more so today, with her skin tan from our two weeks in Puerto Rico. We left after finishing our work on Peggy, making her interior as remarkable as her exterior. Leonard grumbled and moaned about the paint colors, but he helped us all the same, and afterward we got drinks at Mira's bar. He admitted after a couple of Color Me Jealouses that Peggy did look better with a little shine.

"You going to scout out a new house for us to dress up while I'm gone?" I asked.

He tipped his head. "You'd trust me to do that?"

"Don't you know by now that I'd trust you with anything?" I glanced at Delia as I said it, and he knew exactly what I meant. He'd saved her. There might be no debts between friends, but I'd always be in his debt nonetheless.

"You got it, brother," he said, and that last word settled in deep.

When Delia got up to use the restroom, I told him what kind of future I had in mind for Peggy, and his mouth hitched up. "Just like you to get me to do all of that work *for you*." But he didn't hate the idea. Neither do I.

We'd picked a good time to blow town, because—predictably— the news cycle took a liking to the story. Thomas had cracked like an egg once he was in police supervision, and he'd admitted to all of it. Turns out he hadn't tried to brain me—or Delia—with that brick. My near-miss truly was an accident. But then he discovered the great-aunt and uncle he'd barely spoken to for years but had always assumed would be generous to him in their will had a young woman living with them—an adopted granddaughter. And my accident made him think of creating another. So he stole that equipment and tweaked it to set up a couple of potential accidents. He was the one responsible for positioning us on set, which made it easy, especially if he didn't much care about potentially killing other people.

Leonard's theories on Thomas had proven to be on point. He'd been living hard and fast out west, chasing the kind of life he thought he deserved. Spending money he didn't have.

He'd vehemently denied that he had any designs on hurting Doris and Ross once his plan was carried through, but I don't buy it. He clearly didn't give a shit about murdering any number of people on set. Why stop there?

Speaking of Doris, she's taken to the publicity like a duck to water, appearing in the local news and on a few podcasts. She even wrote an op ed about the whole thing for *The Asheville Gazette*. Delia would have preferred not to get involved, but she loves Doris enough not to take away her moment to shine, so she did a bit on the local news with her.

I'd been hoping my name would stay out of it. However, nobody asked, and one journalist wrote about my Romeo and Juliet relationship with Delia—the son of the building magnates who doomed the Newton Building and the best friend of one of the victims.

I didn't like the thought of my parents reading that. Or seeing Delia's face.

I liked it even less when my mother texted me that afternoon.

> What a lovely girl, Lucas.

It felt like a threat, so I hired Deacon on retainer. Just in case they decide to pull anything.

Delia wasn't surprised when her mother popped up, wanting to meet me and congratulate her on—surviving? We had dinner with her the night before we left, many word bombs were dropped, and it ended with the mutual conclusion that there wouldn't be another one anytime soon. Our FaceTime chat with her father, who's on tour with his band, went much better, and it amused me to see his hair really is the same exact shade as hers.

Both Delia and I were relieved to leave everything behind temporarily for our trip. We'd gone to visit Drew, Andy, and Andy's grandmother, whom everyone knows as Mrs. Ruiz because she's much too intimidating to be referred to by her first name. Despite having spent two weeks with her, I'm still not sure what it is.

We had two weeks of bliss. We ate seafood, ran on the beach, drank margaritas, and were generally useless in a way that I usually don't let myself enjoy.

One night, sitting out on the beach, watching our girls dance to music only they could hear, Drew turned and grinned at me. "Got that Drew Affliction bad, huh?"

"Maybe I can co-opt it," I suggested. "It can become the Drew and Burke Affliction."

"No way, man," he said, shoving my arm good naturedly. "Get your own disease."

Delia's the only one who calls me Lucas now. I've decided to reclaim the name I've gone by for my entire life. Leonard's right —

they don't get to have it. I can do my part to make it something to be proud of again.

Part of that involves seeing a therapist. I'm going to start next week. Delia, too, because she's been having nightmares about the attack.

"It's good to see you happy again," Drew had continued, watching me while I watched her. He must've noticed the way I was smiling. Like a damn sap.

"It's good to be happy. It's been a rough go of it."

His mouth hitched into a grin. "So, what about the guys? Who's next?"

"You're asking who's going to fall prey to the controversially named affliction next?"

"Yeah."

"I've got some ideas about that, but I don't want to jinx myself."

"You believe in jinxes now?" he asked, feigning shock.

"Yeah," I said with a laugh. "My mind's really been opening up."

Delia and I got back this Saturday, a week after Labor Day, and now we're on our way to the wrap party for *The Opposites Contract*, which Sinclair is throwing for the cast and crew at Glitterati. Or at least most of the cast and crew. Rumor has it, Jeremy wasn't invited. Thomas won't be coming for obvious reasons, although he'd count himself lucky to be in jail if he knew what I'd like to do to him.

Yes, they finished the damn movie, and people are dying to see it because of the controversy. In fact, the producers have asked Delia if she's interested in doing publicity when it releases. The phrases "star power" and "future opportunities" were thrown around.

To their shock, she refused.

When I asked her why, she said, "It's for the same reason you want to flip houses when you could do something else. I'm already doing what I like."

While we were in Puerto Rico, Mira and Shauna helped her cover her dog-walking duties and the granddaughter jobs that couldn't wait. I also helped her finish a business plan for Grand-daughter for Rent, and Danny's putting together a new website for her. That's what family does.

I feel Delia straightening my collar. "Lucas, your mind is wandering."

"It is now," I say as her fingers brush against my neck, sending need coursing through me. I pull her to me for a kiss, and she laughs into my mouth.

"I'm getting lipstick all over your face."

"Good, then they'll all know who I belong to."

"I think most of the people who'll be there already know."

I tip her chin up to me, hand around her jaw, and kiss her again. Thoroughly. "Let's really shove their faces in it."

She laughs, and I feel the kind of happiness that can only be known by sufferers of the Drew and Burke Affliction.

Yes, I'm taking liberties. No, I don't regret it.

I pull back, deciding there's no time like the present.

"Delia, there's something I've been meaning to talk to you about," I say, taking her hand. "This is another it's-too-early thing."

"I think we're beyond that, aren't we?" she asks, and I can feel myself grinning.

"Bear that in mind. I was... I've been thinking of keeping Peggy for us."

Her eyes widen, but then her mouth purses. "Oh, but you know I can't leave Doris and Ross."

"I know. I was thinking we could talk them into moving in there with us. There's more room than in their current house, and it's in a commercial zone, so I was thinking Leonard and I could open an office for our business there too. The apartment would unofficially be Danny's, because we both know he'd never accept it as a gift."

"Lucas," she says, her eyes getting shiny.

"Your mascara's about to go too. I'm a menace on makeup." I gently trace beneath her eyes, gathering the tears there.

"Happy tears are always worth it," she says, kissing me again. "I love you. And yes, we'll talk to them together. I don't know if they'll agree at first—they're set in their ways—but I have to believe they'll love Peggy. I felt a kinship with her right from when you first brought me there."

"And a house you paint always stays in your heart."

"How positively sentimental of you," she says with a small smile.

"You're the one who's done it to me, so it only tracks that you have to put up with it."

A horn honks three times on the street below us, and I roll my eyes.

"He's probably not going to stop until we go down," Delia says, her eyes sparkling.

"I know you're right."

Still, I kiss her again before letting her wipe off my face. Danny's sitting in the living room with a bowl of popcorn, watching some kind of murder procedural. I think he's a little miffed about having been wrong about that brick, but he's over the moon that one of his favorite crime podcasts has expressed interest in telling the story of what happened on the set of *The Opposites Contract.*

"You sure you don't want to go, buddy?" I ask.

"I'm wearing sweatpants. Doesn't this give me an automatic out?"

"If you want it to."

"Oh, I want it to." He pops a piece of popcorn into his mouth. "You've got lipstick on your face."

"I know. Enjoy being antisocial."

"I will. You look really pretty, Delia."

She beams at him, and that horn honks another three times.

"All right, Leonard. The world is aware you exist," I mutter as we leave the apartment and head to the elevator.

When we get out the door, Delia peers out and then turns to me with wide eyes. "Was that really necessary?"

"I did it for him," I say, laughing. "He said he'd never been to a wrap party before, and since you both saved my life on set, I figured we'd live it up a little."

He's driving an old-fashioned white Rolls Royce, rented from a local classical car company. The company driver is supposed to be behind the wheel at all times, but I'm not at all surprised to see that Leonard managed to talk him around. The car guy is sitting in the passenger seat, the corners of his mustache curled with some sort of wax. He looks like his mood resides somewhere between nervous and amused.

"There you are!" Leonard says as we approach the car. "Get in, and it's off to pick up Constance."

I open the door for Delia. "Your chariot, Sunshine."

Laughing, she says, "You get in first. You wouldn't fit in the middle seat."

She's not wrong, so I slide in first, and she gets in the middle, her side snug against me.

Seconds later we're moving again, speeding a little, and I can tell from the grim set of the former driver's face that he's having some regrets. Leonard behaves himself, though, mostly, and we arrive at Constance's house safely, having run no reds and hit no pedestrians.

She's waiting on the porch for us in a shiny blue dress that makes Delia's eyes light up. I'll bet she helped her choose it. There's a serious set to Constance's face, although the sight of Leonard in the Rolls Royce makes her smile for a second.

"Well, isn't this grand?" she comments as she gets into the back seat beside Delia.

"Just wait until you feel the ride," Leonard says.

The man next to him groans and says, "Maybe I should take over again. You've had your shot."

"Not yet," he blusters. "Not yet. I'll go slower. Below the speed limit. People will be annoyed with me for my lack of speed."

He takes off before the man can deny him.

"What's wrong?" Delia asks Constance. "You look glum."

"Shauna's upset with me."

"But I thought you invited her?" Delia asks. "We would have loved it if she'd come."

"I did, and she refused, but that's not why she's upset."

"Did she see a picture of me?" Leonard asks with a laugh as he maneuvers the car around a turn, heading for Glitterati. The driver's supposed to pick us up at the end of the night, but his face is becoming increasingly pinched, and I'm starting to think we've seen the last of him. "Because that'll usually do it," Leonard finishes.

"Well, as it happens, this *is* about those photos of you," Constance says. "The ones we took in the former fish room."

He glances back, and the man beside him goes white as ghost. "Watch the road!"

"As you know, I refused to explain who you were in the beginning. I thought it would be funny to let them guess for themselves. So people stopped asking after a while. But all of my friends have taken an interest in this wedding Shauna's in, calling her a poor girl, saying she should have gotten Colter to marry her. They were together for two years, you know."

"They sound like assholes," Leonard says flatly.

"Seconded," I offer.

"Well, I agree with you," Constance says, worrying the clutch she's holding. "But I felt the need to defend my girl, so I told them she'd found someone better."

"I don't think I like where you're going with this," Leonard says, glancing back again.

"The road, sir!" the man beside him shouts.

"You're going to be upset with me too," Constance says.

Delia gasps. "You told your friends that Leonard's Shauna's boyfriend."

"And that's not the worst of it..."

There's a screech of brakes as we almost plow into the back of the Buick in front of us, and the man next to Leonard shrieks, "Pull over, this instant!"

Leonard does, his face fairly pale too. We're several blocks away from the bar, but no one objects as we pile out in our party finery.

"You'll never rent from us again," the owner of the car snaps as he takes the key from Leonard.

"That's fair," I say.

The guy drives off, fast, leaving us gathered on the downtown sidewalk, tourists and a few locals streaming around us.

"What's the worst of it, Constance?" Leonard asks tightly, as if nothing had happened between his last question and this one.

She wrings her hands. "One of my friends told Colter's mother, and *she* told Colter, who texted Shauna and told her to bring her boyfriend to all of the wedding events. He said he can't wait to meet him. She's not very happy with me, as you can imagine. I know you won't be either."

Leonard looks at her blankly for a moment, studying her, and then suddenly bursts out laughing. With a shake of his head, he pats Constance on the back and beams at her. "Fuck it. I'll do it. I'll go with her."

I take Delia's hand and squeeze it. She looks startled, her make up a little smudged in a way that only makes her more beautiful, almost wild.

"And so it begins," I say, before lifting her hand to my lips for a kiss.

"You think?" she asks in a small voice.

"I do. The affliction is about to strike again."

What's up next??? Leonard and Shauna in a fake dating, bad boy, wedding crashing extravaganza.
Find out what happens in *You're so Bad!*

about the author

ANGELA CASELLA is a romcom fanatic. Writing them, reading them, watching them—she's greedy, and she does it all. In addition to her solo releases, she's lucky enough to collaborate with Denise Grover Swank. They have three complete series and more co-written projects to come.

She lives in Asheville, NC. Her hobbies include herding her daughter toward less dangerous activities, the aforementioned romcom addiction, and dreaming of having someone else clean her house.

Visit her website at www.angelacasella.com or Angela and Denise's shared website at www.arcdgs.com.

Made in United States
Troutdale, OR
01/04/2024

16688539R00210